The ma   the table did not   Eoin took another
step.

"Bugger off," he said loudly. The man still did not stir.

"Is he asleep?" Ciarán said.

"Probably pissed," Ann said.

He was sitting awfully straight for a drunk man, Siobhán
thought. Eoin was the first to reach the man. Holding the
knife aloft in one hand, he touched the stranger's shoulder
with the other. The man's body shifted, and his head fell to
the side. Eoin yelped, then jumped back and darted to the
front of him. A second later the knife dropped from Eoin's
hand and clattered to the floor.

"What?" Siobhán said. "Is he asleep? But even as she
said it, she knew it was something far worse.

She reached her brother's side. The first thing she saw
was the blood. Not a lot, just enough to form a cloud in the
centre of his chest. Protruding from the man's heart was a
pair of scissors with hot-pink handles . . .

Books by Carlene O'Connor

MURDER IN AN IRISH VILLAGE

MURDER AT AN IRISH WEDDING

Published by Kensington Publishing Corporation

Murder in an Irish Village

Carlene O'Connor

KENSINGTON BOOKS
www.kensingtonbooks.com

KENSINGTON BOOKS are published by

Kensington Publishing Corp.
119 West 40th Street
New York, NY 10018

All Kensington titles, imprints, and distributed lines are available at special quantity discounts for bulk purchases for sales promotion, premiums, fund-raising, educational, or institutional use. Special book excerpts or customized printings can also be created to fit specific needs. For details, write or phone the office of the Kensington Special Sales Manager: Attn. Special Sales Department. Kensington Publishing Corp, 119 West 40th Street, New York, NY 10018. Phone: 1-800-221-2647.

Kensington and the K logo Reg. U.S. Pat. & TM Off.

ISBN-13: 978-1-61773-846-3
ISBN-10: 1-61773-846-8
First Kensington Hardcover Edition: March 2016
First Kensington Mass Market Edition: February 2017

eISBN-13: 978-1-61773-845-6
eISBN-10: 1-61773-845-X
First Kensington Electronic Edition: March 2016

10 9 8 7 6 5 4 3 2 1

Printed in the United States of America

Dedicated to Dermot O'Rourke. I wish you were around so I could thank you in person. I still have the book you gave me—365 Days of Celtic Myths and I used portions of it in this novel. I can still see your infectious smile and hear your boisterous laugh.

To all my Irish ancestors and the people of Ireland.

Acknowledgments

As usual, it takes a village to write a book, and I'm so lucky to have a wonderful pool of people to turn to when I need help. First I'd like to thank my editor John Scognamiglio for proposing the idea for this series in the first place, and my agent Evan Marshall who went above and beyond giving me great notes on early drafts—I so appreciate it. Thank you to the staff at Kensington who work hard on everything from the cover to copy editing, marketing— everything it takes to bring a book to market. Thank you to my friend Daithí Mac Lochlainn for helping me out with Irish phrases. Thank you to Siobhán Hahn for answering last-minute questions. Thank you to Suzanne Brazil for reading an early draft. Thank you to Bridget and Seamus Collins for answering questions and if you didn't have the answers, pointing me to people who did. One such person wanted to remain anonymous but I'd like to thank that person as well. Thank you to James Sheedy and Annmarie Murphy for also being on hand to answer questions. A blanket thank you to the regulars of Maguire's Pub in Woodside Queens, as well as the people of Kilmallock, County Limerick. The original culprits who introduced me to this incredible town—Kevin Collins, Eileen Collins, and by extension, Susan Collins. And a special thank you to my family for their continued support. My sincere apologies if I missed anyone who was generous enough to help me with the first book in this series. The next round is on me.

Pronunciations and Glossary

Pronunciations

Siobhán	Shi-vawn
Seamus	Shay-mus
Ciarán	Keeran
Gráinne	Grawn-ya
Eoin	Owen
Aisling	Ash-lin
Craic	Crack (See meaning in glossary)

Glossary

What's the craic?
The Irish word "craic" means fun, having a good time. It's often mixed with alcohol and/or music: *craic agus ceol* (fun and music). When phrased as, "What's the craic?" it simply means, "What's happening?" or "What's up?"

Trad Session or Trad
Traditional Irish music

Doing my messages
Shopping! Usually food shopping

Deadly
American equivalent: Awesome

Taking the piss
American equivalent: Pulling my leg

Garda, gardai, guards
The local police force in Ireland. Technically known as: An Garda Síochána—Guardians of the Peace. Often referred to as "the guards". Offically: The gardai. (Plural). One guard can be "guard" or garda.

Cheeky
Endearingly bold

Chipper
Irish fish and chips shop. However, "chips" for Americans means French fries. Crisps are potato chips.

Jammers
Packed busy

A right nutter
Crazy

Blotto
Drunk

Leaving Certificate
Completion/graduation of high school

Put on quite a few *stone*
Equivalent to pounds (weight)

Do not get into a *row*
Argument

Kept her *gob* shut mouth

Langered—Drunk

Fisticuffs—fistfight

Runners running shoes

Travelers/tinkers
Also called pavees, or gypsies. A traditionally itinerant ethnic group who maintain a set of traditions. (Wikipedia)

Shift boys
Kiss boys

Chin-wag
Talk/gossip

Black and white pudding
White pudding and black pudding are both sausages (pork meat). White pudding does not include blood, black pudding does.

Mobile
Cell phone

Yoke
A word for when you don't have a word. Equivalent to—

thing—or placeholder for a person. IE: Hand me that yoke. (Thing). OR 'Some yoke'—some person

Pint of the black stuff
Pint of Guinness

Pioneer/Pioneer Pin: The Pioneer Total Abstinence Association of the Sacred Heart (PTAA): Irish organization for Roman Catholic teetotalers. Its members abstain from alcohol. Members can wear a lapel pin—a pioneer pin depicting the sacred heart of Jesus. (Wikipedia)

The truth from a liar is not to be believed.

—Irish proverb

Chapter 1

Siobhán O'Sullivan hurried through lush green fields, adjusting every so often for the bumps and dips of the terrain, imagining that from high above, Kilbane, County Cork, Ireland, must look like an ocean of green, rendering her a mere speck at sea. Before she knew it, she had passed the majestic remains of the ruined Dominican Priory, its Franciscan bell tower rising proudly above the town. Sheedy's cycle shop wasn't far now.

She hugged the medieval walls encircling the town, marveling at how something once constructed to keep violent marauders out could just as easily trap them in. She placed her hand on the ancient stone, relishing the way its rough peaks scraped against her fingertips. It was damp to the touch despite the midday sun. One of the few walled towns in existence, it had endured some of Ireland's most turbulent times and survived. These days Siobhán took solace wherever she could get it.

After ten straight days of lashing rain, the sun was laughing down on them, creating good cheer even in the begrudgers. Shopkeepers swept their footpaths, green thumbs tended gardens, and other folk simply turned their faces to the generous swath of blue sky. Children squealed, and kicked balls, and raced their bicycles through swollen puddles. Shoppers bustled along Sarsfield Street, calling in to the market, and the gift shop, and the chipper, and the hardware store. And, of course, to Naomi's Bistro. They would call out to one another—hello, hi ya, and how ya—and everyone would answer they were grand.

Siobhán had less than an hour before the lunch service at the bistro would begin. Given that children were tasting their first week of summer freedom, and it was a Friday to boot, they were going to be jammers. She picked up her pace, as the shop was just over the hill. If her siblings found out she was sneaking out several times a week to visit a pink scooter, they would declare her a right nutter.

Cows lifted their heads and chewed lazily as she panted by, sheep bleated, and swallows streaked through the sky. Patches of gorse set the neighboring fields aflame with their bright yellow heads, emitting the slightest scent of coconut. By the time she arrived at the shop, Siobhán was out of breath. She'd better stop eating so much brown bread at the bistro or she would have to buy a colored track suit and join the race-walking ladies in the morning. Surely their wagging tongues burned more calories than their aerobics. Siobhán laughed to herself and pushed the door to the shop open, hoping the jangle of the bell would disguise her labored breathing.

She looked at the counter, expecting to see Séamus Sheedy break out in his customary grin. Instead, there stood Niall Murphy. His dark hair, normally cut short, hung almost to his chin, giving him an unruly appearance. He seemed taller, too, or at least more filled out. Even before the bad business with Billy, Siobhán had always felt on edge around Niall. Maybe it was his eyes—technically brown, but so intense, his pupils so enormous that she always thought of them as black. She wasn't prepared for the shock. What was he doing here?

It was impossible to look at Niall without a thousand dark memories swarming in. Just when she thought she was on the mend, there he was again, the sniper of grief aiming a killing blow at her heart. Instantly, no time had passed at all. No time since that cruel morning almost one year ago when Niall's brother, Billy, got into his sporty red car, absolutely blotto, and slammed head-on into her parents. They died on impact. Billy was charged with drunk driving and sent to prison, and Niall took off for Dublin. Where, for some reason, Siobhán had just assumed he would stay.

She wanted to back out of the shop, but he'd already trained his dark eyes on her. Just then, Bridie Sheedy's head popped out from the other side of Niall. Séamus's wife was so petite Siobhán hadn't seen her at first.

"Hallo," Bridie called out. "How ya?" Despite an obvious attempt to sound cheerful, Bridie's voice wobbled, and Siobhán got the distinct feeling that she had just interrupted something. What on earth was Bridie doing standing so close to Niall? The two of them couldn't be sneaking around, could they? Surely not. Bridie was mad about Séamus, despite their age difference; everyone knew that.

"Grand," Siobhán said, doing her best to avoid Niall's stare. "How are you?"

"Not a bother." A smile broke out on Bridie's face, and this time it seemed genuine. With her head of brown curls and sparkling green eyes, Bridie's presence eased the tightness in Siobhán's chest a wee bit. Her smile didn't waver, but her tiny hand fluttered to her head, where she adjusted a knitted blue flower stuck in her hair, one she'd no doubt made herself. Bride was always a walking advertisement for her homemade wears.

It was odd to see her in here, surrounded by grease, and wheels, and dirty rags. She was normally at Courtney Kirby's gift shop, where she sold everything from jewelry to hand-made scarves. And when she wasn't at Courtney's she was perched on top of a stationary bike at spinning class. Siobhán would much rather ride a scooter; it never made sense to her why anyone would want to pedal like mad atop something that was never going to go anywhere.

Bridie picked up her bedazzled handbag, whisked out from behind the counter, and grabbed Siobhán by the arm. She had a surprisingly strong grip for such a little woman. "Would ye mind keeping my secret?"

Siobhán extricated Bridie's clawing fingers from her arm. She was the porcelain variety of pale and bruised easily. "What secret?"

"Don't tell Séamus I was here. I'm begging ye."

"Oh." *Jaysus, she didn't want to be part of that kind of secret.* Was Bridie cheating on Séamus? With Niall? Right here in the shop?

Bridie must have noticed Siobhán's face go scarlet, for she gasped and then laughed. "No, no, pet. Nothing I'll be needing to confess to Father Kearney." She continued to laugh, and Siobhán couldn't help but laugh with her. "Niall was helping me order a gear for Séamus." Séamus was an avid road racer, always darting about town on his bicycle. He used to compete in actual road races and had loads of trophies to show for it. Better than spinning, but Siobhán still preferred the scooters. "A surprise," Bridie continued. "For his birthday."

"Ah. Of course. Not a bother," Siobhán said.

"Grand." Bridie laughed and then kissed each of Siobhán's cheeks. "When are ye going to whittle us a few dainty birds or roses for Courtney's store?" She kept her big eyes on Siobhán without blinking. Siobhán had learned to whittle from her grandfather, who noticed Siobhán had a temper; although her mam was terrified at the thought of putting a knife into her wee hands, her grandfather insisted whittling would be a good outlet for the young hothead. It required patience and concentration, and to everyone but her grandfather's surprise, she was right good at it. She could turn a piece of wood into a tiny singing bird, or a delicate flower, or her personal favorite, a Celtic cross. There was a box underneath her bed with her carving knife and bits of wood. A little here, and a little there, and before she knew it, another marvelous creature would come into existence. But she hadn't felt like whittling since her parents had passed on. It didn't feel right to be so carefree.

Siobhán forced a smile back. "We'll see."

Bridie sang her good-byes over her shoulder and bounced out of the shop. Siobhán had a strange urge to run after her.

Niall darted out from behind the counter and planted himself in front of Siobhán. "What's the craic?"

Siobhán felt her ire rise. *Oh, we've been having some fun, boyo, since your brother slammed head-on into our parents.* "What are you doing here?" she said instead.

Niall glanced around the shop as if the bicycles had ears. "We need to talk."

Siobhán forced a smile. "Here for a wee visit with your mammy?" Nasty woman, that Mary Murphy. Her mam wouldn't want her speaking ill of a neighbor, but she couldn't help it. Mary Murphy hadn't once said she was sorry for what her son had done. Siobhán didn't realize her right hand was curled into a fist until a fingernail dug into her palm.

Niall's face darkened, and an unmistakable look of hate flashed across it as his mouth turned into a slight snarl. "Me mother hasn't been able to work since the town turned against her. You know it yourself. Séamus was good enough to take me on here."

Turned against her? Mary Murphy was the one who had been avoiding contact with everyone. She slipped in and out of Mass, hurried through the shops, and hadn't once come into the bistro since the accident. And here was Niall, blaming the entire town. Did that mean he was back for good? She didn't want to think about that now, and she especially didn't want to think about how her older brother James was going to react when he found out.

This was the problem with positive thinking: the moment she set herself up to be happy, something in her world always came crashing down. He'd ruined her break, the sunny day, her hope. She should just walk out right now, but she didn't want to give him the satisfaction. Without another word, she turned and made her way to the scooters that were lined up at the front window, all shiny and new.

Oh, how she loved the Italian scooters. She stood next to the black one, praying Niall Murphy wouldn't notice when she glanced down the row at her actual favorite, the one in pink. All her life she'd been told redheads couldn't wear pink. But her hair was a darker red, more auburn, and besides, that old notion had changed with the times, hadn't it? Kilbane had mobile phones, and cable television, and iPads, and redheads could now wear pink. Or else she could tuck her hair into the helmet.

Yes, she definitely wanted the pink one. With a basket. That was only practical. She could see herself zipping around town, picking up bread and milk when the bistro ran low, feeling the vibrations of the road in her body, the breeze on her face. Of course, she'd have to be careful in the rain, and she would have to figure out how to keep her siblings off it—

"Aren't you supposed to be in Dublin?" Niall said from behind her. "Starting university?" Siobhán stopped, and turned. Niall was less than a foot from her. Of course, she was supposed to be in Dublin. The whole village knew about her scholarship to Trinity College. After she completed her Leaving Certificate she'd spent two years working at the bistro and saving for University before the scholarship finally came through. Mam and Da even hung her acceptance letter up in the bistro for everyone to see. To add to her luck, her best friends Maria and Aisling had delayed college as well to travel. All three of them would be starting University at the same time, just like she'd always dreamed.

But just a few months before she was to embark on the adventure of her life, her parents were gone. James wasn't stable enough to run the bistro and take care of the three youngest. So it fell to Siobhán. Her best friends, Maria and Aisling, were at Trinity without her. The more time went by, the less they talked. It was too painful to be constantly reminded of the life she thought she was going to be leading.

How one's destiny could change in the blink of an eye. Niall Murphy knew why she wasn't in Dublin better than anyone. Her da's favorite Sean O'Casey quote rose up in her: *It's my rule never to lose me temper till it would be detrimental to keep it.* "I could say the same thing about you," she said. "Why aren't you still in Dublin?"

Niall looked around, even though they were still alone in the shop, then leaned in and lowered his voice. "I was planning on coming to see ye."

"What for?" Couldn't Niall see that she didn't even want to be in the same room with him?

"When can we meet?" He glanced around the shop. "Somewhere private like."

"Never," Siobhán said. Niall stared at her, and she stared back. There it was. She couldn't pretend, couldn't be polite. If he was back in town, that was his business, but she wanted him to stay far away from her and her siblings.

"Don't be like that."

"I have to go." Siobhán headed for the door. Niall blocked her.

"You've turned into a beauty since I've been gone."

Was he hitting on her? Siobhán felt the familiar flush of heat scorch her face. She'd always hated how she blushed at the drop of a hat. When she was younger it was a curse to be so tall, with flaming red hair. But now that she was twenty-two, everything that was once ugly about her had somehow pulled together and blossomed into something beautiful. She still wasn't used to it. It thrilled her secretly, and that in itself was probably a sin.

Imagine Siobhán O'Sullivan succumbing to vanity. Beauty came and went, Siobhán was well aware, but it appeared this was her time, and wasn't it just as much a sin not to enjoy a rose in full bloom? She'd been looking forward to what kind of a splash she could make in Dublin. But she didn't like Niall Murphy looking at her like that, saying those things. Where was Séamus?

Niall brought his face close to hers. She stood her ground despite desperately wanting to back away from him. "Listen to me, gorgeous. It wasn't Billy's fault. He didn't do it."

"Didn't do it?" Fury rose in her as the sight of her parents' twisted white Volvo accosted her once again. "Are ye mental?"

Niall put his hands up, as if surrendering, looked around, and stepped so close she could smell whiskey on his breath. "I have proof."

"Proof?" Instantly she saw Billy's flashy red car zooming around Devil's Curve and barreling head-on into her parents, who had been returning from a weekend in Waterford. When the guards arrived, Billy was found slumped over the wheel, concussed, but alive, and muttering excuses. Later he was found to be three times over the legal alcohol limit.

"Are ye saying someone forced whiskey into him and pushed him into his sporty car? Made him press down harder on the pedal? Ignored all warnings to slow down around Devil's Curve? Is that what you're saying to me?" Her voice was raised now, and she didn't care.

Niall shook his head. He had a wild look in his eye. "There's so much. You wouldn't believe it."

"I don't."

"The proof. It's worth something. You know?"

"I have to go." Siobhán stepped forward, and Niall blocked her path.

"Me mother is in bad health. My brother is rotting away without good legal help." She'd never seen such a look in anyone's eyes before. It was as if he was pleading with her and threatening her at the same time. Like a wounded animal you feared would tear into you the minute you stepped in to help. *Move, move, move.* But she couldn't. Scooters were lined up behind her, and Niall hadn't budged an inch. She was trapped.

"I need you to move," Siobhán said. *Poke him in the eyes.* Is that what she should do if he didn't let her pass?

"Look here. I'd rather give it to you. That's the right thing to do. But he's my brother. And he's locked away for something he didn't do."

"Give what to me?" He wasn't right in the head. Why was she even talking to him?

"I need ten thousand euro." Niall inched even closer.

"Ten thousand euro?" Mad. He was absolutely mad. They barely had a thousand euro in the bank. Not that it mattered. She wouldn't give Niall Murphy the lint from her pocket.

"I figure you must have some money tucked away for college. You said yourself, you won't be needing it now."

"You're despicable," Siobhán said.

"I'm tellin' ye. Yer one would give me twenty thousand euro for it. But I'm trying to do the right thing, can't ye see?"

Siobhán instinctively stepped back, and her backside bumped into the handlebars of the first scooter in line. Before she could even turn around, it tilted over and knocked into the next, then the next, and with surprising speed and clatter, the scooters fell like a line of dominoes. "Jaysus!"

Siobhán reached out to fix the mess, only it was too late. The lot of 'em lay on their sides. Oh, Jaysus, no. Siobhán crossed herself. Were they broken? Scratched? She couldn't afford one, let alone all of them. Why had she come to the shop today?

"You're fine, you're fine," Niall said. He stepped in front of her and pulled the first scooter up. Siobhán held her breath. Niall fixed it so it was standing again, then brushed off the dirt on the other side. Siobhán reached to right the next scooter, but Niall blocked her. "I'll do it. It's me job."

Siobhán stumbled back. It was his fault she'd knocked the scooters over—standing so close to her with alcohol on his breath, ranting about his brother being innocent, propositioning her with lies for ten thousand euro. "You're sick, you know that? You're sick in the head."

The door opened, the bell jingled, and Séamus Sheedy entered, wheeling a mountain bike into the shop. He was a middle-aged man, on the short side, and a good ten years older than Bridie, but he had an infectious grin and a full head of chestnut hair, and cycling kept him trim. "How ya," he called. His grin halted the minute he saw Siobhán's face. He looked from her to Niall, to the mess of scooters on the floor. "Are ye alright, pet?"

"I'm so sorry," Siobhán said. "It was an accident." Séamus shifted his gaze to Niall, still trying to right the last of the scooters.

"It's alright, petal. You're fine." Séamus parked his bike and approached. "What's the story?" he said to Niall.

"It's my fault. I lined them up too close together," Niall said. "So far just a smidge of dirt is all."

Séamus turned to Siobhán with a smile. "There's no harm done, pet. They just need a bit of shining is all."

"I'll get a rag," Niall said. He turned and, with a final look at Siobhán, went back behind the counter.

Séamus grabbed a set of keys hanging by the register and approached Siobhán. "Why don't we make today the day?"

Siobhán was still shaking; she just wanted to flee. "Pardon?" Even with a key dangling in front of her face, she couldn't make out what Séamus was trying to say.

"Why don't you finally take her for a ride?" He gestured to the pink scooter.

Oh, God she wanted to. She wanted to ride out of town and never look back. She wanted to run the scooter directly into Niall Murphy.

"Lunch service will be starting. I'd better get me legs under me." Siobhán headed for the door. She should have never come in. What a silly, silly, girl. What a right joke she was.

Séamus threw open his hands. "There's a discount on the pink one today, seeing how there's a wee scratch."

Siobhán's hands fluttered to her mouth. "Oh, Jaysus," she said. "I'm so sorry. I'll pay for it."

Séamus put his hands up. "I'm just jokin' ye. But she could be yours for a real good price."

Siobhán shook her head. She couldn't think about scooters right now. She couldn't think about anything with Niall Murphy standing right there. Had he really just tried to extort her for ten thousand euro? She should tell Séamus. He'd fire Niall on the spot. But not now. She couldn't think, or even breathe. She just wanted to get out of the shop. She'd sort it all out later. Séamus was still waiting for her answer.

"I can't. But thank you."

Séamus put the keys back and gestured to them. "The keys are here, anytime you want to give her a go," he said with a wink.

"Ba-bye, ba-bye, ba-bye." Siobhán flew out of the shop. She tore across the field, pumping her legs and arms faster, and faster, pushing herself to the point of pain. She ran all the way back to the bistro, and was about to fling herself at the door when Sheila Mahoney jumped out in front of her, wielding what appeared to be a razor-sharp blade.

Chapter 2

It took Siobhán a good minute to realize that the weapon Sheila brandished was a pair of scissors with hot-pink handles. "Go on, go on," Sheila said. She was intimidating enough with her extra padding, platinum blond hair, and heavily lined eyes. Jabbing at her with sharp scissors was overkill.

"They're free," Sheila said in her gravelly voice. Many in Kilbane were health-conscious, but Sheila Mahoney still smoked two packs of fags a day, even while shampooing and cutting hair. Hers was probably the only beauty salon in the entire world where you went in with your hair smelling better than when you came out. Siobhán figured the only reason someone else hadn't opened a rival shop was because most of the townspeople were deathly afraid of Sheila's wrath. Even Sheila's poor husband, Pio, was terrified of her; you could see it in his eyes.

Siobhán reluctantly took the scissors and glanced at the stem. SHEILA'S SALON was stamped on them in black ink. "Grand reopening. See?" Sheila pointed a long blue fingernail at her salon across the street. A new sign jutted out from the top of the door. It was rimmed in the same neon pink as the handle of the scissors. It was only then that Siobhán noticed Sheila's choppy blond locks had a streak of neon pink running through them as well.

Sheila changed her hair color as often as lassies changed their knickers. She had probably been a beautiful woman in her day, but middle age hadn't been kind to her. She'd put on quite a few stone in the past few years, and it seemed the bigger she became, the shorter she cut her hair and the more face paint she slathered on. One couldn't help but look twice whenever she was standing next to Pio, who was the very definition of beanpole. Siobhán wished her mam was here to see what Sheila had done. Screaming pink. It was some sight.

Sarsfield Street was no stranger to color. Shop after shop had façades that were awash in bright yellows, blues, pinks, and green. It helped to keep the folks sane through all the gray days. Siobhán couldn't help but to look up at their sign, a simple wooden frame where NAOMI'S BISTRO was written in black script and outlined in robin's egg blue. The building was painted to match as well—the bottom portion white and the top blue. Many other creative signs dotted the doorways on Sarsfield Street—BUTLER'S UNDERTAKER, LOUNGE, AND PUB was the largest one, almost three feet tall, with a painting of a white-haired gent drinking a pint—but the bistro was the only one with scripted letters and a matching painted frame. Until now. Why, Sheila Mahoney was a little copycat.

"What do you t'ink?" Sheila demanded.

"Lovely," Siobhán said. *Imitation is the sincerest form of flattery; do not get into a row with Sheila.* It was bad enough she was fretting over whether or not to tell James about her dustup with Niall.

Sheila thrust the box of scissors at Siobhán. "Would ye keep these on the counter? For your customers?"

"Our customers prefer to use knives and forks." Siobhán pushed the box back at Sheila.

"They're free." Sheila's voice rose in volume.

"Why don't you take them to Courtney?" Courtney's Gifts was on the opposite side of the street, just down a ways, next to the Kilbane Players, the community theatre.

Sheila wagged her head. "What is wrong with ye? Everyone likes to get something for free. You might think about that the next time you have an extra batch of brown bread."

"I can't take your scissors. We have too many young ones about. Imagine if one of them poked his or her eye out."

"What am I going to do with the rest of these?" Sheila demanded, jiggling the box as if it was Siobhán's fault.

"Cut hair?"

"You need sharper ones for that. These are promotional."

"Maybe you should have gone with candy."

"What does candy have to do with a hair salon?" Sheila barked.

Siobhán jumped. Lord, the woman was a holy terror. "I'm sorry. I can't be giving away sharp objects to our customers."

Sheila shook her fist. "Would you at least point out our new sign and let folks know I'm giving away a free gift with a haircut? Or would that be too much for ye?"

There would be no need. Folks would be able to see it in a hailstorm. "Will do."

"Why don't you take a few pairs for the rest of the six?"

Around town Siobhán and her siblings were known as the O'Sullivan Six. Siobhán hated it, but not as much as she hated the nickname the Irish Brady Bunch, so she kept her gob shut. "O'Sullivans and scissors don't mix." It was actually only Ann she'd be worried about. Still unsteady on those coltish legs, Ann was always falling into things. Although if the scooters could talk they might say the same thing about Siobhán.

"Right, so," Sheila said. She sighed, and remained blocking Siobhán's entryway.

"I'll mention it. I promise."

"T'ank you." Sheila set the box of scissors on the foot-path, next to the entrance. "Can I leave them here, so?"

"No," Siobhán said. She nudged them back to Sheila with her foot.

"Right," Sheila said. She didn't make a move to pick them up again.

"Why don't you place them at your own door?"

"If people were coming to me own door in the first place I wouldn't be needing to give away free scissors, now would I?" Sheila tapped her head, as if she was the only one thinking.

"Why don't you have Pio take them to trad sessions?" Siobhán loved traditional Irish music. Pio played the banjo and, if you were lucky, the spoons. It was amazing what he could do with the spoons.

"If you asked me to keep a platter of brown bread at me salon, I would do it, so," Sheila said. She stared at Siobhán, who simply stared back. Finally she snapped up the box of scissors and hugged them to her ample bosom. "Do you want to give me a platter of brown bread to keep at the shop?"

"I do not." Siobhán made the best brown bread in the village, and everyone knew it.

Sheila snorted and lifted the box of scissors. "Take 'em to the pubs, you say?"

"Why not?"

"A bunch of langered lads running around Kilbane with sharp scissors? Some craic."

"I thought you said they weren't sharp."

"I'm starting to think you aren't either. Free is free."

"My answer is no." Give her long enough and Sheila Mahoney would beat the polite out of anyone, including Father Kearney.

"Your mam and dad wouldn't have turned their back on a neighbor," Sheila said. And with that she whirled around and marched back to the salon, her scissors clinking in the box with every step. It took Siobhán a minute to realize she had a pair clutched in her hand, and then it took considerable restraint for her not to lob them at the back of Sheila Mahoney's head.

The next day the gray skies were back, the rain drummed on the roof and lashed against the windows, and the wind whipped the front bell into a frenzy. It seemed as if the entire town had turned out on a Saturday morning for an Irish breakfast; even Macdara Flannery was there in his garda's uniform. The blue jacket, cap, and tie suited him. He looked proper, and so handsome. She loved the golden decal on the cap—the shield—An Garda Síochána. *Guardians of the Peace.* Her eyes were always drawn to it. The shield. The protector. Intoxicating is what it was. Siobhán tried not to stare—especially since every time she looked his way he was staring at her, and each and every time their eyes locked her stomach gave a little flip. What was it about a man in uniform that she found so irresistible?

He was taller than a lot of lads about town, just over six foot. Siobhán towered over most men in Kilbane at five foot nine, but whenever she stood close to Macdara she felt normal. He was handsome in an imperfect sort of way. His brown hair was always unkempt as if it never met a brush, and his face was often covered in two-day stubble. He had killer black eyelashes and the prettiest blue eyes, a color that stood out against the dark blue of his uniform and the Irish gray skies. Despite women in town going after him, he'd managed to remain a bachelor.

He was once mad about a girl, a blond girl from Australia who'd lived in Kilbane several years back. Siobhán remembered seeing them about town, holding hands or kissing in the rain. The girl had been gone five years now, and although Macdara had dated women since, he'd never stayed with one for very long despite several blatant attempts to domesticate him.

Siobhán had never looked at Macdara in a romantic way, until the day her parents died. He was the one who came to her that awful morning. A series of sharp raps on the door woke her out of a deep sleep. She'd come down in her nightshirt, a ratty old thing that wasn't meant to be seen. For a few heart-stopping seconds she couldn't make sense of the fact that he was at her door in full uniform. They'd stood staring at each other through a thin curtain of rain. Then she stepped back; he stepped in, took off his hat, and placed it over his heart. The first stab of fear pierced Siobhán's heart.

"No," she said, shaking her head before he even spoke. "No." Instinctively she reached out with trembling hands and touched his chest. He clasped his hand over hers and squeezed. She knew then, knew a horror she could not name, but she knew, and she wanted to die.

"I'm so sorry." Despite her silent pleas for him to stop, he delivered the news about the crash with tears in his eyes, and looked at her as if he knew every ounce of pain this was going to cause and would do anything to take it away. When the words stopped, he pulled her into him and held her against his chest while she sobbed. He was wearing cologne, which surprised her. She fit in his arms, which surprised her even more. For one brief second, he even stroked her hair.

Suddenly, he stopped, as if he'd startled himself, as if for a moment he'd forgotten who she was and why he was here. He stepped back, stared at her, and there it was. An undeniable, inappropriate spark. Her parents were dead and she wanted him to kiss her. She didn't know how to forgive herself for that, or if she even should.

Since then, the very air between them had changed. An intimacy she couldn't shove away had filled the gaps between them, and she wasn't the only one appalled by the development. He often looked at her as if he hated her for making him feel again. Surely he didn't want to love a young, orphaned woman suddenly stuck with a family bistro and five siblings to look out for, and she couldn't fall in love with the man who had stirred feelings in her while bringing her the worst news of her life. It wasn't even a real relationship and it was already doomed.

Usually he only visited on weekdays, when he was off duty and the bistro was less crowded. Truth be told, he looked good in his common clothes as well. He was a bit of a clothes horse, which was intriguing. He always wore nicely pressed denims and a stylish shirt.

Did he go into Dublin to shop for the latest fashions? His cologne smelled dear too; she doubted they sold a scent that alluring at the pharmacy in Kilbane. She knew they didn't for one day she went in and sussed them all out, just to see what he was using, and not only did she not come across his cologne, she spent the rest of the day sneezing and being blessed.

Despite her ambivalence, the atmosphere lifted whenever Macdara was nearby. Not that she would ever do anything more than daydream about him. He was too old for her—at least thirty years of age he was—and besides, she wasn't going to spend the rest of her life in Kilbane like Macdara seemed poised to do.

He was sitting by the front window with a heaping pile of food in front of him, a cup of Barry's tea, and an extra helping of brown bread. He caught her eye and smiled. Her cheeks heated up as if she'd been caught doing something she shouldn't. She jerked her head in the opposite direction. *That wasn't odd at all,* Siobhán. *Way to go.* She picked up a few empty plates from neighboring tables and took them into the kitchen. Next she poked at the fire that crackled in the front room before tossing more kindling on it.

Gráinne and Ann had control of the dining room, and the

lads were manning the kitchen. Besides tending to the register, Siobhán's main job this morning was to warn folks to watch their step. For as soon as she wiped up one set of wet prints from the floor, two more feet walked across it.

She had just set the mop in the corner when the bell jangled and in walked Niall Murphy. Before she could even say a word, he strode to the back of the bistro and took a seat at the last empty table. He gave her a look, as if daring her to challenge him.

Siobhán whirled around and burst into the kitchen. "Niall Murphy is here," she announced to her brothers, who turned in unison. Shock was stamped across Eoin's boyish face, but James was deathly still, his expression hard to read.

"Why?" Eoin said. Siobhán shook her head. There was no reason why. Not anymore.

"Well, how do you like that?" James slammed the spatula onto the side of the grill, and Eoin jumped. James had two years on Siobhán, but they were negated by his love for the drink. In many ways he needed just as much minding as the young ones. But he had been doing so well lately. Would Niall Murphy ruin all his progress in one fell swoop? James was finally on the straight and narrow, helping out in the bistro and about to get his six-month Pioneer Pin. Siobhán never thought he could stay sober for that long. She'd die before she'd let another Murphy boy pitch their lives upside down.

"Toss him out," Eoin said with a jerk of his hand. At fifteen, Eoin was already taller than Siobhán. Ciarán, who was supposed to be doing the dishes but was really testing out a toy boat in the sink full of suds, watched the exchange with wide eyes. Siobahn could practically see his ears flapping as he soaked in every utterance. He was still young, thank God, but a bit cheeky at ten years of age.

"Hush," Siobhán said. "We're not like that."

"I'm like that," Eoin said. "That's exactly what I'm like."

His eyes sparked. He often reminded Siobhán of a cannon about to fire, his lanky body bottled up and ready to blow. God help her.

"Niall Murphy," James said, as if testing out the name. His chestnut hair was curled at the edges, testament to the heat in the kitchen. Eoin had the exact same hair, but his was tucked under a backward Yankees cap. He'd never been to New York, let alone America, and had never even seen the team play on telly. But it was a rare day he wasn't wearing that cap. Eoin had a strange addiction to ordering American shite off eBay. But if he limited it to small items and if it kept him from going down the same road as James, Siobhán couldn't see the harm in it.

"I'll do the honors," Eoin said. He grabbed a bowl of potato leek soup and spit in it. Ciarán careened in, plucked up a thick slice of brown bread with soapy fingers, licked it top to bottom, and dropped it on the platter next to the soup.

"Deadly," Eoin said. He and Ciarán high-fived. Ciarán had to stand on his tiptoes to reach Eoin's hand. He was the only one besides Siobhán with dark red hair. But unlike her porcelain skin, he had a mountain of freckles dotting his face.

"Don't be cheeky," Siobhán said as Eoin grabbed a salt-shaker and upended it into a cup of tea. "We're not serving him that. James?"

James nodded, removed the offending offerings from the lads, and upended them into the trash before turning to Siobhán. "What's he doing here?"

Siobhán bit her lip and shrugged. She was dying to tell James what Niall had said to her in the cycle shop, but now she knew she couldn't. If Niall Murphy uttered a word to James about Billy being innocent and wanting ten thousand euro, James would be raging, that was for sure. The sooner Niall Murphy went back to Dublin, the better. "I just wanted you to be prepared. We'll all be polite, hear?"

"Why are we being polite?" Siobhán didn't even hear Gráinne come into the kitchen. She stood in front of her, right hip jutted out, manicured hand on top of it like she was posing for a soap on the telly. Siobhán still wasn't used to how pretty Gráinne was; at sixteen she was a raven-haired stunner. Too bad her personality wasn't anywhere as refined.

"Niall fecking Murphy is in the house," Eoin said. "And we can't even spit in his soup."

"Language," Siobhán said.

"I saw him already," Gráinne said. "I talked to him."

Siobhán felt the hair on the back of her neck rise. "What did he say?"

"Why are you freaking out?" Gráinne said.

"Why are you talking like a Yank?" Siobhán said. Although she knew the answer to that. Internet and the telly. The door burst open and Ann barreled in. At thirteen, she was just a hair taller than Ciarán, and the only blonde of the lot. Their da used to say, "I never did like the milkman."

"There's a row in the dining room!" Ann said. "Niall Murphy and Mike Granger are about to get into fisticuffs!"

Chapter 3

The O'Sullivan Six rushed out of the kitchen and burst into the dining area. Sure enough, Mike Granger and Niall Murphy were circling each other around a table, chests out and fists up.

"A amadáin!" Mike called Niall a fool in Irish.

"Éist do bhéal," Niall replied. *Shut your mouth.*

Siobhán was furious. They were acting the maggot in her bistro. Garda Flannery and Séamus Sheedy circled around them.

"Take it easy now," Macdara said.

"Settle," Séamus echoed. The rest of the patrons were out of their seats, a few standing on them, craning their necks to have a look. Several had their mobiles out and were snapping pictures.

"What's going on?" Siobhán said. She stepped up next to Macdara. He put his hand on her waist and gently pushed her back. "Stop it," she called to the men. "This is a family place."

"I want him out of this town," Mike Granger yelled, spit flying. His biceps bulged under his shirt. He owned the food mart at the end of the street and was living proof that hauling boxes of produce could turn you into a he-man. Mike had been a dear friend of her da's. They grew up together, and even opened their shops at the same time. Siobhán felt a squeeze of love toward him for trying to protect them, but at the same time was ashamed of herself for it. Niall wasn't the one to blame. Like it or not, he had a right to be here. The overhead light shone on Mike's bald head as he circled the table.

"I'm my brother's keeper, is that it?" Niall said. Siobhán froze, praying he wouldn't start in about Billy being innocent.

"Let's take it outside," James said, pushing his way in. Panic seized Siobhán. It sounded like he was including himself in that invitation.

"You are good for nothing, just like your brother," Mike said. Macdara stepped up, took Mike by the arm, and pulled him back. Siobhán glanced at Niall. Sweat dotted his forehead, and the crazy look he'd had in his eyes yesterday was even more pronounced today. Now that Mike was somewhat subdued, he pushed his chest out and looked wildly around at all the people staring at him.

"This is my home too," Niall shouted. "You might have scared me mother, but you don't scare me."

"Nobody has been scaring your mother," Siobhán said. Right? She'd never heard a word about it.

"Of course this is your home too," Gráinne said. She sounded as if she meant it. As if she didn't want Niall to be upset. Alarm bells rang in Siobhán's head, but there was no time to make sense of it.

"Shame on all of yous," Niall shouted, his eyes landing one by one on those gathered around him. "You're all going to know the truth. And by this time tomorrow, you're all going to have to face it." He whirled around, then closed the distance between himself and Siobhán until he was right in her face. "Especially you," he said. "You had your chance."

Macdara and James immediately stepped between Siobhán and Niall. Macdara gave a warning nod to James, and to Siobhán's relief he fell back. Macdara and Niall squared off.

"Niall Murphy." Bridie Sheedy stepped up, despite Séamus trying to hold her back. This time she wore a pink headband with sparkles. "You're better than this. There's no need for a scene."

Niall ignored Bridie and thrust his finger at Siobhán. "You had your chance. Don't forget that."

"What chance?" James said. "Siobhán?"

Siobhán shook her head as if she had no idea what Niall was going on about.

"Get a move on, or hand to God, I will take you into the station," Macdara said. It struck her now more than ever that the guards should be allowed to carry guns. What good would a baton do in a real crisis? The crowd parted as Niall Murphy marched toward the front door. Halfway there, he whirled around and instead headed for the back door. It led to their private back garden, and customers weren't supposed to use that door.

"Hey." James started after Niall, but Siobhán grabbed his arm and held onto him with all her might. She didn't care which way Niall went out as long as he was gone and stayed gone.

That evening the O'Sullivan Six sat in the front room of the bistro, with the shutters thrown open so they could catch the remaining light of the day as they had supper together. The bistro was only open for breakfast and lunch; suppertime was for family.

Niall's appearance had cast a somber pall over the clan, and the argument between Mike and Niall had them all twitching. Siobhán couldn't help but feel there was more to the story. Of course, Mike would be protective of them; everyone in town was, to some extent, but the fight she witnessed had seemed personal. What had Niall ever done to Mike? Siobhán didn't want to think about it during family dinner, so she tried to lighten the mood.

"I'm going to start running," she announced. It was true. She was going to get in great shape; she was going to become a morning jogger.

James looked up from his bacon and cabbage and frowned. "Running what?"

"Running," Siobhán said. "Like for sport."

"Without anyone chasing you?" Ciarán said.

"Are ye joking me?" Ann said. "Why would you ever want to do that?" She flipped her blond braids behind her with disgust.

"When?" Gráinne demanded.

"Early, like," Siobhán said. "Very early."

"Who is going to prep the breakfast?" Gráinne said, eyes narrowing into tiny slits.

"I'll be back in time."

"See that you are," Gráinne said. "Everyone likes your brown bread the best. Even better than Mam's."

Siobhán didn't like to admit that, but it was true. She crossed herself anyway.

"Is it because of what the lads have been saying about your arse?" Eoin asked.

Siobhán's fork clattered to her plate. "What lads? What have they been saying about me arse?"

"Don't answer that," James said. Siobhán glared at him. James shrugged. "Best he learns now," he said. "Best he learns now." When they were finished with the meal, James ordered the rest of them out of the room.

"They're supposed to clean up," Siobhán said, picking up a plate. James took it out of her hand and gently pushed her down in her seat.

"I'll do it myself. But first you're going to tell me exactly what Niall Murphy meant when he said you had your chance, and that we'll see, we'll all see."

"How would I know?" Siobhán said. James gave her a look. She should have known better than to try to lie. James had this uncanny ability to see into her. Even more than her parents ever had. That is, when he was sober.

He plopped into the seat across from her, folded his hands together, and leaned forward. "Spill the beans. All of 'em."

Siobhán looked over his shoulder. Her eyes caught her mam's apron, hanging on the hook behind the register. Usually it gave her comfort. It did nothing for her now. This was bad. She could feel it. "Just some nonsense he said at the cycle shop."

"Are ye still going to see that fecking pink scooter?"

Now that Sheila's shop had gone pink Siobhán had decided she liked the black scooter better. Not that James needed to know any of it. "Is that what you want to talk about now?"

James shook his head. "What nonsense?" He leaned forward, his brow furled. He was a dog who wanted his bone alright, and he'd be at her until she gave it to him.

"He said Billy was innocent. That he had proof."

"What?" James rose from his chair.

"I told you. It's nonsense."

"Go on."

"That's pretty much it."

"Siobhán O'Sullivan."

"He said he could get a lot of money from yer one, but he wanted to do the right thing and sell it to me first."

"A lot of money from who? Sell what?"

"I don't know. He was talking nonsense. He just said 'yer one.'"

"Are ye jokin' me?" James was practically bouncing around the room.

"He's mental. I mean it. Sick in the head."

"He's mental, alright. If he's not, he will be when I get

through with him." Fists curled, James headed for the door. Siobhán threw herself at him and grabbed his arm. He yanked it away.

"Don't," she said. "I'm begging you." Siobhán literally dropped to her knees. James turned around.

"Get up."

"I need you. We need you."

"If you think I'm going to let that arsehole threaten me sister and spread nasty lies about our parents, then you must be the one who's mental."

"It's not worth it. It's not worth everything we've been through."

"Get off the floor." James held his hand out.

Siobhán took it but remained kneeling. "Promise me, James. Promise me you'll let this go."

James sighed, then gently hauled Siobhán to her feet. "I can't promise."

"Promise me," she said again.

He headed for the door. "Lock up."

"Where are you going?" But James didn't answer. He simply headed for the French doors that separated the bistro from the hallway. Once he was in the hall, James was either heading for the staircase on the right, or the main door straight ahead. Siobhán had a feeling he wasn't headed upstairs for a rest.

"Wait. Stay here. Just for tonight." She hurried after him. But he was already out the front door. It slammed behind him. She got back down on her knees. She closed her eyes. She clasped her hands. And for the first time in nearly a year, she prayed.

The next morning, Siobhán was up before the birds. She crept into the room the lads shared. Eoin and Ciarán were fast asleep, but James's bed was empty. Not a crease on it.

He'd been away all night. Did he get drunk? Confront Niall
Murphy? Where was he now? Siobhán had tried to stay awake
and wait for him but had succumbed to sleep just after midnight. She should have called Macdara. She should have gone
looking for him.

Siobhán used her gnawing worry to fuel her first run. She
kept at it, one step at a time. At half four there was a marked
chill in the air, but at least it wasn't lashing rain. The sky
was still dark, and the houses were shuttered. A few street
lamps created a glow along Sarsfield Street. Siobhán liked
listening to the echo of her runners hitting the pavement.
She passed King's Castle in the centre of town, cut right at
the corner, and then slammed into someone's chest.

She jumped back with a half scream.

"Oh, God. I'm sorry. I'm so sorry," the stranger said. He
had an American accent. Siobhán stepped back and took in
the man. The Yank was a tall lad, and was about her age.
Who was he? Where had he come from? *Gorgeous* was the
only word that popped into her head. He looked like a movie
star. If she had known men like him were out running in the
wee hours of the mornin', she would have started a long
time ago. "Sorry," Siobhán's voice was barely a whisper.

"My fault," he said. He flashed perfect teeth. They were
in the town square, the only part of town that was well lit at
night, to keep lads from vandalizing the castle. It was bright
enough to see a dimple appear on the left side of his face.
"Are you okay?"

"Right as rain." She took off again, too flustered to talk.
He couldn't have been in Kilbane long or surely she would
have seen him in the bistro. She'd have to ask Courtney or
Declan about him; they were always the first two to get the
gossip.

"What's your name?" he called after her, but she kept
going. Looks like he'd be asking around town about her as
well. She thought of Macdara and felt a bit of shame flare

through her. It was normal to find more than one man attractive; she knew that, of course, so why was she apologizing to Macdara in her head?

She reached the end of the street and gazed out at the remains of the astounding Dominican Priory set farther back in the field, just across the river. Kilbane's most precious landmark was founded in 1291, donated to the Dominicans, and cared for by the White Knights. The original settlement was said to be comprised of a modest stone chapel and a few wooden buildings. But almost immediately the bishop of Limerick, who was the feudal lord at the time, sent his armies to kick out the Dominicans.

In true Irish spirit, the Dominicans appealed all the way up to the king of England, who granted the monastery back to them. The White Knights became the patrons of the monastery, and their importance and wealth grew under the earls of Desmond, and the priory blossomed as Kilbane became one of the wealthiest and most strategic towns in Ireland. The magnificent cloister was added in the fourteenth century with the stunning five-light east window. The ornate arched structure was separated into five distinct openings by intersecting stone arches. It must have been absolutely stunning when the glass was in place and the sun would strike just so. In the fifteenth century the Franciscan Bell Tower was added and the abbey came alive with sound. Where there is light and music, there are spirits. It must be so for the Dominicans brewed beer and had two stills along the river dedicated to that purpose.

Sadly, when the fortunes of the earls of Desmond began to wane in the sixteenth century, so too did Kilbane's. In the 1570s, during the Desmond Rebellions, Kilbane was attacked and the monastery was burned. Even then, many Dominicans returned. And then came the Reformation and the vicious dissolution of the monasteries by the English king Henry VIII. Despite this, Kilbane stayed strong and the monastery stayed

Catholic. But as the English government took more control, in swept the Cromwellian armies, and twice more Kilbane was attacked and burned. The monastery eventually became a burned-out shell.

But it was the most beautiful burned-out shell Siobhán had ever seen, its turbulent and fascinating history a testament to the Irish spirit. Growing up with it practically in her backyard had inspired Siobhán's love of medieval history.

She was so proud of the amazing piece of architecture. She could spend hours within it, searching for stone carvings of heads and flowers that still adorned the ancient structure. The best bit was in the centre of the choir. There lay the tomb of the last White Knight, Edmund.

Kilbane had much to be proud of, and Siobhán felt as if the history of the town was actually a part of her, as integral to who she was as her blood and bones. If it could withstand everything it had, surely she could withstand a morning run.

But once she reached the monastery, she'd be running in the pitch black. She gripped her flashlight as her feet sank into the soft grass. The path was broken up by little holes, the product of bored boys with sticks and spades. Siobhán would have to watch her step. It wouldn't be such a good start if she sprained an ankle. A horse was grazing by the stream at the far end.

It was a horse that belonged to one of the travelers, or tinkers, as everyone in town called them. Siobhán tried not to use the disparaging term, but it was hard not to be enraged by some of the behavior of the itinerants who set up camp on the outskirts of Kilbane. They didn't pay taxes or electric bills, yet many of them had their RVs rigged up to the power lines, and the areas surrounding their camps looked like junk heaps. They didn't treat their animals much better. This brown and white horse, tied to a tree by a short rope, was so skinny that in the daylight you could clearly see his ribs. Once she'd tried to feed him, and one of the travelers had come tearing across the field to run her off, screaming and hollering at her. All for trying to feed the poor thing!

Presumably they brought the horse here to graze on the grass and drink from the stream. Fortunately, his owners weren't around at this hour of the morning, and Siobhán hurried over with her carrots. The horse whinnied if she got too near, so she dropped the carrots at his feet and turned back to the abbey. She could hear him crunching as she jogged away.

She flicked on the flashlight as she started around the circumference of the monastery. She trained her eyes on the bell tower, where kids often climbed to the top just to get into all kinds of mischief. Teenagers came for a different kind of mischief. Siobhán knew that included James and Eoin, but she was hardly going to fault a couple of teenage boys. Gráinne and Ann claimed that it wasn't their style to make out with lads here, but Siobhán had her doubts. After all, she had come here as a teenager to shift boys or chinwag with her girlfriends about shifting boys. But the kissing was as far as it went. She had never drunk or smoked, or shagged any lad here, but it was obvious the lads and lasses were doing it these days. As if the holes weren't bad enough, one had to watch out for broken beer bottles and other unmentionables.

She kept the light shining just ahead of her on the ground. Large footsteps could be clearly seen in the mud. Had the gorgeous American been running here as well? She looked closer and noticed they were covering up a slightly smaller set of footprints. Maybe he'd been here with a girl. Siobhán gripped the flashlight as she wondered who it might be, and picked up her pace. By the time she'd run around the grounds, she was sweating and a pain was starting to form in her side. That was enough for today. She turned and headed for home. She kept her eyes peeled on the road back home, but there was no sign of the handsome Yank.

Chapter 4

⬥

Siobhán checked her watch as she neared the bistro. Thirty minutes. *That'll do.* The street lamps emitted a soft glow, but it was still dark. However, across the way, the shutters were thrown open in Sheila's salon, and every single light was ablaze. Stranger yet, the front door was wide open. How very odd.

Had Sheila just stepped out? Siobhán looked left and right, but didn't see a sign of Sheila or Pio. She turned her eyes to their bedroom window. Like the O'Sullivans, most of the people who owned businesses on Sarsfield Street lived in a flat above the shop. There was no use living farther away when your hours were so long. But Sheila and Pio's bedroom was dark. Yet there didn't appear to be anyone downstairs. Should Siobhán go over and shut their door? Why, anything or anyone could wander in.

Siobhán started across the street, then stopped. What if they were being robbed? Maybe Siobhán should just go inside her own home and call Macdara.

Just then a little red pickup truck rumbled by. Mike

Granger stuck his hand out the window and waved. Siobhán waved back. Maybe nobody in town could sleep today. Mike usually opened the market at eight. After that, Peter's hardware store would open at nine, and Courtney's gift shop at ten. The only establishments that opened earlier than their bistro were a handful of pubs that catered to the graveyard shifts.

Just then, a figure appeared from around the side of Sheila's salon, hurrying through the tiny walkway that separated it from the chipper next door. It could have been Sheila, but Siobhán couldn't see for sure. The person was wearing a hooded rain jacket, even though there wasn't a drop in the sky. He or she was the right size and height for Sheila, round and short. Definitely had to be Sheila. She was carrying a large rubbish bag with both hands and appeared to be sinking underneath the weight of it.

Siobhán lifted her hand to wave, but Sheila didn't even glance in her direction. Instead she hurried into the salon and slammed the door. Seconds later the shop plunged to black. Strange. Why was she carrying a rubbish bag *into* the shop? Siobhán didn't want to know. Sheila probably wasn't the first wife to go through the rubbish, literally trying to dig up something on her husband. Siobhán liked Pio, but that didn't mean she could vouch for his fidelity. He was, after all, a musician. At least they hadn't been burgled.

Siobhán unlocked the front door of the bistro and slipped inside. She locked the door behind her, passed the staircase leading to their upstairs dwelling, and turned right where French doors led into the entry of the bistro. They wouldn't open for several more hours, but Siobhán wanted a few quiet moments in the space before she showered. She made a beeline for the counter on which sat her pride and joy, a state-of-the-art espresso machine. Despite a few old-timers grumbling about her trying to change up the joint, her cappuccinos were to die for. Siobhán threw open the shutters. If only she could stand here for hours, drinking cappuccinos and daydreaming.

Instead she would have to shower quickly and start the brown bread and Irish bacon. She crossed back to the French doors and was about to head upstairs when she heard voices coming from the kitchen. Her knees locked up as she strained to listen. Someone was definitely in the kitchen. Her siblings wouldn't be awake for another hour. Siobhán grabbed the rolling pin next to the register, held it up to her right shoulder, and positioned herself near the kitchen door. On three, she told herself. *One. Two.*

Siobhán burst through the door before she even hit three. Voices and the clattering of dishes rose to greet her along with the smell of bacon and black-and-white pudding sizzling on the grill. The meaty patties filled the kitchen with a sharp, sweet aroma. Gráinne and Ann were kneading the soda bread, Ciarán was cracking eggs, and Eoin was lording over the grill. Siobhán's stomach rumbled. Running sure did work up an appetite.

"What's this?" Siobhán asked.

"It's a surpise," Ann said.

"Surprise," Ciarán said, jumping into the air with his arms out.

"Take a shower," Eoin said without looking up. "I can smell you from here."

"Look," Ciarán said, tipping his bowl to show her the eggs. "No shells."

"Maith an buachaill," Siobhán said. *Good boy.* Her mam used to say it to Ciarán all the time. Siobhán wanted to keep up the effort. Ciarán grinned, exposing a gap between his teeth. She could eat him up.

"Are you surprised?" Gráinne said.

"You could have knocked me over," Siobhán said. "I was

going to smash someone's head in with this rolling pin."
Siobhán thunked it down on the nearest counter. Four faces
turned to her, beaming. Oh, no. They were up to something.

Last time they'd pulled something like this, Ciarán had
wanted a puppy, Eoin a car (even though he was only fifteen), and the girls had wanted to escape to London for the
weekend. *As if!*

"Go on take a shower and change, will ye. It'll be ready
when you're done," Eoin said. "And wake James while you're
at it."

Siobhán's smile faded. Apparently they hadn't even noticed that James wasn't in his bed. "Are you sure I can't
help?"

"We've got it," Gráinne said.

"Suit yourself." Siobhán whirled around and exited the
kitchen. Maybe there was hope for them, after all.

She was just about to cross through the dining room
when out of the corner of her eye she spotted a figure sitting
in the back dining room. Was it James? Heart pounding in
her chest, she stopped and stared. There was someone there
alright, but it wasn't James. Although she could only see the
back of his head, the man appeared to be completely bald.
Mike? Couldn't be; he'd just passed her in his truck. The
man was seated at the same table Niall had occupied the day
before.

Whoever it was, he was sitting like a statue. She thought
of calling out to the man, but none of it felt right. Siobhán
slowly stepped backward until she reached the kitchen door.
She backed into the kitchen and grasped the doors to keep
them from making a noise as they swung shut.

"You still smell," Eoin said.

Siobhán whirled around and put her index finger over her
mouth. Eoin raised an eyebrow. "Did you invite a friend
over?" she whispered.

"What are ye on about?" Gráinne said.

"Did anyone hear James come in last night?" Siobhán said. "Did he bring a friend?"

"I think I heard him," Ann said.

"You were dreaming," Gráinne said.

"Who has the mobile in here?" Four faces stared at her, uncomprehending. The O'Sullivan six shared three mobiles between them, a rule her parents threw down and one Siobhán had been too heartsick to break. James had commandeered one and Siobhán the other. That left the younger four squabbling over the third. Siobhán's was upstairs in her room. The work phone was next to the cash register. She was going to have to rethink the three-phone rule.

"Gráinne always has the phone now," Ann said.

"Shut your gob," Gráinne said.

"Why do you need our mobile?" Ciarán asked.

"Quiet. Did any of you invite a friend over?" Siobhán asked.

"None of us have friends," Gráinne said loudly.

"Shh." Siobhán bypassed the rolling pin and snatched a large knife off the counter.

"What are you at?" Eoin said.

Siobhán shushed them again. "Turn off the grill. And stay in here."

"But we've only started," Ciarán said. "It's still mooing."

"It's pig, you eejit," Eoin said.

"Oinking, so," Ciarán said.

Siobhán waved her arm. "There's some yoke out there."

"But we're not open," Ciarán said.

"What yoke?" Eoin stepped up and squared his shoulders. She was grateful he was tall, like James, and awake.

"You're giving me a fright," Ann said. Her blue eyes were wide, strands of her blond hair stuck up in the back like antennas. Siobhán was going to have to give her a trim soon.

"Not me," Ciarán said. "Let's give him a wallop!"

"You're staying here," Siobhán said. "Eoin and I will go."

"You're taking the piss," Gráinne said. Her eyes were wide too, her dark hair pulled back and held with a band.

"There's some yoke just sitting in the back dining room," Siobhán whispered, pointing.

"Did he see you?" Eoin said.

"His back was to me. I think he's asleep."

Eoin grabbed an even larger knife, and before Siobhán could stop him, he hit the door. Out of the corner of her eye, she saw Gráinne grab the rolling pin, and before long the O'Sullivan clan was armed. Ann had a spatula, and Ciarán lofted a tea kettle. Siobhán didn't know if he was going to serve the stranger tea or scald him. She wanted to yell at the younger ones to go back into the kitchen, but maybe they were better off staying together.

Siobhán flipped on the light to the dining room as they poured into the front room of the bistro. Makeshift weapons aloft, they inched toward the stranger. Whoever he was, he was wearing a gray pinstriped suit. The only suits they saw in here were after weddings or wakes. Not even Sunday Mass. The light didn't cause him to stir. Whoever he was, he must be dead asleep.

"Hey," Eoin yelled. "You there."

"Put your hands up and slowly turn around," Ciarán said. They all stopped and glanced at him. "*CSI*," he whisper-yelled.

"On how many episodes of *CSI* did they take down the criminal with a tea kettle?" Siobhán asked.

Ciarán shrugged.

The man at the table did not move. Eoin took another step.

"Bugger off," he said loudly. The man still did not stir.

"Is he asleep?" Ciarán said.

"Probably pissed," Ann said. He was sitting awfully straight for a drunk man, Siobhán thought. Eoin was the first to reach the man. Holding the knife aloft in one hand, he touched the stranger's shoulder with the other. The man's body shifted, and his head fell to the side. Eoin yelped, then jumped back, and darted around to the front of him. A second later the knife dropped from Eoin's hand and clattered to the floor.

"Jaysus," he cried out. He planted his fists in front of his mouth.

"What?" Siobhán said. "Is he asleep?" But even as she said it, she knew it was something far worse.

"Feck!" Eoin said. "Feck, feck, feck." He bit his fist.

Siobhán reached his side. The first thing she saw was the blood. Not a lot, just enough to form a cloud in the centre of his chest. Protruding from his heart was a pair of scissors with hot-pink handles.

Siobhán let out a scream. "Oh my God, oh my God." She couldn't stop saying it.

The dead man's eyes were wide open, like two black holes staring into an abyss. Siobhán screamed again and slapped her hands over her mouth as if to shut herself up.

"What?" Gráinne yelled. "What?" The three younger ones tried to move forward to see, but Eoin held them back.

Niall Murphy. Oh, God in heaven. The dead man was none other than Niall Murphy.

Chapter 5

Siobhán had wished Niall Murphy dead so many times since yesterday, and now here he was, as if mocking her. If only she could take back every evil thought. Had she caused this somehow? Or had it been James?

No, don't even think such a thing. Siobhán crossed herself. Not James. He would never do such a thing. *Would he?* The terrible thoughts pierced her like stinging nettles. Oh, God. Nobody deserved this, not even Niall.

"Gráinne, call the guards. Ann and Ciarán, watch out the front window for them," Siobhán said. She wanted them all to focus on something, anything, other than the body in the back of the bistro.

"I want to see, I want to see," Ciarán shouted.

Siobhán pulled him into her. "No," she said squeezing him tight. "No."

Gráinne came running back into the room. "Garda Flannery is on his way."

"What did you say?"

"I told him we had a break-in."

"That's it?"

"He'll catch on when he's here, won't he?" Gráinne gave her a withering look. Siobhán didn't have time for her teenage attitude.

Just then Ann came tripping down the stairs. Her face was even paler than usual. "James isn't in his room."

All of her siblings looked at Siobhán. "He never came home?" Eoin asked.

"Not a word to Garda Flannery," Siobhán said.

"Why?" Ciarán said.

"It's *our* business, that's why," Siobhán said.

"Niall Murphy?" Gráinne said. Her voice rose and cracked. "Are ye sure it's him?"

"It's him," Siobhán said. "By God, it's him."

"No," Gráinne said. "No, no, no, no." She rushed toward the body, but Siobhán threw out her arms and blocked her. Gráinne wailed.

"Settle," Siobhán said. "Settle."

"It can't be Niall, it can't be," Gráinne said.

"It is," Siobhán said. "It definitely is." *And why are you acting like you've lost a dear friend?* Siobhán didn't like it, didn't like it at all, but now was not the time to grill her younger sister. Girls got crushes on bad boys all the time. Thank God, he was never going to get the chance to take advantage of her. Siobhán crossed herself. Awful, thinking such things of the dead, but she couldn't help it.

"You hated Niall, didn't you?" Ciarán asked Siobhán.

"Hate is a strong word," Siobhán said.

"Do you think someone was running with the scissors?" Ciarán said.

"What?" Siobhán stared at her youngest brother. He was deep in thought. So much for keeping him from the body; he'd obviously had a peek.

"You aren't supposed to run with scissors," he said.

"No," Siobhán said. "You're not."

Suddenly, he pointed at her. "You were running. And you hated Niall. Were you running with scissors?"

"No, I wasn't running with scissors," Siobhán said. "And I didn't hurt Niall Murphy."

"Why?" Gráinne said. "Why?" Her body was shaking.

"Everyone outside now," Siobhán said. "Some fresh air will do us good." Siobhán ushered them out the door. They huddled on the footpath. Murdered. In their bistro. The sun might have been rising, but it was going to be a dark day. A very dark day indeed. Siobhán rang James on his mobile. It went to voice mail. She left a message telling him to come home. There was an emergency.

She didn't want to call Declan O'Rourke, the publican at James's favorite watering hole. Soon news of the murder would spread like wildfire. No use alerting anyone to the fact that James wasn't home last night. Not until she had to. Siobhán knew he couldn't possibly have anything to do with Niall's murder, but tongues would wag. *Please come home, James. Come home.* Where in the world was he?

The local gardai station was just down the street, and Macdara was at the bistro within five minutes. It was early still, and he looked as if he'd just been roused from bed. His hair was wavier than she'd ever seen it and sticking out of his cap like weeds growing through cracks in the pavement. Siobhán had an urge to pat it down. A second gardai car pulled up, but only Macdara had stepped out of his vehicle. For a second everyone just stood and stared at each other.

"A break-in?" Macdara said, looking everywhere but at Siobhán. "Everyone alright?"

"Niall Murphy is dead," Gráinne wailed.

"Dead?" Macdara said, finally meeting Siobhán's eyes. "Niall tried to break in?"

"No," Siobhán said. "Well, we don't know. He was just sitting in our back dining room."

"And you killed him?" Macdara asked, voice tinged with the first sign of panic.

"Of course not," Siobhán said. "He was dead when we found him."

"Murdered," Ciarán said. "With scissors."

Macdara took off his cap and scratched his head. "Are ye jokin' me?" The five shook their heads in unison. "Where is he?"

"Still sitting in the back dining room," Siobhán said. Macdara raised his right eyebrow, then gestured to the door.

"Let's have a look." Siobhán opened it and let Macdara go in first. The rest filed in after him. Siobhán told her siblings to stay in the front room as she followed Macdara to the threshold between the spaces. Macdara took in the body from a distance and gave a low whistle. "Niall Murphy? You sure?"

"We're sure," Siobhán said.

"Dead," Ciarán said. "As a doornail."

Siobhán turned and silenced him with a look.

"In a suit?" Macdara said.

Dressed for his own funeral, Siobhán thought. *God, how awful. I'm so awful.*

"You sure it's murder? Not a heart attack?" Macdara asked. The look on his face said he was thinking of every Irish breakfast he'd ever had at the bistro and adding up the cholesterol. So far he had not ventured into the back room, and the other two members of the gardai were standing in front of their vehicle smoking and having a laugh. They hadn't pulled up expecting a murder. And why should they? There had never been a murder in Kilbane in her lifetime. The only one she had ever heard wind of was way before she was born. A woman was murdered in the bathroom of a pub. It was the husband who done it. Story goes she came to drag him home and he wasn't having it. He killed her in the ladies' room. After he did the deed, he sat in his regular stool and drank a pint while waiting to be arrested.

Bet it was the best pint of his life, her da had joked only once before getting the death glare from their mam.

Oh, boy, Sheila Mahoney was not going to be happy to see her scissors used in this manner. Guess they were sharper than she realized. Had Pio taken them to the pubs last night like Siobhán had suggested? Were they going to blame her? Should she confess to that bit now?

Why was Macdara just standing there? Shouldn't he have gloves, and crime-scene tape, and a camera, and a notebook? Siobhán stared at him, trying to convey these things, but for once he didn't seem to notice her.

"Do we call Butler's to pick up the body?" Siobhán asked, hoping to jolt Macdara into action.

"We do nothing until the detective superintendent arrives," Macdara said, taking out his mobile. "He'll have to declare it a crime scene. Then the state pathologist will have to come out, and she'd be coming from Dublin."

"Until then, he just sits there?" Siobhán said.

Macdara tilted his head. "I don't think he has anything else in mind." He walked a few feet away and placed his call.

"Oh, Jaysus." She sounded just like her mam, but she couldn't help it. Niall Murphy would be sitting there for some time. The bistro was ruined. Siobhán crossed herself and tried to shove the thought out of her head. Macdara finally approached the body. He reached into his pockets, as if to pull out a pair of gloves but came out empty-handed. Siobhán gestured toward the kitchen. "I have some disposable gloves. Will those do?"

"Yes, please," Macdara said. Siobhán nodded but didn't move. "Can you get them now?"

"Sorry." Christ, what a right eejit she was. She whirled

around and hurried into the kitchen. She retrieved an entire box of gloves from the supply cabinet and sprinted back with them.

"Can you take a pair out of the box?" Macdara said. Siobhán did so. Macdara nodded as he put them on. Siobhán stepped back with the box. Macdara circled around until he was standing directly in front of Niall. "Did ye touch anything?" he asked glancing up. "Anything at all?"

"No," Siobhán said. "I don't think so."

"I touched his shoulder," Eoin said. "To wake him up, like. It didn't work." Macdara frowned. Siobhán said a silent prayer.

"And our DNA is going to be all over the place," Ciarán said. "Because we own the place, like." Macdara raised his eyebrows. Siobhán and Eoin shot Ciarán a look. Ciarán shrugged. "Well, we don't technically own it, but we have a long lease, like." He looked up at Siobhán. "Don't we?" His big eyes, his freckled nose, his pale Irish complexion. She never wanted him to grow up. She ruffled his hair.

"A hundred years, like," she said. Actually there were sixty years left on the lease. But Alison Tierney, who'd inherited the property after her father died, was desperately trying to find a loophole, even hired fancy lawyers from Dublin to nose into the lease. Alison wanted to sell the property, but so far no one was willing to yank the business away from the O'Sullivan Six. Besides, no one wanted to lose out on Siobhán's brown bread. But a murder on the property—that might just be a game changer. The worst day of Niall's life might just be Alison's best. Who would eat at the bistro now? Siobhán didn't have to be psychic to guess that a murder on the premises was anything but appetizing.

Macdara looked up as if a brilliant thought had just occurred to him. "Where's James?"

"Sick," Ann said.

"He's out," Siobhán said.

"Watching telly," Ciarán said.

Macdara cocked his head. "Well, which is it?"

"He's out sick. Probably watching telly," Eoin said. Siobhán looked at him. *You're welcome,* he mouthed.

"Rouse him, will ye? I'll need statements from all of you." Macdara took out his mobile phone and placed another call. Out the window, the other two guards snapped to attention, tossing their cigarette butts into the street and running for the door. Macdara didn't even turn around. He was staring at Siobhán. "James?"

"He's not here," Siobhán said. She wasn't going to lie. It would make things worse. Besides, Macdara knew James couldn't hurt anyone. Not really.

Macdara gestured to the ceiling. "I thought he was out sick watchin' telly."

"No. He's just out," Siobhán said.

"Did ye ring him?" Macdara said.

"Straight to voice mail," Siobhán said. "I think he forgot to charge it. You know yourself."

Macdara pointed to Niall's chest. "Are those your scissors?"

"No," Siobhán said. "I don't know."

"Which is it?" Macdara stared at her.

"Sheila's been tossing them out like candy the past two days. I took a pair, but I can't be sure those are mine."

"Will you check around for them?" Macdara said.

Siobhán nodded. "Ann and Gráinne, will ye look around for the scissors? Last I remember they were in the cabinet under the register."

"Gráinne had them last," Ann said.

"Did not," Gráinne said.

"You had them last night," Ann said.

"Liar," Gráinne said.

"Am not," Ann said, hurt stamped in her voice.

"Just look for them," Siobhán said. Gráinne grabbed Ann

by the arm and pulled her out of the room. Siobhán wanted to call James again, but she didn't want Macdara to pick up on her stress over it.

Siobhán pointed at Niall's head. "I don't know if that means anything."

"Go on," Macdara said.

"He wasn't bald when he was in here yesterday," Siobhán said.

"You think that's relevant?" Macdara said.

"Course I do. He must have gone to Sheila Mahoney."

Macdara stared at Niall's head. "He could have done it himself, no?"

"I suppose so. Easy enough to check, isn't it?"

"I suppose it is."

"It's settled then. You'll be needing to talk to Sheila straightaway."

Macdara shifted in place and ran his hands through his own hair. "Hold on. Are you saying Niall went to the salon, got his head shaved, then Sheila Mahoney stabbed him in the heart with a pair of her own scissors and dragged him across the street, into the bistro, and set him up in one of your chairs, like?"

"Of course not," Siobhán said. "But folks spill all their secrets to their hairdressers, don't they? I bet Sheila knows why he was getting himself shaved and all suited up." Should she tell him about seeing Sheila this morning running into her shop with a rubbish bag?

"Right, so," Macdara said. "Why was Sheila passing out scissors?"

"Grand reopening. They match the hot pink on the background of Sheila's new sign," Siobhán explained. "She wanted me to keep a box of the scissors by the register, but I told her no. So she was going to have Pio hand them out at the pubs during his sets." Siobhán left out the bit about being the one to suggest it.

Macdara looked up as if he could see across the street from back here. "Sheila has a new sign?"

"She copied ours, so," Siobhán said, trying not to sound bitter.

"She copied our sign?" Ann said, returning with Gráinne from the front room. "Bollix. Are ye gonna let her get away with that?"

"Did you find the scissors?" Siobhán asked.

"No," Gráinne said. Ann folded her arms and stared at the ground. Macdara wrote something down in his notebook. Siobhán was dying to know what it was. She turned to Gráinne. "Will you take Ann and Ciarán over to—"

"Hold up," Macdara said. "I'm going to need everyone to stick around."

"Yes!" Ciarán said.

"Hush," Siobhán said. "Show some respect." Siobhán was glad he wasn't frightened, but she certainly didn't want him enjoying this. Who knew being a parent was so hard?

"Should we finish breakfast?" Ann asked.

"No," Siobhán said. "We won't be open today. Unless you're hungry?" Ann shook her head no, quickly followed by the rest.

"Do you always start breakfast this early?" Macdara said.

"No," Siobhán said. Why *were* they all in the kitchen so early? She glanced at the young ones.

"We were doing it for Mam and Da," Ciarán said. Siobhán's eyes filled with tears. The one-year anniversary. Technically the one-year anniversary of the crash was in three days. But the O'Sullivan Six had decided to celebrate the last day the eight of them were together.

They'd all had breakfast before Naomi and Liam left for Waterford. The last breakfast they'd ever share. Everyone had been in such a hurry. Their dad joked that the eggs were too hard. "Like bullets," he said. "Your mam is in such a hurry to buy a fancy crystal bowl." Mam had given him a

look, then when he buried his face in his plate without another word, she let a little smile escape her lips.

They sat and ate together; then, when everyone was finished, there were kisses good-bye. Her mam never left a room
without kissing someone on the cheek. Then she started wor-
rying and going on about emergency numbers. She gave them
the number for the hotel. And her mobile. And her da's mobile (neither of them had ever actually used their mobiles,
but this wasn't mentioned by any involved). Then she gave
them the number to the Waterford Crystal factory in case
they were taking a tour when Siobhán tried to call, and that's
when her da threw up his hands and said, "Oh, for feck's
sakes, will ye stop?" Then Siobhán laughed and herded her
mother out the door. And the worst bit of all was the relief
she'd felt when they were gone. She loved her parents but
felt she was due for a bit of a break. A bit of a break, imagine! Now she'd give anything—anything—to have even one
single moment back.

"We were supposed to have a special breakfast," Siobhán
said to Macdara. "To honor our parents." Macdara watched
her with those probing eyes of his until she looked away.
How was it he always made her feel as if he could read her
mind? She couldn't believe her siblings were making the
breakfast. Shame on her. Siobhán had forgotten all about it.
Because she was too busy obsessing over Niall Murphy.
*Billy didn't do it. I have proof. You had your chance. Don't
forget it.* Oh, God. She should have told someone. Could it
have something to do with why he was killed? She swallowed hard.

Macdara was still talking. "And when you first came
down, you didn't see Niall in the dining room?"

"It was dark," Gráinne said. "We didn't even look over."

"Went straight into the kitchen," Ann said. Siobhán didn't
know why, but everything that came out of Ann's mouth

sounded rehearsed. She wanted to tell the kid to relax. Macdara looked at her as if expecting her to say something.

"And where were you?" he said when she didn't.

Alibis. Was he actually asking them all their alibis? He was good. Subtle. It didn't dawn on her until now that that was what he was doing, and she was surprised by how much it hurt. What did that mean? Did she have feelings for Macdara Flannery? He was a garda. It was his job to solve the crime, and they were standing at the scene of the crime. It could be one of them. That's what he was thinking. That's what everyone would soon be thinking. Even she was thinking it. James. Where was James? Oh, God. She suddenly longed for Father Kearney. He would comfort her. He would assure her that no one was thinking any such thing. "I was running," Siobhán said.

"But not with scissors," Ciarán interjected.

Macdara stared at him for a moment, and then threw his head back and laughed. He had one of those laughs that warmed you up inside. He finally settled down and looked at her.

"Running?" he said. "Running what?"

Chapter 6

"Running," Siobhán repeated. "For sport, like." Macdara continued to stare. "Is that so hard to believe?"

Macdara turned red and shook his head. "It's just . . . you seem fit to me," he said under his breath.

Siobhán flushed. He went from accusing to flirting? Why was she always the most attracted to him at the worst possible times? She was inexplicably angry with him. "I didn't see him when I first came in either. I was going back upstairs to—" She stopped. Macdara knew James was gone, but he didn't know that when James left last night, he was furious and probably had gone out looking for Niall Murphy. Macdara also didn't know Niall had threatened her and asked for ten thousand euro. How had things gotten this complicated this fast? And why was she so afraid to tell him now?

"Went upstairs to . . . ?" Macdara probed.

"Take a shower," Siobhán said quickly, praying none of the younger ones would contradict her. "That's when I saw him. We called you straightaway."

"Not straightaway," Ciarán said. "We freaked out for a

few minutes. And then went to get James and he wasn't in his bed, and then we tried to call James, and then we called you."

Typical, Siobhán thought. *Just typical.* Maybe Macdara wouldn't think a thing of it. Macdara turned to Siobhán. "James didn't come home last night?" *Or maybe he'd notice right away, like.*

"Do you think he did it?" Ciarán said. "And that's why he's not here?"

"Ciarán!" Siobhán said. Why hadn't Macdara let her send him away? Ciarán wrinkled his brows. Siobhán wanted to hug him, and kill him.

Siobhán tossed her head back. "James is a grown man, Garda Flannery." Macdara flinched at her switch to formal address. She'd never called him Garda Flannery in his life. Oh, God, she was making a right mess of this. Even she was starting to feel guilty, like she was the one who'd done it and she just couldn't remember actually doing it. Was that possible? Could she have killed him in her sleep? *Don't be daft. Besides. There's very little blood. If he'd been killed here, there would be a lot of blood.* Wouldn't there? "He isn't always home with the likes of us, if you know what I mean." Siobhán tried to don a sexy look. Macdara frowned. Shoot. She wasn't any good at seduction either.

Macdara pulled out his notebook again. "Are ye saying he has a girlfriend?"

"I suspect," Siobhán said. *Suspect? Why did she use the word* suspect? "But he's never brought her around."

"He'd want to be here," Ciarán said. "He'll be so shocked."

"That he will," Siobhán said. "That he will."

"Unless he did it," Ciarán said. "And then he already knows."

Macdara knelt down in front of Ciarán. "Is there any reason to think James would have done this?" he asked gently.

"No," Siobhán said. Ciarán's eyes widened as if a little common sense had just crept in. He shook his head.

Macdara straightened up and adjusted his notebook just as the other two guards came in from the back garden.

"There's some trampled grass back there, alright," one said.

"Like a body was dragged?" Macdara asked.

"Quite possible," was the answer.

"Do we have any crime-scene tape in the vehicle?" Macdara asked. One hurried out to check while Macdara herded the O'Sullivans to the seating near the fireplace. "Do you remember hearing anything? Any noises in the middle of the night or early this morning?"

"I thought I heard glass breaking," Ann said. She turned to Gráinne. "Remember?"

"What?" Siobhán said.

"'Tis true," Gráinne said. "Ann woke me up to see if I heard it too."

"Why didn't you wake me?" Siobhán said.

"Because you don't sleep in our room," Ann said.

"Tell me exactly what you heard," Macdara said.

"It sounded like it came from down here. Like someone had thrown a rock through one of the windows," Ann said.

"Why a rock?" Macdara asked.

Ann shrugged. "Why are ye asking me? I didn't throw it."

"Ann," Siobhán said.

Macdara held up his hand. "She's alright," he said.

"Could it have been a brick?" Ciarán asked Ann. "Or a shoe?"

"A brick, maybe," Ann said. "Definitely not a shoe."

Ciarán nodded with a very serious expression on his wee face, then pointed to Macdara's notebook. "Are ye going to write that down?"

Macdara shifted uncomfortably and scribbled something out. "Let's start again. You woke up because you thought you heard glass breaking. Like someone threw a rock into one of your windows. Or a brick. Definitely not a shoe."

Ciarán and Ann nodded their encouragement. Gráinne looked at Siobhán and rolled her eyes. If it was a better time, Siobhán would have laughed. Macdara looked around at the windows, as did the rest of them, but all of them were intact.

"The back door was locked when the other guard went out to the garden," Macdara said.

"We always lock up," Siobhán said.

"Did Niall have a key?" Macdara asked.

"Of course not," Siobhán said. She turned to Ann. "What time did ye hear glass breaking?"

Ann shrugged. "I dunno, exactly. Just that it was the middle of the night, like." Her blond hair was a rat's nest, but she still looked so sweet and innocent. When she wasn't talking, that is. Her attitude was almost as snippy as Gráinne's. The girls were becoming strangers day by day.

"Middle of the night," Macdara repeated.

"That sounds about right," Gráinne said. "Like late middle, not early middle."

"That's very helpful," Siobhán said. Gráinne played with her hair and nodded solemnly as the sarcasm zoomed right by. Siobhán prompted Ann. "Then what?"

"I woke Gráinne up, asked her if she heard glass breaking downstairs; she called me a stupid eejit, shoved me, and told me to go back to sleep," Ann said. She slid a look to Gráinne. *Told ye.*

Gráinne threw her arms up. "It was the middle of the night, for feck's sake. I thought she was dreaming."

"So you shoved her?" Siobhán said. She didn't know whether to focus on that or the language. How did she get here? She didn't have a clue as to how to be a parent.

"It's good they didn't come down," Macdara said. "I'd hate to think if they'd"—he cut the rest of the thought off. Ciarán was staring at him with saucer eyes.

Come in at the wrong time and witnessed a murder. Siobhán shuddered to think what would have happened.

"And none of you let Niall Murphy inside?"

"Of course not," Siobhán said.

"Could he have had a key?" Macdara asked again. Had he forgotten he asked it earlier, or was he trying to catch them in a lie?

"Definitely not," Siobhán said. "But we keep a spare in the back garden."

"Where?" Macdara looked to the door.

"In a glass jar buried in the corner of the garden closest to the door."

Macdara made note of it. "We'll check to see if it's still there." Siobhán wanted him to run out and check this very second, but she kept her gob shut. Nobody liked someone else telling them how to do their job.

"Do you think Niall was here to see one of us?" Gráinne suddenly cried out.

"Why would he be here in the middle of the night to see one of us?" Siobhán said.

Macdara was staring at Gráinne. "Can you think of any reason?"

"Of course she can't," Siobhán said. What was he trying to say? Gráinne just shook her head and looked away.

"Maybe he was hungry," Ciarán said.

"He was probably langers," Ann said. "And he didn't know it was the middle of the night."

"Maybe he tripped and fell on your scissors," Ciarán said, turning to Siobhán.

"And then got up and calmly sat in one of our dining chairs?" Siobhán said. She didn't mean to, but they were starting to sound like a bunch of daft eejits.

"Maybe he had just enough life in him to sit down," Eoin said. Eoin mimed sitting down.

"We don't even know that they're our scissors," Siobhán reminded them. Ann shot a worried look at Gráinne. Gráinne glared back. It gave Siobhán a sinking feeling. She'd have to remember to ask what that was about when they were alone.

"The killer could have brought the scissors with him," Ciarán said.

"Premeditated murder," Gráinne mused.

Macdara was staring at all of them, mouth open. "We watch a lot of *CSI*," Ciarán said.

"Right," Siobhán said. "But it is true. We know for sure now he wasn't stabbed here." Macdara stiffened, but he didn't respond right away. Uh-oh. She got the distinct feeling he was browned off. At her? What did she do?

Macdara turned to the young ones. "Do you have anything else to add, you three?" Ciarán, Ann, and Gráinne shook their heads. "Why don't you go upstairs, now. Give us minute here." They stood obediently. Siobhán would have had to ask at least three times.

"Can we watch telly?" Ciarán asked.

"Quietly," Siobhán said. "And no *CSI*."

"Why not?" Ciarán said.

"Because we're living it," Gráinne said.

"I want to stay," Ann said.

"You heard Garda Flannery. Up with you now," Eoin said. Gráinne stomped off, followed by Ann, then Ciarán. He kept looking back.

"Tell me everything," Ciarán said before disappearing out the French doors. Macdara turned to Siobhán and Eoin.

"Where do you keep your mop?" Macdara said.

"Our mop?" Siobhán said.

"We'll need to see if anyone's been tidying up after themselves lately," Macdara said.

"Are you serious?" Siobhán said.

"I'll get it," Eoin said. He started for the kitchen.

"Hold up," Macdara said. "We'll do it. From now on, you don't go anywhere I don't approve; you don't touch anything." Macdara glanced outside. "There hasn't been a tragedy like this since . . ." He stopped.

Her parents' accident. Siobahn bit her lip and looked away.

Macdara came up and put his hand on her shoulder. The weight of it sent shudders through her body. "I'm sorry. This is happening at the worst time for all of you."

Tears filled Siobhán's eyes, and she stepped away. He was still Macdara, but in this case he was a guard first. She'd best not forget that.

"Siobhán," Macdara said quietly.

She didn't dare meet his gaze. There were too many people around.

One of the other guards came out of the kitchen, pushing the mop and bucket. "It's here. It's clean."

Siobhán looked at Macdara. *Take that.*

Macdara nodded and turned to Siobhán. "Start from the beginning," he said. "Where did you say James went last night?"

Chapter 7

Once the detective superintendant arrived and declared it an official crime scene, the bistro instantly transformed into a beehive of organized chaos. Siobhán watched, fascinated, as the guards dusted, gathered, photographed, and conferred.

Macdara found Siobhán by the counter. She wondered if it was hard for him to let outsiders take over. That's how she would feel if it were her. She wasn't even a member of the gardai, and she was itching to step in. But he seemed more concerned about her.

"We found the key in the back garden still in the glass jar."

Siobhán swallowed and nodded, even though she couldn't process what that meant for the case. How did the murderer get in?

"After we're done with the scene, would you bring that jar in and make sure you don't keep a key outside anymore?"

Siobhán nodded again.

"Are you okay?" His voice softened to a concerned whisper. He was no longer speaking as Garda Flannery but as Macdara, her friend.

"Who's going to tell his poor mam?" Mary Murphy had already withdrawn from the town after the accident. How in the world was she going to cope with this news? Although Siobhán had secretly never liked the woman, she couldn't imagine the pain this was going to cause. Especially with her only other son in prison. If Naomi O'Sullivan were here, she'd be thinking and praying for Niall's mam. Siobhán would do the same.

"We're sending guards to the house as we speak. They'll break the news as gently as possible."

"I wouldn't wish it on anyone," Siobhán said.

"You know yourself," Macdara said.

Siobhán glanced at a stream of light snaking in through a gap in the closed shutters. "Folks will be wondering why we're not opening." She didn't mean to take away from Mary Murphy's pain, but this was going to shake the community of Kilbane to its core. Not to mention ruin the bistro. Their livelihood. Without it, how on earth would the O'Sullivan Six survive?

"I've got a bit of good news," Macdara said.

Siobhán waited. *Please tell me Niall did accidentally fall on the pair of scissors.*

"The pathologist is already in Cork for a conference. She's on her way as we speak."

"That's a relief," Siobhán said. The sooner the body was out of here, the better.

"Since the spare key was still in the jar, just where you said, I have to ask you again. Are you sure there isn't any chance at all that Niall Murphy had a key?"

"Why would Niall have a key to our bistro?" She sounded snappy, but who wouldn't after hearing the same question at least three times? The very thought of Niall having a key to the bistro set her on edge.

"There's no sign of a break-in," Macdara said. "Either he used a key or someone let him in."

Siobhán shook her head and threw her arms open. "Did you check Niall's pockets for a key?"

"Excellent observation." He turned and yelled over his shoulder to one of the Cork guards, who didn't look any older than James. "Check his pocket for a key, will ye?"

"I'm sure he doesn't have a key. If he had a key, I certainly didn't know about it."

"If he had a key?" Macdara said. "So you're saying he might have had a key?"

"I don't know what I'm saying!"

Macdara's face softened. "It's a right shock. Finding a dead man in your dining room."

"'Tis," Siobhán said. In her mind she started cataloging the keys. They each had one, of course, so that made six. Her mam was a trusting sort, so there was no telling how many neighbors had spares. After all, they had keys hanging on hooks behind the register belonging to other folks in town. People looked after each other in Kilbane. It wasn't unusual to phone a neighbor to ask them to pop in and check on such and such if one was going to be late getting back home or to their shop. Spare keys were far from being a smoking gun.

Not to mention the number of times James lost his key after a night in the pub. Why, they might as well have kept their doors wide open with the number of people who could have had access to the locks. Siobhán didn't want to deal with any of it. James was the oldest; he should be here trying to figure this out.

She picked up her mobile, and this time she dialed O'Rourke's, praying that Declan could tell her where to find James. The phone rang and rang, but nobody picked up. That was odd. Siobhán couldn't recall a single time that Declan hadn't answered on one of the first few rings.

Hating to do it, she sent Eoin to see what he could find out. He came back twenty minutes later, out of breath and sweating.

"Well?" Siobhán said. They were standing outside on the footpath, having been kicked out the moment the state pathologist arrived. At least she was here.

"O'Rourke's is closed," Eoin said. "I tried to look in the windows, but I couldn't see a thing."

Years of dirt will do that to a pub, Siobhán thought. "O'Rourke's is closed?" She'd never known that to happen. Ever.

"I even went around back. It's all locked up."

Declan only closed on Christmas. She hoped he was alright. "Why don't you try one of the other pubs?" Siobhán said. "Someone will know what's going on."

"What do I say if they start asking me questions?"

"Tell them you're looking for James, or ask them if they've heard about O'Rourke's being closed, but not a single other peep," Siobhán said. "Sometimes the best way is to answer a question with a question."

"Answer a question with a question?" Eoin tilted his head in confusion.

"Exactly," Siobhán said. "You've got it."

"Can I buy a pint?"

"Absolutely not," Siobhán said. He'd be of legal drinking age in a few years. And, of course, he was probably sneaking a few with the lads when they were out. But she certainly wasn't going to condone it, and she prayed he didn't take to it like James had.

"I don't have a good feeling about this," he said as he headed off. Siobhán squeezed her eyes shut. Neither did she. But the first thing she had to do was look after the younger ones. It wasn't going to be healthy for them to stay here. She called Bridie.

"Is it true?" Bridie said in lieu of hello. "Is it Niall? Is he dead?"

"How did you know?" Siobhán asked.

"Courtney, of course." Siobhán should have guessed. No one would be surprised if they discovered that instead of veins, Courtney was wired with communication cables. She was always the first to know everything. "Are you alright, petal? I'd be going out of my mind."

"I need a favor," Siobhán said.

"Say no more," Bridie said. "Pack their bags and bring them over." Siobhán nodded even though Bridie couldn't see her through the phone. Friends knew what you needed before you even uttered a word. That was the Kilbane that she knew and loved.

"I don't see why I have to go," Gráinne said as they trudged over to Bridie's, suitcases in hand. "I'm sixteen." Why were they always telling her how old they were, as if she couldn't count?

"You like Bridie," Siobhán said.

"We'll get to make things," Ann said, her eyes sparkling. Gráinne rolled her eyes and shoved Ann. "I'm not going to make anything."

"Hey," Ann said.

"Don't shove your sister," Siobhán said. She shoved Gráinne.

"Are we ever going home again?" Ciarán said.

Siobhán took his hand. "Of course," she said. "Of course." Bridie and Séamus lived a few streets back, down the street, a right at the post office, up the hill, and a left at the yellow house. They were one of the few who didn't live above their shop; in fact, they were a good driving distance from it. Séamus didn't mind; it gave him another bike route.

And Bridie didn't spend much time at the cycle shop anyway. Except, of course, she was there the other day. With
Niall. Siobhán wondered if she had any clue as to who could
have done this.

Oh, no. What if someone found out that she had argued
with Niall at the bike shop? Would people start to think she
had something to do with his murder? When Séamus came
in, he could definitely see that she was upset. Would he say
something to Macdara? Should Siobhán confess that bit to
the guards first?

Before Siobhán could decide whether or not she should
mention her argument with Niall to Macdara, the Sheedys'
door swung open. They hadn't even stepped into the tiny
yard. Bride had been watching for them. She stood on her
porch with a big smile, although Siobhán thought she looked
strained. Just like she did at the bike shop the other day.

"I made ham and cheese toasties," she called out.

Siobhán kept her eyes forward and a fake smile plastered
on her own face. Behind her, Ciarán groaned, and Siobhán
gave the back of his arm a soft pinch. He looked at her.

Cheese toasties? he mouthed. Bridie was known to have
burned more than her share of toasties in her lifetime.

Behave, she mouthed back. It wasn't poor Bridie's fault
that her brood all considered themselves culinary geniuses.
Surely after everything else they'd been through, they would
find a way to survive Bridie's ham and cheese toasties.

Siobhán didn't even step inside the door. She had to get
to Declan's and see what was going on. If he still wasn't
there, she'd try the next pub. Finding James was her top pri-
ority.

"What happened?" Bridie said. Her eyes were rimmed in
red as if she'd been crying. Siobhán had almost forgotten
that Bridie had been fond of Niall. She felt guilty for not
grieving his death. But there was too much water, too big of

a bridge to cross in order to shed a tear for Niall. Maybe someday. But she did want to find his killer, and she hoped that counted for something.

"They'll fill you in," Siobhán said. "I have to get back into town."

"But I already poured you a cuppa," Bridie said. "And a biscuit."

"Another time. And thank you. Thank you so much for minding them." Bridie threw her arms around Siobhán even though it meant she had to stand on tiptoe to do it.

"I can't believe it. He had just come home. He was a good lad. I know you don't want to hear that, but it was true. He might have been a bit misguided, but he loved his brother, and his mammy, don't you know? He had good in him, he did. He was a good lad." It was as if Bridie were stuck on some kind of loop, and it sounded as if she were trying to convince herself of Niall's goodness.

Maybe Siobhán had a stone in her heart. She couldn't quite play along.

"It's a terrible shock," Siobhán said. "There are no words."

"A killer in Kilbane," Bridie said. She placed her hand on her heart. "Who could it be?"

"I can't imagine," Siobhán said.

"Why was Niall at your bistro? Did he pay you a visit last night?" Bridie's curiosity was natural, of course, and in her place Siobhán would have been doing the same thing, but it felt wrong to gossip about it before all the facts were in.

"No," Siobhán said. "Nothing like that. It was a true surprise seeing him there." She stopped herself before sharing anything else. "Were you out at all last night? Did you see or hear anything out of the ordinary?" Siobhán held her breath. What she really wanted to know was if anyone had seen James.

"Séamus was at O'Rourke's," Bridie said. Siobhán took one look at Bridie's face and knew Bridie knew something about James.

"Is Séamus here?" Siobhán asked.

"He's at the shop," Bridie said. She put her hand on Siobhán. "It's just a little slip," she said. "If he gets to a meeting they'll sort him out."

Just a little slip. Oh, no. No, no, no. Siobhán had been praying she'd been wrong. He'd been doing so well. Nearly six months sober. Why? Why had he thrown it all away? And would this be the start of another bender? One that might last for months, or years, or the rest of his life?

Tears stung Siobhán's eyes and she bit down on her lip to keep them contained. "James was at O'Rourke's? Are you sure?"

Bridie's face crumpled. "You didn't know? Oh, pet, I'm sorry. No wonder you look so pale. Séamus said he tried to convince James to go home. He did his best."

"I'm sure he did."

"A slip is all it was. He'll get himself sorted. You'll see."

Siobhán wasn't so sure. "I just need to find him."

"Find him? He didn't come home?" True alarm rang out in Bridie's voice.

"He's a young man; he doesn't always come home," Siobhán said. "You know yourself." She didn't want Bridie thinking James had anything to do with Niall's murder.

"Do you want me to call Séamus? Ask when was the last he saw him?"

"Not yet. I'm going to pop into O'Rourke's."

"I bet it's jammers with gossip," Bridie said, shaking her head.

"That's just it. Eoin popped by a bit ago and said the place was closed up, like."

"O'Rourke's? I've never known it to close."

"Same as I." Why was it closed? Was Declan tending to

James? Was he okay? "Anyway, I'm going to have a look-see."

"You've had to grow up so fast." Bridie had tears in her eyes. "You're like a little mother bear, protecting her cubs."

She didn't feel like it. "Does a mother bear ever want to clobber her cubs?"

Bridie laughed and absentmindedly rubbed her stomach. "I hope I find out soon. I'm sure they do." Siobhán shouldn't have said that. Courtney had hinted that Bridie and Séamus had been having trouble having kids. Séamus had an older son, so rumors flew that the problem conceiving was all on Bridie. She was the mothering type too. Ann was right; there would be crafts.

"Thanks again. I'd better get on." Siobhán started to leave.

Bridie stepped forward. "So it's true? He was found *inside* your bistro?"

"Please, we're still trying to sort everything out," Siobhán said. "I promised Macdara I wouldn't wag my tongue all over town."

Bridie abruptly pulled away. She looked as if her feelings were hurt, but she quickly put on a smile. "Of course. Please. You'll be back to spend the night too, won't ye? There' s a bed here for ye."

"Thank you. I'll see." Siobhán couldn't think about anything but finding James. She hurried away from Bridie before she too succumbed to the comforts of tea, and biscuits, and ham and cheese, and knitted flowers, and headbands with sparkles.

Chapter 8

By the time Siobhán reached O'Rourke's, there were already half a dozen twitching men pacing in front of the locked door, drooling for their pints. The cream-stone building was a Kilbane institution. The window boasted Declan's collection of Laurel and Hardy memorabilia, and the interior was filled with posters of John Wayne and other old-time movie posters.

Declan, a hearty man with a laugh to match, was in his seventies now, but the only giveaway were the wrinkles in his broad face and the couple of front teeth that had packed up and moved out of his mouth. When he laughed, exposing the gaps and filling the room with his boisterous sound, one couldn't help but laugh back. He was a man seasoned in the language of operas, and plays, and movies. It was fitting, his job front and centre as a publican, for Declan had been entertaining the folks in Kilbane for the past fifty years. He was a kind soul, the first to offer an ossified lad a ride home, but he was just as quick to cut down any lad who got too big for his britches. Declan, like most institutions, demanded a fair amount of respect. He was equally loved and feared.

Siobhán stood just behind the pacing, smoking men, gawking at the CLOSED sign. In all her life, Siobhán had never seen the other side of the OPEN sign. Two of the men were prattling on about the tragedies that must have befallen Declan. Theories seemed to range from heart attacks to kidnappings to alien abductions. Siobhán kept her head down, for next the conversation turned to the guards, and what was more than one vehicle doing parked in front of Naomi's Bistro? Could Declan have popped in for a bit of brekkie and had a heart attack? Siobhán wanted to lash out and proclaim that Declan did not die of a heart attack from breakfast at Naomi's, t'ank you very much, but she couldn't afford to draw unnecessary attention to herself.

Just then the window above O'Rourke's screeched open, and Declan's big face popped out. "Go 'way," he called down.

"Are ye alright there, horse?" one of the regulars called up to him.

"I'm sick as a small hospital," Declan called back. "And me lad called in as well. It's going around, it is."

Great, Siobhán thought. That's all they needed, on top of everything else, for one of them to get a bug. "Declan," she yelled up, "can I have a word?"

Declan looked at her, and their eyes locked for several seconds before he offered her a slight nod. "I'll sort it out, petal," he said. The look he gave her was a warning. James was with him. Declan wasn't sick; he was sorting out James.

Siobhán nodded and hurried away just as the men pacing in front of the pub realized who she was and started asking her why the guards were parked in front of the bistro.

This was bad, she thought, as she headed back. If Declan had to close the pub to see to James, it was bad. Was he hurt? He would call an ambulance if James was hurt, wouldn't he?

A squat vehicle from Cork University Hospital was parked directly in front of the bistro. Siobhán was glad Niall's body would be removed, but their place of business was now an official circus. Gossip was no doubt already flaming through town. They might as well have set off firecrackers. Neighbors were starting to gather on the street, necks straining for a look-see, and curtains were twitching up and down the block.

"And so it begins," Siobhán whispered as she gazed across the street at the crowd. Siobhán was surprised at their restraint. She half expected someone to cross over to them to ask what had happened.

She wondered who would be the first to traverse the invisible barrier. Her money would be on Courtney Kirby. Some said she opened her gift shop just so she could gossip with the locals. But she had a heart of gold, Courtney. She couldn't help it if she lived for drama. She would be equally propelled by the need to comfort as well as to be the first to get the story. She was Kilbane's ambassador of news, both good and bad, and she accepted the position with the reverence of a queen.

Siobhán glanced at the salon. It was still dark. She'd forgotten to tell Macdara about seeing Sheila this morning. She still wasn't sure if she should even mention it. Surely Sheila wouldn't murder anything but a person's hair.

Siobhán's thoughts once again landed on Niall's mam. The poor dear. No matter what Siobhán thought of her, no mother deserved news like this. Should Siobhán go see her? She lived out in the country, apart from the town, but only a ten-minute drive along the back road. These days she only ventured out when she ran out of smokes, which she bought by the carton. Once again Siobhán looked over at the eager faces across the street. Friends. Patrons. Neighbors. Standing among them could be a killer.

It didn't seem possible. These were people they'd known all their lives, stood next to a dozen times at the market, or prayed with in church, or served in the bistro. And as if that thought weren't bad enough, it occurred to Siobhán that the folks in the crowd were probably thinking the same thing about them. That one of the O'Sullivan Six could be a killer. Her parents would be turning in their graves!

Just then Courtney Kirby stepped out into the street, sashaying toward Siobhán, all hips and breasts and bouncing pearls. Her mousy hair was now mahogany-red, thanks, Siobhán assumed, to Sheila.

"Ah, chicken," Courtney called out. "What happened?" Courtney fixed her eyes on Siobhán and put her hand on her heart. "It's not James, is it?"

Siobhán could not believe it. She knew full well who had died, had already leaked it to Bridie, and now here she was pretending as if she didn't have a clue. "We're all fine."

"Thank heavens. You gave me such a fright."

"Please, lower your voice," Siobhán said

Courtney did no such thing; in fact, her next question was almost at a shout. "Who is it? What's the story?"

"There's been a murder." If Courtney wanted to pretend she didn't know the gossip, Siobhán was going to play it for all it was worth.

"Murder?" Courtney said. "In Kilbane?" A definite murmur went through the crowd gathered across the street, and more folks were coming, streaming down Sarsfield in both directions. "Who was it?"

"You'll know soon enough. We need to let the guards do their job."

"Rumor has it it was Niall Murphy," Courtney whispered.

"And exactly where did that rumor start?" Siobhán asked.

Courtney leaned in and actually cupped her hand behind her ear, where a string of cubic zirconia dangled. She often loaded up with accessories from her shop. When Siobhán didn't offer any gossip, Courtney dropped her hand and lowered her voice. "I heard from Helen, who was having a chat with Patrick O'Shea, who was doing a bit of business this morning with Father Kearney when . . ."

Siobhán shut out Courtney's chatter and looked around. Where was Macdara? The doors opened with one of the men from Cork University Hospital backing out, holding one end of a stretcher. On it lay Niall Murphy in a body bag.

Courtney cried out. "Oh, oh, oh, oh," she said over and over.

Mike Granger stepped out of the crowd and toward them. For a second she was distracted by his shiny bald head.

"Siobhán," he said. "Pray tell, who is it?"

Why did everyone in town suddenly sound as if they were rehearsing lines from a play? She got the feeling that Mike knew exactly who it was. Or was she imagining things?

"Please," Siobhán said. She took a step toward the crowd. "Out of respect for the family, let's not start gossiping."

"Is anyone from the family here?" Mike said, turning back to the crowd.

"We've all just come from Mass," Courtney said. "Well, most of us," she added, with a lingering look at Siobhán. The O'Sullivans hadn't been to Mass much since her parents had passed, but instead of stating this, Courtney simply fluttered her fake eyelashes at Siobhán. One got stuck, and Courtney literally had to force the eye back open with her fingers. Siobhán had completely forgotten it was Sunday. She even spotted Father Kearney in the crowd, face pinched in worry, arms clasped in front of him as if in perpetual prayer.

"Where are the rest of the six?" Courtney asked.

"At Bridie's," Siobhán said. *All except one.*

Later, back safely inside the bistro perched with Siobhán near the fireplace with steaming mugs of tea, Macdara repeated his findings. They hadn't found any signs of a break-in, no broken glass, no splintered door. There was some trampled grass in the backyard, and it was possible Niall was killed out there and then dragged inside. The pathologist would examine his suit for streaks of dirt and grass. But the spare key had been found inside the glass jar in the garden, just where Siobhán said it should be. Macdara was on his way out, as were the rest of the guards. The state pathologist would perform a complete autopsy at Cork University Hospital.

"Still no sign of James?" Macdara asked.

"I'm working on it," Siobhán said. There she went again, keeping secrets from Macdara. But she wanted to talk to James first, and she had to trust that Declan was handling whatever shape James was in at the moment. She'd seen her brother hungover. He probably didn't even know his own name, forget answering questions about a murder.

"Looks like I have my next assignment," he said.

"Why is it so urgent you find James?" Siobhán knew why, of course, but she wanted Macdara to know that James didn't do it.

"I'm sure you'll be wanting him home," Macdara said tactfully. "There's no need for you to handle this on your own." The minute the door clicked shut behind him, Siobhán felt a sense of dread come over her as she surveyed the bistro.

Only scraps remained of the day's incident. A few bits of crime-scene tape, abandoned coffee cups, and dirty boot prints all over the front dining room. At least they'd put booties on when they reached the section in the back where Niall was discovered. There was still a crowd outside, which is why Siobhán drew her shades—the first time she could ever remember. Her mobile rang. It was Declan. Siobhán answered right away.

"James is here, pet," he said the minute she answered. "But he's a bit rough."

Relief crashed over her for the briefest of seconds. "Thank you."

"'Don't thank me. I've called the guards and the HSE."

"The paramedics? Is he okay?"

"I found him behind the pub. Behind the rubbish bins. He was out cold from the drink, but looks like he took a beating as well."

"A beating?"

"He'll be a bit bruised, alright, but nothing broken. He's awake now, but not making much sense."

Siobhán knew all too well. "You don't have a bug, do you?"

"I'm fit as a fiddle, pet. I was out for a smoke when I found him. I kicked out the stool huggers and turned over the CLOSED sign while I saw to him. I wanted to delay the floodgates as long as I could."

"Thank you. I'll be right over."

"Don't, petal. The paramedics are seeing to him. Looks like he's refusing to go to hospital, so he'll be home soon. I just wanted you to know."

"Thanks, Declan." Siobhán stood in the front of the bistro, and a few seconds later, Macdara showed up. She'd hoped he had gone to speak with Mary Murphy, but it was obvious he was waiting for James as well.

"Do you want to wait inside?" Siobhán said. "Have another cuppa?"

"I'd rather one of your fancy coffees," Macdara said. "I get the feeling I won't be sleeping much the next few days." They entered the bistro but stuck to the front room. Siobhán made them cappuccinos, and it was the first time it didn't bring her joy. They slurped in silence. When they were almost finished, they heard the front door open. Seconds later, James stumbled into the dining room.

"Siobhán." His clothes were disheveled and dirty, his hair matted. But it was his swollen eye and bloody mouth that made her gasp.

"James." She rushed up to him. "James, James. Are you alright?"

"I'm fine," he slurred. "Don't you worry about a t'ing.

I'm in perfect form." He stumbled forward and grabbed the back of a chair. It slid away from him, and he had to two-step not to fall. He failed at this as well, stumbled, and then collapsed to the ground. Siobhán stood over him, seething.

"Look at the state of ye," she said. And at the worst possible time. Macdara made a move to help him up, but Siobhán's arm shot out in front of him. "Leave him."

James opened one eye and groaned. "Is it true?" he asked, looking up to her. "Is Niall Murphy really dead?"

Siobhán kneeled down. "You should be ashamed of yourself." She reached for his face, wanting to examine the wounds.

"Don't touch him," Macdara said.

"Don't touch him?" Siobhán said.

Macdara stepped closer and peered down at James. "Is every guard in this town a right eejit? How could they let him come home? He's covered in blood."

Siobhán's head snapped back to James's dirty clothes. "No. That's just . . ." She stepped closer. Oh, God. Macdara was right. It wasn't much, but there were drops of blood on James's shirt. Startled, her eyes locked on James. "What happened?" she demanded.

"I don't know," James said. "I don't know."

"You blacked out," Siobhán said.

James squeezed his eyes shut. Then nodded.

"Tell me everything you do remember," Macdara said. He put on a glove, then helped James up and sat him in a chair. Siobhán couldn't help but stare at the glove, then at the pad of paper and Biro in Macdara's hand as he waited for James to speak. Should Siobhán warn him to keep his gob shut? Was her brother in big trouble?

"I went to O'Rourke's," James said. He glanced at Siobhán. Shame was stamped across his face. "I'm sorry."

She nodded.

"Continue," Macdara said.

"Can I get washed up first? Have a cup of tea?"

"Of course," Siobhán said. She should have said something to warn him. But she didn't want Macdara to think James had anything to hide.

"No," Macdara said.

"What?" Siobhán turned to Macdara, hand on her hip.

Macdara pointed to James's shirt. "It's evidence."

"Evidence?" James said as if he didn't understand the word.

"He didn't kill Niall," Siobhán said. "You know that. It's James. You know him."

"Kill Niall?" James said. "Me?"

Macdara ignored James and turned to Siobhán. "Do you want people to think he got away because I let him wash off evidence?"

"It's probably his own blood. Look at his mouth. Clearly he's the one who took a beating last night!"

"I think I got in a fight with someone," James said, as if Siobhán had never spoken. "In the alley behind O'Rourke's."

"What was your first clue?" Siobhán snapped, unable to contain her sarcasm. James tried to frown, but he was so hungover he couldn't even pull that off.

Macdara stood. "I'm going to have to take James into the station."

"Why? If you want, I'll put his clothes in a bag, and you can just take them," Siobhán said.

"The detective superintendent is going to want to question him. Come on, Siobhán. You have to let me do my job."

"He's right," James said. "Where are the others?"

"They're with Bridie and Séamus."

James nodded. "I'd rather he take me now. With them gone."

"Don't talk like that. You'll be back before they are."
Siobhán glanced at Macdara for confirmation, but for once

he avoided her eyes. "Can I get him a fresh set of washing, or are ye going to send him home in his birthday suit?"

James laughed. Siobhán silenced him with a glare.

"Go ahead," Macdara said.

James put his hand out as Siobhán started to walk out of the room. "How is Gráinne?" Alarm bells rang inside Siobhán's head. Why was he specifically asking about Gráinne? The panicked look on his face confirmed it. He knew something. He was hiding something. How she wished Macdara wasn't here. Was Macdara going to think it odd that James was asking specifically about Gráinne?

"Upset," Siobhán said carefully. James stared at her, as if trying to tell her something. She glanced at Macdara, who had his head buried in a notebook. *Thanks be to Jaysus for once he wasn't paying attention*. As if he could feel her thinking about him, Macdara suddenly popped his head up, then pocketed his notebook.

"Go on," Macdara said. "Get the change of clothes." Siobhán hurried upstairs and threw a pair of his denims and a shirt into an overnight bag. She was tempted to write him a note, but she couldn't think of what to say, and what if Macdara found it first? She had to keep her temper in check. She hurried downstairs and started to hand the bag to James. Macdara took it instead. "Let him have some headache tablets," she said. James looked like death warmed over.

Macdara nodded. When they were almost to the door, James stopped and looked at Siobhán.

"Don't spend a quid on a solicitor, you hear?"

"James?"

"Not a quid."

Siobhán turned to Macdara. "You'd better let him wash up after you collect your evidence. And give him water, and headache tablets, and a bit to eat, and a soft cot—"

"I'll mind him," Macdara said. "In the meantime, you make

sure to mind yourself and the young ones." When Macdara and James were almost out the door, James stopped and turned.

"What?" she said.

"Lock yer windows and doors," he said.

"I will, so."

Macdara didn't look convinced. "He's right. Call Séamus. Have him replace the locks."

Siobhán nodded. This was good. This meant Macdara didn't think James did it. It was a stab of relief. On the flip side, it meant he thought there was a killer still out there. A killer who might be coming back for one of them.

Chapter 9

The next day, the young ones were back, and they had scrubbed the bistro clean, said prayers, and set up crosses and candles in the back room, on the very table where Niall had been found, but Siobhán still couldn't get the horror of death out of her mind. Maybe Father Kearney could come and give the space a blessing. They held hands around the table and said a prayer for Niall and his family. Then they prayed for James. That helped a little.

Ann and Gráinne were pumping out a constant stream of tears. Ann's tears were because James was once again back at the gardai station being questioned (the first attempt was all but impossible with James experiencing the terrors after so much drink), but Gráinne seemed to be crying for a different reason. She seemed to be crying over Niall. Siobhán took a seat next to her and leaned in.

"What is going on with ye?" she whispered.

Gráinne's head snapped up. "What do you mean?" She didn't bother to whisper; she was full-on yelling.

"We're all shaken up, but you're crying as if you've lost a dear friend." *Or a boyfriend.* Hand to God, if Siobhán found out that Niall had been sniffing around her sister, she'd wish him alive just to kill him all over again. A shameful thought, she supposed, but the honest truth. Like it or not, this brood was hers to protect. Siobhán braced herself. "Was there something going on between you and Niall?"

Gráinne shot out of her chair. "Don't be daft!"

"Don't speak to me like that."

"You're not my mammy."

"But I am your guardian."

"So what?"

"So I deserve a little respect!"

"Not if you go around accusing me of terrible things, like, you don't."

"It had to be asked. You're crying as if the love of your life just died."

"We've known Niall our whole lives!" Gráinne said. "How can you be so cold-hearted?"

Ann and Ciarán were looking on, wide-eyed. Siobhán had better back off. No use rattling everyone up even worse than they already were. She'd forgotten how volatile Gráinne could be. If she wanted answers, this was not the way to get them. "Settle down. I'm only asking."

Gráinne wiped her tears, and hiccuped. She's still so young. Just a girl. Siobhán went to hug her. Gráinne turned her back on the gesture. "Why aren't you crying? Why aren't we all crying?"

"Should I be crying?" Ciarán said.

"I'm crying," Ann said. "I've been crying a lot."

"See?" Gráinne wailed, pointing at Ann. "So why are you just giving out to me?"

Pick your battles. This wasn't getting her anywhere. If Siobhán was going to confront Gráinne again, she'd have to wait until they were alone.

"I just don't like seeing you in such a state," Siobhán said. Gráinne folded her arms across her chest and sat back down. At least she hadn't stalked off to her room. It was best to leave it for now. It seemed every time she opened her mouth lately she said the wrong thing. Maybe she wasn't cut out to be minding young ones.

"I'll wet the tea," Ann said.

"Good girl." Siobhán took a deep breath and made her way to the front window, trying to settle herself down and collect her thoughts. Across the way, she spotted Sheila Mahoney dashing into the salon and slamming the door shut behind her. Now there's someone she needed to have a chat with. Niall's recent head shave, not to mention the scissors plunged in his heart, warranted a fair look at Sheila. Yet Macdara was focused only on James.

Did Sheila even know that her scissors were the murder weapon? Macdara would be raging at her if she gave away evidence. She wouldn't say a word about the scissors, or anything else. She would simply take in information. Should she grab a Biro and paper to take notes, or would that look too official? She'd sneak them in her pocket and write everything down the minute she was on her own. It couldn't look like she was investigating, which, of course, she wasn't. Paying a visit to Sheila was the neighborly thing to do. They all had to band together, keep each other safe.

Siobhán grabbed her handbag and ordered her siblings to stay upstairs. She was met with protests until she said they could watch all the telly and eat all the sweets and crisps they wanted, but they were not to come down in any circumstances. She forbade them to answer the door or the mobile. She had to promise puppies, and cars, and trips to London, but at least she was able to get out of the bistro.

She headed straight for Sheila's shop. She definitely should have told Macdara about Sheila's strange activities this morning; maybe then he wouldn't be so focused on James. She would make up for her mistake. The quickest way to free her brother was to find out who really killed Niall Murphy.

Siobhán hurried across the street and tried to open the door to the salon, but it was locked. Siobhán looked at the window. The curtains were drawn tight. At this time of day they were always thrown open. Where was Sheila? Not only had she expected it to be open; she was convinced the shop would already be full of ladies there on the pretense of getting their hair done just so they could stare at the bistro across the street and gossip. It was looking as if everyone was at the pub. Siobhán pounded on the door.

On the third bang the curtain finally twitched. "Sheila. I know you're in there." Siobhán made sure her voice was loud. Sheila would be forced to open the door just to hush her up. "It's Siobhán. We need to talk." The curtain twitched again, and this time Sheila's round face appeared. Her eyes went wide, she put a plump finger to her lips, and a second later the door swung open. Before Siobhán could say another word, Sheila grabbed her arm, yanked her inside, then slammed and triple-locked the door. Next she jammed a chair underneath the doorknob, then made sure the curtains were drawn tight.

When she whirled around to face Siobhán, she was out of breath. But it was Siobhán who got a fright. For the first time, maybe ever, Sheila wasn't wearing a lick of face paint—not mascara, not rouge, not heavy black eyeliner, not lipstick, not foundation, or even cover-up for the dark circles underneath her eyes. Definitely not a pretty sight. A cigarette dangled from her fingers. Her fake nails had even been stripped off, and the jagged short ones revealed her to be a biter. Siobhán wasn't surprised.

"Are ye well?" Siobhán asked. It was the only thing she could think to say.

"I am, yea. Why wouldn't I be, with a killer on the loose?" Sheila's voice rose and wobbled. Smoke from the cigarette curled up and soured the air. She seemed right mental, and

Siobhán had an urge to flee. Her eyes flicked to the fortified door and covered windows.

"You closed the shop?"

"Everyone has closed their shops," Sheila said. "Out of respect, like." Siobhán glanced at the chair jammed into the door. "Just because we're fierce scared as well doesn't mean we didn't do it out of respect."

"Of course," Siobhán said.

"Would you like a cuppa and a biscuit?"

"Yes, please."

"Sit down, sit down." Siobhán turned to the salon and was momentarily stunned to see that it was clean. Remarkably clean. The scent of bleach hung in the air. Had Niall been murdered here and that's why they'd done such a thorough cleaning? She'd have to tell Macdara about this straightaway. The pristine shop floor was a sharp contrast to Sheila's naked face, chewed nails, and ratty bathrobe.

Siobhán looked around. Was she meant to sit on a styling chair? There weren't any other options. Siobhán hoisted herself onto the edge of one as Sheila turned and tended to the kettle. A small cooker had been installed in the shop just for tea. Their real kitchen was upstairs, where she and Pio lived.

Siobhán felt instantly comforted as she watched Sheila crush out the cigarette so she could tend to tea and biscuits. It didn't matter what was happening in the world; there was nothing that couldn't be softened with a spot of tea. "Milk and sugar?" Sheila asked.

"Yes, please, just a drop and a pinch." The clink of the spoon and the solid feel of the saucer as Sheila handed it to her helped Siobhán breathe a sigh of relief. Outside it began to rain, and it sounded like a bucket of pebbles slowly being tipped out over the roof.

Her mind flashed to their back garden. Would the rain be washing away evidence? Had the guards missed anything?

Her hands instantly warmed as she wrapped them around the mug. Sheila leaned against one of the sinks with her own mug of tea, and for a few seconds they slurped in silence.

"Tell me everything," Sheila barked just as Siobhán was starting to relax.

Siobhán hesitated. She was the one who was supposed to be asking questions. But she couldn't afford to rile Sheila up. *Sometimes you have to go along to get along.* "I got up early that morning for a run," Siobhán started.

"A run for what?" Sheila furled her eyebrows in utter confusion.

"A run, like," Siobhán said. "For sport." Sheila's frowned deepened. Siobhán kept going. "When I returned, I noticed a light on in your salon, and the door wide open."

Sheila suddenly stood straight, sloshing a bit of tea onto her robe. "What?" She shoved a biscuit into her mouth and let it sit there for a moment as if attempting to plug up a leaky spout. Crumbs trickled out onto her ample bosom. She didn't make a move to wipe them off.

Siobhán had an urge to yank the wee biscuit out of Sheila's piehole, see if a confession would burst through. She was dying to tell Sheila that it was her hot-pink scissors sticking out of Niall's chest, just to gauge her reaction.

"I was worried you'd been burgled. I was going to call the guards when I saw you hurrying up through the passageway."

Sheila plucked the biscuit out of her mouth, tossed it on the counter, and withdrew a packet of smokes from the pocket of her robe. "You saw me, did ye?" she asked as she stuck the cigarette in her mouth and lit it.

"I did indeed. You rushed into the shop, slammed your door, and your lights went off."

Sheila blew the smoke directly at Siobhán. "Did you tell Garda Flannery?"

"Why would I tell Garda Flannery?" What a funny thing

to ask straightaway, not to mention the menacing tone with which it was said. Siobhán tried to keep her face still. She was a better poker player than Sheila.

"You said you thought I'd been burgled. So why not call the guards?"

"I was headed back to the bistro to do just that when I saw you coming up alongside the salon with the rubbish bag."

Sheila shook her head furiously, tossing ashes into the air. "What does any of this have to do with the murder?" Her voice was gravelly and deep. She stared at Siobhán, and that's when Siobhán noticed it. Sheila had a faint bruise under her left eye. Was that why she wore so much makeup? Was Pio a violent man? He certainly seemed harmless enough, but as her mammy always said, you never knew what was going on behind closed doors. It was hard to imagine that skinny husband of hers, the man who could make a set of spoons sing, giving her a punch. But you just never knew. Siobhán resisted the urge to cross herself. "Well?" Sheila barked. Siobhán started. She'd forgotten the question.

"Well?" she repeated. When in doubt it was best to nod and smile or answer a question with a question.

"Why are ye going on about me when Niall was murdered in your bistro?"

"We don't know for sure that he was murdered in the bistro. In fact, I think he was murdered out back and—"

"What does this have to do with me? What were you doing spying on me, for feck's sakes?"

"I wasn't spying. I was worried about you, that's all." Siobhán's eyes landed on a broom propped in the far corner of the room. Why on earth does Sheila look like death warmed over yet the salon was scrubbed as if she was expecting the queen? Something was definitely not right here.

"How was he killed?" Sheila asked.

With a pair of your scissors. The ones you were handing out all over town like you were sharing a bag of sweets.

*How do you like that? Now we can't narrow the suspect list
at all.* Siobhán needed to change the subject, get control of
the conversation. "How did Niall seem when you shaved his
head?" she asked casually.

Sheila crushed out her cigarette and stepped closer to
Siobhán with a menacing glare. "What did ye say?"

"Did Niall say why he wanted it all shaved off? Was he
going to a wedding, or a funeral, or—"

"How did you know he was here?" Sheila's head darted
left and right as if she was expecting someone, perhaps Niall
himself, to jump out from behind one of the chairs.

"Who else would he have gone to for a cut and a shave?"

Sheila opened and shut her mouth like a fish trying to decide whether or not to chomp down on the bait. "You're
right, of course," she said, finally deciding she wanted the
worm. "Of course, he came to me. Everyone comes to me."
She stepped even closer. "Except the O'Sullivans. Always
cutting your own hair, aren't ye?" Before Siobhán could
leap out of the chair, Sheila sunk her nicotine-stained fingers
into Siobhán's long, red locks, roughly drawing her fingers
through them.

"That hurts." Siobhán squirmed in the chair. "Our mammy
liked to cut our hair. It's nothing personal. I just want to carry
on the tradition."

*The last thing that manky woman should have is a pair of
sharp scissors in her hands,* her mammy always said about
Sheila.

"You could use a wee trim. Sit back." Sheila shoved
Siobhán's head back into the sink. The back of her head
thunked against the porcelain rim, and pain shot through
her skull. "Idle hands entice the Devil to hold them," she
sang. She reached to her left, and before Siobhán knew what
was happening, she was staring at a pair of scissors with hot-
pink handles.

"No," Siobhán said. She struggled to get up. Sheila held her down.

"What's the matter with ye?"

"I can't get my hair cut." *Was Sheila going to stab her through the heart as well? Right here, right now? Why hadn't she told anyone where she was going? She doubted the young ones would even miss her, not when they had endless telly, and sweets, and crisps.*

"Why can't ye get a hair cut? You don't think I can do a good job?"

"It's not that, like."

"You t'ink yer hair is so special? Would ye look at the oldest O'Sullivan girl, with hair like fire?" Sheila twisted her hair even harder. Jaysus, she was mental. Siobhán never should have come. Was Pio upstairs? Should she yell for help?

"It's not that." She wished her hair was really made of fire so she could set Sheila aflame.

"Then what is it?"

"It's like you said. We need to show respect today for Niall. Especially me."

"Why especially you?"

"The poor lad was found murdered in my bistro. How would it look if the next day if I was in here getting me hair done?"

"Like you're getting ready for the funeral," Sheila said. She finally loosened her grip on Siobhán's hair.

The funeral. Oh, God. Not another one. After her parents' funerals, Siobhán hoped it would be at least a decade before she ever had to go to another one.

"I'll tell ye what," Sheila said, stepping back. "I'll tell ye why Niall was getting his hair cut if you let me get my hands on yours."

"Another time?"

"Then I'll tell ye another time as well, like."

Shite. Siobhán needed to know. For James. "Will ye also tell me about the black rubbish bag I saw you carrying into the shop that mornin'? And why your door was wide open, and your lights blazing one minute but plunged into the black the next?"

"I'll tell ye everything," Sheila said. "Do we have a deal?"

"Please just a wee trim." Siobhán's plea came out with a squeak. *Was that what Niall asked for and instead Sheila shaved his head?*

"Brilliant." Sheila threw an apron over Siobhán, tied it around the back of her neck to the point of choking her, and shoved her under the water to either drown her or shampoo her. Siobhán gritted her teeth, praying that she would have enough hair left to cut, as it felt like strands were being ripped from the roots. She was pretty sure she didn't have as pretty a head as Sinéad O'Connor, and she didn't want to find out.

She silently scolded James. If only he'd stayed in that night, Macdara would surely be the one over here questioning Sheila. James had better appreciate the sacrifice she was making. Sheila continued to be rough, but Siobhán didn't give her the satisfaction of crying out. When she had been brutally shampooed and conditioned, Sheila began wringing out her hair, and that hurt even worse. Then came the raking with a giant brush, and next the dreaded scissors.

Siobhán flinched as she flashed on poor Niall again. Would she ever get that image out of her head? She squeezed her eyes shut as Sheila began to snip. *This too shall pass*, she said to herself. *This too shall pass*. If only she believed it.

Chapter 10

True to her promise, Sheila began to talk as she worked. "Niall came in around seven that night. I think he'd had a few pints at O'Rourke's. He wanted it shaved off, all proper like."

"Did he say why?" Siobhán moved her head, trying to see in the mirror, but Sheila grabbed her by the chin and yanked her eyes back to hers.

"No peeking."

"Sorry."

"Niall just said he needed to look his best."

For what? Or who? "Was he wearing a suit?"

"Why would he be wearing a suit?" Sheila froze mid-cut. "Was he wearing a suit when he was killed?" Curiosity oozed from her pores.

"No," Siobhán said quickly.

"He must have been. Why else would you ask me that?"

"You didn't ask him why he needed to look his best?"

"I'm not a Nosy Nellie," Sheila said.

"Of course not," Siobhán said. "But you must have been curious."

"I assumed he was sweet on someone."

"Any guess who?"

"How would I know?"

Siobhán sighed. This wasn't worth getting her hair cut. "Why were you up so early, and what about the rubbish bag?"

"I wasn't up early; we were just getting home. Pio played at Fitzgerald's until the wee hours of the morning."

"And the rubbish bag?"

The scissors started to move faster. Siobhán glanced down at the floor and was horrified to see a sea of red hair. She cried out.

"What in heavens?" Sheila yelped.

"Are you cutting it short?"

"No fussing until after you've seen it."

"I asked for a trim. That doesn't feel like a trim." It was true. Her head felt light. Way too light.

"You said you were a runner now. Runners need short hair."

"I don't want short hair."

"Hush now."

Siobhán hated her. She hated her. "What about the rubbish bag?"

"I broke a vase. Pio threw out the pieces before I could collect 'em. I wanted to try and glue it back together."

"What happened to your eye?" The question spilled out of Siobhán before she could stop it.

"None of your feckin' business." Sheila slammed the scissors down and got out the hair dryer. She turned it on full heat and practically scalded Siobhán's scalp. Only this time, Siobhán let herself yelp. Sheila ignored her. After drying and wrestling her hair with a brush, Sheila turned her around to face the mirror. Siobhán braced herself to hate it, to see that she was practically bald, or looked like a lad. Instead, she couldn't believe the image in the mirror.

It wasn't as short as she feared. It fell just below her chin, with soft, jagged layers. She couldn't believe it. She looked stunning. Sophisticated even. This would have been the haircut she would have wanted for her first day at college. Tears came to her eyes.

"You hate it?" Sheila said.

Siobhán's hands fluttered around, as she touched it all over. "I love it."

"You mean it?" Sheila's voice softened.

Siobhán nodded. "I really mean it."

An actual smile crept across Sheila's face. She straightened her robe and stood up tall. "Well, then. Maybe you'll let the young ones come to me too."

"I will indeed," Siobhán said. She continued to stare in the mirror as Sheila went to the corner and got the broom. When she removed it, Siobhán noticed a pile of broken glass. Was that the vase Sheila was on about?

Siobhán tried to think through what Sheila said. She and Pio had come home in the wee hours of the morning. Somehow Sheila broke a vase. Pio threw the pieces out. Sheila fetched them. Had they been having a row? Sheila got mad and threw a vase? Did Pio hit her? Then what? They went to bed and Sheila shook the broken pieces out onto the floor? Did that make sense?

Siobhán would have to try and make sense of it later. What else? Niall had his hair cut, wanted to look good for something. Although that wasn't really all, was it? Why did the place smell like bleach? Not to mention that Niall was killed with a pair of her scissors. Maybe Pio had a dark side. Maybe Sheila was sleeping with Niall, and Pio killed him in a drunken rage. Maybe Niall had broken into their salon that day and the shards of glass were actually from a broken window.

"Go on with ye now," Sheila said. "I'm done cutting and I'm done talking."

Just then, Sheila sneezed, and a memory came hurling

through Siobhán's mind: Sheila at the calling hours for her parents' service. She'd stood too close to the flower arrangements and starting sneezing. "I'm allergic," she'd said when Siobhán glanced over at her. "I feckin' hate flowers. I don't even own a vase." Why would someone who hated flowers, and never owned a vase before, go to such lengths to glue one back together? If it was anyone else, maybe for sentimental reasons. But Sheila wasn't a sentimental gal. Siobhán had once seen her crush a cigarette out in one of her wedding photos. If it were just the vase, it wouldn't be that big of a deal. But when you took into consideration the bleach, the bruise, and how she was hurrying back into her salon with a rubbish bag just before Siobhán discovered Niall in their bistro—it was all just too odd to ignore.

Siobhán had to go to Macdara and tell him to come to the salon straightaway. She handed over her credit card and practically vibrated as she waited for Sheila to charge her. When it was done, she thanked her and flew out of the shop, and didn't stop running until she'd reached the gardai station.

"You just missed James," Macdara said the moment Siobhán stepped into his office. "He's back home. For now."

"I'm not here about him," Siobhán said, hating how he said *For now*.

"We'll see what we're dealing with when the results come back from his shirt," Macdara continued.

Siobhán didn't want to think about that, and arguing about it now might only distract Macdara. "I went to question Sheila."

"You did what?" Macdara stood up and approached Siobhán. She'd never seen his nostrils flare before. Macdara's office was tiny, and in any other circumstances she would have been all aflutter to be this close to him. Now she just wanted to get away. She wasn't used to him being angry with her, let alone apoplectic. Still he was mighty attractive, even now. She wanted to cross herself, but she didn't want him wondering why. She was definitely going to have to go to confession after all of this.

"I'm only telling you what I observed when I went to get my hair done." She nervously touched it as Macdara's eyes flicked to her hair, then her face, and she couldn't help but notice his eyes lingered on her lips.

"It suits you," he said gruffly, then looked away.

"Thank you."

"Let me get this straight." His voice was clear and stern again. "There was a murder in your bistro a few days ago, your brother is our top suspect, and you just happen to decide to get your hair done?"

"Top suspect? I thought you were just questioning him."

Macdara sighed. "Please, sit," he said.

"No."

"If the blood on him matches Niall, he's going to be arrested. You need to prepare yourself for that."

"He didn't do it. You know James. You know he didn't do it."

"I don't know that at all. Neither does he."

"What?" What had James been saying?

"He says he doesn't remember a thing. He can't say whether he did it or not."

Why couldn't he have just kept his gob shut? She was going to kill him. She'd better stop using that expression. But she was. She was going to kill him. She put her hands on her hips. "Aren't you supposed to have a solicitor present when you're being questioned?"

"He didn't ask for a solicitor." Macdara sat in his chair and turned to his computer as though signaling that the conversation was over.

"You should have advised him to get one."

"I have a job to do. Whether you like it or not."

"James didn't ask for a solicitor because he has nothing to hide. Doesn't that count for anything?"

"I talked to Declan. He said James and Niall were in a heated argument that night. Almost came to fisticuffs right there in the pub."

"But it didn't?"

"Declan and Séamus broke it up. Threw them both out."

"What time? Was Niall wearing a suit?"

"I can't give you information on an ongoing investigation."

"So what if they had a bit of a scuffle? That's probably where the blood came from. But wouldn't there have been way more blood if he had been the one who stabbed him?"

"There wasn't any blood on Niall's face, love. If James's shirt has Niall's blood on him, it came from the wound in his heart."

Siobhán felt like she had just been stabbed. "It's James's blood. From his own mouth. Or his nose. You'll see. It has to be."

"We'll find out soon enough." Macdara said.

"So that's it? You aren't even going to question anyone else?"

"I've got work to do," Macdara said, gesturing to the door.

Siobhán leaned on the desk. "If James had killed Niall in some kind of drunken blackout near the pub, why would he drag his body all the way to his own bistro?" It didn't make sense.

"Niall could have followed your brother home. Could have even stumbled in the door after him. Who knows. Maybe it was even self-defense."

"Ann would have heard the commotion. If she heard glass breaking, she certainly would have heard a violent struggle. And again—he couldn't have been killed in the bistro—"

Macdara's head shot up. "Why couldn't he have been killed in the bistro?"

"Where's the blood?"

"Someone could have cleaned up."

"Sheila's place smells like bleach. Not ours. And you and I both know the guards checked our place thoroughly for more blood. The grass was trampled out back—I think from where he was dragged. Are you sure you didn't miss any evidence out there?"

"Do I come into the bistro and tell ye how to make brown bread?"

"That's not fair."

"I have work to do."

"If Niall followed James home, and James killed him in some kind of drunken self-defense, then why wasn't James up in his bed? You're saying he sobered up enough to clean up the blood—blood you didn't find, by the way, or our bistro would still be a crime scene, and you know it—then what? Would he leave his bloody clothes on, go back to the pub, and pass out in the back of O'Rourke's until Delcan finds him there? Then pretend not to remember any of it? In what universe does any of that make any sense?"

"Maybe he did sober up. It would be natural to be afraid of what he'd done. Try to cover it up. Pretend he can't remember."

"Why would he do that?"

"To get away with murder."

"I cannot believe I'm hearing this."

Macdara threw his hands up. "I'm not jumping to any conclusions until all the facts are in."

"Except for the conclusion that my brother is guilty." Macdara ignored her and began pecking away at his keyboard. "When will the autopsy results be in?"

"This is a murder investigation, not a show on telly. Everything has to go through Cork City or even Dublin, depending. Things will take however long they will take."

Siobhán bit her lip. If her da was alive, he would have gone with James. Macdara wouldn't have tried questioning James without a solicitor then. Maybe he wouldn't even have James's clothes to test in the first place. "Please. Go talk to Sheila. Go now."

"I don't take my directions from you."

"Why? Because I'm a woman? My place is in the kitchen, is that it, yea?"

"Don't twist my words. You're not a detective superintendent, or a garda, or a blood expert. I feel for ye. I do. But I can't get distracted." He stared at her for a moment, then looked away.

Stunned, Siobhán headed for the door and yanked it open. She was about to storm out when she turned and took a deep breath. It would be wise to hold her temper, just like her da and Sean O'Casey always said. "I'm telling you, something isn't right. Sheila was the one cleaning with bleach. Not us. Niall was in her salon the night he was killed. And she had a black eye, and there's broken glass on the floor, which she said came from a vase, but she's allergic to flowers. And on the morning of the murder I saw her running into her shop with a rubbish bag. Who brings a rubbish bag *into* their home?" Macdara's head snapped up, and he looked at her.

"And you're just telling me this now?" he asked.

Siobhán shook her head. "I forgot."

"Blarney, you forgot." He got up from his chair and approached her. "That's called interfering with an active investigation."

"Really? Because it doesn't look like you're interrogating anyone but me brother."

"Right now I'm interrogating you."

"What do you mean?"

"I mean you're the one with a temper. You admitted Sheila forced you to take a pair of the scissors, and you were the one who found the body."

"What are ye saying? Are you accusing me of murdering Niall?"

"It's crossing me mind."

"Well, uncross it. I could never do something that vile."

"But you can keep important information from me."

"I told ye, I forgot."

"And I called blarney on ye, Siobhán O'Sullivan."

He was close. Close enough to kiss. He was also furious. "Yes, Garda Flannery?"

"What else are ye hiding from me?"

Chapter 11

Siobhán stood still for what felt like a lifetime. Macdara's eyes never left hers. If she didn't tell him everything now, he'd never be on her side again. It was now or never. She took a deep breath. "The Friday before he was killed I got in a bit of an argument with Niall."

"You did, did ye?"

"At Sheedy's cycle shop."

"What's the story?"

"Niall Murphy was trying to extort me."

Macdara kept still. "What?" His voice was almost a growl.

"He asked me for ten thousand euro."

"What exactly did he say?"

"He said he had proof that Billy was innocent."

"Are you joking me?"

"That's what I said. Of course it was madness. You were there. At the accident site. There's no doubt it was Billy who killed them, is there?"

Macdara suddenly lunged forward and took Siobhán's hands. She was startled, then ashamed, as a shiver of attraction ran through her. "There is no doubt, Siobhán. Billy ran into your parents. He was drunk. He was in the car. There was no one else. I don't know what Niall was on about, but there is no doubt."

Siobhán nodded as tears filled her eyes. She'd done so little crying; she was terrified that once she started she'd never be able to stop. She bit her lips and pulled her hands away. "Niall mentioned someone else who he said would pay him twenty thousand for his proof. So he was extorting or blackmailing someone else too. Maybe he or she killed him."

"Who was this other person?"

"I don't know. That's why I said he or she. Niall just said 'yer one.'"

"Yer one."

"'Yer one would pay me twenty thousand for it.' That's exactly what he said."

"I can't believe I'm just hearing this now."

"I thought it was madness. I still do. But you should look through his things. See if you can find anything."

"Mary Murphy will put up holy hell, if I try to blacken Niall's name during the course of this investigation. I can tell ye that right now."

"Even if it's to find her son's killer?" Macdara gave her a long look. "Does she know James was here for questioning?"

Macdara nodded. "She was in the station when they brought him in."

"And she thinks he did it?" Macdara's look said it all. Of course, she thought James did it. There had been bad blood between their families ever since the crash. "I can't believe this is happening. I can't believe any of this is happening."

"Did James know about your run-in with Niall?" Siobhán looked away. "He knew. He went out that night to find Niall, didn't he?" Macdara's fury was back. Siobhán just didn't know when to stop.

"I didn't say that," Siobhán said. "You can't say that I said that."

"So, that's a yes. Damn it, Siobhán. You're making this worse."

"How?"

"James went out all cocked and ready to fire at Niall. That's damning evidence."

"So is extortion. Niall was extorting or blackmailing someone else. Maybe that someone was willing to kill to protect his or her secret."

"What secret are ye on about?"

"I don't know! You're the guard. You figure it out."

"I told you there is no doubt that Billy caused that accident."

"That doesn't mean he wasn't going around extorting other people. He knew me well enough to know what buttons to push. How do we know he wasn't torturing several others with different lies? And why did he need ten thousand euro? With that suit, and that much money? What if he was running off with someone? What if they had intended to marry? Isn't it usually the spouse who does it?"

"Damn it, Siobhán," Macdara said. "I'm the one who should be asking these questions."

"Finally," Siobhán said. "At least we agree on something." She could still feel the heat of his glare as she took the opportunity to make a dramatic exit. She probably shouldn't step on his toes. But if he wasn't going to do his job, she would have no choice but to do it for him.

The O'Sullivan Six gathered in the bistro and cozied up to the fireplace, as if seeking warmth wherever they could find it. Gráinne's eyes were swollen from crying. Ann was biting her nails. Eoin was pacing. Ciarán was hopping about, unable to keep still. Siobhán was watching every few seconds out the window as if she'd be able to figure out how it was going with Macdara and Sheila. She'd seen him go into the salon about an hour ago. James was the only one not in motion; he was lost in thought, staring into the fire.

They'd been over and over James's last recollection. It wasn't much; he remembered going to O'Rourke's and having that first drink. After that, everything else was gone.

"We need to talk to Gráinne alone," James said, snapping out of his catatonic state.

"We do?" Siobhán said. Her heart clenched. She knew something was up with Gráinne and Niall. She didn't want to hear it.

"What for?" Gráinne asked.

"I want to stay," Eoin said.

"Me too," Ann said.

"Can I watch telly and eat crisps?" Ciarán asked.

"All of yez upstairs now," James said, sounding very much like their da. "And don't make me say it again."

"We never used to keep secrets," Eoin said with a disgusted look before herding Ann and Ciarán upstairs. James was looking at Gráinne. A feeling of foreboding washed over Siobhán.

"Bits and pieces of the evening are coming back," he said.

Siobhán lunged forward. "Do you know who beat you up?"

James shook his head. "I just remember Niall goading me."

"About what?" *Billy not causing the accident.*

James looked at Gráinne. "About you. Niall told me, Gráinne. He told me."

"Told you what?" Siobhán said.

Gráinne just looked at the fire, tears running down her cheeks.

"What is going on?" Siobhán pressed. She was wrong; she did want to know. Imagining all sorts of scenarios was worse.

"Niall and Gráinne have been writing each other this past year," James said. "Isn't that right, Gráinne?"

"Oh my God," Siobhán said. "No."

Gráinne stepped forward, clutching her hands. "You didn't know him. He wasn't bad. He wasn't bad at all."

"How did this even start?" Siobhán asked.

"He sent us that letter after Mam and Da died," Gráinne said. "And I wrote him back."

Siobhán had forgotten about that letter. In fact, she hadn't even finished reading it. She hadn't wanted his sympathies. "Were you in love with Niall?" The thought made her cringe.

Gráinne shook her head violently. "Don't be daft. We were friends. That's all."

"Did he mention being romantically involved with anyone?" Siobhán asked. "Do you know any reason he would have been in a suit?"

Once again Gráinne shook her head. Siobhán wondered what she was hiding, because it was obvious there was something. "Were you supposed to meet him that night? Was he coming here to see you?"

Once again she just shook her head.

"Let me see the mobile," Siobhán asked.

Gráinne looked horrified. "Why? You think I'm lying?"

"I think you're skirting the truth."

"What does that mean?"

"Garda Flannery thinks James killed Niall. You have to tell us everything you know."

"We were friends. Writing letters. That's all. I hadn't even seen him until he came into the bistro and everyone got in a fight with him."

A fight that started with Mike Granger. Siobhán had forgotten all about that. She needed to talk to Mike, find out exactly what had triggered that fight. She remembered being surprised at how upset Mike was. As if he was personally affronted by the sight of Niall. Siobhán glanced at Gráinne.

She wasn't telling the whole truth either. She knew her sister well enough to know that.

"Go get the mobile," James said.

"I won't." Gráinne actually stomped her foot.

"Do it," James said. Gráinne whirled around and sprinted out the door. Seconds later they heard her furious stomps on the stairs.

"She's going to erase everything first," Siobhán said.

"I know," James said. "But we can hint that we're sending it somewhere where people can retrieve messages. Maybe it'll scare the truth out of her."

"And what do you think the truth is?"

James shook his head as he walked over to the window. "Hey," he said, his voice perking up. "Macdara is across the way talkin' to Sheila and Pio," he said. "It looks serious."

Siobhán ran to the window. Sure enough, Macdara was standing just outside, with a very unhappy-looking Pio and Sheila. Just then, Sheila's head swiveled, and she looked directly at the bistro. If her eyes were explosives, the place would have been blown to smithereens. Uh-oh. Maybe this was a good time to pop into the market and talk to Mike Granger. Anything other than face Sheila's wrath again. She'd leave that to Macdara. She lied to James about needing a bit of fresh air and slipped out the back door.

Chapter 12

Mike's Market was on the same side of the street as the bistro, but was situated at the end—or the beginning, depending on which direction one was headed. It was small, but it stocked most everything one could ever need, and as usual it was filled with people doing their messages. Siobhán hurried past the fresh veggies, spuds, packets of crisps, chocolates, and meats, and headed for the back of the store, where Mike had a small office. The door was closed. Siobhán knocked.

"I'm busy," she heard him call. Who could have known that murder would turn everyone in Kilbane into a recluse?

"It's Siobhán O'Sullivan. Please. I need to speak with ye." A few seconds later, the door opened a crack, and then Mike quickly pulled her into the office and slammed the door behind them.

"How ya keeping?" he said. "Can you believe dis now?"

She didn't know whether he was talking about the murder, or the crowd in his market. "Ah, sure, lookit," she said.

The office was small, but unlike Macdara's orderly space, this one was messy and cramped. Soft-drink cans lined the desk, along with empty crisp wrappers. Diet Coke. He always drank regular as far as Siobhán could remember. When had he switched? Come to think of it, he was looking a bit trimmer. Good for him. He'd stopped smoking last year as well. A man of perpetual improvements—good on him. He had his cap on this time, which was a bit of a relief as Siobhán tried not to think about the vein on the top of his bald head.

Papers were piled on the only chair across from Mike's desk. He removed them, then stood for a moment, trying to figure out where to put them. Finally he settled for a spot on the floor. "Sit, sit," he said. Siobhán did. He folded his arms across his chest, leaned back in his chair, and just waited.

This was so hard. Questioning people who were neighbors, and friends. After her parents died, Mike let them buy food without having to pay right away. It seemed every month they were stretched after paying Alison Tierney the rent. They literally owed him. Siobhán didn't want Mike to think she suspected him of murder, but she had to find out more about the fight he had with Niall. Was it possible Niall had been trying to squeeze money out of him, too? Every little drop of information was a clue. "This has been quite a shock," Siobhán said.

"Indeed," Mike said. "Although . . ." He stopped talking and then shook his head.

"Although?"

"I'm not entirely surprised. The lad was trouble. Just like his brother."

"Who do you think did it?"

Mike looked at the ceiling as if the name of the killer was written there. "Niall didn't have too many friends in town."

"Being a begrudger is a far cry from being a murderer," Siobhán said. "I just can't imagine one of us a killer."

"Who says it's one of us?"

"Well, there aren't many strangers in town." She suddenly thought of the good-looking man she'd passed on the footpath the morning of her run. So tall. Those blue eyes. Like a movie star, he was. In the wake of the murder, she'd forgotten all about him. "There is a fellow I saw the other day who wasn't from here."

"A real good-looking one?" Mike asked. "Tall? About your age?"

"That's the one," Siobhán said, feeling her face flush slightly.

"Chris Gorden. He's a Yank by way of New York. Here tracing his Irish roots." Mike produced air quotes around "Irish roots."

"How long has he been here?"

Mike scratched the top of his cap. "I'd say he showed up about the same time Niall came back. C'mere to me. Would ye look at dat? I think you're onto something there." Mike beamed at her as if she'd just solved the case. Siobhán wasn't convinced.

"Why would a Yank kill Niall?"

"Why do the Yankee Doodles do anything? Maybe he's lying about the reason he's in town. Maybe he was in Dublin with Niall. Could have followed him here. Surely whatever malarkey Niall was up to in the city, it was no good. You know yourself."

Siobhán hadn't thought of that. It didn't have to be one of them. The Yank from New York or an outsider from Dublin. There were a lot of drug-related murders in Dublin. Maybe Niall was in debt to a bad sort. Maybe that's why he was going around trying to extort money. He was desperate. Drug dealers were after him if he didn't pay. And they'd managed to find him.

But why leave his body in their bistro? That didn't seem much like a nasty drug dealer. Still, it was a possibility. She'd have to mention it to Macdara. If he was still talking to her.

"You seemed awfully angry with Niall that afternoon at the bistro," Siobhán said, trying to keep her voice as light and un-accusing as possible.

Mike lifted his eyebrow, then leaned foward. "Did I now?" he said.

Siobhán nodded. She hated the Irish way of answering most everything with sarcasm disguised as a question. Was he trying to give her a gentle warning? She forced herself to press on. "What started the argument? Do you recall?"

Mike leaned across the desk. "Why, Siobhán O'Sullivan, do you fancy yourself a detective superintendent?"

"Of course not."

"Then why do I feel like I need my solicitor?" He grinned, but there wasn't any warmth in his eyes.

"I'm just beside myself with finding his body in our bistro. I guess I'm acting the fool, trying to keep myself occupied."

"Why don't you concentrate in the kitchen? Whip up a nice batch of brown bread. You've a special talent with baking alright."

"Thank you." Siobhán gritted her teeth and curled both fists. "I was very touched by how you stood up to Niall for us the other day. No disrespect to the dead." Siobhán crossed herself.

Mike nodded, then leaned back, looking a lot more relaxed. *He fancies himself a protector. That's his key.* When he spoke again, it was with an air of confidence. "I told Niall he should be home with his poor mammy instead of bothering the likes of you." He shook his head, then adjusted his cap and reached for his can of Diet Coke. He jiggled it, then put it down and tried the next one. It too must have been empty, for he opened one of his desk drawers and brought out another can. The sound of it popping open filled the tiny space. Siobhán was forced to watch as he horsed it into him all at once, then let it down with a simultaneous belch. "I was sorry to hear about James having a right slip. Ah, but it's part of the process, like. I'll get him back to a meeting, I will."

Siobhán nodded. Mike was a Pioneer too. Hadn't had a drop of the drink in years. He'd not only been there for them at the bistro, he'd been there for James during some of his darkest days. Maybe he had been just protecting them from the likes of Niall. And here she was, suspecting him of murder. She hated this. Every single bit of it. Mike clearly didn't want to answer her question about why he was so angry with Niall, and she couldn't afford to make another enemy. She changed the subject instead. "Have you seen Mary Murphy in here since?"

"Father Kearney picked up her carton of fags. Says she barely let him in the door."

"Oh, no," Siobhán said.

"I've been looking the other way when it comes to her bill the past few months. I told Niall he should be ashamed of himself, not taking care of his mammy in her time of need." He sighed as a forlorn expression took over his face. "If I had known he was going to be murdered I would've minded me own business."

"I didn't know things were so bad." Billy's legal bills. Niall had said as much. She would have to make an attempt to see her, no matter what kind of reaction she got. It was the only decent thing to do. Not that Mary had come to see them after her parents died. No matter. Her mam would want her to pay her respects. But there wouldn't be a funeral until the body had been released, and as Macdara had stated, the investigation would take as long as it takes.

"Speaking of paying the piper," Mike said. "Have you given some thought as to what you're going to do now?"

"You mean the bistro?" Siobhán asked.

Mike nodded.

"Do you think we're finished?"

"I just assume folks won't want to eat where a murder occurred."

"I don't think he was killed there."

Mike arched his eyebrows. "No?"

"I think the killer is setting us up."

"How so?"

"I'm not supposed to talk about the details of the investigation. But once the facts are in, I think it will be clear that he wasn't killed inside the bistro."

"I won't say a word. I just hope it's in time."

"In time for what?"

"Alison Tierney. She's been gunning to get your lease revoked since her father died, hasn't she?"

"You're right, you're right." Was it possible that Alison killed Niall just to shut down the bistro? That was preposterous, wasn't it? Why was it every time she turned around there was a new suspect? How could they launch onto James so quickly with all these leads? She would have to pay Alison a visit. Siobhán stood. "Thanks for listening." She stopped at the door. "You were up awful early yourself that morning," she said. "Just like me." Her mind flashed on his truck rumbling by, Mike waving out the window.

"Ah, right," he said. "I was checking out a possible prowler."

The hair on the back of Siobhán's neck stood up. "How do you mean?"

"Declan gave me a bell. Said he was out having a smoke when he saw a few lads creeping around the back of the store." O'Rourke's was directly across from the back lot of the market. If only the alley had faced the store, then maybe Mike would have seen Niall and James fighting and been able to break it up. Or maybe he would have seen Niall leaving James in the alley. Then again, maybe it was Niall who Declan saw creeping about the back of the market. She was going to have to talk to Declan as soon as possible, too.

"Did you catch anyone?"

Mike shook his head. "They were gone by the time I arrived. I saw footprints alright. Looks like there had been several of them."

"How many?"

"At least two. But possibly three."

Siobhán had seen footprints around the abbey that morning as well. Was it the same culprits? Had Niall been running around with someone? Or running from someone or more than one someone?

Had the killer been following Niall, waiting for the exact right moment to strike? Maybe it wasn't purposeful at all that Niall's body was brought to the bistro. Maybe Niall had run to their place because someone was chasing him through town. God, this investigating stuff was tiring. For every question she asked someone, three or four more raised their ugly heads. She thanked Mike for his time. When she stood up, she accidentally brushed a pile of papers off his desk. They fell to the floor and scattered.

"Sorry, sorry." Siobhán squatted down to pick them up.

"I'll get them, no bother," Mike said. She heard a chiming that she assumed was Mike's mobile pinging. Siobhán started to gather the pile of scattered papers. Just as she lifted the last one, something fell out from between the pages in her hand. A maroon passbook stared back at her. It was an Irish passport. Was it Mike's? Before she could mind her manners, she opened it. Niall Murphy's face stared back at her.

Chapter 13

Could the man she'd lived down the street from all her life be a killer? A shiver of fear ran through Siobhán as she stared down at Mike, who was thumbing his mobile. She shoved the passport under the other papers and set them back on the corner of his desk.

"Sorry," she said to the top of his cap.

Mike finished with his phone and glanced at the papers on the desk. "It's alright, luv. The place is a right mess. I need to hire a secretary." Siobhán could almost see the passport underneath the pile of papers, glowing like a possessed eye. She couldn't think of a single reasonable explanation for the fact that he had a dead man's passport on his desk. Maybe he would tell her if she just asked the right questions. *Every person is like a lock*, her da used to say. *If you want to spring them open, you just have to find the right key.*

Siobhán cleared her throat. "Besides the footprints, did you find anything else out back?"

A thick crease formed across Mike's forehead as he frowned. *Uh-oh, she had just put him on high alert.* "Like what?"

Siobhán shrugged, as if she were just reaching for straws. "Maybe one of the lads dropped something?" *Like his passport?*

Mike reached down, pulled another can of Diet Coke out of the drawer, and popped it open. "I have several deliveries a week. Trucks are always pulling in and out, and lads are often acting the maggot, smoking, and all sorts of shenanigans. There's cigarette butts, bottle caps, broken glass, rubbish—if the lads from the other night dropped somethin', I'd never be able to pick it out from the rest of the lot."

"So nothing out of the ordinary, then?"

Mike stood. He was short, but he was powerful. In fact, it looked as if he'd been lifting weights. "Sure, lookit, I'd best be back to work."

"Thank you," Siobhán said as she backed up to the door.

Mike cocked his head. "For what?"

"Your time."

"I always have time for you, pet. You know that."

"Thank you," Siobhán said again. Did she sound frightened? It felt like it was taking forever to get out of here. She had to track down Macdara, and he had to get over here straightaway and confront Mike about the passport. Would he lie? Try to hide it? And if so, which one of them would Macdara believe?

Before leaving, she snuck around the back of the shop and scoured the yard. Mike was right. It was a dumping ground. Gum, empty packets of crisps, cigarette butts, bottles. Mike could certainly stand to tidy up more, but other than that, nothing seemed amiss. She shivered again as she thought of Niall's passport buried on Mike's desk and crossed herself as she hurried to find Macdara.

The woman who answered the phone at the gardai station said Macdara was out for a spot of lunch. Since the bistro wasn't open, that left the chipper, or Jade's, the Chinese restaurant. Then again he could have brought his lunch from home, but she didn't picture Macdara as much of a domestic. She did indeed find him at Jade's, sitting in a booth near the window, about to tackle a bowl full of noodles and other mysteries. Siobhán had never been one for Chinese food. She was like her mammy in that respect—a classic.

She approached Macdara's table and waited until he looked up at her. "Just the person I wanted to see," she said when he finally did.

For a second he looked thrilled. "Business or personal?" he said, looking into her eyes.

"Business," Siobhán admitted, feeling her cheeks heat up.

The thrill was gone. He let his spoon clink in his bowl, then picked up his set of chopsticks and broke it in half. "How did you find me?"

"It's a pretty small village and we're not open for lunch, so I took a chance."

"What can I do for you, Miss O'Sullivan?"

She flushed again at his sarcastic use of her name. She couldn't let him goad her. Or distract her. "You need to go over to Mike Granger's shop right away. Go directly to his office."

Macdara let out a laugh and shook his head. "I do, do I?"

"Yes. He has—"

He jabbed his chopsticks in her direction. "First, you insist I question Sheila, which I just did, by the way. And now you're telling me I have to talk to Mike Granger?"

"I was just there and he has—"

"What were you doing there?"

Siobhán hesitated. She couldn't admit she was checking into Mike Granger or Macdara would be furious with her.

"I was doing my messages. Picking up a few bits and bobs is all."

Macdara eyed her head to toe. "Where are they?"

"Pardon?"

"If you say you went over for a few bits and bobs, why aren't you carrying a bit or a bob?"

"I-I."

"You. You. You were back at it, weren't you?"

"No. No. While I was in the shop, I realized I'd forgotten my handbag, so I had to leave. I'll pick them up later."

"Mike would have let you take your items home and then go back and pay."

"Course he would. I just didn't want to take advantage. But listen. While I was there—"

"So if we went over right now, you and me, you're telling me there would be the bits and bobs you were going to purchase sitting right there on the counter?"

"I didn't get that far. I realized I forgot my handbag before I even started. Only thing is—"

"I knew it. I knew there was a thing."

"I got to talking with Mike in his office—"

Macdara held up his hand. "I told you to stay out of this."

"He has Niall Murphy's passport."

"What?" As upset as he was at her, this bit of news stopped him.

"It's on his desk underneath a bunch of papers. He doesn't know I saw it."

"Christ."

"I'm not saying he did anything to Niall. The night of the murder, Declan saw a few lads sneaking about the back of his shop. Maybe one of them was Niall and he dropped the passport." *Except if that were the case why hadn't Mike told her about it?*

"Why would Niall have been carrying around his passport?" Macdara said.

"Excellent question," Siobhán said. "You should get right on it." Macdara pulled out his wallet, threw money on the table, and started for the door. Siobhán followed. "Didn't even get my fecking fortune cookie," he said.

"Sorry," Siobhán said. "You could ask for it. And a doggie bag, too."

"You've ruined me appetite. And I know what the fortune cookie would say. *Beware of the redhead poking her nose in where it doesn't belong.*"

"Very funny," Siobhán said as they headed out the door and back toward the bistro and Mike Granger's. She had to hurry to keep up with him. "What did you find out from Sheila?"

"Stay out of it," he said.

"Did she explain the rubbish bag? The broken glass?"

Macdara stopped, turned. Siobhán almost knocked into him. Their faces were an inch apart. He was just as attractive close up as he was walking away. "When I have something substantial, you'll know. In the meantime, don't you have bigger things to worry about?"

"Like what?" Siobhán said.

"Like how you're going to get folks coming back to the bistro. Maybe you could at least open for tea and brown bread, for a start. And just a wee bit of advice. Don't be accusing your customers of murder."

"You really think they'd come? After everything?"

"I do. Maybe not for the right reasons at the start."

"What do you mean?"

"I mean there might be an idle curiosity about the fact that a crime took place there. Misery loves company—you know that yourself."

He had a point. And did it really matter why they came, as long as they came and paid? Not to mention that if people started to gather at the bistro, they would naturally start to gossip. She could pick up on tidbits that way. Macdara couldn't accuse her of sleuthing if people came to her and volunteered things, could he?

"You're right, you're right. Thank you," Siobhán said.

Macdara looked surprised, and then a flush of pleasure crossed his face. *That's his key*, Siobhán thought. *He likes to be helpful.* "What were you going to get from the shop? I can bring it back for you, if you like."

Crisps, and wine, and chocolate. "It's no bother," Siobhán said. "If I'm going to be opening again I'll have to make a new list anyway." Macdara nodded, and with one last, lingering glance, he left her standing in front of the bistro and was on his way. Siobhán waited until he was out of sight, then turned and started walking from where they came. She had an idea, something that would help bring people back to the bistro. But first, she'd be needin' a stamp of approval from the unlikeliest of places.

Chapter 14

Mary Murphy lived a bit outside of town, about a mile walk once you were past King's Castle and the town streets changed into country roads. When you reached the hill, there was a drive to the left, and at the top sat the Murphys' white farmhouse. In its day, when it had a bit of paint and charm, it was probably something to see. But now it was obvious that nobody with a hammer and nails or any bit of style had been around it for years. The porch was sagging, shingles hung askew from the roof, and the yard had become a junk heap.

It occurred to Siobhán that the lads had resembled their house—good bones obscured by neglect. The boys' father had taken off when they were just wee lads. He was in a traveling band. Took off one day on tour and just never came back. Her heart broke for them, imagining them waiting every day at the edge of their drive for their da. Maybe none of this would have ever happened if he'd stayed to raise them. Maybe they'd have turned out to be nice lads, and maybe her parents would still be alive, Billy wouldn't be in prison, and Niall wouldn't have been murdered.

Siobhán stood at the top of the driveway and glanced at a car parked in the yard. It was covered by an old tarp, but it only took seeing a tiny flash of red for her to know that it was Billy's car. Revulsion washed over Siobhán, and it took everything in her not to spin around and go back home. Mary Murphy was hanging on to the car either because she thought Billy would be back one day and want it, or because she thought she could get something for it. Maybe Siobhán would kick the tires later when she was sure no one was watching. More satisfying would be taking a baseball bat to every inch of it.

Siobhán held a pan of brown bread in front of her like a shield of hope, but despite her offerings, her sense of dread increased with each step she took to the front door. Mary's windows were covered by heavy drapery. This was not a home where people were encouraged to drop by and say hello.

A bicycle was propped up along the porch. Niall hadn't been driving since he'd been home. She wondered briefly if the bicycle was from Sheedy's, and if so, did Séamus know he had it? She wouldn't have put it past Niall to steal a cycle. Even so, Séamus wouldn't be worried about that now, and certainly wouldn't be coming after a mother who lost her son for the sake of a bicycle.

Siobhán rapped politely on the door and then stepped back. It felt like she waited an eternity. Just as she was about to give up, the door opened a crack. All that was visible of Mary Murphy was her straight nose, a single blue eye, and waves of white hair. Despite her demeanor, she had the looks of an aging movie star; she must have been quite the beauty in her day. "Why are you here?" Mary's tone was clear. Siobhán was not welcome.

"I'm so sorry for your loss," Siobhán said. "I've come to tell you that we're absolutely shocked at what happened."

"Are ye now?"

"I know you think it was James. It wasn't. James would never have hurt Niall. Not in a donkey's age."

"They're going to arrest him, you'll see," Mary Murphy said.

"He didn't hurt Niall. You have to believe me."

"I'd like you to leave now."

"I brought some brown bread."

"I don't want it."

"I'd like to invite you to the bistro—"

"Are you joking me?" The door swung open. Mary Murphy glared at her. For such a tiny woman she certainly did pack a lethal stare. The door began to swing shut again.

"For a fund-raiser for Niall."

The door stopped an inch from slamming. Siobhán could hear Mary's labored breath. Then she heard a shuffling, and the sound of a lighter being struck. Soon cigarette smoke snaked out of the tiny wedge in the door. Siobhán covered her mouth and coughed as softly as she could. "A fund-raiser?"

"Yes. I'm sure there will be expenses. And we'd like to help."

The door opened the rest of the way. "Are you trying to bribe me?"

"Bribe you?" How ironic. Given her interactions with Niall.

"Get me to saying that I think James didn't do it?"

"No. James didn't do it, but that's not what this is about. I know what it's like to struggle to make ends meet, only to have end-of-life expenses crop up." It had wiped out their savings, having funeral services for her parents.

"Don't just stand there. If you're going to come in, come in. Shoes on the porch." Siobhán knew Mary's floor would be dirty, way dirtier than the bottom of her shoes, but she was in no position to argue. She tried to hand Mary the brown bread, but Mary didn't move a muscle to take it, so

Siobhán set it on the porch while she unlaced her shoes and left them by the door. Then she picked up the brown bread and stepped inside.

The smell of stale cigarette smoke was so overpowering she almost turned and hightailed it back home. This was worse than Sheila's; at least she had bleached the place up and probably opened a few windows. The smoke in here smelled like it had been trapped for a lifetime, wedged in the heavy draperies and cracks in the floorboard. A deep sadness settled in Siobhán's chest. Niall and Billy must have been miserable growing up here.

"Would you like a cuppa?" No. Siobhán didn't want tea. She wanted to throw the bread and run.

"That would be lovely."

Mary Murphy looked around as if she hadn't expected Siobhán to say yes and didn't know what to do now.

"Sit." Mary pointed to her dining room table. Siobhán sat, noting as she did that aside from the suffocating smoke and unbearable darkness, except for a pile of magazines dumped on a chair in the corner of the kitchen the place was surprisingly tidy. Perhaps back in the day it had been messy because of the boys. She felt seized by pity for Mary Murphy. Whatever she thought of her, she had in essence lost both her sons, and she wouldn't wish that upon any mother in the world.

Mary Murphy stood at her cooker, taking her time putting on the kettle, keeping her back to Siobhán. When the tea was wetted, Siobhán sipped in silence. Mary didn't make herself a cup; she simply leaned against the kitchen counter chain-smoking. Siobhán suddenly didn't know what to say. The questions she really wanted to ask didn't seem appropriate. *Did you know Niall was trying to extort me? Do you have any idea who else he was trying to work over? Do you have any idea why he would say he has proof that Billy is inno-*

*cent? Do you know anybody besides my brother who would
want your son dead?*

"I just want him home so I can bury him," Mary Murphy
said suddenly. "You know yourself."

"I do indeed. That's why I thought we'd have a fund-
raiser. Folks will be wanting to pay their respects as soon as
possible."

Mary Murphy let out a snort. "Will they now?"

"Nobody wanted anything like this to happen."

"James couldn't get at Billy, being he's locked away, so
he took it out on my Niall for what happened to your parents. Everyone knows James's got it in 'im."

Siobhán stood. "That's not true! James hadn't had a drop
to drink for nearly six months."

"But he did that night, didn't he? Right back to his old
ways."

"Aren't you even sorry for what your son did?" Siobhán
hadn't meant to blurt it out, but resentment like hers could
only hold so long.

"What did ye say?"

"You wouldn't even pay your respects. I don't care how
much you love your son. My parents didn't deserve that."

"No," Mary said, dropping her voice. "They didn't. And
I did pay my respects. Just not with everyone's eyes on me,
t'inking there's the woman we blame."

"What?"

"It's always the mother's fault, isn't it?"

Siobhán looked down at her feet. "I don't blame you for
what Billy did. And my mam and da wouldn't have either.
And if James is guilty, then he should pay the price. But I'm
just asking you to let the guards do their job before you go
insisting that my brother is a killer."

"Sit down." Mary gestured to the chair. Siobhán perched on
the edge of it again. Tears ran silently down Mary's cheeks,

and it startled Siobhán to see it. She'd been so wrapped up in her own anger toward Mary Murphy that she had almost forgotten she was human. Siobhán had an urge to take her hand or give her a comforting pat, but she knew her pity would not be welcome.

"When I ran into Niall in the bike shop, he wanted to talk to me about Billy." There it was, out of her mouth before Siobhán could stop herself. But she had to find out what Mary Murphy knew. Was she believing the same crazy ideas as Niall?

Mary's eyes flicked to Siobhán's and stayed locked for a second. Defiance. That was the look. Defiance.

"When are ye thinking of having the fund-raiser?" Mary Murphy said. "We'll need to talk to Father Kearney."

"Of course. Whenever you think it would suit."

"Where will we have it, like?"

"At the bistro. We could make a nice meal for everyone."

"Where my precious boy's body was found?"

"Found. But not killed. And I won't let anyone sit at the table. It would be nice if folks could leave candles, and pictures, and warm wishes, like."

"What do you mean not killed?"

"I don't believe Niall was killed in the bistro. I believe he was brought in. After. I'm sorry."

"Why would ye think that?"

"Because there was very little . . ." Siobhán stopped. She shouldn't have opened her mouth. "There were indentations in the grass out back. Like someone had been dragged." That didn't sound any better at all. It was all macabre, this murder business, no matter how polite you tried to be.

"I see," Mary Murphy said as she crushed out a cigarette.

"I think someone wanted to make it look like we had done it. Someone wanted to frame us."

"And why would anyone want to do that?"

"You mean besides get away with murder?" Mary flinched, and Siobhán once again kicked herself. "I'm sorry. I think they knew people would suspect us because of what happened last year." *And because a few days ago Niall had the nerve to ask me for ten thousand euro to help clear Billy's name.* But nobody else had been in the shop for that exchange, so who else had Niall told and why? Or was Niall killed because he was trying to extort someone else, using yet another lie?

"Billy can't even be here for his own brother's funeral. How do you like that?"

"Did you know that Niall spoke to me about Billy? Did he mention it to ye?" Siobhán had to ask.

Mary Murphy removed another cigarette from her pack. "Niall was a grown man. He didn't tell me who he was talking to or what he was saying. But he was a good brother. And he was a good son." Mary's voice grew in volume. She pointed a finger at Siobhán. "And your brother killed him. Niall didn't deserve to be done like that."

"James didn't do it."

"He was home all night, was he? Is that what you're saying to me?"

"Folks are saying he got in a fight with Niall that night. Although it was James who took the punches—"

"How dare you?"

"There weren't any marks on Niall's face," Siobhán blurted out. She couldn't help it. It was true. If the fight between James and Niall got physical, then Niall had been the only one throwing punches. Had Niall's knuckles been swollen, or was there any evidence that he'd hit James? Siobhán would have to ask Macdara. No good would come from discussing her theories with Mary Murphy, so she brought the topic back to the fund-raiser. "When would you like to schedule the gathering?"

"How's Sunday after Mass?" Mary Murphy said.

"That'll do just fine," Siobhán said. "I'll talk to Father Kearney, and he can help spread the word."

Mary Murphy didn't even get up to open the door. "Don't waste your bread on the likes of me," she called when Siobhán reached the door. "I was never one for it."

Siobhán gritted her teeth and swiped up the pan of brown bread. She'd have to throw it out; surely the smell of cigarette had seeped into its core. Siobhán headed for the door again.

"Say hello to Gráinne," Mary called out in a pleasant singsong.

Siobhán halted as the statement poured over her like a bucket of ice. "What?"

A slow smile crept across Mary's face. It was the creepiest thing Siobhán had ever seen. "She's such a wee dolt. Thank her for me, will ye?"

Siobhán did not blink or breathe for a few torturous seconds. "Thank her for what?"

Mary Murphy simply held the smile and Siobhán's gaze. A chill ran up Siobhán's spine. "Sunday week?" Mary said. The pleasant singsong tone had evaporated.

"Sunday week," Siobhán manage to reply, and then flew out of the house before she could get her hands around Mary Murphy's scrawny neck and squeeze.

Chapter 15

Declan O'Rourke was leaning against the bar and watching rugby on the new HD television that had been mounted on the wall just a few months prior. Siobhán would much rather look at the movie paraphernalia on the wall or even Séamus's racing trophies that Declan proudly displayed on the top shelf. Eleven trophies in all, an impressive collection. One was missing, Siobhán noted with a pang. Last year. Séamus gave up the race two days beforehand to help the O'Sullivans after the crash. Maybe it was good she didn't go to college. She could never imagine that neighbors in Dublin would do such a thing for each other.

Siobhán glanced at the screen again and sighed. She hoped it wasn't an important game or she was going to have even more of a challenge getting anything out of Declan.

"How ya," he said, turning to her when there was a break in the game. "What's the story?" His warm welcome was genuine and infectious, despite the gap in his grin. Siobhán smiled back and took a stool. There were only a few lads down at the other end of the bar, so lost in the game and their pints that they didn't even look to see who had come in.

"Same old," Siobhán said. *If only*.

"You're either here to drown your troubles or you're wanting to see me," Declan said.

"Am I allowed both?" Siobhán said.

"Ah, sure, chicken. What are ye havin'?"

"A pint of the black stuff," she said. Declan winked and set to pouring her a Guinness. She felt a little thrill, having a pint in the middle of the day. And why not? It had certainly been a rough few days.

"'Tis a fierce, nasty business," Declan said while he waited for her pint to settle before pouring the head.

"It is indeed," Siobhán said. This was just the opening she needed. Siobhán maintained an expression of pity for a moment before diving in. "In fact, I was just talking to Mike Granger. He mentioned how you saw a few lads running around the back of his store the night of the murder."

It felt odd to say the word *murder* out loud, and she could've sworn one of the lads at the end of the bar popped his head up on hearing it, but by the time she looked over, he was back to staring at the game. She didn't recognize him; so many of the young lads around Kilbane were suddenly turning into men. And it was only if they came to the bistro regularly that she could keep track of them all. Since taking over the work of her parents, she certainly hadn't been going out to the pubs at night.

Declan set her pint in front of her, and she decided to be happy for the little moments instead of fixating on what could have been. Maybe the neighbors in Dublin wouldn't have treated her like family, as they did here, but there was a whole world of possibilities she knew she was missing.

She would have been spending her evenings at pubs and restaurants, and her weekends shopping on Grafton Street, strolling through Phoenix Park, or hitting the tourist sites. She got so wrapped up in feeling sorry for herself that it took her a minute to realize Declan hadn't answered her question about seeing lads up to no good that evening. His eyes were back on the game. "Mike said I should have a word with you about the lads he saw running around the back of his shop that night."

"Did he now?" Declan looked at Siobhán again. "Are you doing alright, petal? Are you going to be opening again for business?"

"If I do, are you finally going to start coming in?"

"I'm always here," he said. "You know yourself."

"I do indeed."

"But I'll sneak out for your grand reopening. How's that?"

"Very sweet of you. Oh. I almost forgot. I'm going to have a bit of a fund-raiser for Mary Murphy."

Declan's mouth opened slightly. "For Mary Murphy?"

"Well. For Niall, really. It's going to be a while before she can have the funeral, and the expenses will be dear. Niall mentioned she'd been having a bit of a hard time even before this business. So I offered to have a gathering, and she said yes."

"She said yes?" Declan's eyebrows arched up.

"We're going to put aside our differences and honor Niall's memory. It's what me mam and da would have wanted too."

"You're having it at the bistro?"

"Of course."

"I see."

"You know Niall wasn't killed in the bistro," Siobhán said. "Somebody moved him there."

Declan leaned in. He might not have been one for giving out information, but he was always the first to soak it in. "How so?"

"Nothing else makes sense. There was very little blood."

Declan shook his head. "You shouldn't have had to deal with that. Not after what you've been through."

"Anyway, it's Sunday week. I have a feeling you'll get all the folks in here after."

"In that case, I'll show up meself," Declan said. "They can live with the doors shut for a few hours."

"Thank you. Would you mind spreading the word?"

"Will do."

"Thank you."

Declan winked. "I almost forgot," he said. He bent down underneath the counter and came up with a book. Siobhán glanced at it. *The Encyclopedia of Celtic Mythology and Folklore*. Tears came to her eyes. "Thought you might get a kick out of it. I hope you get back to your college plans soon." Declan didn't wait for a reply, instead he busied himself by washing glasses. He knew there was precious little chance she'd be going to college anytime soon.

She hugged the book to her chest. "Thank you."

"Not a bother, chicken."

"Can you tell me what you saw that night?" Siobhán said, lowering her voice and leaving out the word murder this time.

Declan sighed. "I was out smoking a fag when I saw movement around the side of Mike's shop."

"Movement?"

"A few lads running around. I only saw the backs of 'em. But they looked as if they were in a hurry alright."

"Were they short? Tall?"

"Their heads were down, and they were running, so it's hard to tell. Nothing out of the average."

"It doesn't have to be out of the average. Anything will help."

"One of 'em might have been wearing a cap."

That didn't help. All the lads in Kilbane wore caps half the time. "Could one of them have been Niall?"

Declan contemplated the question with some gravity. "I don't know. He was in and out of the pub like always. But he left for the final time around midnight, I'd say. Now that you mention it, there was something different about his head. Was it a cap?"

"Sheila shaved his head just after seven."

"So he might have been wearing a cap to cover it up, like," Declan said, as if they'd solved the mystery.

"But you're not sure?"

"I wasn't expecting there'd be a quiz," Declan said. "Sorry, pet, I can't say for sure."

"But my brother was here."

"You know yourself. He and Niall got into a shouting match at the bar. It would have become physical if the new Yank hadn't have stepped in and pulled them apart."

"Chris Gorden?" Siobhán hoped Declan would say more. "You've met him?"

"Not really. Ran into him is all. Literally bumped into me."

"I bet he did that on purpose," Declan said with a wink.

"What's his story?" Siobhán said casually.

Declan's face lit up as it always did when he was the first to deliver a bit of news. "Tall lad. About your age. Most of the colleens think he's nice to look at."

"He tried to break up the fight?" For an outsider, that was either awfully brave or awfully stupid.

"He tried, I tried, Séamus tried." Declan sighed and turned a rag on the counter.

"So then what? They took the fight outside?"

"Not while I was here, petal. I don't know when or how James ended up beaten in the alley."

"So you never saw Niall and my brother physically fight?"

"No. They cooled off; we all thought it was over. The Yankee Doodle had a chat with Niall. After a bit, Niall seemed to settle."

"Somebody beat up my brother that night," Siobhán said. "If it wasn't Niall, then who?"

"Jameson," Declan said. "That whiskey would be my guess."

"Besides the whiskey. Someone gave him a few punches. He has the bruises to prove it." *And the blood.* "Macdara is convinced it was Niall."

Declan sighed. "They certainly wanted to have a go at each other."

"Please don't take this the wrong way," Siobhán said, "but I wish you wouldn't have served James. He was about to get his six-month Pioneer Pin."

Declan sighed. "It's the worst part of me job. I didn't want to see James drinkin' any more than you did, chicken, but it's not my place to deny a grown man a drink. And I cut him off after the shouting match. If he drank more after that, he didn't get it from me. And I did cut him off. He was raging."

Great, just great. "Did he leave? Go someplace else maybe?"

"If he did, I don't know where, and to be honest, I didn't care, as long as he was outta here. Séamus offered to take him home, but James told him to feck off."

Oh, no. James never would have said that when he was sober. "You said Niall and James were shouting at each other. What was it about?" Siobhán had a pretty good idea, but she had to ask anyway.

"I wasn't paying much attention. When lads are fighting, it's usually about land, lassies, or money, or all t'ree."

Siobhán sighed. "What was Niall wearing?"

"Are ye considering becoming a detective?"

"Sorry. But Macdara says they're looking at James for this. And drunk or not, I know he didn't do it. Niall was wearing a suit when I found him."

Declan's eyebrows arched up again. "A suit?" Siobhán nodded. "Well, I can't tell ye what he was wearing. But I can tell ye this. It sure as feck wasn't a suit."

Siobhán nodded. Just as she thought. Not that she had any more answers. In fact, the more questions she asked, the less any of it made sense. "Did ye ever think we'd have a murder mystery right here in Kilbane?" she said.

"Surely not," Declan said. "Although it's usually the spouse who done it."

"Niall wasn't married," Siobhán said.

"Right, so. Doesn't help us at all," Declan agreed. Siobhán glanced behind the bar and spotted a HAPPY BIRTHDAY banner curled up as if it had just come down.

"Did Bridie throw Séamus a birthday party that night?" she asked. It was a little hurtful she wasn't invited, but maybe they kept it a small affair.

Declan glanced at the banner and shook his head. "That was from a month or so back."

"Oh."

"It would be mighty funny if it had been for Séamus, though."

"Why is that?"

"His birthday is in December."

Siobhán straightened her spine. "Are you sure?"

"Course I am. He complains every year that between Christmas and Saint Stephen's Day nobody pays it much mind." Siobhán just learned a valuable lesson. Publicans may not tell you the big things, but sometimes it was the little things that made all the difference. He had no idea he'd just exposed someone in a lie.

A December birthday. So why did Bridie say the gear was a surprise for his birthday? What had she and Niall really been doing that morning?

Chapter 16

When Siobhán arrived back at the bistro, she was loaded down with bags from the market. She might as well start preparing for the fund-raiser. She'd go mental with too much time on her hands. Ann, Ciarán, and Eoin were playing upstairs, while James and Gráinne were having a chat in the back dining room. Siobhán got the distinct feeling they were arguing. She sighed. Tensions had been high with everyone since this business with Niall, but it was time to confront Gráinne. If there was still something she was holding back, Siobhán had to know what it was. She hurried to put away the groceries, then approached the secretive duo.

James stopped talking the second Siobhán entered the room, and Gráinne looked away, but not before Siobhán could see that she'd been crying.

Siobhán had had it. She faced Gráinne. "What was going on with you and Niall?"

"Again?" Gráinne said. She glared at James.

"Were you—seeing him?" Siobhán hated to ask the question.

"No!" Gráinne flew out of her chair.

Siobhán pulled her back down. She glanced at James. "Was there anything on the phone?"

He shook his head.

"See," Gráinne said.

"You erased everything," James said.

"Start telling us what's really going on," Siobhán said. "Because from where we're standing, it looks like you're heartbroken."

"He was way too old for me." Gráinne rolled her eyes.

"I just came from Mary Murphy. She said to say hello. To you, Gráinne. Why would she do that?"

Gráinne shrugged.

Siobhán threw her arms open. "James is protecting you. And he could go to jail."

"Don't put that on her," James said. "It's my fault for drinking and letting Niall goad me."

Gráinne's pretty face was positively ashen. Siobhán pressed her anyway. "I saw your reaction when we found Niall. It was more than shock. I know you're sixteen, and I'm just your sister, and you have your right to your secrets—"

"T'ank you."

"Under normal circumstances. But this is not normal. And you aren't getting up from this table until you tell me what was going on between you and Niall Murphy."

"Nothing. Nothing was going on between us. Not like you think."

"So what exactly are we missing here?"

"Nothing."

"If you don't tell us, you're grounded."

"You're not my mother."

"She's your legal guardian," James said.

"Because you were too drunk to do the job," Gráinne said.

"Mo náire thú!" Siobhán said. *Shame on you.*

"I deserve it," James said. "But what I said still stands. Answer your sister."

"I won't," Gráinne said. "It has nothing to do with either of you."

Siobhán wished more than anything she were still just a big sister. Gráinne used to come to her with things she didn't want to tell Mam. But all that changed. Now she went to Ann. Gráinne had no clue how much that hurt. Was Ann hiding things from her as well? She'd have to work on her later.

"We're not messing, Gráinne. This is important."

Gráinne stood. "It has nothing to do with the murder."

"How do you know?"

"Because I didn't kill him, and—" she stopped.

"And what?"

"And neither did the other person."

"What other person?"

"It's none of your business."

"Don't you see? Everything is important. Just tell me and let me decide—"

"You're not a detective. I heard Garda Flannery tell you as much. He told you to stop poking your nose into the murder."

"So you'd rather I tell Garda Flannery that I think you're hiding something and let him have a go at you?"

"Siobhán," James said. "Calm down."

"Now is not the time for her to be stubborn and childish. Not when so much is at stake."

"You two are the stubborn ones. I'll tell Garda Flannery what I know. Not you." Gráinne took off and was soon out the door of the bistro. Siobhán started after her. James grabbed her arm.

"Let her cool down."

Siobhán stopped and turned to James. "Do you think they were? Romantic, like?"

"It looks that way, doesn't it?"

"I could kill him. She's only sixteen." Siobhán stopped, looked at James.

"I felt the same way. But I didn't kill him. At least I don't think I did. I couldn't do that. Could I?"

James looked at her for a desperate second. Siobhán put her hand on his arm. "Of course not. Of course you couldn't."

"How do you know?" Wild pain was reflected in her brother's eyes.

"I *know,*" she said, turning his chin so that he'd look her in the eye. "I *know.*" James nodded, then slumped back into a chair and buried his face in his hands. Siobhán sat and proceeded gingerly. "Declan says Niall left the pub before you. He also said Séamus tried to get you to go home. Do you remember that?"

James rubbed the bridge of his nose with his hand, then massaged his forehead. "Do we have any headache tablets?"

"I think I've used them all up."

"I'll go to the store."

"Do you remember fighting with Séamus?"

"Fighting with him?"

"Not physically. I guess he tried to accompany you home, and you told him to feck off."

"Oh, Jaysus. There's another person I owe an apology to."

"Maybe we can pay them a visit later." Siobhán was dying to talk to Bridie again. "I take it you don't remember?"

"I know Séamus was there. But no, I don't remember that bit."

"So somehow you ended up back in the alley, and someone beat you up."

"Someone?"

"How do we know it was Niall? Declan assumed it was because you were fighting earlier—"

"And because I had drops of his blood on me."

"We don't know that yet. It might be your own blood, like."

"We'll know soon enough." James drooped like he had the weight of the world on him.

"You should have never let them take your clothing."

"Why? I want the truth as much as anyone. If I did this—"

"You didn't."

"But if I did, I'd want to know. I couldn't live with meself if I did it."

"There's no way you fought with him in the alley without getting a punch in yourself. And Niall didn't have a scratch on him. You know. Apart from the scissors, like."

"So who beat me up?"

"Maybe the killer."

"Why?"

"To frame you."

"Maybe you should let Garda Flannery handle this."

"Because I sound crazy?"

"A wee bit, yea."

"I'm doing this for you, James!"

"And I thank you, but I don't want you running around stirring up the pot. It's not safe."

"I'm convinced you didn't have a physical fight with Niall."

"Are you even listening to me?"

"Think, James. Do you remember anyone else hanging around that night?"

"No. I don't remember a thing. Why?"

"I think the killer beat you up to make it look like you fought with Niall. You could have even been passed out while he beat on ye."

"If you're right—and I'm not sayin' ye are—but if you are, then someone went to a lot of trouble just to set me up."

"To get away with murder."

"But what if Niall was coming here to see Gráinne? What if he tried something, and—" James stopped, shook his head.

"You think Gráinne killed Niall?" Ann said.

Siobhán and James looked up. Ciarán, Ann, and Eoin stood before them. They all seemed to be waiting for an answer.

"No," Siobhán said.

"He does," Ann said, pointing at James.

"He's worried that Niall came here to see her that night. That's all. And whether she knew it or not, maybe he did," Siobhán said. "But that's only if he was stabbed here. Which I have my doubts. Because there was hardly any blood. But even if he was here when he was alive, there's no doubt that somebody else stabbed him. Gráinne wouldn't have had the strength."

"She's pretty strong," Ann said.

"Not strong enough to come up behind someone with a pair of scissors and jam them into his heart," Siobhán said.

Ann gasped and put her hands over her mouth.

James looked at Siobhán. "How do you know the killer came up from behind?" he asked. Siobhán pulled out the chair where they found Niall.

"Sit there," she said to Eoin. After a squint and a shrug, he did.

Siobhán stood behind the chair. "He was found sitting here. So assuming he was alive when he came in, we might also try assuming that he was alive when he sat in the chair. Like he's waiting for someone."

"Gráinne," Ann said.

"There's no other reason he'd be sneaking into our bistro."

James looked doubtful. "So supposin' for a minute he did manage to get in. Why is he just sitting in the chair, like?"

"That was my question," Eoin said.

"Maybe he was waiting for Gráinne to come down. Maybe that's what she's hiding."

"She would have told me," Ann said.

"Can we just move past that for a second? I want to play this out." The others remained silent as Siobhán backed up. "The killer could have followed Niall here. He already has the scissors in his hand—" She began to sneak up on Eoin from behind.

"Or she," Ciarán said.

"Excellent point," Siobhán said. "He or she comes from behind." Siobhán held her hand up as if she was carrying the murder weapon. "And before Niall even turns around, the deed is done." Siobhán quickly imitated the scissors going into Eoin's heart.

James stood up and paced around. "You wouldn't need as much strength, coming up from behind like that."

"That's true," Siobhán said. *Would you look at that. Instead of proving her sister couldn't have done it, she'd just discovered the opposite.*

"So it could be a woman," Ann said.

"It looks that way, so" Siobhán said. *Even a woman as tiny as Bridie.*

"Wouldn't Niall have heard someone sneaking up on him?" Eoin asked.

"He had drink in him; he could have been sleeping," Siobhán said.

"But if it were Gráinne, she would have had to come down the stairs. She'd be coming up in front of Niall. Not from behind," James said.

"Unless they struggled first and he was only put in the chair after," Eoin said.

"She didn't have a scratch on her, either. Even if she is hiding something about Niall, she didn't kill him any more than you did," Siobhán said to James.

"Then what is she hiding from us?" James asked.

"I know what she was hiding," Ann said. Everyone looked at her. "She got a text in the middle of the night. That's what woke me up. Not the glass breaking."

Siobhán stepped up to Ann and put her hands on both her shoulders. "Are you sure?"

Ann nodded, eyes wide. "Will I go to jail?"

"Of course not. Why would you go to jail?" Siobhán asked.

"Because I didn't tell Garda Flannery about the text," Ann said, tears spilling out of her eyes.

Siobhán knelt in front of Ann and wiped her tears. "It's okay. Do you know who the text was from?"

"No. I swear. I have no idea." Ann shook her head violently. Her reaction seemed a bit extreme. Either she was still afraid she was going to be arrested for lying, or she *was* lying. Siobhán was trying to figure out how to get more out of her without Ann having a complete meltdown, when a man cleared his throat, startling all of them. Siobhán whirled around. John Butler from BUTLER'S UNDERTAKER, LOUNGE, AND PUB stood in the bistro. His expression suggested that he wanted to tower over them, but his stature undermined him. John Butler hadn't been blessed in the height department. As usual, his white hair was slicked back, and his thick black glasses were halfway down his nose, which forced him to peer down through them, always giving Siobhán the impression that he thoroughly embraced the idea of looking down on people despite lacking the actual inches to do so. In his right hand he clutched a gold-tipped cane that was his constant companion. With his gray trench coat and matching top hat, he always struck Siobhán as a character in a play. And she wasn't far off; he often did act in the local productions of the Kilbane Players. He swept off his hat and rested it on his chest. For a split second, Siobhán wondered if he was here to challenge one of them to a duel. "Hello," he said. "Please pardon the intrusion."

"Hello," the O'Sullivans answered in discordant unison.

"Siobhán, it's most urgent that I speak with you. Would you mind stopping over when you're done with . . . ." He gestured at the air around them. "Whatever it is you're doing?"

Chapter 17

Butler's Undertaker, Lounge, and Pub was situated in an old stone house. The bar was the first room you entered when you walked in, although the atmosphere was a bit more somber than the other pubs about town. It boasted the same dark wood, to be sure, but heavy drapes on the windows, a pair of flowered sofas, and boxes of tissues propped up on nearly every available surface distinguished it from the typical pubs. There was an adjacent room, separated by a curtain, where viewings and funerals were held, and Siobhán didn't even want to think about the mortuary in the basement. Her parents were taken here after the accident, as was pretty much everyone else in town who died. Butler had no competition, and he was the fourth male in his family to, literally and figuratively, undertake the family business.

He gestured to one of the sofas. Siobhán perched on the edge, her handbag taking up more space on the sofa than she did. She hadn't realized how exhausted she was until she sat on the pillowy cushions. Between the soft music, the plush sofa, and the box of tissues on the table in front of her, she felt as if she could lie down and have a good cry. Maybe sleep for days. It was better not to get too comfortable.

"I'll get right to the point," John Butler said. "I heard you're having a fund-raiser for Niall on Sunday week at the bistro."

News traveled fast. Looks like Siobhán wouldn't have to spread the word at all. "That's right. I've already spoken with Mary Murphy, and she's agreed. I hope to see you there."

"May I ask you a personal question?" John Butler arched one of his theatrical eyebrows.

"You may."

"Why are you having a fund-raiser for Niall? After what that family has put yours through?"

"Because it's what my mam and da would have wanted."

"Very well then. Am I to assume the proceeds will be for his burial services?"

So that's what this was about. Why wasn't he dealing directly with Mary Murphy? "Yes, that was the intent."

"So I thought. May I suggest that you deal directly with me? I'll speak with his mother and handle her choices for the services, of course, and then I can send you the bill directly."

"I see."

"It won't be for the full amount, a deposit has already been put down for a portion of it."

"Mary Murphy?"

"No."

"May I ask who?"

"You may, of course." He stopped and waited.

"Well, who was it?" Siobhán asked.

"I'm afraid that information is confidential." John Butler crossed one leg over the other.

If not his mother, who would pay for a portion of Niall's

funeral? And why? "Would you be willing to divulge the name of the person to Garda Flannery?"

Butler put his hand over his heart. "Whatever for?"

"It's just odd, don't you think? Niall wasn't exactly loved by the town. Why would someone pay for part of his funeral?"

"Why are you having a fund-raiser for him?"

Because James is the top suspect in his murder, and I don't want the town to think we have anything to hide. Because he was found, maybe even killed in our bistro, and I want to replace that memory with a more positive one so I don't have to shut my doors forever. "I told you. I believe it's what my mam and da would have wished."

"You are doing it out of the goodness of your heart. There's no reason to think that this other donor isn't doing the same thing."

"But if Garda Flannery asked you directly, as part of his investigation, you would have to tell him, would you not?"

"I suppose so. But Garda Flannery hasn't asked me, and he doesn't even know to ask me, because you're the only person I've told about it. And I've already asked you to keep this between us. Which I assume you are going to do, aren't you?"

"I just think it could be important."

"I assure you, it's not."

"Perhaps if you could truly assure me by telling me the name, I wouldn't have to go to Garda Flannery."

Butler stood up. "I won't take any more of your time. If the fund-raiser is to help with Niall's service, I implore you to deal directly with me."

Siobhán stood as well. It was obvious she wasn't going to get John Butler to spill his secrets. But he was willing to talk about Mary Murphy, so she continued along that line of inquiry. "Is there any reason to think that if the money went directly to Mary Murphy, your portion would not arrive in a timely manner?"

Siobhán was trying as politely as possible to find out if Butler was worried that Mary Murphy wouldn't pay him at all. Niall did hint that she was desperate for money. Was she also trying to get a better solicitor for Billy? Had she been aware of Niall's crazy accusations? Siobhán should have questioned her harder when she'd had the chance.

"I don't wish to speak ill of anyone. But, as you know, this death business is a delicate business."

"As I know?"

"Sorry. I just mean you've been through the grief process yourself. People aren't always able to handle the business end of it. I'm afraid Mary Murphy falls into that category. And, please, don't let this leave this room, but there's been some talk of her hiring a new solicitor for Billy. A quite expensive one at that."

"Where did you hear that?"

"Forgive me. I didn't mean to speak out of turn. People don't realize the service we struggle to provide. Of course, I'm thrilled to say that most of the residents of Kilbane are in good health. Everyone is aging gracefully. Good for them. But not so good for business. I need to get paid, or I'm afraid I'm going to have to shut my doors."

"I didn't realize things were that bad."

"As I said, times are changing. People are exercising, and eating healthy. You can't smoke in the pubs anymore. I've heard even you have taken up running."

Even me?

"And did you see that Mike Granger had kale in his shop? Kale. Can you believe dat?" John Butler looked absolutely devastated. "There just aren't enough people dying around here anymore."

"I promise to deal directly with you, but you have to tell

me who put the deposit down for Niall. If I agree there's nothing suspicious, I won't go to Garda Flannery."

Butler sighed. "He was working at Sheedy's cycle shop. Did ye know that?"

"I did," Siobhán said.

"Bridie Sheedy brought in his last paycheck is all."

"Oh."

"So you see, nothing amiss at all."

"You're quite right. That was the decent thing to do."

But as Siobhán walked home, she couldn't help but turn it around in her mind. Bridie Sheedy had lied to her about Séamus's birthday. She hadn't wanted Séamus to know she was in the shop that day. Now it was her bringing in the paycheck and not Séamus. Had Siobhán's original suspicions been correct? Had Bridie been having an affair with Niall? Despite the age difference, such things did happen. She'd promised not to say anything to Séamus. But now she wasn't so sure. She wasn't sure of anything anymore.

Siobhán was halfway back up the street when she realized she'd left her handbag on the sofa. She hurried back and walked in. John was no longer in the sitting room, so she picked up her handbag and started to leave.

"I need that loan," she heard John say. She looked around. He was standing in a small vestibule just off the main sitting room. "Whatever amount, but I'd prefer something north of twenty thousand euro." Siobhán froze. Twenty thousand euro? She heard Niall's voice in her head.

Yer one would give me twenty thousand euro for it.

Was it just a coincidence? Or had Mary Murphy picked up extorting where Niall left off, and John Butler was "yer one"?

Siobhán didn't realize she was frozen in place until suddenly John Butler whirled around and caught her. He frowned deeply, as if she had been deliberately eavesdropping. Is that what he thought?

She held up her handbag. "Forgot this," she said.
"Oh my," he said. "How unfortunate."

Siobhán replayed his words all the way home. *Oh my. How unfortunate*. What a creepy little man. She had her purse back, so what was so unfortunate? Or was it a warning? How unfortunate that you caught me? Was it a threat? Was John Butler a killer?

Chapter 18

❧

"Do you think anyone will come?" Ciarán asked as he stood at the window in the bistro gazing out on Sarsfield Street.

"Yes," Siobhán said ruffling his hair. "It's a fund-raiser for Niall's mam. Everyone will come."

The O'Sullivan Six had spent the past two days cooking for the fund-raiser, and here it was, Sunday morning. Siobhán and Gráinne were barely speaking. Gráinne had denied getting a text in the middle of the night, insisting that Ann had been dreaming. This set Ann off on a crying jag and once again put Siobhán and Gráinne at odds. Siobhán wasn't sure what to believe. Ann did have remarkable hearing. But who was to say she wasn't dreaming? Or maybe she heard something else. All Siobhán knew for sure was that this was tearing them all apart. Hopefully putting their minds on helping others would patch things up a small bit.

As soon as Mass was over, the place would begin filling up. It would have been nice if the O'Sullivan Six had shown up for Mass, but there was too much to do to get ready. Father Kearney wouldn't be happy with them, but hopefully he would understand. The next hour flew by as they put the finishing touches on everything. Candles and plates, and silverware, and flowers, and mountains of food. Siobhán was nervous. It had to go well, or no one would ever eat here again, and they might as well just pack up and leave.

The doors were to open at eleven, but at half ten, folks were already lined up to be the first inside.

"See?" Siobhán said. "I told you."

"Wow," Ciarán said.

"Deadly," Eoin echoed. They high-fived. When Siobhán threw open the doors, Mary Murphy was front and centre, dressed all in black, including a hat with a black lace veil. Once she made her entrance, everyone else began to spill in after her. It wasn't long before the bistro was filled with voices and goodwill.

"Holy cow," Ann said, weaving her way through the crowd until she spotted Siobhán. "Do we have enough food?" They turned to look at the tables behind them, piled with eggs, and bacon, and black and white pudding, and ham, and brown bread, and potatoes. It was quickly disappearing as people made their way down the line.

"We'll keep an eye on it and make more if we have to," Siobhán said, dreading the thought.

"Can we afford this?" James said.

"We can't afford not to," Siobhán said. Ciarán was hanging out next to the tin marked DONATIONS.

"He's worried someone is going to steal it," Eoin said.

"No one is going to steal it," Siobhán said.

"The killer might," Eoin said.

"That's how we'll catch him," Ann said, eyes wide and hands clasped. "Oh, I hope the killer tries to steal the money."

Siobhán shook her head. They were all going a bit insane. James was now weaving his way toward Siobhán as well with a grim look on his face.

"What's wrong?" Siobhán asked.

"They all think I did it," James said.

"Are they saying that?" Siobhán asked.

"Of course not. I can just tell. Do I have to stay?"

"Tongues will wag harder if you hide," Siobhán said.

James lowered his voice. "I fought with Niall. And everyone knows it. I wish I could take it back." Siobhán wanted to hug her brother, but he'd never allow it. Not when he was feeling vulnerable.

Siobhán kept a smile on her face while speaking in a whisper to James. "A lot of people fought with Niall. The town knows what he was like. We'll get through this. Do it for us."

James nodded. "Can I at least stay in the kitchen?"

"Mingle a little longer. Then you can hide in the kitchen." She left her brood all gathered by the front, picked up the tea kettle, and began to make the rounds. It was a relief to see their neighbors back in the bistro, and quickly every table was filled except for the one where Niall was killed. Already anticipating as much, they'd placed a picture of Niall on the table, along with a candle, a rosary, a Celtic cross they'd bought on their trip to the Aran Islands, and a guest book to sign. She wondered if the killer would end up signing it. Would he or she be so bold? Not that you could tell a killer by his or her handwriting. Still, it was a disconcerting thought, the killer being among them, offering comfort, eating and drinking and chatting like he or she was just another neighbor, hiding in plain sight.

In between running back and forth to the kitchen, refilling cups with hot water, and making cappuccinos, Siobhán chatted with her neighbors and friends, but she was quick to extricate herself whenever the conversation turned to the murder. She didn't want Mary Murphy—or Macdara Flannery, for that matter—to think she was holding this fundraiser just for the gossip.

Speaking of Macdara, he had yet to make an entrance. Was he on his way, or was he out investigating the case? She longed to see him, but when that familiar warm flush shivered through her at the very thought of him, she convinced herself that his presence would help deter a killer. That was the reason he was on her mind, nothing more. She was still silently wrestling with her feelings for Macdara when she found Bridie by her side, tears spilling out of her eyes.

"This is so nice of you," Bridie said. "I can't believe it. I just can't believe it." Her tears seemed genuine, and Siobhán forgot all about grilling her about her lies. Today was a day of mourning. Siobhán hugged Bridie.

"You were good to Niall too," she said.

"How do you mean?" Bridie suddenly sounded on edge.

"You gave him a job in the shop."

"Ah, right. It wasn't for long." Tears pooled in Bridie's eyes.

"Did Niall ever mention being afraid of anyone?" Siobhán asked before she could stop herself.

"You're wondering who could have killed him," Bridie said. It was a statement not a question.

Siobhán nodded.

"I've been wondering the same thing." Bridie clutched Siobhán's hand and squeezed so hard Siobhán had to bite her tongue to keep from crying out. "Going over and over it in my mind. At first I thought maybe it was someone from his time in Dublin." Bridie took out rosary beads, giving Siobhán the perfect opportunity to retract her hand.

"It could have been, don't ye think?" Siobhán said.

"Except he never mentioned having trouble with any Dubliner," Bridie said. Siobhán wanted to ask her if she'd ever suspected Niall of being on drugs, but she feared that was crossing a line. Bridie seemed to like Niall, and Siobhán couldn't afford another enemy.

"Did you ever get that gear for Séamus?" Siobhán asked.

"Yes," Bridie said quickly. Almost too quickly. "I haven't given it to him yet, so please, not a word."

"How was Niall able to help you?"

"Pardon?"

"You said he was helping you order the gear."

"He asked Séamus about his broken one for me. If I had asked, Séamus would have been suspicious."

"Is his birthday coming up?" Siobhán smiled despite the pain in her stomach. She hated this charade.

"It's been a year since Séamus has raced," Bridie said, expertly skirting the real question. Who knew Bridie Sheedy would be so adept at avoiding the truth? Siobhán had better be careful or Bridie was going to get defensive.

"I'm sorry," Siobhán said.

"Whatever for, pet?"

"He gave up racing to help us out, didn't he?" Siobhán knew the bistro wouldn't have survived had Seamus and Bridie not stepped in after the accident to help them out. It was probably the first year Seamus hadn't competed. Maybe they owed him a trophy.

Bridie put her hand on Siobhán's shoulder and patted it. "You're not the only reason."

"Why else?" Siobhán really wanted to know. It sounded like there was a story there.

Bridie stretched her neck like a gyroscope and scanned the room. "There's Courtney!" she cried out as if Courtney had been missing for ages. "I need a word. Excuse me, Siobhán. The food is lovely, just lovely."

Bridie hurried away. She definitely meant to get away from Siobhán. She had really hoped to eliminate her as a suspect, but Bridie was acting too squirrelly. Why wasn't anyone in this town normal? Siobhán set to mingling again, and as she maneuvered through the crowd, she spotted Sheila and

Pio lingering by the back door; even from a distance, they looked clenched, like vibrating coils about to spring.

Where was Macdara? Did he say something to Pio and Sheila to make them look so defensive? Were they angry with her? She didn't want to face them until she found out. She'd had enough surprises to last a lifetime. But Macdara wasn't anywhere in sight, and Pio and Sheila were openly glaring at her. It would look even worse if she didn't go over to say hello.

Siobhán took a deep breath and headed over to the surly couple. "I'm getting a lot of compliments on my hair," Siobhán said, touching her locks, hoping flattery would melt the glacier that was Sheila.

"Well, if it isn't our nosy neighbor," Pio said.

"Me?" Siobhán said.

Pio stepped forward. "You think we killed him, is that it?"

"Of course not," Siobhán said in a low voice. "But now's not the time."

Sheila put her hand on Pio's arm. "For once I agree with the hothead. Now's not the time. We're here to support Niall's Mam."

Pio didn't advance again, but he didn't back up either. His eyes were bloodshot, and he had the look of a man who hadn't been sleeping. He was such a talented musician. She was even hoping he'd play the spoons for them. Looked like those utensils were not coming out today, and thanks be to God; given his demeanor she shuddered to think what he would do with them if he had the chance. Siobhán had better start mending fences. If not for her, then at least for the sake of the business.

"I don't know what Macdara told you. I was concerned when I saw the door to your shop wide open and all your lights blazing. Then Sheila came running up the side of the house with a rubbish bag. And then there was a pile of broken glass in the salon. It struck me as odd, that's all." She left out the bit about Sheila's black eye and the smell of bleach. It *was* odd. She was right to say something.

"Sheila already told you. She broke a vase. Truth is—"

Sheila clamped down on his arm. "Don't," she barked.

Pio's eyes blazed. "She thinks we're murderers! While her brother is the one that did it!"

"Quiet," Siobhán said. "James did no such thing." People were starting to look their way. This was so inappropriate. "Let's step out into the garden, shall we?" Siobhán opened the door and was prepared to shove the two of them out if she had to, but to her surprise they stepped out willingly. There was only one patch of wildflowers growing out back, and Siobhán purposefully moved toward them. Pio started to follow, but Sheila remained rooted to the spot.

"See!" Siobhán said.

"See what?" Sheila said.

"You're allergic to flowers."

"So?"

"So why would you go to the trouble to glue a vase back together when you're allergic to flowers?"

Sheila began to blink rapidly. Pio sucked in his lips. They definitely looked guilty.

Sheila turned around and went back inside. She slammed the door shut. Pio looked at Siobhán. "I understand you're having a rough time of it since your parents passed. So we're going to forgive you." He pointed at Siobhán. "Once," he said, sternly. "No more." Then he too, turned and went back inside. At least he didn't slam the door. Siobhán went back inside as well, and immediately James came up to her. Sheila and Pio were still standing in the spot by the door.

"Is there a problem here?" James looked at Siobhán, then at Sheila and Pio. This was all Siobhán needed, James getting into an argument. She took his arm and guided him away from the surly couple.

"It was you, wasn't it? Who killed Niall?" Pio called after James. Siobhán whirled on him.

"This is a fund-raiser for Niall. Don't you dare start a scene."

"He's the murderer," Pio said pointing at James, wobbling as if he was dancing with himself. Was he drunk?

"I'll have Garda Flannery throw you out." Siobhán glanced around. Where was Macdara?

"Why don't you let me do that right now?" James said. Séamus and Mike caught Siobhán's eyes. Within seconds they stepped up and formed a protective barrier between James and Pio. Séamus squared his shoulders, and Mike actually flexed his biceps.

"Everything alright here?" Séamus asked.

"They were just leaving," Siobhán said, pointing to Sheila and Pio.

"Let's go," Sheila said. "She's out of brown bread anyway." She grabbed onto Pio's arm and started hauling him toward the door. But before they could make their escape, Mary Murphy stepped in and blocked their path.

"You," she said, pointing as Sheila. "How could you pass out deadly weapons to everyone in town?"

Sheila threw her hands up. "They weren't meant as weapons. Scissors is all they were. Siobhán is the one who suggested I pass them out at the pubs." Everyone looked at Siobhán. She wanted to deny it, but she'd reached her quota of lies for the day. She hung her head instead.

"You should have kept track," Mary Murphy cried out. "You should have kept track of every single person you gave one to."

"If it hadn't been the scissors, it would've been something else," Pio said.

"But we'd have fewer suspects then," Mary said. Siobhán was slightly relieved. Did this mean Mary Murphy wasn't convinced it was James? What changed her mind?

Father Kearney cut into the group. He was a portly man with a cherubic face. He smiled like a shepherd who was trying to stop his flock from going over the edge of a cliff. "Let's remember why we're here," he said. "To honor the memory of Niall. To support a mother in her time of grief. Let's not allow one tragedy to beget another."

"Thank you, Father," Siobhán said. "Maybe you could lead us in a prayer."

"I can indeed." Father Kearney put his arm around Mary Murphy and began to gather folks around the table with Niall's picture. Sheila herded Pio out of the bistro. Siobhán watched them through the window. The minute they were outside, Pio shook free of Sheila's grip and she stumbled. He didn't even reach for her. Sheila called after him, but he didn't look back. He opened the door to their home, and a second later it slammed shut in Sheila's face.

Siobhán felt horrid. They were definitely having marital strife. Could they also be killers?

Chapter 19

Siobhán turned back to the crowded room. Father Kearney was still leading the prayer. Gráinne and Ann were nowhere to be seen. Ciarán and Eoin were making the rounds, and so was James, although Siobhán could tell he wanted nothing more than to flee. When the prayer was finished, she looked up to find Courtney Kirby beside her.

"Can you spare a minute?" Courtney said, flicking her fake eyelashes about the room. Her tone didn't have the usual excitement.

"Of course," Siobhán said. "How are you keeping?"

"Grand, grand. But I need your ear for a minute."

"Certainly," Siobhán said. "But if it's about whittling for the store, I'm not ready."

Courtney put her hand on Siobhán's shoulder. "Take your time, pet. It's not that at all."

"What is it?"

Courtney glanced around once more. "I can't tell ye here. Too many eyes and ears, if you know what I mean." That was ironic coming from gossip-loving Courtney, but Siobhán kept her gob shut. "Can you meet me in my shop? In about an hour?"

"I should be able to sneak away," Siobhán said.

"I'll see you there. The sign will say CLOSED. Just knock three times, will ye?"

"Three times," Siobhán repeated. "No bother."

Courtney's eyes darted around the room again. Who was she looking for? Why was she so nervous? Siobhán would make sure she asked her when they were alone. Macdara stepped up behind them, and Courtney slipped away.

"What was that about?" Macdara said, watching as Courtney took her leave.

"You noticed it too," Siobhán said.

"She looked as if she'd just had the fright of her life," Macdara confirmed.

"Everyone's on edge," Siobhán said. "There's a killer among us."

"I'm working on that," Macdara said. "Question is, Are you?"

"Whatever do you mean?" Siobhán kept her eyes wide, hoping it would make her look like an innocent lamb.

"Have you let it go, like I asked?"

"Yes," Siobhán said. It wasn't exactly a lie. It wasn't her fault if people were coming to her with information, was it? She'd better steer this ship in a different direction. "What have *you* found out?"

"A garda gathers information; he doesn't give it," Macdara said. Siobhán batted her eyelashes. "Do you have something stuck in your eye?" he asked politely.

She put her hand on his arm. He cocked his head and looked suspicious. She dropped her arm. "Please," she said. "If I can't investigate, I have to hear how it's going. It will help calm my nerves."

Macdara sighed. "Just this once," he said. "After this you're cut off. Got it?"

"Got it."

He stepped closer and lowered his voice. "Sheila and Pio seem to be having domestic problems alright. But I don't think it has anything to do with Niall."

"I thought the same. Anything else?"

"What?" His eyes flicked to hers and remained steady. "Nerves not calm yet?"

She couldn't help but smile. "Getting there."

"You could've charmed the snake out of Eden," Macdara said with a shake of his head.

"I won't say a word to anyone. Cross my heart and hope to die."

"I do not need you saying that," Macdara said, putting his hand up as if to stop her. He moved even closer and dropped his voice to a whisper. "You were also right about Mike Granger. He did find Niall's passport behind the shop."

"He admitted it?"

"First thing. Said he'd be meaning to call me about it, but then it got buried on his desk, and he had forgotten about it until you came in and knocked over his papers."

Siobhán didn't buy that for a second. Did Macdara? She didn't want to antagonize him, so she tucked that one away. "Did you find out why Niall was running around with his passport?"

"I had a word with Declan. He said Niall liked having it on him. Said it was a reminder that he wasn't going to stay in this country a second longer than he had to."

"Where was he going to go?"

"It was just talk. But Australia, it seems."

"Billy always talked about going to Australia," Siobhán said.

"It seems to fit. Niall carrying it around for motivation. A little hope that he would get his brother out of jail and they'd take off for down under."

Instead he was really *down under*. Siobhán shivered at the thought. "Does Mike know I saw the passport?"

"If he did, he didn't mention it."

"Doesn't it seem odd? That he would forget he had a murder victim's passport?"

"I can't arrest someone for odd behavior," Macdara said. "If I could, there would barely be anyone left in town."

Siobhán let it drop for now. "So someone was chasing Niall that night. It must have been the killer."

"Declan couldn't say who the lads were. In coats and caps on a dark night, it could have been anyone."

"What about footprints?"

"Too much time has gone by. Too many people walk around the back of that shop."

"Declan said there was a Yank in town," Siobhán said. Why wasn't she telling him she ran into Chris Gorden that morning? Because she was afraid Macdara would pick up on the fact that she'd found him very attractive. Not that there was anything wrong with that at all.

"Chris Gorden?" Macdara's eyes narrowed. "I thought you said you were done snooping."

"I happened to run into Declan, and he happened to mention that the new Yank got into an argument with Niall in the pub that night."

Macdara sighed. "He seems like a decent fellow. He's renting a room across from the gardai station. That doesn't strike me as something a killer would do."

"That's exactly what a killer would do. Hide in plain sight."

"I'll talk to him. I take it you've never seen him in here?"

Siobhán shook her head. "That's odd too, don't you think? A man who doesn't like an Irish breakfast? Why come to a little town like ours if you don't want to get to know the locals? What is he doing here anyway?"

"I think he's some kind of writer."

"Writer?" Siobhán said.

"He's here writing a book. That's what I heard."

"What kind of book?"

"I don't think it's a murder mystery, if that's where you're going. Some kind of history book."

"Irish history?"

"Celtic myths, or so they say."

Celtic myths. One of her passions too. Now she really wanted to see this Yank again. "He's here alone?"

"Are ye asking me if the lad is single?"

From his tone, Macdara was obviously browned off with her. But she couldn't let that distract her. "Maybe we should go talk to him now. While everyone else is distracted."

"We? There's no we."

"You, then."

"I'm here to pay my respect to Niall." And to my brown bread, Siobhán thought. But some things were better left unsaid. She glanced at the clock on the wall. She had thirty minutes before she had to meet Courtney. She could use a little fresh air.

"I'd better slip into the kitchen," Siobhán said. "Wouldn't want to run out of brown bread." Macdara put his hand on her arm. A bit of a shiver ran through her.

"I'm getting the blood results in tomorrow," he said.

"Declan said Niall left the pub before James. He wasn't wearing a suit. He didn't look like he had been in a fight. And James was in no condition to be chasing Niall through town. So even if James has a bit of Niall's blood on him, so what? It just means the killer put it there. To frame him. The same reason they brought his body to the bistro."

Macdara shifted, then looked away.

"Tell me," Siobhán said.

"I have preliminary results from the pathologist. She said

the blood coagulated around the blades of the scissors. That's the reason there wasn't much blood. He could have been killed in the bistro."

"And if he even has a drop of Niall's blood on him, they're going to arrest James, is that it?"

"Yes," Macdara said, making sure he kept eye contact. "That's precisely it."

Chapter 20

Siobhán stood outside Courtney Kirby's gift shop. Some people said the only reason she kept her shop open was to get the goods on everyone else. Often she'd been spotted with binoculars around her neck, checking out the street. "Just trying out the product," she'd say if anyone dared confront her about the peeping. Siobhán wondered if she had seen something suspicious the night Niall was murdered. Was that why she'd wanted to talk to her? Siobhán took a deep breath and knocked three times.

The curtain twitched, and Courtney's face came into view. Definitely acting strange. Who else would be knocking three times at the exact time she'd told Siobhán to knock three times?

Courtney disappeared from the curtain, and a second later Siobhán heard the sound of locks being unbolted. Three of them, to be exact. The door opened and Courtney stepped back to let Siobhán in. A little bell tinkled as she entered. The shop was tiny, the smallest one in town. But Courtney had done a good job arranging the space, and so it didn't feel as claustrophobic as one might think. The walls were painted a lovely pale green, and every inch of space was taken up by cheerful items, many homemade. Jewelry, and scarves, and lotions, and handbags, and picture frames—a ladies' shop, to be sure.

"Can I get you a cup of tea?" Courtney offered straightaway.

"That would be lovely, thanks," Siobhán said. It would give her another minute to peek around the shop, see if anything looked amiss. But the shop was tidy, and if anything was wrong with Courtney, it wasn't reflected in the décor; the place was as bright and cheerful as ever. Siobhán could spend hours in here, touching the fabrics, smelling the perfumed soaps. Even now, with an investigation going on, she was drawn to a row of ladies' scarves in the middle of the aisle. They were handknit, colorful, soft things, more decorative than for warmth. They looked like items one might find in a shop in Dublin. Siobhán ran her fingers through a black one with little streaks of silver.

"Those are Bridie's," Courtney said coming into the room carrying a silver tray with their cups of tea and a package of biscuits.

"They're gorgeous," Siobhán said.

"It would suit you, alright, with your new haircut, missus."

"I wouldn't have anywhere to wear it."

"Nonsense." Courtney set the tea down on the counter next to the register and swooped in. Before Siobhán knew what was happening, the scarf was around her neck. "You're a proprietor now. Why don't you wear it in the bistro? I can see ye making your fancy cappuccinos in this, I can."

Siobhán laughed, then peeked at the price tag. Seventy-five euro. Oh, my. They were so dear.

"They would be double that in Dublin," Courtney said.

"I'm sure they would." Siobhán took the scarf off and gently put it back on the stand.

"I'd hate to see it gone by the time you change your mind," Courtney said.

"You wanted to see me?" Siobhán said.

"I hear you're looking into the murder," Courtney said. "Do you have any leads?"

"I'm afraid I don't," Siobhán said. Really, what kind of sleuth did Courtney take her for? She was here to get information, not give it. "Did you hear anything or see anything the night of the murder?"

"Are you sure you don't want that scarf? She won't be making more when they're gone. Not with the black and silver bits." Courtney batted her eyes as if she wasn't trying to exchange commerce for information.

Siobhán couldn't believe it. If every shop owner tricked her into buying something or getting something done before they talked, she'd be broke in no time. She sighed and took out her credit card.

"Lovely," Courtney said, swiping it out of her hands. "Will you be wearing it out?"

"No thanks," Siobhán said.

"I'll just wrap it up then." Courtney snatched the scarf from the stands and expertly folded it into pink tissue paper. She talked as she wrapped. "Such a shock, finding Niall like that, I'm sure," Courtney said with a shudder.

She'd already come out and asked Courtney why she'd called her here, and that didn't work. Maybe Courtney needed a little coaxing to start talking. "Did you hear anything that night? Or see anyone?" Siobhán asked, trying to keep her voice light and chatty.

Courtney shook her head. "I might have me eyes peeled during the day, but I sleep as heavy as they come. I was dead to the world." Too late, Courtney heard what she said, then gasped and slapped her hand over her mouth.

"Relax," Siobhán said. "We all say things like that."

Courtney crossed herself and handed Siobhán the scarf.

"But there is something. And I wanted you to hear it from me first."

Finally, she was going to get to the point. However, Siobhán didn't like the sound of it already, nor did she like the pitying look in Courtney's hazel eyes. "Hear what?"

"The day before Niall was killed, he was in the shop. I caught him trying to lift a necklace."

"Trying to steal it?"

"Stuck it in his pocket and headed for the door."

"Which one?"

Courtney went over to the wall where the necklaces were hung. She pointed to one with a dazzling pink gem.

"He tried to lift that necklace?" Siobhán couldn't make sense of it.

"Got all the way to the door when I confronted him."

"You were at the counter, and he just stuck it in his pocket with you standing there, like?"

"No, I was coming from the back, just having me afternoon tea. Bridie had just gone to lunch, but she left without telling me first. Niall thought he was free and clear."

"What did he say when you stopped him?"

"What could he say? Caught red-handed. He tried to say that he thought no one was here to pay, but when I put out my hand, he didn't have the money on him."

"Did you report it to Garda Flannery?"

"No. I just told him never to come back into the shop."

"What did he say?"

"He said, 'It would be my pleasure,' and then he called me a name I will not repeat."

"He did not."

"He did. Turned nasty straightaway."

"Who do you think he meant to give it to?" *Not, Gráinne. Don't say Gráinne.* Was it Gráinne? Is that why Courtney thought she wasn't going to like it? "Maybe it was for his mam," Siobhán suggested lamely.

Courtney blinked her fake eyelashes. "It's definitely not the kind of thing you give your mammy."

"Probably not."

Courtney sighed. "Should I tell Garda Flannery? Do you think it's important?"

"Tell him what? You said you don't know who he was going to give it to."

He had his hair cut. He was in a suit. He was stealing a necklace. There was definitely a woman involved. Please don't let it be Gráinne. Maybe he just thought it was something he could sell. Siobhán would accept any explanation, no matter how implausible, just so her sister wasn't involved. She glanced around the store. "Do you think he took anything else? Is anything else missing?"

Courtney gasped. "I didn't even think of that." She grabbed a sheet from underneath the counter, along with a pen, and began examining items and checking them off. Courtney was still avoiding whatever it was she had to say. Siobhán tried another approach.

"What did Bridie say when you told her what Niall had done?"

"What makes you think I told Bridie?" Courtney opened her eyes wide.

"She's your employee, and Niall had been working at the cycle shop. Surely you told her?"

Courtney's eyes remained wide, and she stared at Siobhán without blinking. If she was trying to pull the innocent lamb routine as well, Siobhán was going to lead her to the slaughter. Luckily, Courtney was more than willing to keep talking. She leaned in close to Siobhán and lowered her voice.

"That's the strangest bit," Courtney said. "When I told Bridie she didn't believe me."

"Surely she did."

Courtney shook her head. "She might as well have called me a dirty liar. Said I must have misunderstood. Said Niall was a good lad. Why, if I didn't know better, it almost sounded like she fancied him."

"You told her that you caught him red-handed and that he didn't have the money on him?"

"I did, of course. It gets even stranger." Excitement was evident in Courtney's voice.

"Go on."

"Bridie said she told Niall he could take it. That she'd take the cost of it out of his next paycheck and pay me back, like."

This time Siobhán gasped. It wasn't like Bridie to encourage someone to steal. "Wouldn't she have told you that before Niall took the necklace? And if it was true, why didn't Niall explain that when you caught him?"

"Exactly," Courtney said. She walked up and clasped Siobhán's hands. "So I'm not crazy. That doesn't make a lick of sense, does it?"

"No. Bridie was obviously covering for Niall."

"Thank the lord. I truly thought I was losing me mind."

"And Niall never did take the necklace again?"

"He didn't have the chance. I told Bridie she could take it, of course, but she didn't. She was red in the face and shortly after said she wasn't feeling well and would I mind if she went home."

It was becoming more obvious that Bridie and Niall were having an affair. Was he stealing the necklace for her? Did Bridie realize that and that's why she lied for him? Siobhán had to confront Bridie. She'd have to do it alone because if Bridie had been having an affair, she certainly wasn't going to admit it in front of Séamus.

"Leave it with me," Siobhán said. "I'll see if I can make any sense of it." Siobhán started for the door.

"At first I thought Bridie might be sweet on Niall," Courtney said. Siobhán stopped. There it was again. That pitying tone.

She turned around. "Until I found out who the necklace was really for."

And here they were. Truth time. "It wasn't for Bridie?" Siobhán couldn't hold onto her patience much longer.

"Think about it. Bridie works here. She could have anything she wanted at a discount. It wasn't for Bridie."

"Who then?" She sounded agitated now, and she couldn't help it.

Courtney fluttered her lashes. "It's a bit delicate."

"Go on." This woman could turn a saint into a sinner.

"It's personal, like."

Siobhán stepped into Courtney's personal space. "Personal? To me?"

Courtney swallowed hard and nodded. Oh, God. Courtney wasn't trying to be infuriating at all. She was afraid. She was afraid to tell her. Siobhán stepped back and exhaled. "You aren't going to like it," Courtney said shaking her mahogany-streaked head. "You aren't going to like it one bit."

Chapter 21

"Why are we at this stupid castle again?" Gráinne asked, bending over to catch her breath. She and Siobhán had just finished the arduous climb up the limestone bluff to the ruined Conna Castle, eighty-five feet tall and looking out over the River Bride. A pleasant drive from Kilbane, Conna was removed enough to give Siobhán and Gráinne a bit of breathing room from prying eyes and wagging tongues. Courtney had taken pity on Siobhán and insisted she take her car so the two of them could have this little outing. Siobhán hadn't driven more than a few times in her life, and not at all since the accident. The clutch took some getting used to, but they had made it here alive.

The view from the top of the hill was extraordinary. Ireland's green hills undulated below them, covered in a gentle mist. In 1653 the castle was consumed by a blaze that took the life of the steward and his three daughters. Siobhán said a little prayer for them every time she read the plaque, and she read the plaque every time she came.

"Mom used to bring me here when I was little," Siobhán said. "I love this stupid castle."

Gráinne shrugged, then looked genuinely interested. "I didn't know that."

"It was just the two of us. When I was the only girl." Siobhán laughed, and finally so did Gráinne. "We'd come up here, and I'd run around the castle, then we'd walk into town and have lunch. I thought it would be nice for the two of us to continue the tradition."

"And?" Gráinne put her hands on her hips.

"And that's it. Oh." Siobhán brought the little box out of her handbag. "And I wanted to give you this."

Gráinne stared at the box like it was poisonous. "It's not my birthday."

"Doesn't have to be your birthday for me to say thank you."

"Thank you. For what?"

"For not running away."

"Excuse me?"

"You're sixteen. I'm sure it crossed your mind."

"I'm in school."

"Of course. But I couldn't help thinking. If it were me."

"It was you. You were supposed to be in college."

"And once I was out of the nest, you were supposed to be the oldest girl, getting special attention from Mam and Da." Siobhán thrust the box forward again.

After a stare down, Gráinne reluctantly took it. Siobhán watched her face as she took in the necklace from Courtney Kirby's gift shop. Tears came to her eyes.

"How did you know?"

Siobhán shrugged. "Just a guess. Here." She helped Gráinne put the necklace on. "Ready for lunch?" The two of them made their way downhill. The pink gem glittered against Gráinne's ivory skin.

"They aren't really going to arrest James, are they?" Gráinne said once they were seated in a downtown pub with cheese toasties and curried chips.

"Macdara said it was looking like a sure thing."

"But they can't think he would actually murder Niall. He wouldn't, would he?"

Siobhán dropped her toastie. "Of course not. That's why I have to find out who killed Niall. That's why I have to find out everything about him. Who he talked to since he came back to town, what he said, and why."

"Surely it can't all be important."

"Maybe not. But there's no way to know. It's like putting together a puzzle. The tiniest piece can bring the entire picture into focus."

Gráinne stabbed at her chips with her fork. "I wasn't his girlfriend."

"Then why did he try to steal that necklace for you?"

Gráinne gasped. "How do you know that?"

"Courtney caught him."

"How did she know it was for me?"

"Bridie told her. Apparently Niall confessed it to her when she confronted him."

"It wasn't romantic. I swear. I was helping him. I can't even believe he remembered me mentioning the necklace. That's kind of sweet." She bit her lip, and tears came to her eyes.

"Helping him how?"

"You aren't going to like it."

Siobhán had been hearing that a lot lately. "Okay."

Gráinne finally let her fork fall to her plate. "You promise you won't get mad?"

"I'll try."

"That's not the same thing."

"How can I promise when I don't know what you're going to say?"

"See? You're getting mad already."

"I'm frustrated. So what if I get mad? I'll get over it. I love you no matter what. I love all of you no matter what."

"I've been writing to Billy Murphy in prison."

It was the last thing on earth Siobhán expected her sister to say, and the shock jolted all promises out of her system.

"You what?" She didn't realize she'd yelled it until all heads in the place turned to her.

"See?" Gráinne said.

"Why? Why would you be writing to Billy?"

"At first I just wanted to know if he was sorry. It was a pretty mean letter."

They'd all been through so much. Gráinne didn't even like to write. So for her to sit down and compose a letter . . . well, it meant something. Siobhán had failed. She hadn't noticed how much they were all suffering. All her focus had been on running the bistro, continuing a normal routine, biting back the bitterness of giving up on a college education. She'd missed Gráinne's desperation. Of course she wanted answers. She was too young to realize that sometimes there weren't any.

"I take it he wrote back."

"Straightaway. I couldn't believe it. At first I wasn't even going to open it. You don't know how many times I almost burned that letter."

"What did he say?"

"At first just the usual things. How sorry he was. How he was never going to drink again. How he wished he'd died instead of Mam and Da."

"Did it help? Make you feel better?" Tears dripped down Gráinne's face. She shook her head. Siobhán reached out and took her hand. "I'm not mad."

"You're not?"

"No. I ache for you. I ache for all of us. Because there are no answers. There's nothing Billy could have said that would bring back Mam and Da. Sometimes life is cruel."

"Father Kearney says that God always has a plan. Do you believe that?"

"I don't know. I do know that we were loved. That if they are looking down on us, they'd still want the very best for us. Which is why we can't let James go to prison for something he didn't do."

Gráinne nodded. "Billy and I have been writing for the past six months. He started telling me things. I started to believe him."

"He told you he didn't do it."

"How did you know?"

"Because Niall told me the same thing. Tried to get me to give him ten thousand euro for Billy's defense."

"I'm sorry. I'm sorry."

"Just get it all out. You'll feel better."

"Niall knew I was writing Billy. He was so thankful. He kept saying what a good person I was. That I was doing the right thing. He said he was going to get a good solicitor, one of the best, and help free Billy. He said if I went with him to talk to this solicitor—"

"Where?"

"Dublin."

"When?"

"That afternoon."

"What afternoon?"

"The same day he was killed. That afternoon. I was going to have our anniversary breakfast, and then I was going to meet Niall at the cycle shop. We were going to catch a taxi to Charlesville to catch the train to Dublin."

"Was that why Niall was in a suit?"

"Yes. He said he was going to put it on as soon as he got home from the pubs just in case he overslept. He told me to dress up as well, like. He wanted the solicitor to take him seriously."

So that's why he had on the suit and his head was shaved. It meant he'd made it home after he left O'Rourke's. Why did he come back out again? "Do you know why Niall was at the bistro so early?" Gráinne shook her head. "Did he text you that night?"

Her eyes went wide with terror.

"You have to tell me."

"He did. He said he had to tell me something. I didn't answer. It was the middle of the night, like!"

"I think he wanted you to hear about his fight with James before James had a chance to tell you," Siobhán said. "So you wouldn't change your mind."

Gráinne nodded. "He said it meant everything that I was coming with him."

"Was the text before or after Ann woke you up about hearing glass breaking?"

"Before," Gráinne said. "And I was terrified it was Niall breaking in."

"Did you text him back?"

She nodded. "I told him I wouldn't see him until that afternoon at Sheedy's cycle shop."

"And did you hear back from him?"

"No. He didn't text back."

"Did you hear anything after Ann woke you up? Did you go downstairs?" Tears came to Gráinne's eyes again. "What is it?"

"We put on headphones and listened to a story on tape," Gráinne said. "It was my idea. I was terrified Niall was downstairs, and I didn't know what to do. I didn't want to hear anything more, and I didn't want to go down there."

"Why didn't you wake me?"

"And tell you I thought Niall Murphy was downstairs waiting for me? Are you daft?"

"Settle," Siobhán said. Had the gardai found a phone on Niall? Siobhán hadn't thought of that before. Surely if they had found his phone they would have questioned Gráinne about those texts. It means they didn't have it. Did the killer take it? "Do you know the name of the solicitor he was going to meet with?"

"No," Gráinne said. "I swear."

"Did Niall tell you he had some kind of proof that Billy didn't do it?"

Gráinne nodded. "A video."

"A video of what?"

"He said there was a witness to the accident. That they filmed a portion of it. He says the video proves that Billy isn't responsible."

"Did he say who the witness was?"

"He said it wouldn't be safe for me to know."

Outrage threatened to suffocate Siobhán. The liar. Despicable. "Did he show you this video?"

Gráinne shook her head.

"Did he tell you anything else about what he was going to do with it and when?"

"No. I asked him over and over. He said he needed time."

Time. Time to get the money. After which his lies wouldn't matter. And he and Billy would be off to Australia, or God knows where.

Gráinne looked at Siobhán with pleading eyes. She instantly looked like a little girl again. "Do you think he was killed because of me?"

Startled, Siobhán looked at Gráinne. "Because of you?"

"Niall said if I told the solicitor I believed Billy was innocent, it would help. Maybe the killer knew. Maybe that's why Niall was left in our bistro. They were trying to warn me, like. Get me to stop helping Billy."

Siobhán put her hand over Gráinne's. "Niall was a liar. You telling a solicitor you believed in Billy wouldn't have changed the facts. He was drunk. He was the only one in the car. Macdara said there isn't any truth to what Niall and Billy have been saying."

"James drinks too. What if it were him who killed someone's parents? Would we hate him?"

Siobhán sighed. "You're asking a lot of complicated questions." Gráinne played with the necklace. "How did you mainly communicate with Niall?"

"Texts."

"Can I see them?"

Gráinne looked away as a deep blush rose in her cheeks. "I erased them all. After."

"After he was killed."

Gráinne swallowed and nodded. "I was afraid people would think it was me who killed him."

"We have to tell Macdara what you just told me."

"Does it help?"

"It tells us why Niall was in a suit and had his head shaved. And I think it means Niall came to the bistro that night to confess his fight with James. Make sure you were still going."

"Why would he do that in the middle of the night?"

"Why do lads do anything in the middle of the night? Because they're full of drink. Only the killer followed him to the bistro."

Gráinne shivered. Siobhán quickly reached for her hand and held it. "I won't let anything happen to us," she said.

"Niall didn't act like he wasn't making it all up," Gráinne said. "About Billy being innocent."

"I agree," Siobhán said.

"You do?"

"If the two of you really were going to meet a solicitor, if that's why he needed ten thousand euro—"

"He told me he needed twenty thousand euro," Gráinne interrupted.

"He asked me for ten. Guess he was giving me a discount."

Gráinne's eyes brightened up. "Maybe because I was helping."

"Not the point. He needed a lot of euro. That means something or someone convinced him of his brother's innocence. I don't think it was true, of course, but maybe someone had him fooled. Maybe someone made up a witness or lied about having a video. Maybe they told Niall it would get his brother off. Only they weren't going to share it with him unless he gave them twenty thousand euro."

"That's a lot of maybes."

"But it's better than no maybes."

"So who do you think it was? Who was tricking Niall Murphy, and why?"

"Whoever it was, they needed to get their hands on a substantial amount of money." *John Butler? To keep his business open?*

"We find that person, and we find the killer." The tears were gone, and Gráinne's eyes actually started to sparkle.

"There's no we."

"There is now."

"No. You are to stay out of it."

"I'm part of this family too."

"But I'm your legal guardian. I won't let anything happen to you."

"I won't let anything happen to James."

"You can help by writing down everything that was said between you and Niall, and even Billy. Write Billy again. Ask him if he knew where Niall got this crazy idea."

"I could pretend I still believe he's innocent."

"That would be a huge help."

"What if Billy doesn't know?"

"One thing at a time."

"Do you think we're on to something?"

"I do."

"I do too. Are you going to tell Macdara straightaway?"

"I don't know."

"Do you still like him?"

"What are you on about?"

Gráinne grinned, and she flipped a strand of her black hair back with a flourish. "Your face matches your hair. I rest my case."

What a cheeky thing to say. Siobhán raged silently and paid the bill. Gráinne sang to the radio on the way home, while Siobhán tried to think of a good retort, something to convince Gráinne that she wasn't in love with Macdara Flannery, but nothing came to mind. She was so lost in thought she almost didn't see John Butler dashing out in front of the car until Gráinne screamed. Siobhán slammed on the brakes, stopping just short of knocking him down.

"I hope Courtney has good motor insurance," Gráinne said. Siobhán's heart pounded in her chest. She was never going to take somebody else's car in her hands again. Imagine, another accident. What was she thinking? Courtney was probably looking out her window too, just in time to see her almost wreck her car and kill John Butler. That would be some bad luck, to kill the town undertaker.

John's face had a sickening green tint as he gaped at Siobhán through the windshield. He was the one in the middle of the street, like.

Siobhán stuck her head out the window. "Sorry. I didn't see ye."

"My fault," he said, holding up his hand. He hurried out of the way and took off down the footpath at a fast clip.

"That was weird," Gráinne said. "I thought for sure he was going to take your head off."

"Me too."

"I would have if I were him."

"He just darted out in front of me."

"Certainly was in a hurry."

"Certainly was." Siobhán kept her eyes on him. He was headed in the direction of the bank. Was he still trying to get a loan for twenty thousand euro? It was obvious Niall was no longer blackmailing him, so who was? Had Mary Murphy picked up where her son left off? She could tell Macdara to check it out, but he was already browned off with her snooping. Sometimes old adages were true. *If you wanted something done well, you had best do it yourself.*

Chapter 22

She was daft, that's what she was. Completely mental. There was no other explanation for why she was lurking in the back of Butler's Undertaker, Lounge, and Pub while her siblings were about to go into the front so they could distract him. She hadn't wanted to involve them, but she couldn't do it alone, and they were just as determined as she was to help James.

She would sneak in, find Butler's office, and see if there was anything about a loan, or any paperwork that reflected a need for twenty thousand euro. And then what? Was it a crime to need twenty thousand euro? Who in town didn't need twenty thousand euro? She'd have to find something else, something to connect him to Niall.

It took twenty minutes of hiding behind a bush on the side of the house before the back door opened and a lad stepped out. He wedged a concrete block between the door and its frame, stepped a few feet away, and lit a cigarette.

Gráinne would text when they had Butler preoccupied. Gráinne was the one who insisted that wouldn't be a problem. "We'll tell him Ciarán is terrified of death now, and we thought seeing the business end of it would calm him down."

"I'm not terrified of death," Ciarán insisted. It took a bit of coaxing to convince him to pretend he was. Maybe this was all a horrible idea. Siobhán's nerves were twitching, and she just wanted to get it over with, but the lad smoking his cigarette was staying close to the door. How was she going to get him to move away? She could throw a rock, but that was silly. He wasn't a dog that would trot over to investigate. Right? He'd probably look to see who threw something, not where it landed. God, they made these things look so easy on telly. She didn't even see any rocks lying around.

A text beeped in from Gráinne. Siobhán glanced at the lad, but thank God, he hadn't heard it. She immediately switched her mobile to vibration mode. Why hadn't she thought of that earlier? She wasn't built for breaking and entering. Or even just entering. Are you in? He's letting Ciarán lie in caskets.

For heaven's sakes. She was a terrible guardian. Lad out back smoking. Too close to door.

A few seconds later she got a reply. Eoin coming.

Great. She was getting them all trapped in a life of crime. Terrible, terrible parenting skills. What was Eoin going to do? He was more likely to aim a rock at the lad's head, and then she'd have two brothers in jail.

A minute later, Eoin strolled around back, passed Siobhán huddled by the side without even a glance and approached the lad. Eoin was pointing and shouting, and soon running across the field with the lad following.

Siobhán didn't have time to guess what whopper of a lie had incited that; instead, she darted to the back door. Once through, she pulled the concrete block in behind her and thought, this is it, as the door clanged shut behind her. She was in the cellar storage room, and immediately the smell of chemicals, probably embalming fluid, overwhelmed her.

She coughed, then threw her hands over her mouth to stifle the sound.

She tiptoed through the storage room, past bottles, and linens, and long plastic tubes—Jaysus, she didn't want to know—and then stepped into a second room, larger than the storage area. This was the preparation room, no doubt, for in the middle was the furnace, and there was a large drainage sink on one wall, along with several steel gurneys about the room, and at the other end the refrigeration unit for the bodies.

She hurried through the preparation room, looking left or right, for any clues at all. Ridiculous, she scolded herself. Absolutely insane. She was grateful business was slow; she certainly didn't want to run into a dead body. What she did know, from multiple visits here while making the arrangements for her parents, was that just beyond this prep room was a foyer that led to John Butler's office.

Siobhán shivered. It was freezing down here. She crossed through the preparation room to the foyer. Just beyond was the door to Butler's office. From here she could see that it was shut, and through the gap under the door she could tell the lights were off. What if it was locked? The previous times she'd been down here the door had been open. Her phone buzzed and she jumped. At least she was in the right place if she died of fright.

You in?

Yes

She was in alright. But what in the world was she think-ing? She was too jumpy. This was madness. She had turned and started back the way she had come when a woman's voice called out from the direction of the office. "Help. Help." It was as plain as day, and every single hair on the back of Siobhán's neck stood at attention. Shite. She couldn't pretend she hadn't heard it, could she? She hightailed it back to the office door before common sense could grab hold of her.

"Hello? Hello?" Siobhán put her ear to the door. Whoever the woman was, she was still talking, but Siobhán couldn't make out what she was saying. Maybe she was tied up and couldn't open the door. Siobhán turned the doorknob, and almost to her disappointment, it swung open. There wasn't anyone there, yet she could still hear a voice. She stood in the doorway, taking in the empty office, perplexed.

"How did ye like that?" the woman's voice said. "I'm going to scream. Untie me. You brute." A girlish laugh filled the room. A blinking red light drew Siobhán's attention to the desk. An answering machine. The voice was coming out of an answering machine. Unlike Mike Granger's office, John Butler's desk was wiped clean except for the answering machine and a single blue folder in the center of the desk. "I'll see you soon." The answering machine clicked off. Siobhán's heart continued to thump in her chest. What was that? Who was that? She was already in; should she look around? At least open the blue folder and have a peek?

She took a few steps beyond the door. The woman on the phone sounded like a lover. Siobhán had taken John Butler for a lifetime bachelor. Or maybe it was just too creepy to think of him with a woman. There were even rumors that he was gay.

Siobhán took another step in and reached for the folder. She opened it. It was empty.

A book lay on the desk underneath the folder, along with a set of handcuffs. Why did John Butler have handcuffs? Siobhán leaned in to have a look at the book. *Bad Boy in the Bedroom.* Oh, Jaysus. That explained the handcuffs. And the message. And that's what she got for snooping. She dropped the book and placed the blue folder on top of it.

Next she crossed herself, took a step back, and bumped into the door. It slammed shut with a bang that continued to echo inside her head. She glanced at the ceiling. Had they heard that? Her phone vibrated. It had to mean yes, they'd heard it. She reached for the doorknob, turned it, and pulled. It was locked. How was that possible? Maybe she was just nervous, maybe it was just stuck. Siobhán tried to open it again. Just as she managed to pry it open, her phone vibrated, making her jump. Another text from Gráinne.

John's coming!!!

She had just started to type back when she heard someone clomping down the stairs. Her eyes darted around for a place to hide. The desk didn't have a back, so it was no use hiding under there. There was nothing other than a bookshelf and a filing cabinet. The footsteps clomped toward the door. More people seemed to be clomping down the steps. They sounded like a herd of clumsy cattle. Her brood, no doubt, trying to stop John from entering his office. Why hadn't she listened to Macdara and just kept her nose out of it?

Siobhán flattened herself behind the door and threw her hands up to protect her face.

John Butler's voice rang out. "I asked you to wait upstairs."

"Don't go into that office," Ciarán yelled.

"What?" John Butler was on high alert. *Feck.*

It was still open a crack; she'd forgotten to shut it. Before she could formulate a better plan, the door swung open. Siobhán screamed and darted out. She slammed into John Butler's chest. He screamed along with her, in a pitch so high Siobhán expected to hear dogs barking in response.

"Sorry, sorry," Siobhán said. John Butler clutched his chest and bent over, as if trying to catch his breath. From this vantage point, Siobhán could see that he had a massive amount of gel in his hair. No wonder it never moved. Behind him, Ann, Grainne, and Ciarán stood grim-faced and wide-eyed.

"I told ye not to open it," Ciarán said.

"What on earth is going on here?" John said. His fear had dissipated; he was browned off now.

"I heard a woman yelling for help," Siobhán said.

"In here?" John's eyes darted around the office.

"Turns out it was just on the phone," Siobhán said, pointing to the red light blinking on the answering machine. "But the door shut behind me, and I thought I was locked in." John reached out as if to push Play. Siobhán clamped down on his arm.

"No," she said. "It's a lady friend." She tried lifting her eyebrows to make her point. John frowned and reached for the phone again.

"A lady friend doing a bit of role play," Siobhán said.

"What are you on about?" Ciarán said.

John turned to Siobhán. A light must have gone off in his mind for he backed away from the machine, then glanced at the blue folder, or more likely the book it was covering up, with a blush. "What were you doing down here to begin with?"

"Yes," Gráinne echoed from outside the office. "What are ye doing here?"

"Looking for you guys," Siobhán said.

"Down here?" John said.

"I texted Gráinne, and she said you were giving her a tour of the mortuary," Siobhán said. "Obviously it was a little white lie."

"I was only foolin'," Gráinne said. "Can ye see my nose growing?"

"Why would your nose be growing?" Ciarán said.

Gráinne put her hands on her hips. "Seriously? Has she never read ye *Pinocchio?*"

"Who?" Ciarán said.

"The wooden puppet, like," Ann said. "Mammy once read it to us."

"I don't remember," Ciarán said.

"Remember yer one they called Jeep or something like, and the wee grasshopper with spectacles?" Ann said.

Siobhán felt like she was watching a spectacle right now.

"No," Ciarán said.

"Geppetto," Siobhán said.

"Like the ice cream?" Ciarán said.

"No," Siobhán said. "That's gelato."

"You've never read it to me," Ciarán said, looking very much aggrieved. John Butler glared at Siobhán as if she was responsible for what came out of their pieholes. He lifted his gold-tipped cane and whacked the top of the desk as hard as he could. Everyone jumped. "What are you doing here? And if I don't believe you I'm going to call Garda Flannery!"

Siobhán put her hands up, then herded her brood out the door. "It was an honest mistake. When you listen to yer message you'll see why I thought your lady friend was in need of help." She emphasized "lady friend" so he would get the point.

"Why don't we take this conversation upstairs," John said, with another red-faced glance at his answering machine. "Unless you want to go through me drawers?"

"God, no," Siobhán said. John reddened even more, and from the flash of heat across Siobhán's cheeks, so, it seemed, did she. John Butler exited his office and herded them upstairs. It smelled like baby powder, and dampness.

Siobhán wanted to go home, but John's face was set with determination. She was going to get to leave when he said so. Siobhán asked Gráinne to take Ann and Ciarán home.

"I want to stay," Ciarán said. "I want to see what he says."

"See what I say about what?" John said.

"Was Niall Murphy blackmailing you?" Gráinne said.

"Blackmailing me?"

"Go home," Siobhán said to Gráinne.

"We would have been home if you had just asked him in the first place," Gráinne said.

"Why would Niall Murphy have been blackmailing me?" John sputtered. His head bobbed, and his pale complexion turned slightly gray. He looked like a man who'd seen not one, but many ghosts.

"We'll ask the questions here," Ciarán said.

"Hush," Siobhán said. She turned to John. "Rumor has it Niall had been bullying people into giving him twenty thousand pounds."

"Bullying how?"

"Something about a video. Pretending to have evidence of wrongdoing."

"Just what are you accusing me of?"

"Murder," Ciarán said.

"Oh my God," Siobhán said turning to her siblings. "You have to keep your gobs shut."

Eoin walked into the room. He was flushed. John pointed at him. "Where did he go? Was he snooping around my place too?"

"I was just out havin' a smoke," Eoin said. Siobhán glared at him. She wanted to sniff his breath but figured now was not the time and place. He'd better not start smoking. Her parents would never forgive her if she didn't stay on top of that. This wasn't fair. She didn't want to deal with any of this.

John Butler pointed at Siobhán, his finger shaking with rage. "I'm calling Garda Flannery and having you arrested for breaking and entering."

"You opened the door and let us in," Gráinne said.

"All except one," John said, pointing at Siobhán again. "And you set me up. All of you."

"We didn't mean any harm," Siobhán said. "We just wanted to ask you a few questions."

"I heard you were sticking your nose in where it doesn't belong," John said. "Fancy yourself a detective superintendent, do you?"

"You would do the same thing if a dead body turned up in your home." Siobhán stopped when she remembered who she was talking to. "I mean, if you weren't an undertaker, like."

John yanked out his wallet and pulled out a receipt. "I don't know where you've picked up your techniques, but you've forgotten the first rule of any murder investigation." He shoved the receipt at her.

"What is this?" Siobhán said. It was a receipt from a hotel in Cork stamped with the date and time.

"My alibi," John said. "I wasn't even in Kilbane the night Niall Murphy was stabbed."

And right then Siobhán knew what it felt like to be the biggest eejit on the planet. Alibis. She'd been so focused on motives, means, and opportunities, she'd forgotten all about alibis.

Ciarán stepped up to John Butler and stuck out his hand for a shake. A perplexed John Butler weakly accepted the ritual. "We'll take ye off the list straightaway," Ciarán said.

"List?" John Butler said.

"We'd better get our legs under us," Siobhán said. "Your next brekkie is on the house." And before John could call the guards, or Ciarán could explain how they'd started a list of suspects that pretty much included every single soul in Kilbane, Siobhán hustled her brood through the funeral home and out the front door.

Chapter 23

The next morning, Siobhán had just officially unlocked the front door of the bistro for their grand reopening when Macdara entered in uniform. He stood in the doorway like a man about to deliver bad news. Siobhán gestured to his usual table, but he didn't make a move. Instead he shook his head and glanced around. Siobhán's heart clenched as the thought stabbed her in the heart. *He's here for James.*

"Would you like a cup of tea and some brown bread?" Siobhán said. She glanced outside and noticed folks queued up on the footpath.

"I asked them to wait," Macdara said. "I'm sorry."

"No," Siobhán said. "No."

"The blood on James's shirt was a match for Niall's."

"Drops of blood," Siobhán said. "Just drops."

"I told ye what the pathologist said. Drops are enough."

"He's being framed."

"The order has come down from the detective superintendent." Macdara glanced toward the stairwell leading to their bedrooms. "Please tell me he didn't skip town."

"Of course I didn't." James stepped into the room.

"You can't do this," Siobhán said, turning to Macdara.

"It's alright," James said.

"It's not." Siobhán didn't know whether to beg, scream, or pray.

James walked up and took Siobhán's hands. "No crying. No fuss, ye hear? As long as you and the rest of the six are okay, then I'll be okay."

Siobhán squeezed his hands. They were so cold. He was frightened to death but doing his best to be brave. "I'll get you out. I swear."

James winked at her and gave her a peck on the cheek. "Nod and smile," he said softly. "Just nod and smile." He turned to Macdara. "Can we do this outside?" Macdara gave a nod, then put his arm on James's elbow and started to guide him out.

"Wait!" Ciarán came barreling out of the kitchen, followed by the rest. They threw themselves at James.

"He'll be home in no time," Siobhán said, prying them off. Faces were already staring in, gobbling up their misfortune. And although it took only a matter of seconds, watching James get marched out to Macdara's car, as the folks outside watched, was the second-darkest moment of Siobhán O'Sullivan's life. And then, in they came.

Siobhán wanted to close and lock the doors forever, yet here they were, her friends and neighbors, filling up the seats. They knew better than to ask what had just happened, and so the conversation that filled the room was about the weather, and the latest game, and the state of the Irish economy, and the latest horse race or hurling match; they talked about everything and anything other than James, and the O'Sullivans, and murder. It made the nightmare that much more surreal. Siobhán didn't realize she was standing still until Eoin got her moving.

"Come on," he said, touching her elbow. He was holding out an apron. It was her mam's. Siobhán took it with a nod, biting the side of her mouth to fend off the tears. Eoin and Ciarán headed to the grill, Ann began seating people, and Gráinne took up residence behind the counter. Siobhán took a deep breath, put the apron on, and got to work. She smiled, and delivered Irish breakfasts, wetted the tea and made cappuccinos, and chatted with folks about nothing, as if her heart weren't breaking, as if it were any other day. For the first time in a while, she had no interest in asking anyone questions, and she realized with a sinking heart, as she held the kettle and poured endless cups, that despite what her mam always said, it simply wasn't true. Not *everything* in life could be made better by a biscuit and a cup of tea.

Siobhán had never been so relieved to see a shift end. They were as busy as a pub on Saint Stephen's Day. And although her siblings retired upstairs or went outside to play, Siobhán knew that, for her, rest and relaxation would have to wait. John Butler had taught her a fierce lesson. In order to find the killer, Siobhán was going to have to start collecting alibis. That meant dividing her time between the bistro and visiting everyone on the list. It would be impossible to do if she had to walk everywhere. She was going to have to get a scooter, even if it meant Alison Tierney wasn't going to get her rent on time. It was going to cause an uproar from their uptight landlady, but Siobhán didn't have a choice. As soon as the breakfast shift ended, she headed straight for Sheedy's cycle shop.

Séamus was behind the counter, sorting through a box of racing gloves. He held up his hand, showing off a neon green one that he'd slipped onto his right hand. "Glows in the dark," he said. "Isn't it brilliant?"

Did he really need neon gloves for the store? Or was he covering up swollen knuckles? Had Séamus beat up James?

Could he be the killer? Maybe he'd found out Bridie was having an affair with Niall.

"Can I see that?" Siobhán asked.

"Sure, pet." Séamus picked a glove off the counter.

"Actually I meant the one you're wearing."

Séamus tilted his head quizzically but took off the glove just the same and handed it to her. Siobhán slipped it on and pretended to admire it before sneaking a peek at Séamus's right hand. It was white and smooth, not a mark on his knuckles. "Thanks." She took off the sweaty glove and handed it back to him.

Then she began to cry. Suspecting everyone of murder was taking a giant toll on her. Séamus was instantly out from behind the counter, opening up his arms for a hug. Siobhán didn't realize how fragile she was until she felt his touch. She almost broke into pieces.

"What is it, pet?" He stepped back and searched her eyes.

"They just arrested James."

"You're joking me." Séamus sounded as angry as she was. Finally. Maybe he could help, talk some sense into the gardai.

"Just now," Siobhán said.

"For what?"

"Why, for Niall's murder."

"But that's impossible." Séamus began to pace. "I saw him that night. He couldn't have killed a fly. He was in no shape. No shape, I tell ye."

"Thank you. Thank you." Siobhán felt some weight lift off her.

"For what?"

"For believing in him. Even Macdara is starting to think James did it."

Séamus cocked his head. "Because of the fight at the pub?"

"That's right. You were there that night. Did you see anything that might prove James didn't do it?"

"No, pet. Last I saw James, he was stumbling out the door, ranting and raving. I tried to give him a ride home, but he refused."

"Did he say he was going home?"

"Ah, pet. I couldn't understand a word he was saying," Séamus said. Tears came to Siobhán's eyes. She nodded. Séamus came over and placed his hands on her arms. "I'm tellin' ye the God's honest truth. He wasn't in any shape to go stabbing anyone."

"Tell Macdara that."

"Now you know yourself that Macdara isn't calling the shots. It's the detective superintendant we need to have a good old chat with."

"Will you do it? Nobody takes me seriously."

"I will, pet. Can't promise anything. But I'll tell him what I just told you."

"Make sure you tell him that you didn't see any physical confrontation between them, will you?"

"But someone roughed up James that night," Séamus said. "If not Niall, then who?"

"I think it could have been the killer."

"I don't understand."

Siobhán hesitated. She didn't want to tell him about the drops of blood on James's clothing. She didn't want to lose one of her only allies.

"I don't know what I'm saying," she said. "The more I try and figure it out, the more I wrap myself up into knots."

"I wish your da were here," Séamus said. "He was always good in a crisis."

"He'd be so grateful that you believe in James. And so am I."

"I can't tell the detective for sure that James and Niall

didn't come to fisticuffs. But I'll make sure and tell him that none of us witnessed it."

Siobhán nodded. "What time did you go home?" She hoped it didn't come out like an accusation.

"It was about half one. I know because Bridie nearly took me head off." Siobhán laughed. "Ask Macdara to have a look at the CCTVs if he hasn't already. They'll show me leaving about half one."

"Séamus. I hope you don't think—"

Séamus held up his hand. "It's alright, petal. I know about the list. I heard we're all on it."

Oh, God. Everybody knew. She wasn't being slick at all. Would she get the truth out of anyone now? "Ciarán made up that silly list. I just wanted to keep him busy during all this. The thought of losing James is unbearable. I hope folks in town don't think we're horrible people!"

"Ah, no, petal. Everyone is on edge. I'll even help ye ask around. It's alibis you're after, is it?"

"I guess it's a good place to start. John Butler was in Cork the night of the murder, so he's off the list."

"I knew there was a list." Séamus winked.

Siobhán laughed. "Ciarán's list," she repeated. "For distraction, like."

"I still think the ticket is with the CCTVs. Maybe they'll help find the real killer."

There aren't any cameras on the road behind our bistro. And Mike Granger said the lads he saw were wearing caps. She doubted the cameras would help all that much, but she kept that to herself. He was only trying to help.

"Do you need assistance getting a solicitor?" Séamus asked.

"Maybe. But for now I also need the scooter." Séamus raised his eyebrow. "I'm going to have a lot of people to go and see. Regarding James and all. Plus I'll have to run errands for the bistro. We're down a man, you know your-self."

"Say no more, petal. I want you to have her. The pink one, is it?" Séamus turned to the set of keys hanging on the wall.

"Actually I think I'll take a black one." It would be much easier to blend in if she wasn't flashing around on pink. And besides, pink was the color of the scissors that killed Niall. She hated pink now. Séamus removed the key, and Siobhán handed him a credit card. It was to be used for bistro emergencies only.

"What if you hold off on payment until James is back with ye?" Séamus suggested gently.

"I can't let you do that."

"You're not letting me, I'm insisting."

"No. I want to pay."

"You don't have to. You might need it for a good solicitor."

"Please. You know what my da would say. The O'Sullivans pay their way."

"Alright, petal." Séamus took the credit card. "But if you ever need anything . . ."

"Come to the bistro tomorrow for breakfast. Bring Bridie." Maybe Siobhán could get her alone and ask her a few more questions.

"We will be there with bells on." Séamus swiped her card through the reader on the counter. Something must have flashed across the tiny screen, for when Séamus looked up at her, she saw pity in his eyes. "My machine isn't working today." He handed her back the card, then handed her the key to the scooter.

"But . . ."

"But nothing."

"The card was declined, wasn't it?"

"I wouldn't use it again, pet. It's asking me to cut it up."

Great. Another death by scissors. God, she was awful. Séamus took her hand and placed the key in them. "This isn't charity. You'll pay me as soon as you're back on your feet."

"I can't. It's too dear."

"Siobhán O'Sullivan, you know your Celtic myths."

"So?"

"What did the druids believe was the most sacred of virtues?"

"Embracing the goddess of nature?"

"The other one."

She knew where he was going. "Hospitality," she said reluctantly.

"Hospitality!" he said. "So would ye, please? Allow me to be hospitable?" Technically, he was being generous, not hospitable, but Siobhán wasn't going to insult him by pointing this out. Seamus placed his hand over his heart. "You'd be doing my eternal soul a great favor."

"You've done so much for us already," she said.

"That's the way your Mam and Da would have wanted it."

Siobhán nodded as the tears formed, afraid that if she spoke she'd tell him again that she couldn't take it, and she had to. She needed the scooter. She couldn't go borrowing Courtney's car anymore, especially since she'd almost run over John Butler with it.

"I know exactly what's wrong with ye," Séamus said snapping his fingers.

"What?" Siobhán had been staring into space. *Oh, Lord. Did he know she saw Bridie in here with Niall that morning? She should have told him. She could still tell him. Right. Man loans you a scooter, and you tell him you think his wife might have been fooling around with a murder victim? Get ahold of yourself, Siobhán.*

Séamus gestured to the key in her hand. "You don't have any idea how to ride her, do ye?"

Siobhán looked at the key. For a second she'd forgotten

all about the scooter. Imagine that! "Is it that obvious?" she said.

Séamus grinned and pulled a helmet from under the counter. He must have seen the look of dread on her face. "The helmet comes with yer purchase."

"Liar," Siobhán said.

He winked at her. "Why don't we take her to the field out back. Give her a go?"

Siobhán did her best to put all thoughts of murder out of her mind for now so she could concentrate on riding the scooter. It took a few tries to keep from tilting over, but after some encouragement and instruction from Séamus, Siobhán started to get the hang of it. She was horrified to realize that, for a second there, zooming up and down his field, she was actually having fun.

"Don't take her over fields if you can help it," Séamus warned. "Too many holes in the ground. If you catch one just right, you could flip right over. I wouldn't take those fields even in me motorcycle. And remember. Any vehicle can be dangerous. Especially in the rain. Mind yerself." A worried look came over his face as if he thought she would act the fool and get herself killed.

Siobhán smiled. She'd seen that very look of worry on her own da's face many a time. "I will indeed."

He gestured to the shed behind the shop. "I've got a motorcycle in me shed if you ever want to upgrade. She's twice as fast." He treated her to another wink.

"I think I'll stick with this wee scooter."

"You're all set then. See you for breakfast." Siobhán was almost out the door when she remembered. She turned. Séamus was heading down the hall out to the back. She followed. He must have sensed her for suddenly he whirled around.

Siobhán gave a yelp of fright, even though she was the one who had startled him.

"You alright, pet?" he asked, hand to his heart.

"So sorry," she said. "Didn't mean to startle you."

"Did you forget something?"

"Yes. Macdara wanted me to ask if you'd be willing to change the locks at the bistro."

Séamus dropped his hand, and a look of relief washed over his face. "I will indeed," he said. "What if I get to it after we have that breakfast?"

"The meals are on me," Siobhán said. "Or no deal."

Séamus winked. "If you sneak up on me like that again, I'm afraid it's going to be me last meal," he said with another pat to his heart.

Siobhán took it slow driving home, feeling the impact of every jostle of the wheels on the road. Despite a couple of bumps, she rather enjoyed the wind in her face. It was a gray day, but at least it wasn't lashing rain. She wondered what her friends and neighbors would say when they saw her on the scooter. They wouldn't know it was on loan, and Séamus certainly wouldn't tell them. Siobhán didn't know what was worse, being a borrower or being thought of as being wasteful at a time like this. Oh, they would talk, she could hear them now.

Buying a scooter when her brother's been hauled off to jail. Some cheek!

A scooter, when they're so dear, like. I heard she hasn't even paid the rent this month.

Buying a scooter so she can snoop into our lives. They have a list, did ye know dat? And we're all on it! Every one of us suspected of murder. And her brother the one in jail, like.

Siobhán tried to cut out the thoughts. She didn't realize where she was headed until she found herself coming up along on the cemetery. It had been too long since she'd paid a visit. She parked the scooter under a birch tree, entered the small cemetery, and headed for the back row, where her parents lay. She should have brought her whittling knife and some wood. She'd been wanting to make her mother a bluebird. Next time. She didn't even have flowers. They would understand.

She knelt on the soft grass beside the headstones, clasped her hands in prayer, and in a voice no louder than a whisper, she told them what was happening to them and to James. And then she promised them, swore on her life, that she would fix it. She would find the real killer, and she would fix it.

Chapter 24

The following day, once again it seemed as if all of Kilbane was in the bistro, their plates filled to the brim. Now that the initial shock had worn off, appetites had ignited. Comfort was sought, especially here, in the place where it all began. Sweets, and potatoes, and shepherd's pie, and oxtail stew, and bacon and cabbage, and her brown bread, of course, and cuploads of Barry's tea— it all helped ease the stress just a wee bit. Fear had a way of burning up calories; so did lookin' over yer shoulder every few steps to make sure a fella wasn't following you with a pair of hot-pink scissors.

Every table was taken, except for the one where Niall was found. It was still filled with prayer cards, candles, and photos. Whatever grudges folks had had against him in life were cast aside in death. In supporting Niall's memory, they were taking a stand against a killer. Bustling from table to table, ferrying comfort, for a second Siobhán almost felt back to normal. She even made herself a cappuccino.

She was carrying a tray filled with dirty plates back to the kitchen when someone plowed into her. She dropped the tray, and it smashed to the ground with a clatter. She yelped, and several other tense patrons let out little cries of their own.

Siobhán looked at the person who had caused the collision and found herself staring up at the Yank, who was, hands down, the best-looking man she had ever seen. Absolutely gorgeous. At least six foot two, with black hair, and although she wasn't a fan of romance novels, her mam had been, and there was no other way to describe them, and she felt ashamed for even having the clichéd thought, but what other words were there for it? He had right smoldering green eyes, like.

"I'm so sorry," he said, bending down to pick up the plates. Chris Gorden, that was his name. What a nice accent. Not obnoxious at all.

"No bother, I'll get it," Siobhán said. He jerked back up, and she realized she'd sounded harsher than she intended.

"I'm always running into you," he said. "Literally."

"Eoin," she yelled toward the kitchen. "Ciarán."

"I'm on it," Eoin said, coming out of the kitchen doors, followed by Ciarán with a broom and dustpan.

"Wouldn't want you to cut yourself," Siobhán said, gesturing to the broken plate. *One death in here was more than enough.*

"Again. So sorry." He smiled. Gawd, what straight white teeth Yanks usually had, like little white picket fences. His were no exception. And there was that dimple again too.

"Not a bother," Siobhán said, friendlier this time. She wanted to smile, but she could feel someone's eyes on her. She looked up to find Macdara watching them from his table a few feet away. His eyes may not have been smoldering in the romance sort of way, but he was looking at them as if he would have set Chris Gorden on fire if given the chance. Would you look at that. Macdara Flannery was fierce jealous.

The American stuck out his hand. "I'm Chris."

Siobhán wiped her hand on her apron and shook. "Siobhán O'Sullivan."

"I know," he said with an even bigger smile. "How's the running going?"

He was the first person who had asked her about it seriously. No jokes, titters, incredulity, eye rolls, or the slightest hint of sarcasm. She liked that even better than his perfect teeth. "Slowly but surely. Do you run every morning?"

"I'll tell you the truth." He stepped forward and lowered his voice so that he was almost whispering in her ear. It felt a little dangerous, having someone so good-looking so close. "I'm around the priory a lot. It's amazing. Beautiful." His eyes sought hers, then his gaze dropped to her lips. Siobhán felt heat rise to her cheeks even though she'd done nothing wrong.

She laughed nervously and took a step back. Macdara was still glaring in their direction. Chris was still talking. Some investigator she was; she'd totally lost track of what he was saying. *Rule number one: do not start fantasizing about the suspects.*

"To be among such rich history. To stand in a place where there are gravestones that say, 'Here lies a knight.' I mean I guess you're used to that here. But for me? It's magical enough being in a place where there's no McDonald's. But to have that beautiful abbey in your backyard? I can't stay away from it."

"At that time of the mornin'?"

His eyes lit up. "It's the best. Have you ever seen the sun rise over it?" Of course she had. She'd seen the sun rise over it, the sun set behind it, the rain kiss it and make it shimmy, the fog shroud it and render it mysterious, and a few rare snowstorms that made it downright mystical. He thought just because they lived around it and among it all their lives that they didn't appreciate it? He was wrong.

But he wasn't really asking her about it, so she just let him keep talking. "My God. There's nothing like it. Anyway. That morning, I wasn't actually out for a run."

Siobhán's ears perked up. "You weren't?"

"I was just coming back from the poker game. I was a bit drunk. But not too drunk to notice a gorgeous redhead running toward me." He flashed that darn disarming smile again.

Houlihan's. That was the only pub that held all-night poker tournaments. The players were fierce serious about it too. The Yank must have money and a bit of sense about him if they were letting him join the ranks. And it would certainly be an easy alibi to check. Anyone who'd spent all night in a poker tournament couldn't have been the killer. "Did ye win?"

"Lost every last nickel," he said with a sheepish grin. Siobhán didn't realize that they were just standing there staring at each other until she felt a bump at her backside. She whirled around to find Gráinne grinning at her. Why, the cheek! She did that on purpose.

"Sorry," Gráinne said. "Couldn't help it, like. With ye both just standing in the middle of the floor, like, eyeballing each other."

Siobhán would have been mighty tempted to give Gráinne a slap if they hadn't been surrounded by witnesses. She turned to Chris, hoping he wouldn't notice her cheeks were once again aflame. "If you'd like a table, I was just clearing that one," Siobhán said gesturing to it.

"Thank you." By now Eoin had removed the plates and tray, but Ciarán was doing a poor job of sweeping up the bits. Ear-wagging was what he was doing.

Siobhán took the broom and dustpan and nudged him back to the kitchen. When she followed, a few seconds later, Ann and Gráinne accosted her. They were all shiny hair flippin' and big eyes twitchin'.

"Who's that?" Gráinne said with her signature hip jut even more pronounced.

"Who's what?" Siobhán said.

"That gorgeous man," Ann said. Her hair was straightened, held back with a headband. When did she stop wearing the braids? What else was Siobhán missing?

"Don't go gawking at the customers now," Siobhán said.

"You were the one gawkin'," Gráinne said. "You were positively drooling, like."

"Go away with ye," Siobhán said. *Oh, Gawd. Was she?* "He's American. His name is Chris."

"Is he a movie star?" Ann asked.

"Don't be daft," Eoin said.

"He could be, like," Ann said.

Siobhán agreed, but she didn't want to get in the middle of it. She'd often suspected that Eoin was self-conscious about his looks. He didn't have James's build or Ciarán's sweet face. He was a bit of an ugly duckling; Siobhán hated even thinking it, but it was true. She hoped he could just feel good about himself and that he'd meet a nice girl who loved him for who he was inside.

"Back to work," Siobhán said. She glanced at the clock on the far wall. "We've still another hour to go."

"We should stay open longer today," Eoin said. "Make up for lost time."

"No. We need to get back to our routine." And by that she meant her scooter. She was dying to ride it again. And she had to start collecting alibis. It was no good chatting about it in the bistro. Very unprofessional to ask for alibis when all people wanted was brown bread and Barry's tea.

Siobhán returned to the dining room but let Gráinne take Chris's order. Macdara was still there, and the last thing she needed was to give him another reason to be browned off with her. She was just going back to see if he wanted more brown bread and tea when she caught Ciarán at his table, chatting away.

"Would you like to see our list of suspects?" Ciarán said loudly to Macdara. Several heads turned their way. Ciarán grinned through it, oblivious of the effect he was having on the twitchy patrons.

"He's just jokin' ye," Siobhán said pinching the back of Ciarán's arm. "We don't have a list of suspects."

"Ow!" Ciarán said. He yanked his arm away and looked up at her. "We do so. It's in the kitchen taped to the back wall."

"I thought you were going to drop this," Macdara said to Siobhán in a low voice.

"John Butler didn't do it," Ciarán said, totally unaware of how loud he was. "He has an alibi."

"I thought the butler always did it," someone remarked under their breath, evoking laughter from the table. It died down the second Siobhán fixed them with a glare.

"Does he now?" Macdara said.

"He was in Cork City the night of the murder," Ciarán said. "We should have checked that before breaking into his office."

Siobhán grabbed Ciarán's arm and whispered into his ear. "Shut up." This time Ciarán got it. He shuffled off to the kitchen.

"Please tell me you didn't break into John Butler's office," Macdara said.

"When can I visit James?"

"They should be done processing him today. I'll give them a call and see when visiting hours are."

Siobhán poured more hot water into his cup and set another plate of brown bread down but kept her hand on the plate as if she might yank it away. "Have you found out anything on the case at all?"

Macdara glanced at the brown bread. "That's none of your business."

"I was about to take my break. Would you like to see our garden out back?"

Macdara glanced at Chris Gorden's table. "Are you sure it's me you want to ask?"

"I'll see you out there," Siobhán said.

"I'm not talking shop," Macdara said.

"Nobody asked you to," Siobhán said. She took off her apron, set it over the counter, and headed out to the back-yard.

The air was fresh, and the sun was out. Siobhán gazed around the yard, taking note of where the gardai had trampled the grass and the flowers. A rectangular patch where they used to have a vegetable garden was withered and brown. They hadn't kept it up; there was too much to do. Macdara's eyes landed on her scooter, parked just outside the back door. She really wanted to bring it inside.

"Did you get the locks changed?" Macdara asked, as if reading her mind.

"Séamus is going to get to them," she said.

"I'll have a word with him," Macdara said. "The sooner the better."

Siobhán put her hands on her hips and studied him. "Why, Garda Flannery."

"What?"

"You wouldn't be so worried about me safety if you thought James was the killer."

Macdara kicked the ground with the tip of his boot, digging up dirt. "It still doesn't look good for him." He glanced at her scooter. "Is that yours?"

"With James gone, I need it to run errands."

"Be careful. Don't ride it in the rain."

"That would be almost every day, like."

"It's not safe in the rain."

"I'll be careful. What have you learned since we last talked?"

"Nothing to worry your head about," Macdara said.

"What did Sheila say about the rubbish bag and the broken glass?"

Macdara sighed. She was wearing him down. "Sheila and Pio were having a domestic. Sheila threw a vase. It shattered against the wall. Pio threw out the broken glass, but she went to fetch it to see if she could put it back together."

"Sheila's allergic to flowers."

"So you keep saying," Macdara said.

"It's true. She can't have them in her shop. So why would she care so much about a vase?"

"Maybe she puts artificial flowers in it."

"I've never seen her do that."

"Damn it, Siobhán. I can't arrest someone for throwing a vase or bringing a rubbish bag inside the house." Macdara swiped off his cap and slammed it against his thigh.

"What about her black eye?"

"They didn't admit to that, now, but it doesn't look recent. A week maybe. I'll drop off a number of a professional I know who deals with domestic situations. But the rest will be up to her. Although for all we know, Sheila's the one doing the abusing. She must have twenty stone on him."

"That's not nice."

"The world isn't always nice. You know yourself."

"What if Niall was blackmailing the two of them? They could be co-murderers."

Macdara stared at her. He wasn't as traditionally handsome as Chris Gorden, but she liked his rough edges . . . as long as they weren't aimed at her. Right now he was looking at her as if he felt sorry for her. She didn't like that either.

"I'm sorry you didn't get to go to college."

"What are ye on about?" she asked.

"You've got a good mind. And a good heart. You should go to college."

"Who would mind the young ones? Run the bistro?"

"I'm just saying. I hope you find a way."

"Well, right now I'm trying to find a killer."

"That's not your job. It's mine."

"What else have you got?"

"I think you're onto something about Niall blackmailing someone else. I'm trying to follow up on that."

"Don't forget to ask them where they were the night of the murder."

"Why, thank you very much. Don't forget to preheat the cooker."

Siobhán shook her head. Macdara smiled. She smiled back, then turned away when the eye contact lasted a bit too long. She meant what she said. She was trying to catch a killer, and there wasn't time for anything else. "What do we know about the Yank?"

"The one you were flirting with in there?"

"I was not flirting."

"You were flirting."

"You catch more flies with honey."

"Yea? Well, why in the feck would you want to catch flies in the first place?" He had her there. "What do you know about him?" she asked again.

Macdara sighed. "The usual shite. Said he's traveling around Ireland, taking a year off college, looking for his family crest, writing a book, for all I know."

"Any connection to Niall?"

"Could be."

"Like what?"

"I don't know. I just said 'Could be.'"

He was definitely jealous. "Did you check the CCTVs?"

"Yes," he said after what seemed to be a silent deliberation. "I'm in the process of checking all the CCTVs."

"In the process? Meaning you haven't checked them?"

"What should I be looking for? The killer to stare into one of the cameras and confess?"

"Séamus said he left O'Rourke's at half one and headed home. You can verify that. And maybe one camera will prove that it wasn't James chasing Niall around town."

"Who said anything about chasing?"

"I think the killer was chasing Niall. That's how they ended up back here." Once again Siobhán looked around the garden.

"It rained that night," Macdara said. "We couldn't get any footprints."

Siobhán's eye landed on the glass jar where the spare key had been hidden. Although Siobhán had long since removed the key, the jar was still resting on top of the hole where it had been originally buried. The gardai hadn't considered it evidence because nothing had seemed amiss at the time. But something about the way the sun was shining on it set off alarm bells. There was definitely something not quite right about it. It wasn't the same jar. It looked close enough, but theirs had a green tint, and this one was blue. She gasped.

"What?" Macdara said. She ran up to the jar. She held it up.

"It's not the same jar."

"Are you sure?"

"Positive. Our old jar was impossible to open. The lid was rusted shut. You would have had to break it open to get the key. Wait. Gráinne and Ann heard glass breaking, remember?"

"You think it was someone smashing open that jar?" Macdara said.

"I know it was. They replaced it, hoping we wouldn't notice." And she almost didn't. She was going to have to keep her eyes open every second. "Whoever killed Niall must have known where we kept the spare key."

"Any idea who?" Macdara didn't look convinced, but at least he was considering the idea.

"It would be easier to list the people who *didn't* know where we hid our spare key. Anyone who was ever back here chatting with my mam could have seen it."

"Check with your siblings. Make sure they didn't break the jar and were afraid to mention it."

"This could be our big break."

"How so?"

Siobhán shoved the jar at him. "I don't know. Check it for fingerprints. Take it house to house and see who has a matching set of jars."

"Everyone has jars like these. I think there are three or four in my cupboards alone."

"But it's something, isn't it?"

"Everything is something," Macdara says. "Until it's proved to be nothing."

The back door opened, and Ann poked her head out. "Alison Tierney is here to see you," she said. "And she looks as if she's swallowed a French frog." With that, Ann whirled around and let the back door slam.

Macdara looked at Siobhán for a long time. "A French frog?"

"I never have any idea what's going to come out of their gobs next or why," Siobhán said shaking her head. Macdara started to laugh, the second time Siobhán had heard him do that. Soon she was laughing with him.

"A French frog," Macdara said again as they went back inside. "Do you think he wears a wee beret?"

"Le croak," Siobhán said.

Chapter 25

Alison Tierney was seated at the table by the window, dressed in a lovely cream suit with matching heels and handbag. Her dark hair was shiny and straight, as if she'd just stepped out of a salon. When Siobhán arrived, she was texting on her mobile.

"Sit down," she ordered without even looking up. Siobhán wished she were holding the tea kettle so she could pretend to stumble and give her a bit of a scalding. Just a touch.

"I'd rather stand. We're very busy, as you can see."

Alison set her phone down and scanned the bistro as if she'd forgotten where she was. Macdara stood by the back door, watching them. Alison zeroed in on him; then her eyes flicked back to Siobhán, and the corner of her lips curled up. Siobhán couldn't tell if it was supposed to be a smile or a snarl. "It's a bit of a surprise, isn't it?"

"What is?"

"To see others dining in a place where a man has been murdered." She said it loud enough for others to turn their heads.

"Lower your voice. Those aren't even the facts."

"What am I missing?"

Siobhán bent down. "He wasn't killed inside the bistro. He was brought here. Someone is trying to set us up."

"That's not the talk in town."

"How would you know? You don't even live in this town."

"Gossip flows the same way the wind blows."

Up your arse. "If you're here about the rent, I'll have it to ye by Monday week."

"And yet you just bought a brand-new scooter."

What a Nosy Nellie. Now Siobhán really wished she had the tea kettle. "That was a work necessity."

Alison's perfectly tweezed eyebrows raised in surprise. "I didn't realize it took a scooter to run a bistro," she said. "Silly me."

"It does when you have errands to run and you're down a man."

"Speaking of James," Alison said. "I'm truly shocked to hear what he's done." She put her hand over her heart.

"Excuse me?"

Alison reached into her fancy alligator handbag and produced a stack of papers, which she smoothed out across the table with the relish of a blackjack dealer. "As the oldest, James is the only one on the lease since your parents departed." Departed. As if they'd packed up their suitcases and sailed away on a ship.

In an instant Siobhán wondered whether James had killed Niall. It was only on account of the rage she felt toward Alison at that moment, the likes of which she'd never known. She could imagine it now. How darkness could sweep one up in its funnel cloud and cause a person to do something she never imagined she could.

"Did you hear what I said? Without James, this lease is no longer valid."

"That's nonsense."

"There's a clause. If James abandons the property, the lease is null and void."

"I'll sign a new lease. Is that what you want?"

"No. I want you out."

Even if a new owner were willing to continue to rent the space to the O'Sullivans, they would never get the generous terms that Mr. Tierney had given her father. Those terms were the only reason they could afford to keep the bistro going. Without it, they would most likely have to close their doors.

"Your da would have never done this to us."

Alison waved her hand like she was brushing away a fly. "My father was too soft. He felt sorry for your father and the lot of you. I'm a businesswoman. This isn't personal."

She was probably right about that. Because in order for it to be personal, Alison Tierney would have to be a person. She was a robot. An imposter. A monster with a manicure. She had a rich husband and two kids. They lived in a neighboring town, and it seemed Alison found a way to work into every conversation the fact that she didn't live in Kilbane. They had one of those fancy limestone mansions. She probably didn't even need their rent money, yet here she was wielding the sword.

"Sit down, Siobhán, I'm not nearly finished."

Siobhán sighed. She sat. But she kept herself perched on the edge of the chair. Gráinne came over with a tea kettle. She exchanged a look with Siobhán.

"Would you like a cappuccino?" Gráinne asked.

"From here?" Alison said. She laughed. "No thanks."

"I was talking to my sister," Gráinne said.

"I'd love a cup, thank you," Siobhán said. Gráinne smiled and left. "I have the best cappuccinos in Ireland. I dare say I would hold me own with Starbucks."

Alison's eyes flicked over to the cappuccino machine. Siobhán didn't even like her looking at it. She scooted her chair over, hoping to block her view. "It looks like a very expensive piece of equipment."

"You have to spend money to make money."

"How many cappuccinos do you make?"

"Loads," Siobhán said.

"How many do you sell?"

Shite. She had her there. She was mostly the one drinking them.

"I'd say they double my energy, allow me to do the work of two," Siobhán said.

"And now three?" Alison said. Siobhán just stared at her. "With James gone?"

"He won't be gone for long," Siobhán said. "My brother didn't stab Niall Murphy in the heart with a pair of scissors in his own bistro." Even though Siobhán kept her voice low, she still crossed herself after her utterance.

"I'm sure he didn't either."

Siobhán was glad she didn't have the cappuccino yet; she would have spit out a mouthful. "You are?"

"Of course. Your brother isn't a killer." Alison waved her hand again.

"Thank God." So the woman did have some decency after all. Either that or she knew James was innocent because she was the killer.

"But between you and me, I don't trust the gardai to do much investigating when they've got a perfectly good scapegoat in jail." A creepy smile illuminated her pinched face.

"Garda Flannery wouldn't do that to James."

"Garda Flannery." The snarl was back. "Yes. I see the way you two look at each other."

"There's no way."

"I don't blame you. He's sexy."

"There's no way."

"But sexy or not, he's not a detective superintendent, is he?"

"So?"

"So if the detective superintendent thinks they've got yer man, then there isn't a thing Garda Flannery can do about it. No matter how much he wants to." She gave Siobhán another look.

"I have to get back to work." Siobhán started to stand. Alison reached out and touched her hand.

"Please. I have a proposition that I think you'll want to hear."

Siobhán sighed, then sat.

Gráinne brought her the cappuccino.

"Do you need me on the floor?" Siobhán asked Gráinne.

"We're sorted," Gráinne said. "Take all the time you need."

Alison watched Gráinne walk away. "She looks like a woman now." *She doesn't always act like it*, Siobhán wanted to say, but not in front of the likes of Alison. "Do you still want to go to college?"

Why was everyone asking her about college? It was starting to get on her nerves. "I have a lot on my plate," Siobhán said. One glance at Alison's empty place setting and she wanted to add, *unlike you*. As if it were beneath the woman to eat here. As if they didn't have the best brekkie in town.

"I finally have a buyer," Alison said. "For the bistro."

"What?" Siobhán shot out of her chair, bumping the table and rattling the cappuccino. Frothed milk sloshed out the side. Siobhán wished it would leap onto Alison's pristine suit and stain it with a T for traitor.

"His finances check out. I'm afraid he wants to set up his own business in the space, but he's willing to give you time to vacate."

"Time to vacate?"

"To figure out what you're going to do instead. Why don't you go to college like you planned?"

"You're the one who would make money on the sale of

the property—that is, if you're telling the truth about a buyer. But we'd have nothing. You can't do this. We have a lease."

"James had a lease," Allison said emphatically.

"Has a lease," Siobhán answered with equally gusto. "I'm telling ye he's going to be out soon."

"He'll have to be out in thirty days."

"Or what?"

"Or you're all out."

"You're despicable."

Alison reached out again to touch her hand. Siobhán yanked it away. She stood. "I'm not the enemy. In fact, this is for your own good."

"Kicking me and my four siblings out is for my own good?"

"Go to college. Move everyone to Dublin. Get out of this small town."

"This is our home. Our livelihood."

"I told you. I have a proposition."

"We're not leaving."

"Agree to it now and I'll buy you out of a portion of your lease."

"What does that mean?"

"I'll give you ten thousand euro from the sale."

Ten thousand euro. The exact amount Niall wanted from her. "Why would you do that?"

"Because I'm not heartless. It's not even much in today's world, but it's fair."

"Kicking us out of home and job, that's fair, is it?"

"Take the offer. In the next twenty minutes it goes away."

"That's not fair."

"I don't have time to waste. If I don't sell now, who knows when I'll have another buyer."

"Who is this buyer?"

Alison began to blink rhythmically as if sending an SOS

signal to someone at a neighboring table. Was the buyer here in the bistro? "I can't say."

"You won't say."

"Ladies?" Macdara said from behind Sibohan.

Siobhán jumped and whirled around.

"Don't go sneaking up on a person like that," Siobhán scolded. Alison had twisted her pear-shaped.

"Sorry. Is everything alright here?"

"Alison just offered me ten thousand euro to abandon the bistro and move out of town," Siobhán said.

"What?" Macdara looked truly shocked.

"Apparently she has some sort of mysterious buyer."

"Who?" Macdara demanded.

"She can't say," Siobhán said. "But the timing is interesting, don't you think?"

"What are you on about?" Alison asked. Her eyes narrowed to slits.

"It's almost as if someone placed Niall's body here thinking it would put us out of business."

Alison screeched her chair back and stood. "I don't like what you're implying."

"I'm not implying," Siobhán said. "I'm stating it outright." She turned to Macdara. "She's talking about a clause that if James 'abandons the property' the lease is null and void. Just when did you find this clause? Before the murder? Or did you add it right after?"

"What exactly are you accusing me of?" Alison said.

Siobhán spoke to Macdara as if Alison wasn't there. "Ten thousand euro she offered me. The exact amount Niall was trying to extort from me."

"You are out of your mind," Alison said.

"We're not going anywhere," Siobhán said. "Get out of my bistro." Siobhán started to walk away.

"You're making a mistake," Alison said.

Siobhán whirled around. "I'm sure I've made a lifetime of mistakes in the past year. But this isn't one of them."

The two women glared at each other until Alison's phone dinged. She read the text, and a look of alarm came into her eyes. She practically flew from the table, and before one could say "Hail Mary" she was out the door. Her figure sprinted by the window, and Siobhán watched, intrigued, as she practically dove into her car and peeled out. You could hear her tires squeal all the way down the street.

Siobhán turned to Macdara. "Is it me, or was that odd?"

Macdara shifted. "She did seem to be in a bit of a hurry." He went outside and stood on the footpath, staring in the direction where Alison had taken off. Siobhán went up to the window, and Gráinne and Ann followed. They watched him watching the road.

"Odd," Gráinne said.

"Totally odd," Ann added.

"You should follow her," Gráinne said.

Siobhán hushed her, then leaned into her sisters. "My thoughts exactly. Are you two okay holding down the fort?"

"We've got this," Gráinne said. "See what the witch is up to."

"Be nice," Siobhán said, although she couldn't agree more.

Siobhán was almost out the back door when someone grabbed her arm. She whirled around to face Macdara.

"Where's the fire?" he said.

"We're out of tea," Siobhán said. It was the first thing that came to her. Out of tea. What a ridiculous notion. Macdara must have thought the same thing, for he frowned. He was still touching her elbow. Siobhán gently extracted herself, smiled, and shot out the door.

Chapter 26

Siobhán revved up her scooter and took off in the direction Alison had headed after she peeled out. Soon she spotted Alison's silver SUV just beyond King's Castle, taking a left at the end of the street. By the time Siobhán caught up and took the left, the SUV was out of sight. This particular road continued out of town, or you could take another left on Hardy Street, which bordered the back of the town, just beyond the wall. Siobhán would take the left, and if there was no sign of Alison, she would simply take the loop to the next entrance gate and go home.

As soon as Siobhán took the left, she spotted Alison just ahead. She was just on the other side of the Dominican Priory, and it struck Siobhán where Alison might be headed. Had Alison been going home, she would have continued straight ahead. Had she been going anywhere in town, she would have stayed inside the wall. So, barring any other friends she might have who lived along this road, there was one destination that stood out. Mary Murphy's house was halfway down this street, to the right up on the hill. But why in the world would Alison be visiting her?

Just when Siobhán thought she had it figured out, Alison's car pulled over to the side of the road. Shoot. Siobhán would either have to turn around or pass her. If she passed her, she would be caught. There weren't enough other redheaded young women on scooters in Kilbane. She hadn't really been thinking the clandestine part through.

Just then someone approached going the opposite direction on a bicycle. The rider was wearing a helmet, but Siobhán immediately thought of Séamus. Alison had been speeding, and she was lucky she hadn't run him over. Siobhán reduced her speed enough to have a gawk, and just as she neared, the rider removed his helmet.

It wasn't Séamus at all; it was the Yank, Chris Gorden. She would have recognized his movie-star looks from even farther back. Was he pulling over to see if Alison needed help, or was this an arranged meeting? If only they had been on the other side of the wall, there would have been a place to hide.

Then again, the first town entrance was just beyond where they were standing. If they were there long enough, Siobhán could try and get to a point on the opposite side of the wall where she could eavesdrop. If she left her scooter a ways away and kept to the ground, she might go undetected.

The perfect place to park her scooter would be the Kilbane Museum, which was situated at the end of the road that led to the field bordered by the wall. It was a tiny museum, to be sure, but a local treasure. Filled with Kilbane history and memorabilia, including the Troubles and the potato famine, the museum was staffed by locals who took turns volunteering. Siobhán loved spending afternoons riffling through its crates of old photographs and trinkets. She pulled up alongside it and turned off the engine.

Before the murder, Siobhán wouldn't have thought twice about parking on the footpath without a lock and chain, but

Niall's death had changed all of that. She still didn't have a lock and chain, but she would definitely worry about it.

It wasn't possible to put a price on peace of mind, but Kilbane's had been shattered. Love they neighbor had now become Be very wary of your neighbor. Siobhán looked across the field and tried to estimate the distance from the museum to where Alison and Chris were meeting. Before heading off, she glanced in the window and saw Bridie standing in the museum's back room. She was standing near the attic, and the ladder was pulled down.

The few times Siobhán had volunteered, there was no need to go upstairs among the dusty boxes. She wondered what Bridie was doing. She would have to pop in when she was done listening in on Alison and Chris. Not that she was going to come out and ask Bridie if she and Niall had been having an affair, but maybe she would think of something.

Siobhán hurried across the field, ducking as she went, hoping Alison and Chris would still be there by the time she reached the place where they were talking. The tinker's horse was out, farther down the field than usual, and Siobhán wished she had a carrot. It would have been the perfect cover were she to be spotted. She supposed she could pretend to be feeding the poor thing a carrot, but decided that was just too cruel to the horse. Besides, if he nipped at her when she did have treats, he'd probably chomp a finger off to punish her for coming empty-handed. When she was about twelve feet from her destination, she dropped to the ground and began crawling through the grass.

As she crawled toward the stone wall, she could only pray no local residents were out in their back gardens, and so she was a wee bit relieved when it started to rain. Between the mist and the fact that her red hair was tucked up in her helmet, maybe no one would spot her. By the time she reached the wall, her linen pants were soaking wet. She was going to have to start carrying a change of clothes. She finally reached the wall, huddled against it, and strained to listen. In addition to the pattering of the rain, she could hear the swoosh of traffic on the road, and it was only after several seconds that Alison's high-pitched voice rose above the din. At first, Siobhán only caught a few words. *Bank. Obligations.* And then a phrase: "It's only a matter of time."

"Are you sure they want to leave?" Chris asked. "I didn't get that feeling today."

"I told you to stay away," Alison said.

"But why? If it's as you say."

Alison said something about it being a delicate situation, and something about bittersweet. Then she mentioned the bank again. Just then Siobhán felt something strange bump into her backside, followed by a snort. She gave a little cry and whirled around to see the tinker's horse directly behind her, sniffing at her backside. She thought only dogs did that. She heard Chris say something about the horse, then heard footsteps. She flattened herself against the wall just as Chris reached his hand over the wall to stroke the horse. It whinnied and rubbed its nose against his hand. *Would you look at that, the tinker's horse didn't try to bite the Yank the way he did her. The cheeky little bugger.*

"Who owns him?" Chris asked.

"A tinker. You don't want to be touching it. It's probably diseased."

"His ribs are showing."

Alison launched into a mini-tirade about the travelers, like most in town would, and Siobhán couldn't help but wonder how it sounded to the American. Like they were all a bit prejudiced? The truth was, they were, and listening to the disdain in Alison's voice made Siobhán feel slightly ashamed.

"If I wasn't convinced it was James who stabbed Niall, I wouldn't be surprised if it was one of the tinkers," Alison said.

"You think James did it?" Chris asked.

"He's been arrested. The gardai wouldn't do that for no reason, don't you think?" *How dare she? Telling Siobhán she knew James didn't do it, now spreading rumors that he did.*

"I don't know. I only met him that night in the pub. He just didn't seem like he was in any shape to pull it off."

"He blacked out is what I heard. Doesn't remember a thing. Even more reason to believe he did it," Alison said.

"I don't know. I think scissors to the heart requires a bit of coordination," Chris said.

Siobhán wanted to cheer Chris on. He was thinking this through logically, unlike a lot of people in town. How could she go on serving all these traitors who thought her brother was a murderer? Maybe she should move her entire brood to Dublin.

"Maybe he sobered up by the time he killed Niall," Alison said.

"Maybe," Chris said. He didn't sound like he believed it.

"I must be off," Alison said. "Will you sit tight another couple of months?"

"If it's as you say, I will," he said.

"Naomi's Bistro won't last past the summer," Alison said. "I can promise you that."

Siobhán was seething by the time she arrived at the museum. Her scooter was still there, propped on the footpath next to the front door. For a second Siobhán could bask in the lie that Kilbane was the charming town it had always been. Full of Irish cheer, and a thousand welcomes. One thousand welcomes and one wee killer. And one soul-killing landlady.

Won't last past the summer. The nerve of that woman. And the Yank. She'd been so caught up in the fact that he'd been defending James that she hadn't pieced together the rest until now. The Yank wanted to buy the bistro. So much for his flirting, and so much for his lies about traveling around Ireland for the fun of it. And there probably wasn't a book either. What else might he have been lying about? If Chris Gorden had money, and was flashing it around, Niall Murphy might very well have been sniffing around him.

This Yank was definitely a threat. Buying the bistro out from under them! The cheek of him. How dare Alison Tierney do this? Maybe she indeed was the killer. She certainly stood to profit. Maybe that's why she told Siobhán she thought James was innocent but was telling everyone else a different story.

Siobhán had a feeling that she was dealing with a very smart killer. Why couldn't the culprit be one of those dumb ones who get caught on camera really mucking it up?

Either way, she had to stop Alison Tierney from selling the bistro. And Alison had made it clear that unless James was out in thirty days, their lease would default and she would be free to sell it. James would never forgive himself if he thought his arrest made them lose the bistro. He might never recover from it. Siobhán had to find the killer. She had to get them out of this living nightmare.

Siobhán opened the door to the museum, hoping Bridie was still in. The door squeaked, and the smell of days gone by came back to life. She wished she had more time to go through the place; she never got tired of the old photographs of people gathered in the town square, stretches of land where houses and shops now stood, stories of the soldiers who fought and died. But memory lane would have to wait for another day.

Bridie wasn't anywhere to be seen.

Siobhán glanced at the ladder. It was still pulled down. She strained to listen but didn't hear a peep from above. Had Bridie left? The door was supposed to be locked after anyone left, but it wasn't unusual for one to forget.

"Bridie?" Siobhán called out. "It's Siobhán. Are you up

there?" Upstairs, she heard the sound of something being dragged. She froze. It was followed by footsteps, and then there was a loud crash, followed by a woman's cry. Siobhán ran to the bottom of the ladder.

"Hello?" she yelled up. "Are ye alright?" There was no answer. Why wouldn't she answer? Why hadn't she just gone home?

Siobhán took a deep breath and stepped onto the first rung of the ladder. Just then she looked up to see a large box hovering above the opening, directly above her head. Before she could react, the box came hurtling straight at her and slammed into her temple before crashing to the floor and scattering heavy tomes every which way.

Siobhán cried out as pain roared through her skull. She was still clinging onto the ladder when the first wave of dizziness hit her fast and hard. She swayed and fell to the floor. Was it Bridie up there? Had she done that on purpose?

Siobhán lifted her head, and through the little window she could see her scooter. Behind her the ladder creaked. Whoever had dumped the box of books on her head was on his or her way down. If it was the killer, Siobhán was never going to make it to the door in time.

But that wasn't going to stop her from trying. As pain thudded through her head and the world around her turned slightly fuzzy, Siobhán began to slither along the floor to the exit.

Chapter 27

"Stay there," a female voice bellowed out. Siobhán froze mid-slither. "Oh my God."

It was Bridie. Siobhán recognized her voice, but her head hurt too much to turn it around.

"Did I do that?" Bridie appeared in front of her, alarm planted on her face.

"A box of concrete slammed into me head."

"Oh my God, oh my God." Bridie wrung her hands. "I had no idea you were there."

"I yelled."

"I didn't hear you." Bridie knelt down. Her hair was falling out of her pink sparkly headscarf and the top several buttons of her blouse were buttoned wrong. "Let me see." Bridie gingerly removed Siobhán's hand from her temple. "You have a goose egg, alright," she said. "You need ice."

"What were you doing up there?" Siobhán asked as Bridie helped her into a sitting position.

"I wanted to go through those books, but they were too heavy to carry down." A crash came from upstairs, then footsteps.

Siobhán cried out. "Is there someone else up there?" She took in Bridie's disheveled state again, the buttons on her blouse all awry.

Bridie glanced at her top, and for a second she looked stricken. Then she started to laugh. "Please, don't be telling stories. You'll know yourself when you're married. You have to find ways to keep it exciting. And no one ever comes into this place anymore. I thought, of course, that we'd have a few minutes to ourselves."

"You're saying it's Séamus up there. Right?"

"Course it is." Bridie's eyes narrowed. "Who else would it be?"

Siobhán ignored the question. "Why isn't he coming down?"

"He'd be redder than me right now if he had to face ye."

"But you said you didn't know I was here."

"I'm sure he knows now; we haven't exactly kept our voices down." Bridie offered Siobhán her hand and helped lift her up. "There's no ice here. Do you want me to drive you home?"

Siobhán glanced at the ladder, then at the books splayed on the floor. They were thick volumes. That box could have killed her. Who was really up there with Bridie? Seeing as how it almost cost her her life, she deserved to know. "May I have a word with Séamus? Seeing as he's already here?"

Bridie turned red and shook her head. "I told ye. He'd be too embarrassed."

"Séamus," Siobhán called out as loud as she could.

Bridie stepped back as if she'd been slapped. "What are ye doing?"

"No more games," Siobhán said. "Who is up there?" Siobhán took a step toward the ladder, but Bridie cut her off.

"I told ye. Me husband."

"Séamus," Siobhán called out again.

"What in the world is wrong with ye?" Bridie said, hands on hips.

"Everything is wrong with me. My parents are dead. My brother is accused of murder. And that handsome Yank is in cahoots with Alison Tierney to buy my bistro!"

"What?"

"I just heard them talking about it. I already knew she was up to something. She told me that technically James has abandoned the property and soon the lease will be null and void. Now I know why she's so eager to shove us out."

Bridie looked truly distraught. "She can't do that. We won't let her."

"You should have seen the look on her face when she came into the bistro and saw folks were still coming. She thought Niall's murder would scare them off for good."

Bridie gasped.

"What?" Siobhán asked.

"You don't think she killed Niall, do you?"

"To put me out of business?"

"She's been after that property ever since her da passed."

"I know. And I don't like her. But murder is a stretch, don't you think?"

"Money is always a motive for murder," Bridie said.

So is love, and betrayal, Siobhán thought. *For all I know, it isn't even Séamus up there. Maybe Niall found out you were having an affair and was blackmailing you.* "Séamus?" Siobhán called out. She stepped closer to the stairs and called again.

"What are you doing?" Bridie said.

"I have to know it's really him up there."

"Excuse me?"

"When I came into the cycle shop that day—you looked like I'd just caught you at something. Like you were up to no good."

"I told you. Niall was helping me buy a gear for Séamus's racing bike."

"His birthday is in December."

"What are ye driving at?"

"Who buys birthday presents six months ahead of time?"

"Just what are you accusing me of? Murder?"

"I'm just trying to make the pieces fit."

A second later came the clomping of boots, and Séamus popped into view. He was red in the face alright, but he was also sporting his usual grin. Bridie folded her arms across her chest and glared at Siobhán.

"Looks like the two of you are going to be chin-wagging for hours," Séamus said. "And I've got to get back to the shop." He winked at Siobhán, then came down and kissed Bridie on the cheek.

"How's the scooter working out?" Séamus asked.

"It's grand," Siobhán said.

"Good on ye." He kissed Bridie again, and was out the door.

The minute it shut, Bridie grabbed Siobhán's hand and began to pull her toward one of the cupboard doors. Was she going to shove her in there?

"I have to get home," Siobhán said. "They need me at the bistro."

"This will only take a few minutes."

Bridie unlocked the door and swung it open. Siobhán stepped back. She'd grab an old fork to defend herself if she had to. There was a tray of them on the next shelf over. Imagine, historic flatware.

Bridie stepped back. "Have a look," she said.

Siobhán stepped forward and looked into the cupboard. The shelves were crammed with boxes of all sorts and sizes. Some of them were wrapped. It was like a miniature gift shop. Siobhán spied another black and silver scarf. So much for it being one of a kind, she thought. Courtney had literally pulled the scarf right over her eyes.

Bridie snatched a package off the shelf and tossed it to Siobhán. She caught it. The return address was from a cycle

shop in Dublin. "It's the gear. Open it if you don't believe me."

"I believe you," Siobhán said, tossing it back to Bridie.

"I always buy me presents in advance," Bridie said. "I
like knowing they're here, ready to surprise someone."

"That's very sweet."

"Did you really think me capable of murder?" Bridie
asked. She tossed her head of curly hair and for a second
looked flattered.

"I thought Niall might have been extorting you," Siobhán
said. "Like he was me."

"What are you on about?"

"I'd rather not say. It was all a big lie anyway."

"Séamus and I have been there for you. You're like family to us. I can't believe you would think that of me. Come to
think—why would you bring your young ones to me if you
thought I was the killer?"

Bridie had her there. Siobhán hated that she'd just hurt
Bridie. "I didn't think you were a killer. I just thought
maybe you were holding back a piece of the puzzle."

"How so?"

"It was just the look on your face when I walked in on
you and Niall. You looked as if you wanted to crawl under
the floorboards."

"I was nervous Séamus was going to walk in and ruin the
surprise." Bridie put the package back on the shelf. "They
let me have this cupboard. Otherwise Séamus would find
everything."

"Those are all gifts?"

"Nah. Some are items to sell in the shop. Courtney likes
to hold some back. Make them seem like one of a kind."

"I know she does," Siobhán said. She suddenly remembered the new glass jar in the garden. "Does Courtney carry
mason jars at her shop?"

"You'd have better luck at the hardware store," Bridie said.

"But did she have any? And did anyone buy one lately? Or maybe one has gone missing?"

Bridie shook her head. "Not that I'm aware. Why?"

"One of ours broke," Siobhán said.

"The one in the garden?"

"That's the one," Siobhán said. She knew it. Everyone who was ever out there with Mam knew about their secret hiding place.

"I miss yer ma," Bridie said. "I used to love our chats in your back garden. The kids would be running around, getting into things, she'd be kneeling on the ground, planting away, still able to carry on a conversation." Tears came into Bridie's eyes. She took a step toward Siobhán. "I didn't kill Niall. You have to believe me."

"I believe you." Siobhán wasn't sure if she did or not, but Bridie was so intense it seemed like the right thing to say. "You mentioned we weren't the only reason Séamus quit competitive racing. What was the other?"

Bridie looked around the shop as if checking to see if any of the pictures on the walls were listening. "I was the other reason. I read that his racing shorts, not to mention sitting on the seat of a bicycle like that day in and day out for so many hours a day, could reduce the numbers of his little swimmers. I thought maybe that was the reason I haven't been able to conceive. There. That's my secret. Are you happy now?"

"I'm so sorry," Siobhán said. "You would make the best mother."

"Aside from being a killer and all?" Bridie smiled.

"Yes," Siobhán said. "Aside from that." Might as well joke about it, although Bridie was still hurt. Hopefully she'd eventually forgive her. "I'd better get me legs under me," Siobhán headed for the door.

"I wasn't even home," Bridie called after her. Siobhán stopped.

This was news. Didn't Séamus say she gave out to him for coming home at half one? Was Bridie about to lie to her? Again? "Where were you?"

"I spent the night in Charlesville. It was my sister's anniversary. I was minding my niece and nephew. Ring her and ask her if you'd like. She'll tell ye I was there. And Séamus was with Declan all night so that's our alibis sorted."

Except Séamus had already given Bridie an alibi. One she was now contradicting. It was no use calling the sister; of course she would lie for Bridie. Siobhán was right back where she started from. Gawd, this was a thankless job. Should she confront Bridie with her lie? No. They had somewhat patched things up. Confronting her without any additional proof would just get her riled up again and defensive. Besides, Bridie would probably just come up with another lie. Siobhán would do a bit more digging first, let Bridie think she trusted her again.

"I'd best get me legs under me," Siobhán said again. Bridie followed her to the door, then put her arm on Siobhán's before she left.

"We won't let Alison Tierney take the bistro from you. Unless . . ."

"Unless?" Bridie's fingertips were ice cold on Siobhán's arm. She had an urge to shake her off, but she'd offended her enough in one day.

"Unless you don't want to carry it on?"

"How could you ask me such a thing?"

"Please don't take offense. I'm only thinking of you. It would be natural if you still wanted to go to Dublin. Start your life."

"I wouldn't leave my brothers and sisters."

"Of course not. But they could go with you."

"Alison said the same thing."

"Did she now?"

"But all she wants is the money. I bet the Yank is willing to pay a fortune."

"I'll ask Courtney," Bridie said. "I'm sure she knows more than either of us."

"Thank you." Normally Bridie would have hugged Siobhán, but this time she kept her distance and simply nodded. *Oh, Jaysus.* It was beginning to look like accusing folks of murder might have made Siobhán a good sleuth, but it also made her a terrible, terrible friend. And Siobhán knew more than anyone that there had been many, many times in her life when she couldn't have survived without a friend. She had a sudden ache for Maria and Aisling. Hadn't they heard about the murder by now? Why hadn't they called? Because they were in Dublin, and their lives were going on without her. Siobhán would have to try and give them a call—remind her best friends that she was still alive.

Chapter 28

"Mary Murphy is having a wake?" Siobhán asked Macdara for the third time. "Like from days gone by?" The traditional Irish wake, in which the body was laid out in the home and people celebrated the life of the deceased, was a thing of the past for most of modern Ireland. Instead the funeral Mass and burial were the norm. Her parents had spoken of the Irish wakes of old, and her da especially always had entertaining stories to tell.

She'd always secretly wanted to experience an Irish wake, but when it came to Niall and the way he passed, she thought it was terribly morbid. Then again, maybe the killer would show up at the wake. For Siobhán, it would be a perfect excuse to see all the potential suspects in one place.

"She waited so long to get the body back I think she just wants to have him close for a while," Macdara said, taking off his cap and running his fingers through his hair. He looked tired, and she had an urge to sit him down and give him a proper cuddle. But, of course, that was just as inappropriate as Mary Murphy holding a wake for Niall.

"I have a feeling she's using the funds you raised to host

it," Macdara said. "She's even hired Pio's band to play." It was ironic, alright. Niall Murphy put down every bit of music that wasn't screeching. She remembered him once listening to Pio play the spoons. *The bollix! Pure shite.* Niall went on for another ten minutes, colorfully advising exactly what Pio should do with those spoons. He'd never know that Pio would have the last laugh.

"Ah, sure lookit," Siobhán said, "I don't mind how she spends the money. It's John Butler you should be worried about."

Macdara raised his eyebrow. "I thought he had an alibi."

Siobhán bit a smile back. If she didn't know better, it sounded like Macdara was actually starting to listen to her. "He was very insistent that all the monies go directly to him. He doesn't trust Mary Murphy to pay for the services."

"We'll let them sort that out for themselves," Macdara said.

"This is going to be the strangest wake anyone has ever been to."

"I was thinking the same thing."

"What?"

Macdara shook his head. "You have that look in yer eye."

"What look?"

"The look that says you're thinking Niall's wake is the perfect place to continuing your snooping."

"I was thinking no such t'ing."

"I'll be keeping my eye on you."

"I look forward to it." They locked eyes. A zap of fondness seized Siobhán as they openly regarded one another. Macdara broke off the connection, and without another word he was out the door.

A few nights later, most of the folks of Kilbane were inside Mary Murphy's farmhouse, with Niall laid out in his bed, once again in a suit. Only this one was darker and looked like a thing of the past. Siobhán wondered if it had been his father's. Candles flickered in the bedroom, and Siobhán couldn't help but stare at the crucifix laid across Niall's chest and the rosary beads clutched in his hand. *So pale, so cold. So temporary.*

In the old tradition, the bed sheets were pulled out and hung to the ground. She avoided looking at his chest, for every time she thought of it, she saw that flash of hot-pink protruding from his heart. *Heartbreak. The method of killing feels like heartbreak.*

Now was not the time. Siobhán crossed herself, knelt, and said her prayers. She was about to leave when she heard several footsteps approaching, and angry voices. Whoever was coming in, they were arguing. They would clam up the minute they spotted Siobhán. She squatted down and slid underneath the bed, directly under Niall's reposed body.

She could barely fit, and to make matters worse the confining space was filled with dusty old magazines. Siobhán was definitely going to sneeze if she stayed under there for long.

"You. Of all people to lie to the guards," the male voice said. "Not to mention the rest of us."

Siobhán realized with a hitch in her heart that the voice belonged to Eoin.

"I told James. He begged me not to tell."

And the second voice belonged to Ann. Siobhán crawled out from under the bed. "Begged you not to tell what, like?" she demanded, as she got to her feet and began brushing dust from her black dress. Ann screamed. So did Eoin.

"Shhh," Siobhán said. "It's just me." Ann kept screaming. Siobhán clapped her hand over her sister's mouth. Ann jerked out of Siobhán's grasp, throwing her off balance. She stumbled back and bumped into one of the bedside tables.

"Watch out," Eoin yelled. Siobhán whirled around just as the candle on the table toppled over.

Siobhán lunged for the candle, but it was too late; a little flame was already licking at a lace doily as smoke and the smell of burning fabric rose into the air. Eoin leapt forward, and before anyone could tell him not to, he was grabbing at the bed sheet, pulling on it, as if he was going to use it to douse the flames. Niall's body slid stiffly to the left as Eoin tugged on the sheet.

"Stop that," Siobhán said to Eoin. "Find water," she shouted to Ann.

"What in heaven's name is this?" Father Kearney stood in the doorway, a bible clutched to his chest. "Jaysus, Mary, and Joseph," he said as he stared at flames. His eyes then slid to Niall's body lying sideways on his deathbed.

"Oh Jaysus, what are ye doing to my boy, my precious boy?" Mary Murphy pushed her way into the room, a cigarette in one hand and a bottle of whiskey in the other.

"Water," Ann shouted running into the room and knocking into Mary Murphy. Whiskey sloshed on the floor, and Ann yelped.

"Something burned me," Ann said.

"Her cigarette," Siobhán said. "Hurry, douse the flames." Ann reached for Mary Murphy's whiskey.

"Not alcohol," Siobhán yelled. "The pitcher of water on the dresser!"

Ann grabbed it and poured it over the dancing flames. There was a hiss, and then the fire was out. Water dripped down the side of the table and onto the floor. In the other room, the band struck up and began belting out a rousing rendition of "The Irish Rover." Eoin, who had a beautiful voice, but only used it to calm himself down when he was nervous, began to sing along.

On the fourth of July eighteen hundred and six

We set sail from the sweet cove of Cork . . .

"My poor boy, my boy, my wonderful boy," Mary Murphy cried. Siobhán glanced over at Niall. What was she on about? Sure, he was in a new position, but otherwise he wasn't the least bit disturbed by the commotion.

"I'm sorry," Siobhán said. "We were saying a prayer, and I backed into the table." She stared into Mary Murphy's eyes without blinking. She had just lied in front of Niall, his poor mother, and Father Kearney. She was going to have to go to confession.

"It's bad enough you couldn't even bother cleaning yourself up to pay your respects," Mary said, eyeing the streaks of dust on her dress. "But you almost set him aflame. If he had wanted to be cremated, I would have done it myself."

Siobhán gasped at the comment, but as Mary Murphy drew closer, the smell of whiskey reminded her of the state of mind Niall's mam was in.

Ann started to pray out loud as Eoin and Father Kearney straightened Niall's body. *"The Lord is my shepherd, I shall not haunt."*

"What?" Siobhán interrupted. *Did she just say* haunt*?*

"He leadeth me to greener pastors—"

"For feck's sake, Ann, has it been that long since we've gone to Mass?"

Father Kearney cleared his throat. "The 23rd Psalm isn't part of the Roman Catholic Mass," he said, sounding quite affronted.

Siobhán cocked her head. "Are you sure?"

"Quite sure," Father Kearney said.

"It has been awhile so," Siobhán said. "Thanks for clearing that up, Father." Father Kearney nodded, then frowned.

Eoin's voice intruded into the room.: *"She'd got several blasts, she'd twenty-seven masts, and we called her the Irish Rover."*

"I still don't get what I said wrong," Ann said.

Siobhán turned to Ann. "It's want, and pastures. Not haunt and pastors."

"Are ye sure?" Ann turned to Father Kearney, who simply stared.

"We know it's not part of Mass, Father, but surely you can help us out," Siobhán urged.

"It's want, and pastures," Father Kearney said reluctantly.

"That's odd," Ann said.

"Greener *pastors*?" Siobhán said. "What in the world would that mean?"

"I thought it meant one that was more pure. Fresh, like."

"I have been a terrible guardian," Siobhán said.

Father Kearney put his hand on Siobhán's back, and then Ann's. "Perhaps we should give Mary Murphy a bit of peace?"

"Of course."

Just as Father Kearney began to herd the O'Sullivans toward the door, Mary Murphy threw herself on the bed next to Niall, sobbing. "I thought wakes were supposed to be happy, like," Eoin whispered.

"Shh," Siobhán said. Just as they'd almost reached the exit, Ciarán bounded up. Siobhán could tell by the looks of him that he'd been stuffing himself with sweets.

"What's the difference between an Irish wedding and an Irish wake?" he said, upbeat.

"Not now," Siobhán said.

"One less drunk," Ciarán exclaimed. Mary Murphy wailed louder. Father Kearney pinched the bridge of his nose.

"I don't get it," Ann said.

"I'm sorry, Father Kearney," Siobhán said. "Please forgive us."

"Amen," Ann said. Siobhán felt so traumatized that for a moment she forgot all about Ann and Eoin's exchange. What secret was Ann keeping? It was even more infuriating that James knew something he hadn't told her. It was hard enough figuring out this murder without her own kin turning against her. Didn't they know she was doing this all for them?

The second they were home, Siobhán was going to have to get to the bottom of it. Just as they entered the sitting room and Siobhán was considering having a gawk at the food table, someone touched her arm. She turned to find Chris Gorden standing in front of her. He looked so handsome in his suit that for a second Siobhán forgot she was standing in front of the man who might put them out of business.

"I was hoping I would see you here," he said.

"I won't be staying long," Siobhán said. "I have a bistro to run."

"I'm sure you could close for a day," Chris said.

"You'd love that, wouldn't you?"

"Excuse me?" Chris tilted his gorgeous face like a curious dog.

"I don't care who you are, or what you're doing here. But if you think you're going to buy that property out from under us, you've got another think coming." She started to walk away. Darn him. She really wanted to try Courtney's soda bread. Chris grabbed her arm. Siobhán yanked free and glared at him.

He held his hands up and backed away as if he was slightly afraid of her. "I was told you wanted to sell the bistro."

"You were lied to. It's our home. It's our family business. Everyone knows that."

"I didn't know."

"That's because you don't belong."

"I'd like to."

"Then stop making deals with Alison Tierney. She's been out to get our property ever since her father died."

"I didn't know anything about this." He looked around. "Again. She said you wanted to sell. That you'd be off to Trinity College in the fall."

"That was the plan before my parents were killed in a car accident and I was left to take care of my siblings and the bistro. If I left now they'd be orphans. Alison knew my plans had changed."

"Oh my God. I am so sorry."

"I don't want your pity. I'm just telling you like it is. That bistro is the only thing keeping me and my siblings fed, and housed, and clothed."

"Alison must have misunderstood."

"Guess again. I told ye she's been trying to kick us out ever since her father passed away. He had a generous lease agreement with my father. Because, believe it or not, folks around here used to look after each other."

"I believe it. I'll back out of the sale."

Siobhán put her hands on her hips. "The town loves Naomi's. Whatever you put there would fail. Nobody would support you doing a thing like that to us."

"Did you just miss the part where I said I'll back out of the sale?"

"Just like that?"

"Of course. Alison assured me you wanted to sell."

"We don't."

"Which is why I'm going to back out of the sale."

"I see."

"You still look rather pissed."

"Are you really into Celtic myths?"

"Okay, non sequitur, I can deal. I take it you've been asking around about me?" His grin turned wolfish.

"I've been asking around about everybody," Siobhán said.

"So I've heard. Am I on your list? I have to be, right? As an outsider?"

"I have no idea what you're talking about." He was actually at the very top of the list, and not by name; he was listed as: The Yank.

"Why don't you go on a date with me, and I'll tell you everything there is to know about me."

Siobhán's heart tap-danced even though she was shaking her head no. Why was her heart doing that? Was it beating this fast because she liked the Yank or because she was terrified that Macdara would find out and think she liked the Yank? "This isn't a good time."

"I heard. I'm sorry." He moved in closer and bent down so that he could whisper in her ear. It made her shiver. She prayed Macdara wasn't here and watching. She hadn't seen him, but the house was packed, and he could be anywhere. "I saw your brother that night. He wasn't in any shape to murder anyone."

"I know," Siobhán said. She took a few steps back. "But knowing it and proving it are two very different things."

"If anyone can prove it, I bet you can," Chris said.

"You don't even know me," Siobhán said.

"I know enough," Chris said.

The Yank smiled, and Siobhán grabbed a bottle of whiskey off the table along with a glass. She was most generous with the pour. Chris watched her with an amused expression on his gorgeous face. She threw back the whiskey and glared at him. "What?"

"May I be blunt?"

"You're American, aren't you?"

"You are the most gorgeous creature I've ever laid eyes on."

"Oh." An embarrassed warmth spread through Siobhán, and she couldn't think of an appropriate response. She poured herself another glass of whiskey instead. Chris raised his eyebrow. Siobhán held up the bottle. "Do you want one?"

"With you? Absolutely." He found a glass, and Siobhán poured. They clinked glasses.

"Sláinte," Siobhán said.

"May he rest in peace," Chris said.

"Right," Siobhán said. She avoided his gaze. He shouldn't be hitting on her like this at a wake, and she shouldn't be enjoying it so much. "Alison Tierney is going to go absolutely mental."

"I'll tell her I'm looking for something less centrally located," Chris said. With his perfect teeth shining at her, and his dimple so close up, it was hard to tell whether or not he was messing with her.

Chapter 29

Siobhán had completely wasted the opportunities at the wake. She didn't learn a thing apart from the fact that her own siblings were hindering her investigation, she was slightly drunk because she drank two whiskeys but didn't have a bite to eat, she hadn't joined in on a single tune, she'd almost set fire to the deceased, and she'd flirted shamelessly with a Yank.

As the O'Sullivans trudged home, she brooded on her bad luck. "All of our suspects were there, and I didn't learn a single thing."

"What's to learn?" Gráinne said. "Everyone was drinking and singing."

"And telling jokes," Ciarán said. "There once was a man from—"

"Enough," Siobhán said. Ciarán shook his head but clammed up.

"I felt bad for Mary Murphy," Ann said. "I don't think I've cried as much in me life as she did today."

"Especially after you knocked over the candle," Eoin said to Siobhán.

"It wouldn't have happened if the two of ye weren't whispering secrets," Siobhán said. Ann's eyes went wide.

"What secrets?" Ciarán said.

"Yea. What secrets?" Gráinne said, squinting so hard her eyes were like two black slits.

"We'll talk privately when we get home," Siobhán said.

"All of us?" Ciarán said.

"No," Siobhán said. "Miss Ann and I."

Ciarán's hand grasped Siobhán's. It was slightly slimy. She didn't want to know. He started to swing it. "Can I get a puppy?"

"Maybe," Siobhán said.

Ciarán stopped. "Really?"

"Might deter intruders if we had a watch dog," Siobhán said.

"Deadly," Ciarán said.

"I'd rather have a cat," Ann said.

"There's no such thing as a watch cat," Ciarán said. He looked at Siobhán. "Right?"

Siobhán didn't answer, and soon they fell into a rhythm as they headed downhill toward home and a light rain began to fall. Siobhán found herself oddly soothed by the collective sound of their shoes on the pavement—shorter clips from Gráinne who was trying to walk in heels, the shuffle of Eoin's loafers, and the occasional squeak of Ciarán's runners.

Once inside the bistro, Siobhán made a fire, put the kettle on for tea, and turned to Ann.

"I just want to go to bed," Ann pleaded. "Can we speak later?"

Siobhán shook her head. "Out with it."

"Promise you won't be mad?" Ann asked.

Siobhán sighed. She'd certainly heard this request before. "I promise," she lied.

"The text that Gráinne got that night. I peeked. It was from Niall."

Siobhán exhaled. Thank heavens it wasn't anything new. "I already know," she said. "Gráinne told me. This was how long before you heard the glass breaking?"

"Maybe twenty minutes." Tears filled Ann's eyes. Siobhán pulled her in for a cuddle. She kissed the top of her head. "You're not mad?" Ann asked, voice quivering.

"I just want this to be over for all of us," Siobhán said.

"I thought people would get the wrong idea about Gráinne if they knew," Ann said.

Siobhán opened her mouth to half-scold and half-console Ann again when Ciarán cried out from the back room. She didn't even know he was downstairs. Oh God, if there was another dead body in the bistro she was going to lose it. She pulled away from Ann and flew into the back dining room.

"What's wrong?" She rushed in to find Ciarán hovering over the table where Niall was found. It still was a makeshift shrine, filled with little trinkets. He was holding up a folded note. Individual letters had been cut out of a magazine and pasted crookedly onto the page, like a ransom note from a movie.

It made Siobhán's spine tingle, but she was determined not to scare her siblings any more than necessary. She flashed back to the pile of magazines she'd spotted in Mary Murphy's house. Had Mary written the note? Anyone in town could get hold of a magazine. Siobhán was reaching, as usual.

Soon she heard feet pounding down the stairs, and a few minutes later the rest of her brood poured into the dining room. They stared at Siobhán. "He's alright," she assured them. "He found a note is all."

"You put me heart in crossways," Gráinne said, stepping up and ruffling Ciarán's hair.

"I thought for sure there was another body," Eoin said.

"What does the note say?" Eoin asked.

Siobhán took the note and read it out loud.

Stay in the kitchen and out of everyone's business
The first is always the hardest

Oh God, she should have read it silently first. Her siblings' faces were stamped with fear. *When would she ever learn?*

"What first? What's the hardest?" Ciarán asked.

"The first murder," Eoin said. "He's threatening to kill us."

"Me," Siobhán said quickly. "He or she is threatening to kill me. And it's nothing to worry about. Just a sick joke."

One by one the O'Sullivans grabbed for the note to have a look-see.

"Now we've all got our paw prints on it," Ciarán said.

"Gawd, that's true," Siobhán said.

"Should we call Macdara?" Gráinne asked.

"Let's wait," Siobhán said. "I want to think on this."

If it was the killer who left this note, it meant she was on to something. Had the person who left this note attended the wake? Siobhán went to the back door. It was locked as it should be. The front door had been locked when they came in as well. Séamus had already seen to the locks, and this time there wasn't a spare key in the garden. So how had they gotten in this time?

"Could they be climbing up to the bedroom windows?" Eoin said. Siobhán glanced at Ciarán.

"If you say 'little pitchers' I'm going to scream," Ciarán said. "I'm not a baby, like."

"I know. It's just my job to make sure you feel safe."

"He's after you, right?" Ciarán said.

"Right," Siobhán said grimly.

"Then I feel safe." Ciarán grinned. Siobhán wanted to ruffle his carrottop and pinch his cheeks, but she restrained herself.

"Macdara could check around and see if he can figure out how the person got in," Gráinne said. "I think we should call the guards."

"Can we talk this through first?" Siobhán headed into the kitchen, and they all gathered around the back wall, where they had their list of suspects. Siobhán pointed to Mary Murphy's name. "On two visits to Mary's house I saw separate piles of magazines."

"She did it!" Ciarán said. "But why would she murder her own son?"

"She didn't," Siobhán said quickly. Heavens, she couldn't have Ciarán thinking that.

"Then why is her name up there?" Ciarán persisted.

"I thought you were supposed to suspect everyone so I added her name. I don't think she murdered Niall. But she still could have sent the note."

"If we're supposed to suspect everyone, why aren't our names up there?" Ciarán said.

"Can we focus? I'll add our names later if you like." Siobhán turned back to the board. " We all saw the condition, Mary was in at the wake. There's no way that she left the note."

"She could have sent someone," Eoin said.

"It's possible," Siobhán said. "But let's just assume that the person who wrote the note is the person who left it. In that case, I think we can rule her out." They fell quiet as Siobhán put a light line through Mary's name. "Did anyone notice if any of our suspects weren't in attendance? Came in late? Anything?"

"Alison Tierney wasn't there," Eoin said.

"Right."

"And since she owns this building, isn't it possible Séamus gave her a copy of the new key?"

"I don't think he would've done that without letting me

know, but it's a good point. I'll ask him." Siobhán put a tick mark next to Alison's name.

"Sheila came to the wake much later than everyone else," Gráinne said.

"Are you sure?" Siobhán asked.

"Yes. Because Pio was setting up with his band, and one of the lads asked where she was, and he made a joke about taking the chain off for a bit."

"Good catch," Siobhán said. "How long after did she walk in?"

"I'd say at least an hour. And she didn't look happy at all. It was like she knew that Pio was talking shite about her behind her back."

"Language," Siobhán said. She put a star next to Sheila's name. "Did you notice if anyone else was late or left early?"

"Father Kearney went in and out."

"I'd like to think we can safely rule him out."

"Because he's a priest?" Gráinne looked at Siobhán as if she were the biggest eejit alive.

"Honestly? Yes."

Gráinne shrugged but didn't comment further. Siobhán was glad. She didn't want to get into a conversation about naughty priests.

"Bridie and Séamus were a bit late. Séamus made a joke about Bridie taking so long. And Courtney Kirby came in right after. She also said she couldn't stay long, something about needing to take inventory."

Siobhán put a star next to their names as well. "Mike Granger?"

"I didn't see him at all," Gráinne said.

Siobhán looked at the rest of her brood. One by one they shook their heads. Siobhán put a bigger star next to his name. And there was still the matter of the passport. Mike might have satisfied Macdara with his explanation, but Siobhán's gut told her it didn't make sense.

"What about the Yank?" Eoin said.

Gráinne tilted her head and clasped her hands. "He was too busy making eyes at Siobhán."

Siobhán glared at her. "I think he was there when we arrived."

"And he was there when we left," Ann said.

"With a wee bit of drool hanging off his lip," Gráinne said.

"Doesn't mean he didn't slip out," Eion said.

"Because of the drool?" Ciarán said.

"No, Ciarán," Siobhán said. Half the time she had no idea what was going on in that noggin' of his. She turned to the list and sighed. Eoin was right. Anyone could have slipped out and back in. This was getting them nowhere. But it was odd that Mike hadn't shown up. What was so urgent that he couldn't show his respects? She was definitely going to have to follow up on that.

"Declan didn't stay long either," Ann piped up. "Said he couldn't leave the pub for long." Siobhán handed her the marker and let Ann put a star next to Declan's name. When she turned back around, there were tears in her eyes.

"Ah, pet," Siobhán said. "Are you alright?"

"I don't like this," Ann said.

Siobhán put her arm around her sister and held her as she cried.

"I'll make tea," Gráinne said.

"Good idea," Siobhán said, steering Ann out into the bistro and sitting her down near the fireplace. "And how about some cake too?"

"We have cake?" Gráinne said.

"I made it to bring to Mary's and I completely forgot. It's in the kitchen on the rack." Gráinne hurried in to get the cake while Siobhán knelt down and wiped the tears off Ann's cheeks and smoothed her hair. "It's been a rough year," she said. "But remember what mam always used to say?"

Ann sniffled and then nodded. "This too shall pass," she said.

"This too shall pass," Siobhán agreed. She wanted to cheer Ann up. An idea struck her. Something special, just for her. "Wait here." Siobhán hurried up to her room and pulled the whittling box out from underneath her bed. She picked up a hummingbird she'd started quite a while back and her carving knife. Only the details were left to do, and so she began to shave around it, concentrating on the details of the feathers and the needle-beak. Soon, the delicate bird was complete. Maybe Ann would even like to paint it. Perfect.

She raced back downstairs. Her siblings were sipping tea and eating cake. Siobhán's mug was waiting for her at the table, steam curling into the air. "Close your eyes and hold out your hand," she said. Ann closed her eyes and reached out with both hands, palms up. Siobhán gingerly set the bird in it. "Open."

Ann's eyes flew open, and a smile spread across her face. "It's lovely."

"You haven't whittled for a year now," Gráinne said. "You're so good at it."

"For your eyes only," Siobhán said. "Don't say a word to Bridie or Courtney, or they'll be on me about carving them for the store."

"You should," Ann said. "We would be rich."

Siobhán sighed. "Sometimes doing things for money takes all the love out of it."

Money. The root of so much evil. Once again Siobhán thought about Niall trying to extort ten thousand euro out of her. This was key to cracking the case—she just knew it. Who else had Niall been extorting or blackmailing, and why? And now that they were up anyway, should she talk to Ann about what she overheard? Warn her not to tell anyone else that Niall had texted Gráinne that evening? She turned to find her youngest sister nodding off with half a piece of cake still left on her plate. She gently removed the plate, shook Ann awake, escorted her and Ciarán upstairs, and helped them until they were snug in their beds.

"I miss James," Ciarán said just before he fell asleep. "And Mam and Da too."

Siobhán held back tears. She was too exhausted to cry. "Our brother will be home soon," she whispered. "I promise." When she came back down, Gráinne and Eoin were still planted in front of the fire. Siobhán stood, staring into it for a very long time.

"You're thinking," Gráinne said. "It's annoying."

"Tell me more about your correspondence with Billy," Siobhán said.

Gráinne's eyes widened. "What do you want to know?"

"When are visiting hours, and do you think he would agree to see me?"

"Why do you want to see that wanker?" Eoin asked.

Because he might know who else Niall was extorting or blackmailing. "Mind your language," she said.

"I don't know," Gráinne said. "I can ask."

Siobhán nodded. She loathed that Gráinne was communicating with Billy. She for one never wanted to see his face again. But now, with James's life on the line, she had to do it. She had to visit Billy Murphy in prison and get him to explain Niall's scheme. She had to find out every single person he'd been hitting up for money. It might be her only chance to catch a killer.

Chapter 30

Siobhán didn't want anyone but Gráinne to know she was going to visit Billy in prison. Luckily, she had the perfect excuse for going to the prison, seeing as how they needed to see James as well. When Macdara learned the O'Sullivans were going to visit James, he offered to drive them to Cork City. It just so happened that he had some business there himself, and from the city centre they could take the number 8 bus to Cork Prison. When they were finished, they would meet him back in the city and have a spot of lunch before returning home.

Even though Siobhán didn't quite believe Macdara had to be in Cork, for once she didn't put up a fuss. Visiting James was going to be an ordeal for all of them, and she was grateful for the support. She sat in the front of his police car as if she were a member of the gardai, while her four little prisoners cozied up in the back.

During the drive to Cork, they sang along to the radio as rain tap-danced on the roof of the car, and not a single one of them mentioned prison, or murder, or anything remotely macabre. It was as if they had all been craving a little slice of normal. A little slice of heaven, really. That's what normal life was to them now.

Ciarán begged Macdara to put the lights and sirens on, and to Siobhán's surprise and delight he did just that. They laughed as cars veered to the side and faces pinched in prayer greeted them as they sped past. Siobhán could almost hear the collective sigh of relief pile up behind them.

"Sorry, lads, that's all I can get away with," Macdara said, returning to a normal speed and cutting the lights and siren once they pulled far enough ahead of all the others.

"Deadly," Eoin said from the back, a smile tugging at the corners of his mouth.

"Awesome," Ciarán said, sporting an outright grin. Ann giggled, and soon Gráinne joined in. A burst of warmth filled Siobhán, and she gave in to a smile as well. Macdara glanced at her, and their eyes locked, and the warmth spread between them. She looked away first, fearing he would have an accident if he continued to stare at her like that.

Would you look at that, they were happy out. Siobhán had forgotten what that felt like. Imagine. She would hold on to this memory like a nugget of gold until the light could shine again. They would get through this. They would get James back, and they would be a normal family again. *Save your strength for your darkest days*, her mam used to say when Siobhán was bothered over some trifle of a problem— a boy who didn't fancy her, or a friend who didn't invite her to go shopping with the other girls, or a less than perfect mark in school, or heaven forbid she gained half a stone over the holidays. Such were the worries that used to rock her world. Silly, how much time human beings wasted on things that didn't matter. She supposed one couldn't truly appreciate that perspective until one was faced with real problems. And, as usual, Mammy was right. If these weren't the darkest days, Siobhán never wanted to know what was.

She touched the threatening note tucked into the pocket

of her denims as they wound their way through a patch of vibrant trees glowing from the kiss of rain, reminding Siobhán why her home was called the Emerald Isle. The leaves indeed sparkled like precious emeralds. And she knew that, if forced to make a choice, she'd rather gaze upon this beautiful land than wear true emeralds around her neck.

She fixed her eyes on the Ballyhoura Mountains resting in the distance, barely visible through the mist, their earthy lumps as familiar to her as an old friend. She placed her hand on the window and imagined she was touching them. She felt Macdara glance over, but she kept her gaze outward. She couldn't afford being distracted by the likes of Garda Flannery.

Besides, he wouldn't be this nice to any of them once he found out they were keeping new evidence from him. In fact, she wondered if not producing the note was the same as hindering an investigation, but she knew she couldn't tell him. Not just yet. Once he found out, he would keep track of her like patrons in a pub keep track of their pints. She was getting close to the truth; she could feel it. Or at least, they were eliminating suspects, and that was the same as making progress, wasn't it?

Her thoughts returned to Sheila Mahoney, and how she was late coming to the wake. Siobhán didn't know how she would have gotten into the bistro, what with the new locks, but she had that problem no matter who the killer was. They were Sheila's scissors. She went to the trouble to get something out of the rubbish and bring it back into her shop. She said it was a broken vase, but she was allergic to flowers. She had a bruise as if she'd tussled with someone. And she was one of the last people to see Niall Murphy.

What if Sheila had planned the entire murder way in advance? What if that was the sole reason for passing out those hideous scissors, and even changing her sign? So that when she stabbed Niall, everyone would be suspect. Everyone who had access to a pair of her scissors, which was, well—everyone. Just days before the murder Sheila had seen to that.

Was Siobhán on to something? Had the entire thing been a ruse? It was a startling new thought. Maybe the broken glass in the salon didn't come from a vase, as she claimed; maybe Niall had smashed the window, crawled in, and what? Startled Pio or Sheila, who had just returned from the pub, and they stabbed him with the scissors? Wait. That would be self-defense, wouldn't it? And then how did some of Niall's blood get on James's clothing? How would Sheila or Pio even know where to find James?

Pio could have been playing trad music at Declan's that night. He would have seen the state James was in, and that could have led to Pio framing him.

"A quid for your thoughts," Macdara said.

"Just enjoying the scenery," Siobhán said.

"So is he," Gráinne said from the back. "What do you think? Is she beautiful when she's staring out the window like an eejit?"

"Gráinne Kate O'Sullivan!" Siobhán said.

"Pardon?" Macdara said.

"Never you mind. Gráinne's just being smart." Siobhán shook her head but didn't turn around. The cheek of that girl! It was true, though: Macdara had been staring at her almost the entire ride. Macdara coughed and fixed his gaze out the front. Ann and Gráinne tittered in the back.

"How much longer?" Ciarán said.

"Not long now," Macdara answered.

"We would have been there by now if you'd kept your lights and siren on," Ciarán said.

"Hush," Siobhán said. Meeting with Billy was the key to cracking this case. It had to be. Motive was key. Who really wanted Niall dead? Siobhán was convinced it went back to the person Niall mentioned, the one willing to pay twenty thousand euros for some kind of video. Even if the video was a lie, the killer could have fallen for it. And Sheila had certainly been going on about business being bad. Maybe she needed money to pay off Niall. What did he tell her was on the video? Something she'd done? Something Pio had done?

Thankfully Gráinne had successfully set up the visit. Billy would know what Niall had been up to—at least she prayed he did.

Situated behind the Murphy army barracks on Rathmore Road, the pale stone building with bright blue doors looked more like a cheery castle than a medium-security prison. Siobhán was sure it was nothing like a royal abode inside. Still, she was somewhat relieved to see that it had a nice appearance. Hopefully it was just as well-kept inside, and her brother was doing okay. If James was convicted of murder, he'd be sent to Cloverhill Prison in Dublin. There would be nothing cheery about that address. The thought was enough to make anyone shudder. She couldn't let that happen. It would send her to her grave.

Before entering, the O'Sullivans stood outside as if to collectively gather their nerve. "Let's go," Siobhán said and took the first step to the door.

They entered, stepped up to the officer standing just inside, and told him they were there for a visit. He checked Siobhán's ID, and then he teased her siblings for not having motor licenses. She'd brought their birth certificates, and soon they were given a locker in which to put all their belongings, including their mobile phones. Then they waited.

Volunteers with St. Nicholas Trust were on hand to offer tea and a biscuit, and to explain the rules about visitation. They were to go in no more than three at a time, which cut their time down to fifteen minutes for each group. The volunteers doted on Ciarán and Ann, and soon had them laughing. Siobhán could feel the tears welling behind her eyes; she hated this place, no matter how nice they were or what a pretty blue they'd painted the door. She wished she had the power to yank James out of here and never look back. Her visit with James was scheduled first; she'd saved Billy for last.

Should she tell James she was meeting with Billy? It might ruin their visit. Then again, if he heard about it through someone else, it was going to ruin the next visit. She'd play it by ear, see what kind of form James was in first.

"Siobhán O'Sullivan and Eoin O'Sullivan?" a guard called. Siobhán and Eoin were ushered to an electronic door. Inside there was a revolving door and a security checkpoint. They were told to put all belts, jewelry, and anything else metal into the tray. Neither of them had anything that merited an eyebrow raise from the guy holding the scanner. *We haven't had time to dress ourselves up*, Siobhán wanted to say. She also wanted to smack him. He looked so smug.

Once they passed the metal detection, they were asked to stand in position. An officer approached with a dog. Siobhán prayed Eoin wasn't secretly doing drugs. She also prayed Ciarán wouldn't try to pet the dog. Had she really told him they could get one? She'd been so tired. She had a feeling she was going to regret it. Finally, they were sniffed, scanned, and ready to go. The next room was the visiting room. There was a long table divided down the middle by a sheet of plexiglass. At one end of the table two women were visiting a man. Siobhán's heart was racing as they took a seat and waited for James. This wasn't going to work if her meeting with Billy was in the same room.

She wanted to turn and ask the officer about it, but just then a door at the far end opened, and in walked an officer with her brother. She had to slap her hand over her mouth to keep from crying out. He'd lost so much weight already, and there were dark circles under his eyes. But he smiled when he saw them and hurried to his seat.

"How ya?" he said as if he'd just walked into the bistro after sleeping in. How she wished that was the case. He frowned. "Where are the rest of ye?"

"They only allow three at a time, so we have fifteen minutes, and then they'll come in."

"Right, right. Are ye well?"

"We're fair. How are you?" Siobhán instinctively reached to touch him and stubbed her finger on the plexiglass.

"If you start crying I'm leaving," James said.

"Siobhán is on the case," Eoin said. "We've already eliminated John Butler. He was in Cork City the night of the murder." He leaned forward. "With a woman. And they like to hurt each other."

Oh, Jaysus. Siobhán crossed herself and elbowed Eoin. James laughed. "So for once the Butler didn't do it. Is that what you're saying?" James grinned. At least he hadn't lost his wicked sense of humor.

"I don't get it," Eoin said.

"Ciarán will," James said. "I'll use that on him." James leaned forward and lowered his voice. "Listen. I don't want you snooping around."

Siobhán waved him off. "I'm fine."

"She's not," Eoin said. "Someone left a threatening note in the bistro."

"Eoin!" Siobhán said. She could not believe him.

James's smile evaporated. "What did it say?"

"It's nothing," Siobhán said kicking Eoin under the table. "Just told me to stop sticking me nose into everyone else's business. Hardly a threat."

"The first is always the hardest," Eoin said. Siobhán cussed. Eoin didn't flinch.

James shook his head. "Meaning he'll kill again if she doesn't stay out of it."

"Or she," Siobhán said. She glared at Eoin. "What are ye trying to do to me?"

"Protecting you," James said. "Looks like someone has to." He and Eoin exchanged a nod.

"I'm fine."

"What did Garda Flannery say about the note?"

"We don't have time for this. And since you're already upset, I might as well tell ye."

James folded his arms across his chest. "Tell me what?"

"I'm meeting with Billy Murphy today as well."

"No, you're not."

"I am."

"I won't allow it."

"Hate to say this, but you're hardly in any position to dictate what I do."

"Why?"

"He has to know who else Niall was coercing for money. One of Niall's other victims is the killer." Several heads turned her way. Shite. Siobhán forgot how loud she was when she was stirred up.

"Drop it," James said. "I'm pleading guilty."

Chapter 31

Siobhán slammed her fist down on the table.

A guard was immediately at her side. "Do that again and you'll be out," he said.

"Sorry," Siobhán said. Geez. You'd think she was the prisoner. She turned back to James and plastered a smile on her face. "Where did you get the scissors?"

"Pardon?" James looked flustered.

"You said you might be the murderer, so let's explore that idea. Where did ye get the scissors?"

James shifted in his seat. "Didn't we have a pair lying around?"

"Everyone in town who didn't want to face Sheila's wrath had a pair," Siobhán said.

"That means everyone had a pair," Eoin added.

"Doesn't mean I didn't do it," James said.

Siobhán folded her arms across her chest. "Why did you wipe your fingerprints off?"

"What?"

"If you killed him in a drunken blackout, how is it that

you had the good sense to put on gloves or wipe the fingerprints off the scissors?"

"Instinct?"

"Instinct, my arse. You're not a killer whale."

Eoin laughed. The guard looked over and frowned. Apparently only crying was allowed in prisons.

"The other option isn't any better," James said.

"You mean if Gráinne stabbed Niall?"

James swallowed, then nodded.

"Why would Gráinne send her own sister a threatening
note?"

"Maybe because she's scared. She doesn't want you to
find out." James was reaching.

"Why would she kill Niall?" Siobhán demanded.

"I'd like to say the same reason any of us would have
liked to kill Niall, but her reason might have been even more
personal."

"Niall and Gráinne weren't seeing each other romantically," Siobhán said, "if that's what you're thinking."

"How do you know?"

"She'd been corresponding with both Niall and Billy for
the past six months."

James jerked back as if he'd been hit with an electric
prodder. "What for?"

"At first I think she just needed to confront Billy. She
thought it would help."

"At first?"

"Now I'm afraid she believes Niall. She thinks there was
someone else who caused the accident. Someone besides
Billy. Niall told her there was a witness and that he or she
had proof that Billy didn't cause the accident. Some kind of
video."

James shook his head. "This is absolutely mental."

"I know."

"Have you seen this video?"

"No. I don't think there is a video. Although Niall might have believed there was."

"I don't follow," James said.

"Either someone was taking the piss and had Niall believing there was a video that would exonerate his brother—except this 'witness' wasn't going to hand it over unless Niall gave him twenty thousand euro. Or Niall made the witness and the video up to extort money from us."

"Well, which is it?"

"I don't know. That's why I have to visit Billy. See if he can shed any light on it."

"Did you ask Macdara about the accident again?"

"Yes. He insists no other car was involved. He even checked the shops after the accident, just in case someone brought theirs in around the same time." James waited for the answer. "And nothing."

"I told you I remembered Niall goading me that night about Gráinne."

"Right. So?"

"What if?" James's voice cracked, and he couldn't even finish the sentence.

"What if?"

"What if he followed me home and I did kill him? What if I did, Siobhán? What if I did?"

"Shhh. They record every conversation here. Stop talking like that. I told you. You wouldn't have been so neat. The scissors were plunged in once. So precisely. It took strength. From what Declan and Séamus said you could barely put one foot in front of the other. And you certainly wouldn't have wiped away fingerprints. And then what? You stumbled back to the pub and passed out behind it? You would have gone right up to bed. It's obvious you didn't come home at all. Niall was the one who came to the bistro to see Gráinne. And I think the killer followed him there."

"Why would Niall come to the bistro?"

"Because he wanted to tell her about his argument with you before you did."

James folded his arms against his chest. "Again. Why?"

"He didn't want her to change her mind."

"About what?"

"I'll tell you, but you're going to have to stay calm." James followed her gaze to the guard and then nodded. "According to Gráinne they had planned to go to Dublin the next day. To see a solicitor."

"Why would he take Gráinne with him?"

"He thought if a family member of the victims spoke in Billy's defense it would give him a lot of credibility. That's the same reason why he was wearing a suit and had his head shaved. He wanted to be taken seriously."

James clenched his jaw and curled his fists but kept his promise and didn't lose his cool in front of the guard. "Doesn't that suggest that he actually believed that Billy was innocent?"

"Maybe. Which means someone out there had convinced Niall that he witnessed the accident and had some kind of video proving Billy didn't do it."

"Why? Why would someone make up such a sick thing?" Eoin said.

"Money," James said. "Someone, most likely Niall himself, saw an opportunity to make money and stir things up."

The guard stepped up to them. "Time's up," he said. "If he's still seeing the other three."

"He is," Siobhán said. She wished she could hug him, kiss him, reassure him. Instead she put her hand on the glass, and he put his hand on the glass over hers.

"Please," James said, "be safe."

Siobhán bit back tears and nodded. "Slán agat," she said.

"Slán leat," James answered. *Good-bye for now.*

After they said their so longs, Siobhán added a parting phrase, one her mother surely would have said. "Nár laga

Dia do lámh," she said softly. James clenched his jaw as if trying to stop tears from forming in his eyes and nodded. Siobhán only hoped the phrase would comfort him.

May God not weaken your hand.

The room she met Billy in was identical to the one where she had visited James, but to her relief, it was on the other side of the prison. Unlike James, who had lost weight, Billy looked as if he'd gained weight in prison. He had the same dark hair as Niall, but instead of brown, his eyes were blue. He was definitely not the looker in the family, but he didn't have the threatening edge that Niall did. He thunked down in the chair and had trouble meeting her eyes. When he finally did, he tried to offer up a little smile, but when she didn't return any warmth, he became serious. She sat there, watching him, having already decided she was going to make him speak first. He cleared his throat.

"Did you read my letters?" he said.

"No," she said. "But Gráinne did, as you well know."

"I'm sorry," he said. "If I could go back and change things, I would. If I could give my life for your parents, I would do it in a heartbeat. You have to believe me."

"It's too late," Siobhán said. "Even if I did believe you."

"They were good people. They didn't deserve that."

"It sounds like you're admitting you caused the accident," Siobhán said. "So what was this nonsense Niall was spouting about how you didn't do it, and how he had a video to prove it?"

"I played a part in the accident, to be sure," Billy said. "I was drunk too. I admit it."

Siobhán wanted to lash out and scream and cry. But she also needed answers, so she bit her tongue. "So Niall made the witness and the video up to get money, is that it?"

Billy shook his head. "I don't think so."

"You don't *think* so?"

"I don't know whether or not Niall had a video. He said he did, but in all honesty I didn't believe him either."

Siobhán didn't know what she expected, but it wasn't this. She thought for sure Billy would know one way or the other. Or was he lying to her too? "Why didn't you believe him?"

"Because I know when my brother's lying. I think he made up the part about the video so that the person who caused the accident would admit he or she was there."

"He or she?"

Billy shook his head. "I'm not going to tell you who it was. What I will tell you is that I was not the cause of the accident. Another person was. He came out of nowhere, speeding, heading straight for me. I swerved." Billy shut his eyes.

Macdara swore up and down there were no other vehicles involved in the accident. He was lying. But she was going to swallow her rage and see if she could get any morsel of truth out of him.

"Who was it?" Despite her best efforts, Siobhán's voice rose. Luckily the guard at this door wasn't as gruff as the previous one and didn't even glance her way.

"If I told you that your life would be in danger," Billy said.

"It already is. So just tell me."

"I believe the person who caused the accident is the same person who killed my brother. Which means you're only alive because you can't identify this person."

"And Niall could?"

"Of course. I told Niall who really caused the accident. He or she certainly believed Niall had a video. That's why Niall was killed."

Siobhán's head was swimming. "Why didn't you tell Garda Flannery at the scene that you didn't cause the accident?" *And then tell him who did?* Billy was lying through his teeth.

"I was really out of it. By the time I remembered all the details, I was worried it was too late. That nobody would believe me."

You've got that right. "You have to tell me. Or the gardai. Garda Flannery is coming to pick us up—I'll bring him back here and—"

"No," Billy said. He rose from his seat. This time the guard did come over. Billy sat back down.

"Five minutes left," the guard said. That couldn't be right, but Siobhán wouldn't win an argument with a prison guard. She turned to Billy.

"Why won't you tell me who it is?" she pleaded.

"Because if there is a video, you have to find it first. Otherwise it's going to be my word against the murderer's. And who the feck is going to believe me? You don't even believe me, do you?"

"You're not an easy person to believe."

"See? If I talk, no one will believe me anyway—no one but the killer, that is—and then what? What if the killer goes after you, or one of the six, or my mam? I can't take that chance."

"Just tell me, and I promise I will do everything I can to check out what you say and find the video."

"You're going to do that anyway. I can see it in your eyes."

"If you're really sorry, if you care about me at all, you'll tell me who else Niall was trying to extort or blackmail."

"You mean the person who really caused the accident." Billy folded his arms against his chest. "See? You still don't believe me. Without a video, or a confession from the killer, you never will."

"Just tell me who else Niall was extorting."

"I don't have a complete list."

So he was extorting multiple people. God, this was so aggravating. "Give me a partial list."

"Find the video. Or something that will convince you I'm telling the truth. Then we'll talk."

"Where am I supposed to look?"

"Ask Mam if you can have a look around his room."

"I'm sure the police have done that."

"Look again."

"What if there isn't any video?"

"Then nobody is ever going to believe me anyway."

"So just tell me who you think killed your brother."

"You aren't a poker player, Siobhán."

"What does that mean?"

"It means you're much safer around the killer if you don't suspect him or her."

"Which is it? A him or a her? At least tell me that."

Billy shook his head. "One look at your face and the killer will realize I've told you. Then something would happen to you. I guarantee it. But if the killer feels safe, then you're safe."

"Why did you even agree to see me if you weren't going to be helpful?"

"Because I wanted to say how sorry I am."

"Prove it. Tell me who you think killed Niall."

Billy lowered his head. Did he really think he was protecting her?

"Time's up." The guard tapped Siobhán on the shoulder.

"I don't think there's any video," she said to Billy on her way out.

"I don't think there is either," Billy called back. "But the killer thinks there is. Maybe you can figure out how to use that to your advantage."

Chapter 32

It was four days after their visit to the prison, and Friday night in Kilbane. Siobhán tugged on her little black dress as she tried to go down the stairs in heels. She wasn't used to them, that was for sure. She'd even taken the time to straighten her hair, and she was wearing makeup. She felt like she was dressed for Halloween, although she did have to admit that even she'd been impressed when she looked in the mirror. She was definitely a more glamorous version of her, the kind of girl she always imagined she would have been in Dublin. The kids were still at the table, and every one of them gaped at her.

"I didn't know you could look like that," Gráinne said.

"Thanks."

"You're welcome," Gráinne said, the sarcasm flying right by her.

"You look beautiful," Ann said.

"Again, thank you."

"But why are you dressed like that for O'Rourke's?"

"Because she has a date with Garda Flannery," Eoin teased.

"It's not a date," Siobhán said. "It's Friday night." So

what if she also had to ask Macdara if he had found anything on the CCTVs, and also fill him in on her awful meeting with Billy. And if she happened to say that Pio, Sheila, and Mike Granger were her top suspects, and he was to start paying them a closer look, no harm done. And if Pio just happened to be playing there tonight—well, what was a lass to do when there were so many birds? Bring a lot of stones. She was getting close to the killer, she could feel it.

She kissed her siblings good-bye, took a few more jokes directed at her and Macdara, and went out to get on her scooter. A lady wouldn't ride a scooter in a dress, she thought for a second. Then again, she would squeeze her legs tight, it's not like she'd be flashing anyone. Then again, she was going to be having a few drinks. Macdara and Pio had to think this was just a fun night out. She would walk. Macdara would probably give her a lift home anyway.

He can't kiss you good night if you drive home on your scooter.

O'Rourke's was alive with music and people. Siobhán stood just inside, feeling like a party crasher. It was as if everyone in town had had enough of murder, and they were all out to celebrate instead. There was no doubt that the people in this town liked to have a good time. Siobhán smiled when she thought of the typical saying lads here often used: *Up here for thinking, down there for dancing* as they pointed to their head and then their nether regions. Even a murderer couldn't take the craic out of Kilbane.

And the more people she could talk to tonight, the more she could narrow down the suspect list. Chances were good that one of the folks in this room tonight was the killer. She had to do everything in her power to make it look like she was just having fun, to convince everyone she was done sleuthing, yet still get them to talk.

She sensed someone behind her, but before she could turn around, a pair of hands were plastered over her eyes. It could be the killer, trying to drag her out before anyone else had seen her. Thank God for heels. She lifted her foot and brought it down as hard as she could on the foot of the person behind her. The shriek was loud, and female.

The pair of hands immediately fell from her eyes. Siobhán whirled around to see a girl bent over, still shrieking, the foot Siobhán had stomped on raised in pain.

It was Maria. She must be back from Dublin for the summer! And she looked browned off. *Oh, Jaysus*. She had just stomped on her best friend's foot. "I'm so sorry. You gave me a fright."

Maria looked up, her eyes watering. "What is wrong with you?"

"I'm sorry, I'm sorry." She bent down as if examining Maria's foot would help. "I thought you were going to drag me outside and stab me."

"Oh my God. They're right. You've gone mental."

Siobhán straightened up. "They?"

"Mam and Da said you were having a hard time of it. Going a bit nuts with Niall's death. That's why I decided to come home for the weekend and surprise ye."

"I wish you would have told me. I've missed you so much!"

"I thought the surprise would do ye good. Didn't consider it might be bad for my foot."

"I'm sorry. I'm not the only one who's jumpy around here lately. Can you believe it? A murder in Kilbane? And you thought Dublin would be exciting." Siobhán was so happy to see Maria. Now she wouldn't be alone. Maria would be here all summer.

"Dublin is exciting." Maria stood, and gently tested out her foot. "In fact, I'm only back for the weekend. To check on you."

"Just for the weekend?" Siobhán had a million questions stuck in her throat. "You mean you have to pack everything up before you come home for the summer?"

"Let's get a pint into us and start over," Maria said.

"Is Aisling with you?"

Maria shook her finger. "I told ye. Drinks first, news second." Siobhán nodded and looked around. If she had known Maria was here she wouldn't have made a date with Macdara. And he was late on top of it. Should she text him and let him know Maria was here, or just wait and see what time he bothered to show for their date?

"Who are you looking for?"

"Garda Flannery."

"No investigating. We're on the drink tonight, and that's that."

"It's not work-related. Macdara asked me here tonight."

"Like a date, like?"

"I think so."

"You're joking me."

Siobhán didn't like her tone. She'd been dying to see Maria all year, and this was nothing like she imagined their reunion would be. "You don't think he's cute?"

"He's going to stay in Kilbane the rest of his life, and all he's looking for is a woman to pop out his babies. You, on the other hand, are coming to Dublin. Why put him through all that?"

"I can't come to Dublin. I have five siblings and a bistro."

"Don't start. The only way you're stuck here for the rest of your life, Siobhán O'Sullivan, is if you think you are."

"I do. I think I am."

"You're too young to throw away your entire future. But enough of that. Look at you. Your little black dress. You look like a city girl. We're going to have some craic tonight." Maria took her hand and pulled her to the bar.

Declan was over in a jiffy, smiling, setting up coasters. "Trouble is back in town, I see," he said to Maria with a wink. "Where's your third wheel?"

"Right," Siobhán said. "That's what I want to know."

Maria smiled at Declan but didn't make eye contact with Siobhán. "She's in Dublin. In fact, I'm only here for a wee visit meself. We rented a flat near Grafton Street for the summer."

Maria's words were like a thousand paper cuts to Siobhán's heart. Of course they did. They couldn't even bother coming home for the summer for her. And why should they? They were young and free. This was the time of their lives. It came around once. Once. And they knew better than to waste it. Maria was still prattling on to a smiling Declan.

"Aisling's got a new beau. He's Scottish, can ye believe it? I told her he was going to be tight in the pockets, and she said that was just what she was looking for in a man." Maria threw her head back and cackled. Then she got it under control but was still smiling like the cat that swallowed the canary. "She sends her love, but I told her we'd get you to Dublin soon anyway."

Siobhán would have to bite back her jealousy. Easier said than done when her stomach was already flipping inside out. She ordered a Guinness, and Maria made a face. They always got a pint of Guinness when they went out. At least to start.

"I'll have a martini," Maria said to Declan as if they were ordered all the time. "Straight up with a twist of lime."

"How about vodka in a pint glass with a lemon?" Declan said. Maria just looked at him. "Tell you what. I'll throw a wee umbrella in there. A tourist left it here last summer. Been waiting to use it ever since." He flashed his gap-toothed grin, rubbed his hands in delight, then lumbered to the other end of the bar, where he bent over and began rummaging around the shelves.

"How can you stand it here?" Maria said as if she was a tourist herself.

Did she mean the pub or Kilbane? "It's not that bad. And you have to admit we've had quite a bit of excitement since ye left."

Maria waved her hand as if brushing off Siobhán's words. "There are loads of murders in Dublin. Like every week."

Siobhán was sure that was a fine bit of exaggerating, but she kept her gob shut. Maria and Aisling were still her best friends, no matter how much had changed. "You've only been gone since the fall."

"And yet I'm a completely different person."

"You look the same to me." Siobhán was the one who had a new haircut, and a scooter, and had a murderer after her. She didn't want to be bitter, but she hadn't prepared for this. Seeing Maria would have been tough under any circumstance. But Maria didn't even seem to understand the gravity of what was going on. Would she really rather talk about martinis and flats near Grafton Street instead of who could have stabbed Niall Murphy to death?

Declan put their drinks in front of them. Maria did indeed have vodka in a pint glass with a green umbrella set on top like a lid. "Let's get the table in the back," Siobhán said to Maria. Siobhán turned to Declan. "If Garda Flannery comes in, will ye tell him I'm sitting back there."

"Will do, petal," Declan said with another wink. Siobhán wondered if he ever got eyelid fatigue.

Siobhán steered them to a table right by the band. Pio was only a few feet away. Sheila sat in her own chair directly in front of the stage, her legs open wide, her pint glass resting on her knee as she tapped her foot along to the music. Siobhán had to hand it to her; she was very confident for her size, not afraid to take up space in the world. That was how it should be, although Sheila scared the bejaysus out of her.

"Did you ever meet up with Niall in Dublin?" Siobhán asked Maria, trying to sound casual.

"Of course not," Maria said. "I was never friends with Niall."

"I know. I just wondered if you ever saw him about town, or knew where he lived, who he hung out with, if he had a girlfriend."

"Oh my God, you sound like Ciarán. All *CSI.*"

"My brother is sitting in jail for his murder. What do you expect?"

"I'm sorry, I am," Maria said. She placed her hand over Siobhán's. "I heard he confessed."

Siobhán pulled her hand away. "He did not confess."

"I thought he blacked out. Did it in a drunken rage?"

"It's not true."

"Well, the guards think it's him, don't they?"

"They made a mistake. That's why I'm investigating."

"First your parents, now James. I would be a right nutter too. It's too much."

Siobhán leaned across the table and scrutinized her friend. Maria *did* look the same. Very typical pale Irish face with pretty dark hair, and brown eyes. Petite, except for the lungs on her; she had a boisterous voice and an endless thirst for good craic. But she was also her friend, and she'd known James her whole life. If she didn't believe James was innocent, that meant no one else did either. Even if James was released, they would all titter about him as if he'd done it but had just gotten away with it. The only way their lives were ever going to go back to normal was if Siobhán exposed the true killer. She was wasting her time trying to convince Maria of anything.

"Tell me all about Trinity," Siobhán said, and hoped it wasn't obvious, as her friend began to rattle on, that Maria may have had her ear but she was keeping her eye on the rest of the room. Siobhán was just getting the hang of pretending to listen when the band took a break and Pio practically flew over to their table. He stared down at Siobhán, eyes flashing.

"We need to talk," Pio said. Siobhán glanced at Maria. "Not her, you." Pio grabbed Siobhán's elbow and hoisted her up. "Let's go for a smoke."

Chapter 33

"I don't smoke," Siobhán said as he began to drag her to the back patio.

"I'll smoke for ye," Pio said. The patio was no bigger than a few hundred square feet with broken-up bricks and old Guinness signs discarded on the floor. A picnic table that had seen better days housed coffee cans for cigarette butts, but the ground still took most of them. Siobhán coughed and tried to move out of the path of the smoke from the others out to indulge their nicotine habit, which was virtually impossible. Pio lit his cigarette without taking his eyes off her.

"You sounded great," Siobhán said. She tried to smile.

"I heard you were asking around again about that broken vase," Pio said.

"How did you hear?" Siobhán said.

"You can't keep secrets in Kilbane." Pio blew smoke directly at her.

"Some people seem to be getting away with it," Siobhán said.

Pio glared at her. "What's your theory?"

"I saw Sheila the morning of the murder. Coming into the house with a black rubbish bag."

"Broken vase. End of story."

"Sheila is allergic to flowers. Sounds like 'To be continued . . .' to me." He was trying to bully her, and she wasn't going to let him.

"Is that all you've got?"

"Sheila was a right mess the next time I saw her, yet the salon smelled like bleach. She also had a bruise. That was especially disturbing." Siobhán met Pio's gaze head-on.

"Your theory?" Pio repeated.

"Maybe Niall broke into your house that night. Smashed a window. Maybe he attacked Sheila. Maybe she grabbed the nearest pair of scissors, or you did. That would have been self-defense. But then you got scared. So you dragged his body across to our place. Cleaned up. Maybe Sheila threw away something she regretted, then went back to the trash can."

"We dragged his body across the street? How did we get into your bistro?"

That was where her theory didn't quite float. Because in order to bring Niall in through the back garden, they would have had to carry his body all the way down the street, then around back to the road behind their place. "I hadn't completely worked it out," Siobhán admitted.

"I liked your parents," Pio said. "They minded their own business."

"Sheila was hiding something. She was acting very strange."

"Ah, for feck's sakes," a female voice from behind them said. Sheila entered the patio and came up to Siobhán. "You just won't let it go, will ye?"

"It's not a matter of won't," Siobhán said. "I can't."

"You're right," Sheila said. "I was hiding something."

"It's none of her business," Pio said.

"I'm going to tell her," Sheila said.

Finally. A confession? Should she be worried? Neither of them looked as if they were about to kill her. And there were the other smokers. Still, was this how killers confessed to murder? "The glass *was* from a broken vase. But not just any vase. It was the one your parents brought back from Waterford."

The Waterford crystal. After the accident dozens of gifts were found in the trunk of their parents' car. Siobhán couldn't bear to look at them. How could inanimate objects survive and her parents be gone? She'd given them all away, hadn't paid a lick of attention to who took what. "Why would you take the vase when you hate flowers?"

"It wasn't for me. You were giving away all those gifts during such a tough time. I didn't want you regretting it one day, wishing you'd kept something. So I was going to save it for you."

A lump grew in Siobhán's throat. That was actually very thoughtful. Maybe she'd been too quick to judge Sheila. "Well, why didn't you just tell me that earlier?"

"I didn't want to upset you. The fact is that I accidentally broke it. I felt real bad about it. That's why I wanted to try and put it back together."

"I see."

"And I know what else you're thinking. Pio doesn't hit me."

Pio stared at Siobhán, as if waiting for an apology. Sheila held up her beer. "So I like to have a few. Sometimes I stumble home. Sometimes I fall."

"Sometimes she pukes," Pio said. Sheila glared at him. He shrugged. "I'm just explainin' the bleach."

"It's also why Pio had the lights blaring. Said I had to stop trying to stumble in in the dark or folks would start spreading rumors that he was abusing me." Sheila barked out a laugh and smacked Pio across the chest with the back of her hand. "Little did ye know we'd get accused of being cold-blooded murderers instead!" she said. She roared with laughter.

Pio nodded seriously, then pointed at Siobhán. "Can you please eliminate us from your list?"

"Who cares about her list?" Sheila said, leaning left as if she were about to topple over.

"John Butler is off it, and I want off it too!" Pio said.

Sheila's eyes went wide. "John Butler? Drumming up business, was he?" She roared with laughter again.

Oh, God. Siobhán remembered what she hated about small towns. Everyone knew everything. And yet the murderer had managed to keep out of the limelight. "I'm just trying to do what's right," Siobhán said. "For all of us."

"Sure, sure," Pio said. He dropped his cigarette to the patio floor, crushed it with his foot. "Well, now you know," he said. He headed back inside.

Sheila stared at Siobhán.

"I'm sorry," Siobhán said. She wasn't really, but she was still afraid of Sheila.

"There is something I've just discovered," Sheila said. "I put a call in to Garda Flannery, but I haven't heard back." She glanced around the patio as if worried someone would overhear. "And since Garda Flannery is sweet on you, maybe you can give him the news."

"Garda Flannery and I are just friends." Siobhán's voice cracked.

Sheila rolled her eyes. "Since you and Garda Flannery are so friendly, like, I was wondering if you would tell him for me. Just in case he's a bit browned off that I didn't notice it earlier. Because I should have mentioned it. I don't know why I didn't. And the longer I waited, the harder it was to confess."

"Confess what?"

Sheila took Siobhán by the elbow and maneuvered her into a back corner of the patio. Then she leaned in. Siobhán wanted to recoil from the smell of beer and cigarette smoke, but there was nowhere to go. "I'd ordered two different types of scissors," she said in a harsh whisper.

"Okay," Siobhán said. She had no idea why Sheila was so intense.

"One was just for promotions, like the box you refused to take." Sheila glared again as if waiting for another apology. Siobhán remained silent. "The other was actual scissors for the salon."

"For the salon?"

"For cutting hair, like. They still had the same pink handles, but they were sharper. Much sharper. I only ordered three of them. I was keeping them for work, like. After Niall was stabbed, I should have realized the promotional scissors weren't sharp enough to do the job. But I wasn't thinking. I was in shock, like. And the drink has a way of knocking all the sense out of me head. It wasn't until just this morning, when I had an appointment, that I finally noticed one of the salon scissors was missing. I'm betting it was the pair found in Niall."

"Oh my God. Why didn't you tell Garda Flannery straightaway?"

"I did leave him a message to call me straightaway. He hasn't called me back, like." Sheila edged closer. "Do you really think it's important?"

"Important?" *Only three pairs?* "It's everything. Who had access to those scissors?"

"That's just the thing."

"What?"

"I think I know who took those scissors."

And she'd waited this long? Siobhán curled her fist and warned herself to keep her temper in check. "Who?"

"Niall Murphy."

Siobhán exhaled and thought of the colorful saying her

da used to use. *Well, feck me pink with a wide-wash brush.* "Are you sure?"

"You know how he liked to lift things. He was the last client I had that day. When I heard he was killed with pink scissors, I knew those promies weren't sharp enough to do the deed. So I checked on me other scissors. Sure enough, one was missing."

"But you didn't see Niall take them?"

"I just told you I didn't even know they were gone until this morning."

"So why do you think Niall took them?"

"Who else? He loved thieving. Courtney said she'd already thrown him out of her shop for knickin' a few bobs."

Siobhán thought of the necklace he'd been caught stealing from Courtney. Had Siobhán been thinking along the wrong lines all this time? Could Niall's killing simply be revenge for being robbed? How many shopkeepers had he pissed off? Wasn't it likely he was also stealing from the cycle shop? There was that bicycle propped near the porch at Mary Murphy's house. Siobhán didn't know much about racing bikes, but she bet the ones at the top of the line might be worth quite a bit. Did Séamus or Bridie catch him stealing? Is that what she walked in on that morning? And if that was the case, why had Bridie defended him? Why did she give his last check to Butler?

What if he'd stolen much, much more than a pair of scissors from someone? Someone like Mike Granger?

This wasn't helping at all. She was guessing. Grasping at straws. And scissors.

So what if Niall had taken the murder weapon? What did that mean? Did he pull them on his murderer, and somehow they got the best of him? Used them against him? Was there a struggle to reach them first? If Niall hadn't knicked the scissors, would he still be alive?

"Siobhán?" Macdara called out. He stood in the doorway. He and Siobhán locked eyes. He took in her dress, leaned against the door frame, and gave her a lazy smile. It was the sexiest he'd ever looked.

"Speak of the devil," Sheila said. Macdara raised his eyebrow.

"We have news about the murder weapon," Siobhán said. Macdara closed his eyes as if she'd just wounded him. When he opened them, the sexy look was long gone.

Chapter 34

Macdara turned to Sheila. "Do you mind giving us a minute?"

"Not at all," Sheila said. She evaporated. So did everyone else on the patio. They were alone. Macdara stepped closer. He was dressed in lovely dark denims with a dark blue shirt that brought out his eyes. His hair had actually met a brush and looked soft to the touch. His face was so smooth she wanted to run her fingers along his jaw. And he looked absolutely furious with her. She'd never wanted him more in her life.

"I cannot believe you," he said. "Or maybe it's me I can't believe."

"I didn't come here to investigate—"

"You're full of it, O'Sullivan. Although I must say, the dress certainly tells a different story." Siobhán never knew a single gaze could tell so many tales until that moment when Macdara raked his eyes over her with both appreciation and irritation.

"Pio dragged me out here. I was at the bar with Maria. Ask her yourself."

"Maria?" Macdara's head swiveled toward the entrance.

"And before you accuse me of making plans with both of ye, I didn't know she was home. She wanted to surprise me."

Macdara put his hands up. "It's not a bother. I want you to have a good evening." He stepped even closer. "Do you even know how?"

"Sheila said the scissors that killed Niall weren't part of the promotional ones she gave away."

Macdara threw up his hands. "What?"

"She ordered three other pairs for cutting hair. Much sharper pairs. And one of them went missing the night Niall was killed."

"And she's just saying something now?"

"She's been on a bit of a bender, said she didn't notice it until this morning."

Macdara shook his head and ran his fingers through his hair as if there was no longer a point to looking good. "I'll talk to Sheila," he said. "When I'm back on duty. Because believe it or not, there is more to me than being a guard. I actually thought you knew that."

"I do. But even friends talk about things, don't they?"

"Is that what we are? Friends?" He met her gaze straight on.

"Sheila thinks Niall took the scissors himself."

"You're going to be the death of me."

"He was her last client. And you know as well as I do that Niall liked to nick things from shops. It got me thinking. What if that's why he was killed? What if he stole something big from someone?"

"Am I supposed to be worked up about the scissors or the motive here?"

"Can't you be worked up about both at the same time?"

"A few minutes ago when I saw you in that little black dress I was worked up about something else entirely," Macdara said.

An unexpected confidence seized Siobhán, like a sudden gust of wind. She stepped up to Macdara, put her hands on his chest, and looked up at him. "I was looking forward to this too. A Friday night. A proper date."

"Yet here we are—talking shop," he said in a near whisper.

"Because the killer has just been narrowed down to whoever had access to the murder weapon the day before. And if Niall had the weapon on him, it might mean the murder wasn't premeditated. Maybe he meant to kill someone, but whoever it was got to the scissors first."

"Maybe someone he was fighting with that evening?"

Siobhán dropped her hands and stepped back. "It's not James."

"I'll let you get back to Maria."

"I don't want to," Siobhán said. "I'd rather get some air. With you."

Macdara contemplated her for a long, lazy second. "You sure?"

"Just let me say good-bye." She had to get out of here, and Macdara seemed to be in the same frame of mind. Maria, to Siobhán's slight disappointment, didn't put up a fuss when Siobhán said she was leaving. Before they were even out the door, Maria was on her mobile chattering and laughing— with someone from Dublin, no doubt.

Siobhán and Macdara walked without even discussing it and soon found they were headed to the abbey. Were they subconsciously going there to kiss like teenagers? The thought made her laugh.

"What's so funny?"

"Nothing." It was true. Nothing was really funny. They stopped along the bridge over the creek. A few streetlamps shone, offering the night a bit of warmth. The priory framed the background, a solid reminder of the past. Macdara stopped here. Maybe he wasn't going to make out with her after all.

"Why were you late?" Siobhán asked. "For our date," she said without looking at him.

"James wanted to see me," Macdara said.

"What?" This was the last thing she expected him to say. "Why?"

"I wasn't going to talk shop tonight, Siobhán. And even if I was, that thought would have been zapped out of my mind the minute I saw you in your little black dress. But now you've started it. Don't forget that."

"Why did James want to see you?"

Macdara turned to her, and to her surprise he grabbed her hands and held on to them. "Did someone leave you a threatening note?"

Shite. James and his big mouth. Didn't he see she was trying to help him? Siobhán pulled away, dug the note out of her handbag, and handed it to him. He read it, then moved closer to the street lamp and read it again. A shadow fell across his face. When he looked up at her, concern was stamped across his face. "This is evidence. You, of all people, are hiding evidence."

"I was going to tell you tonight." *Was she?*

"You aren't trained. You're going to get yourself killed."

Siobhán pointed to the note. "This means I'm getting close."

"Too close."

"Listen to me, will ye? Even if Niall had the scissors on him, I still think the killing was planned."

Macdara sighed. "If he had the scissors on him, then it's more likely it was a tussle. The scissors dropped. Niall reached them first. If he hadn't, we might have a different victim."

Siobhán shook her head. "I don't agree. The body was staged. And a single jab to the heart? That takes precision, not necessarily passion."

"I've forgotten everything you said except for 'passion,'" Macdara said.

"I think the killer had been following Niall around town. If Niall had the scissors on him, that meant that either the killer didn't bring a weapon, or the minute the killer realized Niall had a sharp pair of scissors on him, he used it *instead* of his weapon."

"Can't be both."

"I think the killer was forced into carrying it out early because he saw the perfect opportunity to frame my brother for the murder."

"Because he witnessed Niall and James fighting?"

"Yes. But not necessarily that evening. Practically the entire town was in the bistro when the argument with Niall broke out."

"That wasn't just your brother. Most of us were arguing with Niall," Macdara said.

"On the evening of the murder, I think the killer was following Niall. He chased him along the road behind our bistro. Perhaps they were the ones running around the back of Mike's store as well. If they hadn't been spotted, maybe Niall would have been killed there."

"So the killer was trying to frame James, or he wasn't?"

"I think the location was opportune. Maybe even the timing of the killing. But the deed itself? It was in the works."

Macdara shook his head. "I know he's your brother. But what if he did it, Siobhán? I have to consider it a likely possibility."

"James was too drunk. Whoever killed Niall had a lot more motor control. And they were coherent enough to wipe away fingerprints and move the body."

"Maybe he had help."

"Help?" She didn't like the way Macdara was looking at her. "What are you saying?"

"I have to look at all angles." His words rang out like a confession. His meaning clicked into place.

"You mean me," she said. "You think I helped James kill Niall."

"I don't want to think it. But I'm supposed to. Because that's my job. And there are six of ye. And don't tell me you don't look out for each other."

"I can't believe this. I'm truly alone. This is why I have to keep digging."

Macdara threw his hands up in the air. "Enough. Enough flying about town on your little scooter, riling everyone up. That's my job. Stick to yours."

"Stay in the kitchen, is that what you mean? Like the note says?"

"Are you saying I wrote that note?" Macdara said. "Who's to say you didn't write the note?" He was yelling. She'd never even heard him raise his voice before.

"Why would I write the note?" Siobhán demanded.

"To deflect suspicion off of James."

"Maybe I could say the same thing about you," Siobhán said. "Because you're a guard, no one suspects you. That's the perfect way to hide in plain sight."

Macdara's jaw dropped open. "Why would I kill Niall?"

"Because he was hurting me," Siobhán blurted out. The meaning behind the statement hung between them as they stared at each other. Macdara looked away first.

"I'm a guard. Our job is to protect our citizens, not murder them. And if I was doing it to keep Niall from hurting you, I certainly wouldn't have left his body in the back of your bistro."

That shut her up. He had a point there. The date was officially ruined. Accusing each other of murder was a definite romance killer. She might as well destroy the rest of it. "Did James tell you anything else?"

Macdara's eyebrow shot up. "Like what?"

"I didn't visit just James that day. I saw Billy Murphy as well."

Macdara cursed. "I knew there was something when I picked you up. I could tell." He reached out and took Siobhán's hand. "What did he say?"

"He stuck to Niall's story. Said someone else caused the accident. But he doesn't know if there really is a video, and he wouldn't tell me who."

"Because he's lying!"

"I guess."

"You guess?"

"I'm not Billy's biggest fan either. But he sounded sincere."

Macdara shook his head. "I'm telling you he and Niall made this story up. He's sticking to it because it's scripted. If there was another car involved in that accident, there would have been evidence. And I don't mean a video or a witness. I mean physical evidence on the ground. Tire marks, paint chips, something. Anything."

"But he even admitted he was drunk."

"You're saying that helps his case? It proves what I'm saying."

"I'm telling you I believed that he believed someone else caused the accident."

"So who was it? If someone else caused the accident, why wouldn't he just tell us who?"

"He said without proof we wouldn't believe him."

"Damn right."

"See? You're proving his theory."

Macdara touched Siobhán's arm. "When I arrived at the scene, Billy wasn't knocked out. He was talking. Kept saying, 'I'm sorry, I'm sorry, I'm sorry.'"

Siobhán shook her head. "I don't want to hear this."

"I don't want to tell you. But I hate the fact that he's pulling this shite. You cannot believe him."

Siobhán chose her words carefully. She didn't want to

upset Macdara more than he already was. "Even if he's lying, he knows something."

"What?"

"The murderer has to be the other person Niall was trying to extort for twenty thousand pounds. Whatever the reason. I think Billy knows who that person is."

"Maybe I can use that," Macdara said.

"How?"

"Pay him a visit. Threaten to charge him with interfering with an investigation, then offer to drop it if he tells me."

"It's worth a try."

Macdara smiled. "Imagine. It's almost like I'm a trained guard."

"When can you see him?"

"I would go right now if I could. Believe it or not, I want to solve this case just as much as you do."

"I believe you. And I never thought you killed Niall. I'm sorry." She wanted to reach out and touch him again, but her confidence was gone.

Macdara looked out toward the abbey. "I'll go tomorrow."

"You carefully checked Niall's room at his mam's, right?"

"Yes," Macdara said. "Why?"

"Did you ever find a smartphone associated with Niall or Billy?"

"No. And before you ask—yes, we're aware that Niall probably had one on him and the killer probably took it."

"And why would the killer do that? Unless they thought Niall had some kind of video on his phone?"

"Maybe it was someone he had business dealings with and they wanted to erase the texts or phone calls."

"So why is my brother still sitting in jail?"

"Because without the phone, we don't have anything but wild theories."

"We have to find it. We have to know once and for all whether or not there's a video."

"We're on it," Macdara said. "We've been on it."

"You'll be busy with Billy. I could check around—"

"No." Macdara stepped closer. "You have to stop. Promise me."

"But . . ."

"Promise."

"Fine." She could tell he was serious. She needed him on her side.

Macdara exhaled. "I'll see what I can get out of him, and I'll look for the phone. You have my word."

"Thank you."

"Are we done talking business? For tonight?" He was looking at her face, her lips. Was he thinking about what it would be like for them to kiss? She was. She'd been thinking about it for a long, long time. Ever since that day a year ago when he'd crushed her to his chest. She nodded. He stepped closer. She closed her eyes. A few seconds later, she felt his lips on hers, softly. They kissed without any other parts of their bodies touching—a wise move, considering that the feel of his lips alone was enough to set every part of her alive with electricity. He ended the kiss, and she opened her eyes. They stared at each other for a while.

"You have no idea how long I've waited to do that," Macdara said.

A little bit of her confidence crept back. "So why did you stop?"

"Because I don't just want you. I *want* you." He meant the whole package. Marriage? A family? Did she want that too? She clasped her hands, almost in prayer, and brought them up to her mouth. "I know," Macdara said. "This isn't the right time. You're going through too much. You're young. You're in pain. There are a million reasons I should stay away from you, Siobhán O'Sullivan, but I don't want to. You have no idea how much I want you. You don't even know how amazing you are. I've literally watched you grow into this unbelievable human being this past year. I know you're a smart and independent woman, but at the same time, I want to take care of you, and the young ones, and everything that entails. I'm going to solve this case. And then I'm going to ask you out again. But don't say yes if you aren't going to be sticking around. Because I am. And I know what I want. I've known for a very long time."

"I feel—," Siobhán started to say.

Macdara put his finger over her mouth. "We solve the case first. We sort this out second. Alright?" She nodded. Anything else, even a single utterance, would likely break her open. And now she had one more desperate reason for wanting to solve this case. Macdara held out his hand. "I'll walk ye home." He laced his fingers through hers as they headed for town.

"Thank you," she said softly.

"For what?"

"For trying to protect me."

"I'm not trying to protect you," Macdara said, squeezing her hand as his voice lifted into a jovial register. "I'm doing my best to protect everyone else in town from the likes of you."

Chapter 35

Siobhán spent the next day focusing on the bistro with some much needed help from Maria. Siobhán insisted the young ones take the day off. Normally they'd only be helping out part-time, but the murder had taken up too much of Siobhán's focus. Giving them a break was long overdue. Ciarán and Eoin were off to a hurling match, while Gráinne and Ann were going to hit the shops in Charlesville. Siobhán felt bad about leaving Maria last night, especially in light of how helpful she was being today.

When the lunch break came, Maria stayed to clean up so Siobhán could head for the bank. She was thankful for the scooter and its little basket. She had just returned and said good-bye to Maria. They were going to go out for drinks that evening to make up for the night before. She had almost finished putting groceries away when she heard her mobile ringing across the room. She hurried to the register, where she'd left it, but by the time she reached it, her voice mail had already picked up.

Courtney Kirby's name flashed across the screen. There was no such thing as a short conversation with Courtney, and Siobhán had a few more things to do before she could put her feet up. She'd hurry through the rest of her to-do list and call Courtney back when she had a spot of time.

It turned out to be an hour later. Aching feet propped up, cup of tea in hand, Siobhán listened to Courtney's voice mail before calling her back. She sounded frantic. Siobhán immediately put her teacup on the table and her feet on the floor as she listened.

"I found out something that's going to crack the case wide open," Courtney cried. "Hurry over." The message cut off. Oh, why had Siobhán waited to listen to Courtney's message? Typical. This was just typical. Was Courtney still there? What was it? Had she called the guards? Siobhán tried to call her back as she hurried out to her scooter. The call went directly to Courtney's voice mail. She called Macdara and was told he was out of the office.

"Did Courtney Kirby call in for him?" Siobhán asked.

"Several times," the girl said. "I left him a message to call her back. Is something wrong?"

"I don't know," Siobhán said. "I'm going to check."

"Call us back if you need us," the girl said. Siobhán headed for Courtney's shop. When she pulled up, she immediately saw that the curtains were shut and the CLOSED sign had been turned around. Siobhán knocked. No answer. The shop, like many in town, had a back garden. The buildings were too close together for her to be able to maneuver herself between them, She would have to ride down the street, make a left as soon as she could, and come up behind Courtney's shop. She was prepared to do that when she saw Bridie coming down the street.

"Do you have a key?" Siobhán asked as she approached.

"I do, luv," Bridie said. "But it's my day off."

"We need to get in."

Bridie stopped and looked at the window. "Courtney isn't there?"

"I knocked," Siobhán said.

"She must have run out. I'm sorry I can't let you in."

"She left me an urgent message. I need to make sure she's okay."

"What kind of an urgent message?"

Siobhán hesitated. Courtney had called her, not Bridie. But this was no time to keep secrets. "She said she'd learned something that was going to crack the case wide open and to hurry over."

"And she's not answering?"

"I pounded on the door."

"Should we call Garda Flannery?"

"I tried. He's out."

"Maybe I should call Séamus."

"Why?"

"You're not the only one afraid of a killer. If you think she's in trouble, he could still be in there."

"Or she," Siobhán said. "How long would it take Séamus to get here?"

"It depends what he's in the middle of." Bridie fumbled in her purse for her mobile.

"Would you just open the door? I'll go in myself."

Bridie sighed. "You're stubborn, aren't ye?"

"I'm worried about Courtney. You have to let me check on her."

Bridie shook her head but handed Siobhán the key. "I'm still calling himself."

"Suit yourself." Siobhán opened the door and pushed it open. It was dark. She listened for any sounds.

"She always keeps lights on," Bridie said. "Even when she leaves." Siobhán felt around the wall for a switch and, upon finding it, flicked on the light. It took a second for her to blink, and another second to take in the room, after which she wished she hadn't. Courtney Kirby was lying on her back on top of the middle display table, eyes open and staring at the ceiling, her arms and legs hanging over the sides. Her expression was frozen as if she were a porcelain doll.

"Courtney," Siobhán cried. "Are you hurt?"

"What is it?" Bridie entered behind Siobhán, then cried out when she saw Courtney. She lunged forward, but Siobhán held her back.

"It's too late," Siobhán said. "Don't touch anything."

It was indeed too late. It took a minute to notice that there was a pair of hot pink scissors protruding from Courtney's chest.

Bridie crumpled to the ground. "No, no, no, no," she cried.

Siobhán wanted to crumple to the ground beside her. Instead, she dialed for the guards. Even as she told them to hurry, she couldn't believe this had happened again. And once more, she was the one to have discovered the body. Why, when she defied the odds, was it always for the worst? Not that this was any time to be feeling sorry for herself.

Poor Courtney. What had she discovered? If Siobhán had only answered her mobile, Courtney might still be alive. Or maybe Siobhán too would be dead. *Hurry, I've got something that's going to crack the case wide open.* Siobhán shuddered. Apparently, she'd been dead right.

Siobhán didn't want to be seen at another crime scene, so as soon as Macdara arrived she gave him her mobile and let him listen to the frantic message from Courtney. Then she jumped on her scooter and was about to head back to the bistro when she spotted Bridie pacing on the footpath. Siobhán stopped to watch her. It took a few seconds to realize that Bridie was talking on her mobile. Of course, she was probably just giving Séamus a ring, but something about the look of panic in Bridie's eyes made Siobhán keep watching.

t was more than just shock at finding Courtney—at least it
ppeared that way.

Bridie looked *guilty*. Siobhán couldn't put her finger on
t, but every time she looked at Bridie or talked to her, she
ad that same nagging feeling—that Bridie was hiding
omething. And so when Bridie slipped away and hurried
own the footpath Siobhán jumped off her scooter, parked it
n the footpath, and followed her on foot.

She kept a decent distance, although it was hardly neces-
ary. Bridie didn't look back once. All those spinning classes
ad apparently paid off for her, as Siobhán had to jog to
eep up. She expected Bridie to either take a turn for the
ycle shop or their home, so she was surprised when Bridie
isappeared into Mike's Market. *All this fuss and she's do-
ng her messages*? What an odd time to pick up your bits and
obs. Maybe Bridie wanted to comfort herself with choco-
ates or biscuits, or maybe she was there for an entirely dif-
erent reason. Siobhán hesitated and then hurried into the
hop. If Bridie saw her, she could always claim to be in
earch of chocolates herself.

She entered in time to see Bridie being ushered into
Mike's office and the door shutting behind them. Siobhán
tood, wondering what to make of that. Siobhán meandered
round the store, hanging as close to Mike's door as possi-
le. But it was of no use; she couldn't hear a word they were
aying. Should she just knock on the door? Just then it swung
pen. Siobhán reacted instinctively and dove for the floor.

"Siobhán?" Mike Granger stood over her.

"Sorry," she said. "I must have slipped."

"Is there a wet patch on the floor?" He looked stricken.

"No. Just my clumsy feet." He held his hand out and
elped her up. Bridie was standing next to him, her face so
ale she looked ghostly.

"I'll tell Séamus to have a word with you," she said to
Mike, then hurried on with a nod to Siobhán.

"Excuse me," Siobhán said. She was done playing games. She caught up with Bridie and looped her arm into hers.

Bridie jumped. "Jaysus. You put me heart in crossways."

"Come to the bistro and have a cup of tea," Siobhán said. "We've both had a shock."

"I can't," Bridie said. "I have to get home."

"You can come in for a cuppa," Siobhán said. "I insist."

"Not today," Bridie said, extracting her arm. They were outside now in front of the shop.

"Do you have any idea how Courtney was involved in all this?"

Bridie stopped. "They're going to have to let James go now. Isn't that enough?"

"What do you mean?"

"Did you follow me here?"

"Of course not. I wanted some chocolates."

Bridie scanned Siobhán. "Where are they?"

"I fell, and then you and Mike came out, and I forgot all about them."

Now Bridie glanced around the footpath. "Where's your scooter?"

"I decided to walk."

"You were following me! Who do you think you are? A detective superintendent?"

"No. I'm just trying to catch a killer."

"To free James, is that it?"

"Of course."

"Then you're finished."

"Excuse me?"

"He obviously isn't the killer, so they'll have to let him go."

"Do you think so?"

"He couldn't have stabbed Courtney from jail, could he?"

"Of course not."

"So James will be free. You can stop now. I'm begging you. Stop."

"I can't. Not with a killer on the loose. I care about Court-ney." *Cared.* Siobhán just couldn't bring herself to talk about Courtney in the past tense.

"We *all* cared about Courtney. I worked closer with her than anyone."

"Which is why I thought you might know something."

"I don't. I told ye." Bridie started to walk away.

Siobhán cut her off. "I think you're hiding something, Bridie Sheedy. No. I know you're hiding something."

Bridie put her hands on her hips. "You know?"

"The day I walked into the cycle shop and saw you there with Niall. The look on your face. It was as if I had caught you."

"We've been through this. I showed you the gear."

"You showed me a large envelope. I didn't open it."

"You're not going to stop, are you?"

"No," Siobhán said. "I'm not." Bridie was right. This was no longer just about James. It was about stopping a killer.

Bridie slumped as if defeated. "I'll have that cup of tea, alright," she said.

This time the bistro was jammers, and nobody hesitated to speculate about the murder. Voices were raised outright instead of hushed. Her siblings were running around like mad, and once again Siobhán hadn't been there for them. She set Bridie up with tea but had to delay their talk. A neighbor down the street, one of the ladies Siobhán had overheard talking about James during the fund-raiser, whisked up to Siobhán and squeezed the life out of her hands.

"I knew James couldn't have done such a t'ing!" she said. "Mark my words, I told everyone. He is not the mur-derer!"

"Thank you," Siobhán said, withdrawing her hands as soon as she could. She threw on an apron and dove right into the kitchen to help serve. They shooed her to the register where she had to engage in talk of the murder while taking care of people's bills. Suddenly everyone was trying to as sure her that they never for one minute thought the murdere was James.

By the time the lunch shift was over and her siblings had scattered for a well-deserved break, Siobhán fully expected Bridie to be gone. She was shocked to find Bridie still at her table. She sank down in the seat across from her. Bridie's eyes were red from crying. Siobhán reached out and touched her hand. It was ice-cold.

"Are you alright, pet?" Siobhán asked.

"It's my fault," Bridie said. "I don't know how. Bu maybe if I had told the truth from the beginning, Courtney would still be alive."

"Tell me," Siobhán said.

"I did buy a gear. But I didn't need Niall's help to do that."

"I didn't think so," Siobhán said. "I'm sure you know more about bicycle parts than he did."

Bridie swallowed and then tilted her chin up and looked Siobhán in the eye. "I was showing Niall our financial rec ords. So he could see."

"So he could see you didn't have twenty thousand euro.'

Bridie gasped. "How did you know?"

"He tried to get me to give him ten thousand euro. I knew he had to be targeting others as well."

"So now you know."

"What did he have on you?"

Bridie squeezed her eyes shut, then opened them. "I did have an affair. Just not with Niall. But Niall found out about it and was threatening to tell Séamus."

Chapter 36

❧❧❧

Was it Mike Granger? Siobhán wondered. She didn't ask. Bridie was ready to talk, and she wasn't going to interrupt her.

"It happened last year. When Séamus was racing day in and day out. Always training. I was stressed from trying to get pregnant and lonely because he was gone half the time. So I let myself be taken in by another man. It was wrong, I know it. I'm so ashamed."

"I see," Siobhán said. She didn't know why she felt so betrayed. Because she didn't want to imagine how much this would hurt Séamus. Because she wanted to think there were some couples out there who actually made it. Because everything was changing.

"Please don't tell him. Everything is better now. He even gave up racing."

"How did Niall find out about the affair?"

"The man I was seeing didn't want me to break it off. Niall overheard us in O'Rourke's one night. The man was drunk and saying things he shouldn't have."

So that's why Mike lit into Niall at the bistro. He was fu-

rious with Niall for holding the affair over their heads. "So Niall was blackmailing the two of you for twenty thousand pounds?"

"He said he'd accept ten from me and ten from the man I was with."

"How generous."

"He said he videotaped our conversation with his mobile."

"Did he ever show you the video?"

Bridie shook her head. "He said I couldn't see it until I had paid at least ten thousand euro."

More reason to support Macdara's theory. Niall didn't have anything on the accident. No proof. No video. He simply knew enough about his victims to know their weak spots. Where they were desperate for information. How dare he? Using others' grief and secrets to his advantage.

"Why in the world did you keep saying what a good lad Niall was?"

"I was hoping if I generated enough positive energy around him, he'd stop. You know what kind of life those boys have had. I'm not trying to make excuses for him."

"Yet that's exactly what you're doing."

"I'm the one to blame. For the affair. I guess part of me felt like I deserved the punishment."

"Next time go to confession instead."

"I couldn't bear to tell Father Kearney what I did."

"You have to tell Macdara."

Bridie swallowed, then nodded. "There's more."

Siobhán leaned in. "Go on."

"The man I was with. His reaction to being extorted might have been very different than mine."

"More aggressive?"

Bridie nodded. "He even stole Niall's passport, thinking he could somehow use that to threaten Niall."

Mike Granger! "Threaten Niall how?"

"This man was convinced that once Niall had the money, he was going to use it to get out of the country. He'd need his passport to do that, of course."

"What was the plan? Take Niall's passport and then what?"

"That's just it. I don't know. He just said he wasn't going to let Niall get away with it."

So Siobhán was right. She knew Mike had been lying about the passport. Bridie had no idea she'd just divulged the identity of the man with whom she'd had an affair. She certainly did have a type. Both Séamus and Mike were older than her, and a bit on the gruff side. And Mike certainly did have a temper. So much for thinking he was standing up for the O'Sullivans that day in the bistro, Mike was furious with Niall for very personal reasons.

"How did Mike even get hold of Niall's passport?"

Bridie's head jerked up. "I didn't say it was Mike."

"I won't tell."

"It's not Mike. I didn't say it was Mike."

Siobhán could hear the panic in Bridie's voice. "I saw Niall's passport on his desk the other day. Macdara knows about it too. Don't worry. I won't tell anyone else. Now how did he get the passport?"

Bridie sighed, and her shoulders slumped. "Niall was always leaving things on the bar. His money, his phone, his passport."

"Why was Niall carrying around his passport?" Siobhán wanted to see if Bridie would substantiate the gossip about Niall leaving the country.

"He said he was going to Australia the minute Billy was out and he had enough money. He was carrying it around like a good luck charm. Anyway, Mike took it off the bar the night of his murder. Even Declan didn't notice. The minute I heard Niall had been killed, I told Mike he had to either give the passport to the guards and tell them everything—or destroy it."

"He did neither," Siobhán said. Had Niall confronted Mike about stealing his passport? Was there a chase? A violent struggle?

Bridie was already on edge; there was no use asking if Mike had had any run-ins with Courtney. Instead Siobhán asked Bridie if Courtney knew about the affair.

"Of course not," Bridie said. "Nobody knew. Except Niall." *And now he's dead.* It hung in the air. Bridie stared at her empty teacup as if the name of the murderer were written in the leaves.

Niall was one thing, but Siobhán couldn't imagine Mike hurting Courtney. They couldn't be dealing with two separate killers in Kilbane, could they?

The first one is the hardest. Oh, God. What if Courtney found out about the affair, or somehow suspected Mike of murdering Niall and confronted him? Could Siobhán really know what he would do if he'd already murdered once and his back was up against the wall? "Did you notice anything different about Courtney lately?"

Bridie twirled her tea cup around the table. "Different how?"

"Did she mention she was looking into the case?"

"She talked about the murder, of course, with just about everyone who came into the shop. You know Courtney. But looking into it? Of course not."

"Then someone who came in must have provided a tip. Were there any folks in recently who stand out for any reason?"

Bridie considered this. "Mary Murphy was in to learn how to use e-mail."

"At the gift shop? Why?"

"Courtney set up her computer in the back and decided she'd let people use it. You know, like an Internet café. For a charge, like. You should have thought of it first."

Siobhán sat up straight. "Forget the entrepreneurial bit. When was this?"

Bridie tilted her head. "Day before yesterday? I believe that's right."

"Courtney showed her?"

"I showed her. And, heavens forgive me, but it was like trying to teach a monkey how to type."

"Who did she want to send an e-mail to?"

"Apparently everyone. Insurance people, Billy's solicitor, I don't know who all. But poor thing. Progress isn't fair to the elderly, is it?"

Siobhán didn't think of Mary Murphy as elderly, but it was true, she was from a generation who didn't think they'd ever need to own a computer just to get along in the daily world. "Did she send any e-mails?"

"That's why she was there, wasn't it?"

Siobhán bit her tongue. "Did you catch a glimpse of any of those e-mails?"

"Of course not."

Siobhán got up and refreshed their tea and biscuits, then sat back down. "Did anyone else make a surprise visit?"

Bridie smiled. "The movie star was in."

The Yank. Siobhán wasn't surprised Bridie was calling him that. "Did he buy anything?"

"No. As a matter of fact, I found his behavior rather odd. He asked a lot of questions about foot traffic and square footage and the like."

"He's interested in buying one of our buildings. Starting up some kind of mystery business."

"Male strippers," Bridie said with a grin.

Siobhán laughed, then stopped. It felt so wrong to laugh when Courtney was gone.

"Sorry," Bridie said. "Poor taste. Still. I'd even give up our chipper to see that."

* * *

Siobhán called Macdara. She didn't expect him to answer, not with a second murder to investigate, but she had to tell him what she'd learned. She crossed herself before betraying Bridie's confidence. It couldn't be helped. She reached his voice mail and spoke into it quickly in case it cut her off.

"I'm not investigating, but as you can imagine, the bistro was buzzing today, and Bridie unburdened herself on me. First, it may be nothing, but Chris Gorden isn't here just to check on ancestors. He's actively sizing up real estate and is in cahoots with Alison Tierney to buy whatever properties he can, including Courtney's gift shop. Second, you may want to have a look at Courtney's computer. Mary Murphy was using it to send e-mails. I don't know if that has anything to do with what Courtney discovered, but it's a place to start. And third—this is the worst bit, and you know I don't enjoy sharing news like this, but it might be important: Mike and Bridie apparently had an affair last year when Séamus was busy with his racing schedule. I'm only telling you because Niall found out about it and was trying to extort both Bridie and Mike Granger for ten thousand euro each. Mike lied to us about Niall's passport. He didn't find it; he stole it. He thought Niall was going to try to leave the country as soon as he got someone—apparently anyone—to give him twenty thousand euro. I don't know if any of that helps, or why anyone would kill poor Courtney—"

Macdara's voice mail cut her off with a loud beep. Great. Even his mobile was reprimanding her now. Siobhán hadn't meant to rattle on. She hated people who left rambling voice messages. But she had to give him everything—who knows which tidbit might just be enough to crack the case—

Crack the case wide open. Those were the exact words Courtney used. As if she had no doubt as to the killer's identity. What had she learned? Who else had she called? Macdara would find her mobile and check it out, wouldn't he?

How Siobhán wished there were a camera on him so she could see what he was doing and learning about the case.

Had Courtney actually been right about the killer? Or had she accidentally alerted her killer? And if she was in his or her warpath, didn't that mean Siobhán could be next? Macdara was right. She should stay out of it. She couldn't put her siblings through any more trauma. But how could she drop it now? It was unfathomable that someone could do this and get away with it. Siobhán sighed and snuck into the kitchen for a slice of brown bread with her tea. Some days it was the little things that got her through.

Chapter 37

Maria came to the bistro the evening of Courtney's murder to say good-bye. She was lugging a huge suitcase. "I can't believe how much stuff I brought," she said. "Just a weekender, and I've filled an entire suitcase." Siobhán laughed and sat down with Maria for a few minutes, dreading the moment when she left again. She kept waiting for Maria to mention the murder. It was all anyone else was talking about, but Maria was behaving as if nothing else in the world existed other than Dublin and Trinity College. Would Siobhán have been just as obnoxious if she had gone?

"I'm sure you heard about Courtney," Siobhán said. "It was the biggest shock of me life."

"The whole town is talking about you. You're like a divining stick for dead bodies."

"I'm like a what?"

"You know those sticks that bend when you get them near water?"

Siobhán just looked at her. Maria shrugged. "Anyway, I didn't want to mention it in case it upset ye even more."

So much for not hanging around the crime scene. Everyone knew she was the first to find Courtney anyway. "It's horrible," Siobhán said. "But I suppose James will be getting out now."

"That means you can come to Dublin!"

"I don't know about that," Siobhán said. After all that had happened, Dublin seemed so remote now.

"I'll tell Aisling you say hello, and that ye hardly miss us because you're too busy tripping over dead bodies." Maria hugged Siobhán before she could respond.

"My Joe Maxi is here," Maria said. Sure enough, a taxi idled at the curb. Siobhán helped her throw the suitcase into the boot, and then they hugged again. Siobhán waved as the taxi pulled away. Gawd, that suitcase was heavy. *Just a weekender, and I've filled an entire suitcase . . .*

Siobhán had a sudden thought. Niall had been dressed up because supposedly he was going to Dublin to see a solicitor. So where was his overnight bag? He must have had one. Even a small one. Gráinne hadn't said whether or not they'd planned on spending the night, but surely he would have had a bag in case things went long or they missed their train? Or even to change out of his suit once the appointment was over. If he did have a bag, where was it? Had the killer removed it from the scene along with Niall's phone? Had he disposed of it somewhere? Hung on to it? Would Mary Murphy know anything about his trip or what kind of bag he might have used? She was hoping she'd be in the bistro after the news of Courtney.

Siobhán hated going all the way out to her house. It was not terribly far in the scope of things, but definitely separate from the rest of the town. It wouldn't be so bad with her scooter. She'd been smart to make that investment.

She still hadn't heard back from Macdara. He wasn't avoiding her because of the kiss, was he? She was glad she had distractions on her mind; otherwise she'd be thinking about that moment even more than she already was. She wouldn't bother Macdara with another phone call about missing luggage until she paid a visit to Mary Murphy to see if she could find out exactly what kind of bag they should be looking for.

There was a stillness to Mary Murphy's house. The curtains were drawn tight against the windows, even in the midday heat. The steps creaked as Siobhán made her way up to the dilapidated front door. The only sound was an occasional clink of wind chimes, which hung askew from a rusted hook dangling over the door. A moldy smell permeated the air. The house had the feel of a child's toy left to rust in the rain.

There was no use peeking in the windows; they were all completely covered. Siobhán tried the door. It was locked. Should she check around back? What did she hope to learn by getting inside the house? Siobhán practiced her excuses as she hurried around to the back. *I heard what sounded like a call for help inside. The door was open; I could have sworn someone said to come in. She was expecting me.*

I was afraid she'd come to the same fate as Courtney Kirby.

Siobhán stopped in her tracks. What if she had? Siobhán didn't want to see another body, not in her lifetime. She should call Macdara again. Would he believe that she was simply paying a neighborly visit? She was pretty sure he was a man with limits. He might have feelings for her, think her the most beautiful woman in Kilbane, but if she continued to defy his order to stop investigating, he could very well never pursue her again.

And if he wanted her so badly, why wouldn't he come with her to Dublin? She could bring the entire brood as well. No, that wasn't how life worked. She was the one who was supposed to leave the nest. How many people ever took the nest with them? Siobhán looked up to find Mary Murphy bursting out the back door clutching a suitcase. Mary had her eyes on the ground, and Siobhán didn't move quickly enough.

Mary Murphy slammed into Siobhán, almost knocking the wind out of her. Siobhán gave a little cry, and Mary let out a scream.

"Jaysus, Mary, and Joseph," Mary Murphy said, stumbling back. "Don't ever sneak up on a person like that again."

"Sneaking? I was standing still."

"What are ye, a tree? What in heaven's name are you doing here?"

"Where are you going?"

"What are you doing in my back garden?"

"Looking for you."

"I'm on my way out, as you can see." Mary brushed past her and headed down the drive. Siobhán hurried after her.

"What's wrong?" Siobhán asked. She had never seen Mary Murphy look so panicked.

Mary whirled around. "How can you ask me that after what happened to poor Courtney?"

"It's horrible. But you seem particularly frightened."

"Mind your own business."

Why was everyone saying that to her? Couldn't anyone think of anything original? Just then a silver SUV pulled up the drive. What was Alison Tierney doing here? She and Chris Gorden stepped out.

"I'm ready," Mary Murphy said. Chris nodded at Siobhán and then heaved Mary's suitcase into the back of the SUV.

"What's going on?"

Mary Murphy shook her head. "You're trespassing on his property now," she said with a nod to Chris.

"You sold it?"

"And everything in it," she said. "It's brought me nothing but hard times. You know yourself."

"She wanted to sell," Chris said. "I didn't push her."

"I'm going to use the money to free my son," Mary Murphy said. "That's all my poor Niall was trying to do, God rest his soul."

"That's what I have to talk to you about," Siobhán said. "Please. Before you go."

"I've nothing to say. Not to you, not to anyone."

"I think I know why you're running."

Siobhán reached into her pocket and pulled out the threatening note someone had left in the bistro. "You sent me this."

Mary Murphy eyed the note like it was a snake capable of striking. "How do you figure that?"

"I remember seeing the pile of old magazines when I was here for the wake." Siobhán wasn't sure Mary had sent her the note, but she wanted to see her reaction.

"Which means anyone who was at the wake had access to those magazines," Mary pointed out.

"Is this note from you or not?"

"It is not. I'd say it's from the killer. Why won't you listen and stay alive?"

Siobhán glanced at Chris and Alison, who were far enough away that they couldn't overhear the whisperings. "You're not concerned about my safety. You're worried I'm going find out that you continued the blackmail that Niall started. You're the one getting too close to the killer. That's why you're running."

Siobhán wanted to add that Courtney might still be alive if Mary Murphy hadn't sent e-mails from her computer, but she didn't have confirmation of that just yet. "But why would you send people threats through e-mail? Didn't you know they could figure out who was sending the e-mails?"

"I didn't know a t'ing about those computers. I thought they were anonymous." Mary's voice shook with fear. So Siobhán was right. Mary had e-mailed the killer. "There's a

Delete button. I thought that meant it deleted whatever you did after you did it!"

"Who did you e-mail? What did you say? Why did they kill Courtney?"

Mary Murphy whirled around and lunged into the front seat of the SUV, then leaned over and blared the horn. "Let's go, let's go."

Siobhán ran up to the vehicle. Mary Murphy rolled her window up. Siobhán kept talking, not caring now whether or not Alison or Chris heard. "Garda Flannery is going to seize Courtney's computer. If you used her account to send threatening e-mails, you have to tell me who all you sent e-mails to."

Mary Murphy rolled her window down a smidge. "I'm doing the smart thing and getting out of this town alive. I suggest you do the same."

"Who did you e-mail? Help me narrow down the list of suspects, please."

Chris looked at Siobhán, then at Alison. "I say we don't give her a ride until she tells us," he said.

"No answers, no ride," Alison said.

Although she was glad Chris stepped in, she couldn't believe how Alison Tierney obeyed him. Movie star looks certainly served him well.

"Mike Granger, Bridie, and Declan," Mary Murphy said. "Your killer is one of those t'ree. And if I had known they were going to t'ink Courtney was threatening them, or if I had known they could figure out where the e-mail was comin' from, I wouldn't have done it. Are you satisfied? I'm sorry. E-mail is the devil's work. Now get me out of here."

"Declan?" Siobhán said. "What did Niall have on Declan?"

"Those are the t'ree I e-mailed. Alison, let's go."

"Billy's car, the furniture, your things? You're leaving everything?"

"I had some things shipped. The rest I never want to see again."

Alison started up the car. "Wait," Siobhán said. "Is one of Niall's overnight bags missing?"

Mary's eyes widened. "Yes, his black bag. I've looked everywhere for it. Why do you ask?"

"He was going to Dublin," Siobhán said. "It's a long day trip. I bet he was planning on spending the night. Which meant he would have needed to pack a bag. And he didn't have one when he was found."

"I bet the killer has it," Mary said.

"Where can I reach you if we find it?" Siobhán asked. She wanted to know where Mary was going.

"You can't," Mary Murphy said.

"I don't think Garda Flannery will be happy that you left. People will talk."

"I've heard worse."

"Can I look inside your house?"

"I told you. It's not mine anymore." The car pealed out, leaving Siobhán and Chris standing in the drive. She turned to look at the house. Home sweet home.

"You're welcome to come in," he said. "If you think it will help."

"They just left you here?" Siobhán said. "No motor car?" She couldn't help it; she glanced at Billy's car.

"I'm not touching that," he said. "Don't worry." He pointed to the bike leaned up against the porch. "Mary said I could use that to get around." Ah, the bike that Siobhán wondered if Niall had stolen. Or maybe Bridie gave it to him. She certainly was going out of her way to placate him. Did Séamus know Niall had the bike? Why did she care so much about that? Because she hated the thought of anyone stealing something that didn't belong to them. Maybe she'd mention it to Séamus. Then again, Chris thought it was his bike now. Was she ever going to learn to stay out of everyone's business?

"What's wrong?" Chris said.

"Niall might have stolen that bike from Sheedy's," Siobhán said. *Let him handle it.*

"If he did, I'll go in and pay for it."

"Thank you," Siobhán said. If he was a killer, he certainly was a polite one. She texted Macdara in case he wanted to follow Alison and stop Mary from leaving. Mike Granger, Bridie, and Declan. What on earth did she have on Declan?

A few minutes later, Chris and Siobhán stood back on the porch. The search of the house had turned up absolutely nothing.

"Now what?" Chris Gorden asked. "Are you going to break into everyone's home and see who has Niall's bag?"

Siobhán shook her head. "It could be in the trash or in the creek by now." The only things she found in the house were cut-up magazines, as she suspected. If Mary Murphy was telling the truth, the suspects were down to three.

"Be careful," Chris said.

"I will."

"You weren't afraid of me."

"What do you mean?"

"You walked right into the house with me. Alone. Unarmed. What if I was the killer?"

"Are you the killer?"

Chris laughed. "No. But you didn't know that."

"Mary Murphy wasn't afraid to talk in front of you."

"And you think she knows who the killer is?"

"I think she believes it's one of those three. Besides, if I turned up dead, Mary Murphy and Alison Tierney would have known it was you. Plus, I texted Garda Flannery and told him exactly where I was."

Not that he'd be able to reach her in time. Siobhán left that bit out. Chris was right. Only an eejit would follow a potential killer into his home all alone. Had she been assuming he wasn't the killer because she didn't want him to be? Too gorgeous to be a killer, he was. But shouldn't the ones she didn't suspect at all be the ones to look out for? Wasn't it always the one you least suspected?

What a sick game. She suspected everyone and no one equally. She wasn't cut out for this. And she was still standing here, chatting away, not a bit afraid for her life. Then again, she'd survived this far she might as well get a bit more out of him. She'd make sure she never put herself in such a vulnerable position again.

"Why did you buy this house?" Siobhán said. "I thought you were looking for a place in town."

"For my business," Chris said. "This will be my home."

"What is your business?"

Chris smiled. "You'll just have to wait for my grand opening."

"I suppose Courtney Kirby's place will be up for sale," Siobhán said. She wanted to weep. Poor Courtney. They had to catch the killer.

"I was thinking I could do with a pint," Chris said. "Would you like to join me?" He gave her a long look. He knew she wanted to talk to Declan. It couldn't be him. She loved Declan. Everyone loved Declan. The town might survive two murders, but she didn't see how anyone would get over it if the oldest living publican in Kilbane did it. Siobhán would have to be careful what she said to him as well. Accusing Declan was right up there with accusing Father Kearney. She sighed and hopped on her scooter. Chris pointed to the seat.

"Mind if I hop on?"

"I've only had it a short while. I'm a bit wobbly."

"I like to live dangerously." Siobhán gave a nod, Chris jumped on the back, and they were off. As she zoomed along the back road, she tried not to admit how good it felt to have Chris's arms wrapped around her waist, and she prayed it would never get back to Macdara.

Chapter 38

Declan flashed his gap-toothed grin, and if he thought it was odd to see Siobhán enter with the Yank, he didn't let on. And why would he? He probably knew more about every person in town than anyone realized. Bartenders didn't talk out of school, and Declan O'Rourke was a large man who didn't suffer fools. What if Mary Murphy had lied about who she had e-mailed? It was definitely a possibility with Declan. But had she lied about all three?

Mike Granger was sitting at the bar. And so was a haggard-looking Bridie. Would ye look at that—all three of her suspects in one place. Just as Siobhán was trying to figure out what to do, her mobile rang. It was Macdara. Declan set a pint of Guinness in front of her.

"Excuse me," she said. "I have to take this call." She hurried out to the back patio and quickly filled Macdara in on her visit with Mary Murphy. Then, to her surprise, Macdara filled her in on what the guards were doing.

"We're seizing Courtney's computer, and Sheila has given us a list of her most recent customers," he said. "And

I'll be able to track Mary Murphy down if I need her. She's moving into an apartment in Cork. Near the prison."

"Don't we have enough for the authorities to let James go?" Siobhán said.

"I've petitioned for his release," Macdara said. "But the sergeant hasn't ruled out the possibility of two killers."

"The chances of that are nil," Siobhán said. "But we do have one blackmailer and one killer."

"How so?"

"Mary Murphy all but admitted she was trying to get the money from those Niall was already blackmailing."

"Through e-mail?"

"She thought the Delete button deleted everything."

"What?"

"Honestly, I have no idea what she was thinking. Guess it was getting time-consuming cutting letters out of magazines."

"Are you saying she sent you the threatening note?"

"No—she said it was the killer. And she thinks the killer is one of the three she e-mailed—Declan, Bridie, or Mike." Siobhán whispered the names even though she was alone on the patio. "The sooner you check Courtney's computer, the better."

"One of those three?" Macdara said.

"I'm just telling you what Mary said to me."

"She could have been lying."

"Don't I know." Siobhán filled Macdara in on the search for Niall's bag and her interaction with Mary. She didn't mention Chris Gorden. Macdara promised to get access to the computer right away. Siobhán let out a sigh of relief. "Something in those e-mails led to Courtney's death."

"If you're right, this will all be over soon. Promise me you'll stay out of it until then." Macdara's voice was soft but strong.

"I promise." Siobhán meant it. She wasn't going to risk her life anymore. Not when so many other lives were counting on her.

"I'll talk to ye later."

"Wait. Do you think Niall and Mary would actually blackmail Declan O'Rourke? I mean, they couldn't possibly have anything on him, could they?" Siobhán didn't even know she was going to ask it until it was out of her mouth.

"You mean besides who has the biggest bar tab in Kilbane and who has ever shifted who?"

Siobhán laughed. "So you do it too."

"Do what?"

"Trust your gut during an investigation. Rule people out based on a feeling?"

"I wouldn't go that far."

"But you think I'm right? If Mary Murphy had known it wasn't smart to send threats through e-mail, then Courtney would still be alive."

Macdara let out a low noise, almost like a growl—a protective growl, if Siobhán had been forced to analyze it. "You have good instincts," he said. "The killer might have thought it was Courtney threatening them. Too bad the killer didn't stop to think that Courtney would be smarter than that. But let me bring this home. I don't want you in harm's way." A few folks wandered out onto the patio, and the noise level rose. "Where are you?" Jealousy crept into Macdara's voice.

"I'm at O'Rourke's."

"In the middle of the day?"

"Folks are on edge. Me included. But I'm headed back to the bistro now."

"I'll ring ye later," he said, and then hung up. Odd, she thought as she headed back to the bar. He sounded different with her this time. More intimate. She was right. He'd be green with jealousy if he knew she was hanging out with Chris Gorden. Was she doing anything wrong?

When she got back to the bar, Mike and Bridie were gone. Great. They didn't want Siobhán questioning them. Nobody wanted to answer her questions anymore.

Wait a minute. She'd just told Macdara that chances were slim that Kilbane had two killers. But what if she'd been wrong? What if Bridie and Mike were in on it together? Kilbane's own Bonnie and Clyde. Suddenly it seemed not only possible, but likely. Bridie would have known about Mary Murphy using Courtney's e-mail, so she wouldn't have mistaken Courtney for the blackmailer and killed her.

Unless. What if Courtney wasn't killed because she was mistaken for the blackmailer? What if Courtney was killed because she read Mary Murphy's e-mail to the killer? *I learned something that's going to crack the case wide open.*

If Bridie and Courtney were so close, why did Courtney call Siobhán instead of Bridie?

Because Bridie was the killer.

My God, could that be it? Could Bridie and Mike be the killers? The more she turned it around in her mind, the more convinced she became. What did she do now? Just wait for Macdara to find the proof?

She glanced at her pint, then at Chris Gorden, who, she just noticed, was watching her intently. "I'm sorry," she said. "I have to go."

"I thought you wanted to talk to Declan," Chris said.

"You want me alibi, do ye?" Declan said from the far end of the bar. Chris Gorden's mouth dropped open.

"He hears everything," Siobhán said.

"I was here, luv, you know that yourself," Declan said.

"With Séamus?" Siobhán said. She wanted to check on Bridie's statement.

"You've asked me this before. Séamus left at half one to run home to the missus."

So Bridie had lied. Said she was at her sister's. There was no doubt. Bridie was a killer. It hardly seemed possible, yet the evidence was mounting. Maybe Mike had kept Niall's passport because they were planning a quick getaway of their own. Poor Séamus.

Siobhán thought of the visit to the museum. If Séamus hadn't been there, would Bridie have killed her, too? Bridie and Mike had motive. They had means. Mike said he saw two lads outside his shop, but Mike could have been one of the lads; he could have chased Niall right down the street, to the back of their bistro. He hadn't gotten up early that morning; he was still up from the evening before.

Bridie and Mike were still in love. That's why they were in the pub together. Were they on their way to the train station or airport this very moment?

"Did Bridie or Mike Granger say where they were going?" Siobhán asked Declan.

Declan raised his eyebrow. "You're making it sound like they were going somewhere together. They just happened in at the same time is all."

"Right. Did either of them say where they were going?"

Declan shook his head and moved away. Siobhán started to leave. Chris put his hand on her arm.

"I heard . . . Bridie, is that her name?" he said.

Siobhán nodded, too worried to speak.

"I heard her tell the man from the store—"

"Mike Granger."

"She said, 'I swear.' Then something about 'tonight.'"

They were leaving. Tonight. She had to stop them; they couldn't get away with this. "Thank you."

Chris smiled. "You might be Nancy Drew, but I'm both Hardy Boys rolled into one."

"Who are they?"

"Never mind. What's going on?"

"I have to go," Siobhán said. She hurried out the front door and called Macdara. It went to voice mail. She hung up. What was she going to do? Wait? Or confront Mike and Bridie?

She exited the pub and ran to her scooter. It looked lower to the ground than usual. She looked closer. Her tires had been slashed; they weren't just low, they were flat as pancakes. Someone had done this deliberately. Mike and Bridie—who else?

She ran toward Mike's shop, then ran around it until she reached the back street—the same route Niall and the killer took that night. Maybe it would help to literally follow in their footsteps. By the time she reached her back garden, she was out of breath. Should she ask Séamus to fix her tires before telling him that Bridie was running away with Mike Granger and the two of them were cold-blooded killers?

Siobhán glanced at the garden. Bridie not only knew about that jar, she'd purposefully misdirected Siobhán by telling her she could buy a replacement jar at the hardware store instead of at Courtney's. Then again, Bridie could have bought the jar at the hardware store as well, like. That bit didn't matter so much. What did matter was that everything was starting to click into place.

Siobhán walked up to the back door, praying her siblings had locked it. Instead, it opened easily. Siobhán stepped into the bistro. Ann and Gráinne were in the front, drinking tea.

"How many times do I have to remind you to lock this door?" Siobhán said.

"All our customers are in the pubs," Ann said.

"I want this locked. Always." The girls nodded.

"Where have you been all day?" Gráinne said. "Is James getting out?"

"I'll tell ye all at the same time. Where's Eoin and Ciarán?" Siobhán asked.

"Eoin's upstairs," Gráinne said. "Ciarán went to the cycle shop."

The news stopped Siobhán in her tracks. The hairs on the

back of her neck tingled. *They had Ciarán.* She had to keep calm, not alarm the girls. "Why?"

"Bridie stopped by, said Séamus had a surprise for Ciarán." *Oh, God. She was using him as bait. Bridie wouldn't harm Ciarán, would she?* "Does Ciarán have the mobile on him?" Siobhán heard her voice crack into a higher register.

"I've got it," Gráinne said, holding it aloft. Why didn't she let Ciarán have his own mobile? Or a puppy? She would let him have one the minute they got him back. Her family was everything. The only thing. Never again would she complain about being stuck here. She wasn't stuck; she was where she wanted to be. They needed her. She'd been so busy investigating she had let her guard down.

She would never ever let Ciarán out of her sight again, and she would kill them, God help her, if they harmed a single hair on his head; she would kill them. She dialed the number of the cycle shop. After so many trips visiting her scooter, she had it memorized. There was no answer. Bridie knew Siobhán was on to her. She could have her. She could do whatever she wanted to her—as long as she didn't hurt Ciarán.

She dialed Macdara again. Once more his voice mail picked up. "Call me," she said, then hung up. She could call the other guards, but what if she was wrong about it all? And what if she was right and they didn't move fast enough? She couldn't leave Ciarán all by himself. She had to go.

"There's no answer at the cycle shop," she told the girls. "I'm going to fetch him."

"You sound funny," Ann said. "What is it?"

"Yes," Gráinne said. "What is it?"

"Lock all the doors and windows. If I'm not back with Ciarán in thirty minutes, you need to call Garda Flannery and tell him to get over there."

"You're scaring me," Ann said. "What's the matter with ye?"

"For once I agree with her," Gráinne said. "What are you hiding?"

"Please. Just do as I say. It's so important. Stay here. If I'm not back in thirty minutes, call Macdara. And if he doesn't answer, call the gardai station and have them send whoever is available."

"Based on what, like? That we haven't seen you for a half an hour?" Gráinne said.

"Make something up. Just get them there."

"Are you saying that Séamus is the killer?" Ann asked, wide-eyed.

"No. I'm not saying that at all." Should she tell them about Bridie and Mike? She didn't want to alarm them further, and she didn't want to falsely accuse anyone. It was better they be wary of everyone. "I don't care if Father Kearney comes knocking on the doors. Do not open them for anyone."

"Not even for Father Kearney?" Ann asked, wide-eyed.

"Just pretend you're not home," Siobhán said. "Until I'm back with Ciarán."

"Should we get Eoin?" Gráinne said, looking toward the stairs.

Eoin would insist on coming with Siobhán. She'd rather he be here to protect the girls. "The minute I'm gone. Stay close to Eoin. But don't tell him where I've gone unless it's been thirty minutes."

"If you won't let us go with you, then you should take Eoin," Gráinne said.

"No. I want him here. Stay here, and do this for me. Will ye? Please. I need you, I really, really need you to listen."

"We will," Gráinne said.

"Cross our hearts and hope to die," Ann said. She slapped her hand over her mouth as the irony registered.

"Thirty minutes," Siobhán said.

"We heard you," Gráinne said, trying to stay brave. "Don't get your knickers in a twist."

Chapter 39

Siobhán thanked God she'd kept up with her running. She'd never sprinted so fast in her life. They wouldn't hurt Ciarán; it was Siobhán they wanted. Oh, please, let Séamus be there. Bridie couldn't hurt either of them if Séamus was there.

A light rain started to fall just as she reached the cycle shop. She crouched low and snuck up to the window. She peeked in.

Ciarán and Séamus were in the front room, sitting on the floor. Siobhán's first thought was that Bridie was standing behind them with a gun. Then she saw that they were working on a bicycle. Ciarán was laughing. Thank God. Should she go in with a nod and a smile and just pretend she needed Ciarán back at the bistro?

Where were Bridie and Mike? What if they were hiding, just waiting for her? Siobhán continued to crouch down and began to move alongside the building. Maybe she'd sneak into the backyard, see if there was any sign of Bridie and Mike.

She scrambled alongside the building and soon reached

the back field. About ten feet away was Séamus's private shed. There was no sign of Bridie and Mike. She was about to go back around to the front when something shiny and gold caught her eye. The shed had a fancy new padlock. Why would Séamus bother with a padlock for a beaten-up shed?

Niall's bag? Bridie didn't use that shed; Séamus said so himself. What did he call it? His man cave.

Her chest tightened, and her heart started to hammer. And her mind began to go over everything anyone had ever said about Séamus and the case.

He hasn't raced in a year. Siobhán assumed Séamus stopped racing in order to help out at the bistro or because Bridie wanted children. But what if it was another reason altogether? Soon Billy's voice, and Niall's, and even Macdara's joined the other ones in her head.

He came out of nowhere. Speeding, heading straight for me. I swerved.

There wasn't any evidence of any other car at the scene.

Billy didn't cause the accident.

There isn't any video.

The killer doesn't know that.

It's usually the spouse.

Séamus hadn't ridden his bike competitively since her parents' accident. There were eleven trophies because he hadn't entered the race this year. He was the one who was supposed to have changed the locks on their back door. He would have kept a key, and that's how he left the threatening note. And, of course, he was in the pub with Niall and James that night.

One by one, clues fell into place with a sickening click.

Niall wasn't really working at the cycle shop. He wasn't just blackmailing Bridie; he was blackmailing Séamus. And not for an affair. Something much, much worse. Siobhán didn't want it to be true, but once the dreadful thought hit, it lodged inside her, and she knew she was right. There was a weight to the truth, a sinking heft that could not be denied. Séamus probably darted out in front of Billy, causing him to swerve into her parents. And Niall knew it. Séamus Sheedy caused the accident, not Billy Murphy.

Memories continued to unravel as Siobhán's heart hammered in her chest. She remembered how tortured Séamus seemed during the days after the accident. How he was at the bistro every day helping out. And now she knew why. The guilt. The guilt had been eating him alive. It was an accident. But he'd caused it, and he let Billy Murphy take the blame for it.

Niall probably realized that if he had gone to the guards with Billy's story it would have been his brother's word against one of the most respected men in town. He'd need proof. So he made up a video, and used it to try and coerce Séamus, get some money out of the deal. And turned Séamus into a real killer.

Bridie hadn't been lying about her alibi. Séamus had lied about his. He'd either forgotten that Bridie had gone to her sister's that night or he never thought Siobhán would check into it. And it was no accident that he had Ciarán with him right now. Ciarán was the bait to lure her in. And now Ciarán was in danger.

She had to play it safe. If she could get into the shed, maybe she could find a weapon. Something. Anything.

She crept around to the back of the shed. There were no gaps in the wood. No window. Nothing. He'd made sure the shed was a fortress. No doubt Niall's overnight bag was inside.

She crouched again and this time hurried back to the shop. She was soaking wet. She had to get inside and get Ciarán. She would play dumb, act as if she was happy to see them both. Laugh about how she'd got caught in the rain with no umbrella. Tell Séamus that Macdara was convinced Mike

Granger was the murderer. She'd say anything she had to to get Ciarán out safe.

She was about to hurry around to the front when she spied the back door. A brick was propping it open. Should she come in the back? Sneak up on Séamus? Why had he propped the back door open? Should she take the brick out? She hesitated, not wanting to make the wrong move.

Easy, Siobhán. Go around front. You don't want to alert him. She crept around the side, reached the front, and opened the door. A smile was plastered on her face even before the bell jingled.

"Hello," she called, praying she sounded normal. "How ya?" Ciarán and Séamus were still on the floor and appeared to be working on a bicycle frame.

"There she is," Séamus said as if he'd been expecting her. He stood and hauled Ciarán up with him. He stood in front of Ciarán as if keeping them apart.

"I need Ciarán at home," Siobhán said. Her voice was shaking. Pretending that Séamus wasn't a killer, wasn't the man who caused her parents' death, was harder than she thought it would be. He stared at her, and in that moment she knew that he knew. Would ye look at that? Billy Murphy had been right. She was only safe if the killer thought she didn't suspect him, and she hadn't been able to pull it off.

Feck. Feck, feck, feck.

"Why don't you go on home now," Siobhán told Ciarán. Ciarán peeked around Séamus to look up at Siobhán. He frowned when he saw her face. It had been too long since she'd played poker. "It's okay," Siobhán said. "I'll be home soon."

"Why can't I wait?" Ciarán said.

"We have grown-up talking to do," Siobhán said.

"About what?" Ciarán asked.

"Go on, now," Siobhán said.

"Let him wait," Séamus said. He put his hand on Ciarán's shoulder. Such a big hand. Such a small shoulder.

"Gráinne made apple pie," Siobhán said. "Ciarán should get there before it's gone."

"I said he stays," Séamus said.

"You don't need him," Siobhán said. "You have me."

"I don't trust you," Séamus said. "Not anymore."

"You could leave now. Hop on one of your bikes and go."

"Go where?"

"Anywhere."

"At my age? After all I've worked for? After all I've built?"

"Everyone knows we're here. My siblings, Garda Flannery, everyone."

"Garda Flannery is off to Cork to pick up your brother," Séamus said. "As far as everyone else goes—'Oh yes, they were here. Siobhán came and picked up Ciarán. Said she was taking him home for some apple pie. They never arrived? That's horrible. I'll join the search team.'"

Fright crept into Ciarán's eyes, making them appear wider. His head snapped toward Séamus. "You're the killer? Why?" Siobhán's heart broke at the sound of Ciarán's voice. Séamus had been like a second father to him. To them all.

"Why don't you tell him, Siobhán?" Séamus said, taking a step toward her. "Let's see what you've figured out." Siobhán went to grab Ciarán's hand, and Séamus blocked her. Had it been close to thirty minutes? She had to keep him talking.

"You were always darting around town on your racing bike. You caused the accident," Siobhán said. "You probably pulled up alongside my parents' car to tease them about how you were faster than them. But by the time you pulled in front, Billy Murphy was barreling through the curve. He swerved to miss you. And slammed into my parents instead."

"What?" Ciarán cried out. "What?"

Séamus shook his head. "It was an accident. A terrible accident."

Siobhán let her emotions get the best of her, and all thoughts of remaining neutral just to get him talking evaporated. More than anything, she wanted to know why. "You just left them there. How could you just leave them there?" Tears stung her eyes.

Séamus looked at her, and for a second she forgot he was a killer. She saw true pain reflected back at her. "They were gone. I checked. I would have stayed with them if they were alive. I would have called the medics. I swear to ye. It was too late. They were gone."

"Billy wasn't gone," Siobhán said. "But you had no problem leaving him there, did ye?"

"He didn't deserve my help. It was his fault. Just because he happened to swerve around me first doesn't mean he wouldn't have hit them anyway! He was drunk; I smelled it on him. He's still the one to blame. I was just at the wrong place at the wrong time."

"And Courtney?" Siobhán said. "You can't say the same thing about her, can you?"

Séamus's eyes seemed to turn into little black holes. He took another step toward Siobhán. "Where's the video?" He held out his hand. "Who was the witness? Who got me on video? What exactly did they see? Or is it just audio? Did they get me teasing Billy?" Words fell from Séamus's mouth like he was a madman. "Give it to me, and I won't hurt either of ye. You have my word."

Oh, God. Séamus doesn't think she figured it out. He thinks she has the proof. "It's not on me," Siobhán said. "It's in a safe place. If no harm comes to me or Ciarán or any of us, I'll let you have it."

"You should have brought it," Séamus said. "I can't trust you now." Séamus turned, grabbed a bike, and threw it across the room. It clattered into a row of them, and they fell in a heap. Ciarán turned to run, but Séamus was too fast. He whirled around and snatched Ciarán up by the waist. Ciarán kicked and screamed to no avail.

"It's okay," Siobhán said, doing her best to calm Ciarán and the cold-blooded killer who was holding him. "Séamus, we'll make this right. I'll make this right. I'll do anything. You know I would do anything to protect my family. Just like you were trying to protect yours, right? That's why you had to kill Niall. I understand. I do."

Séamus put Ciarán down but kept his hand on his shoulder. Ciarán was shaking from head to toe. It took every ounce of strength for Siobhán not to crumple to the ground. "Twenty thousand euro," Séamus said. "And I would have paid it. I wasn't going to hurt anyone else. I was going to pay the bastard. Then he had the nerve to go hinting to you that Billy didn't cause the accident. I knew. As soon as I saw him cornering you in here. I knew I had to do something about him."

"And you framed James for it. You knew he was passed out in the alley behind O'Rourke's. You beat him up. You left drops of Niall's blood on his clothing."

"I'm sorry about that. I really am. But he was the perfect culprit. Blind drunk, fighting with Niall, right across the street from the salon—so it was easy enough for you to get the murder weapon." He stopped, shook his head. "It was so perfect."

Siobhán glanced at Séamus's knuckles again. He grinned. "I wore gloves when I hit him," he said. "I must admit, you made me nervous that day you wanted to have a look at my hand. Checking for bruises. Smart. But I wore gloves. But don't worry; he was already passed out. He didn't feel a thing."

He did the next day, you evil man. She prayed the gardai were on their way. Lucky for her, he seemed to want to talk, unburden himself. "You followed Niall that night through town. Mike Granger saw you. Niall ran to our place. You struggled, and the scissors fell out. Would you have killed him otherwise?"

Séamus nodded. "I had me own knife. Hadn't quite planned on doing it that night, but the stars aligned. Niall and James both langered, shouting in public. And when those scissors fell out, it was like it was meant to be. Don't you see? I was meant to do it. What better weapon than one everyone in town has?"

"Except they weren't the promotional scissors. They were the professional ones from the salon. And there were only three of them."

"I heard. Which is why I had to do a bit of handiwork for Sheila so I could nick another pair. Switched them out with one of the freebies. She didn't even notice."

"Did you kill him in our yard or in the bistro?"

"Snuck up behind him in the yard. He was headed straight for your back door. For all I knew, he was going to break in and hurt one of yous."

How kind of you to intervene. "Hurting us won't help you now. Macdara will know it's you. You've made mistakes."

"Like what?" Séamus seemed genuinely curious. Siobhán just wanted to stall for time. If Gráinne had listened for once in her life, Macdara should be on his way here. She had to keep him talking.

"After you stabbed him in the back garden, you broke our buried jar to get the key and brought Niall inside. On your way out, you cleaned up the glass and returned with a replacement jar of Bridie's. It wasn't quite a match."

"I didn't count on you having such a good eye," Séamus said. "But how does that prove I'm the killer?"

"Maybe Bridie will testify that one of her jars is missing."

"You're reaching."

No, you eejit. I'm stalling. "Mary Murphy used Courtney's computer to continue blackmailing you. Courtney read her message to ye and figured out you were the killer. She tried to warn me."

"I should have known Courtney wouldn't be so stupid as to send an e-mail like that from her own account. I feel bad about her, I really do."

"What did the e-mail say?" Siobhán really was curious. Poor Ciarán was still shaking. She wished he could sneak away.

"She said she knew I caused the accident. That she'd seen the video. That soon everyone would know."

God, what was Mary Murphy thinking? That Séamus would never know who sent it because she deleted it. Ah, it wasn't fair to be so behind the times. Her own mam had never sent an e-mail in her life.

"Why did she have to go poking her nose in where it didn't belong?" Séamus said, still going on about Courtney. "It wasn't just the e-mail. I might have figured that Mary had used her computer. But she called for Bridie. And when I answered—oh, she tried to pretend everything was alright, but I could hear it. I could hear it in her voice. She knew I was the killer. I didn't let on, though. As soon as I hung up, I was on me motorcycle, headed for her shop. Got there just in time. I was going out the back when you were coming in the front door. Had to walk my motorcycle halfway back to the shop so no one would hear it. God, that was close. You have to admit she was asking for it. Still, I feel bad. But not as bad as I'm going to feel bad about the two of you." Séamus looked sadly at Ciarán.

Siobhán wanted to scream. She wanted to lunge and grab for Ciarán. It would never work; Séamus could overpower her in a second. All she could do was plead for their lives. There had to be a little bit of good left in Séamus. "It's over. You're a good man. I've known you all my life."

"He's not good. He's a killer," Ciarán cried.

"Please, Séamus. There is good in ye. I know there is. Please. You don't have to kill anyone else."

Séamus took a step forward. "If I quit now, it will have all been for nothing."

"What's it for now? Your reputation? Your family?" Should she tell him Bridie had an affair with Mike Granger, or would it enrage him even more?

"I've done too many things to protect myself and my family. If I stop now, it was all for nothing."

"You wouldn't get away with it. Everyone will figure it out. You can't kill the whole town."

Séamus took a step forward but kept his hand on Ciarán's shoulder. How she wished Ciarán could turn and run! "I promise I'll make it quick," he said. "But I have to take you out to the shed." He picked Ciarán up again. Ciarán screamed and kicked.

"No!" Siobhán yelled. She held up her hands and stepped forward. "I've already mailed the video to the gardai station."

"Liar." Séamus dropped Ciarán with a thud and lunged for her. Siobhán stepped out of the way, and he fell into a bicycle. She grabbed Ciarán's hand.

"Run," she said. She pushed him toward the back door. "Hurry. Get the brick." Ciarán scrambled down the hall with Siobhán on his heels. Ciarán easily slid between the gap in the door. Siobhán reached down to grab the brick. Suddenly she felt strong hands grab her hair and pull her back. Siobhán kicked at the brick, hoping Ciarán would pick it up. Séamus began to drag her down the hall, back into the shop. "Help!" she yelled as loud as she could. "Help!"

"There's no one for miles," Séamus said.

"There's no video. Niall made it up. There's no video."

"Liar."

"I'm not lying. There's no video."

Séamus maneuvered her to the bathroom door, just off

the hallway. He shoved her into the little room. "Hand me your mobile or I'll find it on ye myself," Séamus said.

She dug in her pocket and handed him her phone. He whirled around and slammed the bathroom door shut, and she heard a key turn in the lock. Then she heard his footsteps down the hall as he called out for Ciarán.

She threw herself at the door and tried opening it. It was locked. She kicked the door, threw her body against it, pounded on it. It didn't budge. There weren't any windows to crawl out of. She scanned the bathroom for something, anything. The lid to the toilet tank. It was the only thing she could think of. She removed it, held it in front of her, and backed up as far as she could. *Here goes nothing.*

She held out the lid and charged the door using it like a battering ram. The door didn't break all the way open, but she heard a screech and the splintering of wood. She backed up and rammed it again. This time a small crack split through the door. A small crack, but a crack. She rammed a third time, and a fourth, and a fifth, and then the crack widened enough to reach her hand through. She dropped the lid, then reached around and unlocked the knob.

Splinters bit into her arm, but her adrenaline was pumping so hard she could barely feel them. She threw open the door and ran out the front entrance. There was no sign of Séamus or Ciarán. Which way would Ciarán have gone? She picked the left side of the shop because it hugged a row of trees and Ciarán would have been attracted to the smallest space. Sure enough, he was huddled against the wall, gripping the brick in his hands and shivering something fierce. She threw her finger up to her mouth when he saw her to stop him from crying out. She grabbed him and sank to the ground, holding him.

"Where is he?" she whispered. And then they heard him.

Chapter 40

❧✗❧

"Ciarán?" Séamus called out. "I've got your sister. Come out if you don't want her hurt." From the sounds of it, Séamus was on the other side of the shop. It wouldn't take long for him to cross to this side. What was she going to do?

"What's he talking about?" Ciarán said. "You're right here."

"Shhh." She had to think quickly. So much for anyone coming to their rescue. Either her sisters couldn't tell time or something was keeping them from getting here. The row of scooters flashed in her mind, followed by an image of the shiny gold keys hanging behind the register. She had to get to them.

She looked at Ciarán. "I have a plan," she said. "But I need your help." He nodded, and she whispered the plan into his ears.

Ciarán took off running out the front. A few seconds later, Séamus darted out after him.

"Macdara is here," Ciarán yelled, just like she'd told him to do. "Macdara is here." Séamus whipped his head around just as Ciarán threw the brick with all his might. It clocked

Séamus on the temple. He roared out in pain and let out a
string of curse words.

Good on ye! Siobhán wanted to cheer, but this was no
time to celebrate. Ciarán ran toward the trees on the left side
of the property.

Siobhán raced inside the shop, propped open the front
door with a wooden board Séamus must have used for that
purpose, and grabbed a key. She fumbled with it, and it fell
to the floor. She grabbed another and and hopped onto the
first scooter in the line. It was one of the pink ones. She in-
serted the key and turned it, but it didn't start. She raced back
and grabbed every single key. Her hands had never shaken
so much in her life. She prayed Séamus hadn't caught Ciarán yet. He was quick, and she'd told him to go into the woods.

On the fifth key the scooter roared to life. She revved the
engine and backed it up, sending bicycles clattering to the
floor. She veered left, then straight, and drove the scooter
right out the front door, praying it wouldn't flip as she drove
it off the landing and down the little hill. It bounced a good
one, but she'd had enough practice and managed to keep it
steady.

Praying, and concentrating with all her might, she headed
for the line of trees where Ciarán was hiding and Séamus
was pacing like a wildcat. At the sound of the scooter, he
whirled around. Siobhán aimed straight for him. It took
more resolve than she'd thought, aiming to mow down a
grown man, but she kept coming at him until he dove out of
the way with a yell.

"Ciarán," she screamed, pulling up alongside the trees.
"Now."

Ciarán darted out from behind a birch and hopped on.
She'd forgotten helmets, but there wasn't any time. She silently prayed to her mam and da to keep them safe.

"Hold tight," she screamed. "Don't let go."

Séamus was running back toward the shop. Siobhán shot

forward, as fast as she could without tipping them over. She hesitated at the road. Behind them a motorcycle roared to life. He was going to catch up with them.

Siobhán hit the gas, taking the scooter as fast as she could once again, and this time she made a beeline for the field. She knew the terrain. If she concentrated hard enough, she could avoid the holes that marred the ground. She knew them like she knew the back of her hand. Maybe Séamus wouldn't be that lucky.

"He's following us," Ciarán shouted.

Sure enough, the throaty roar of the motorcycle gave no doubt that he was upon them.

"Hold on," Siobhán yelled.

They were well into the field now, just along the wall. The scooter bounced along the rocks, and soon the front tire hit a patch of mud and slid to the left. Siobhán tilted her body to the right, concentrating with all her might to keep the scooter from crashing.

In the distance, police sirens blared. It had to be for them. But it was too late for anyone to rescue them. The abbey was just ahead. She veered left just before she reached it, following the outlines of the monastery walls, but leaving enough space in between for a motorcycle. This particular patch was covered in the most holes.

Séamus took the bait, filling in the gap between her scooter and the walls, and was soon right alongside them.

"Hold on," she screamed again. She gunned the scooter, and Séamus hit the gas. He pulled up without a second thought. Seconds later a terrifying screech rang out as the front wheel of Séamus's motorcycle dipped into a hole, tilting the beast until it was straight up in the air, where it remained suspended for a second as though Séamus were a stunt man performing a death-defying trick. And then it began to flip, back wheel over front.

Ciarán screamed, along with Séamus, and for all she

knew, she did too, but Siobhán kept going, even when she heard the terrifying crash.

"He's trapped under his motorcycle," Ciarán yelled.

"Don't look!" Siobhán flew past the little bridge, feeling every vibration as the wheels of the scooter stuttered over the wood. Ten feet more and they would finally reach the road leading to the back of their bistro. Just ahead she saw a group huddled in the street, as if watching for her. There stood Ann and Gráinne and Eoin, along with Mike and Declan. Worry was stamped across each and every face. She screeched to a halt, and they hurried over.

"Macdara is headed for the cycle shop," Eoin said.

"He's a bit late," Siobhán said. "But I'll deny I said it if you ever repeat it."

"Call the gardai and the paramedics. Séamus needs help." Mike and Declan looked toward the field. Siobhán still couldn't bring herself to look back. "But tell them to be careful," she added. "Because Séamus is the killer."

"Why help him?" Gráinne said. "Why not just leave him?"

"Because he's still a neighbor," Siobhán said. "And that's what neighbors do."

Chapter 41

Siobhán was thrilled when James took a second helping of her bacon and cabbage, potatoes, and brown bread. He'd lost weight, and she couldn't wait until he looked like himself again.

"I can't believe you cooked when we have all that," James said with a nod to the kitchen, where several platters were lined up, all brought by neighbors and friends.

"It's your first night home, and nothing beats a home-cooked meal," Siobhán said.

She smiled and glanced at the shuttered windows. They'd seen enough of their neighbors for now. The bistro would be jammers the next few days, possibly the next year, as people gathered to rehash the details.

Séamus was in the hospital with a broken leg and a broken jaw, but he would recover. He'd admitted to the murders, so he'd go straight from the hospital to a jail cell.

Macdara was convinced Bridie didn't have a clue as to what Séamus had done, and Siobhán agreed.

Mary Murphy was cooperating in lieu of being arrested herself. She said she didn't report what was going on to the police because there was no video, no proof. She repeated that she was desperately sorry about Courtney and that if she had had a clue that the e-mail could be traced back to her, she wouldn't have sent it.

Billy was still in prison, for he had been driving drunk, and they would have to wait as an official investigation into the accident was reopened. But Siobhán assumed he would eventually get out. She prayed he'd learned a lesson about drinking and driving.

After dinner, they went to the cemetery, held hands around their parents' graves, prayed, and filled them in on the excitement. Siobhán would whittle a bird for each of them to leave atop the headstones. She would do the same for Courtney, perhaps a flower or a heart.

She missed whittling, and she was sorry she hadn't made something for Courtney when she was still alive. She'd never stop doing it again. Life was too short to let your talents go to waste. Maybe death was a necessary nudge, a reminder to love, whether it was a person or a wee block of wood. The ancient druids believed in nature and hospitality. Siobhán was eager to embrace life again. Her parents would want that for her. So would Courtney. She'd bring them all back if she could, even Niall. But since that was out of her hands, she could at least try not to waste a single moment of her life. A life that was surprisingly full, even though it was simple. Or maybe because it was simple.

Sometimes one could think too much. Siobhán grabbed James's hand as they walked, holding it like she did when they were children, and he accepted the gesture without complaint.

"You can go to Dublin now," he said as they headed home. The others were ahead of them, jumping over puddles, laughing, racing each other, doing what kids did on a summer evening in Ireland. Soon they were back on Sarsfield Street and almost at the bistro.

"I know," Siobhán said. "Except I want to stay." She didn't even know those words were going to come out of her mouth, but once they did, she knew them to be true. It didn't mean she would never go to college; it just meant that right here and right now she was exactly where she needed to be. Maybe she would enroll in an online course, something she could handle in between her other duties. She was going to look into programs straightaway.

"I just want you to know that it's an option from now on," James said.

Just ahead Macdara was coming toward them. His eyes sparkled when he saw Siobhán, and he broke out in a grin.

"Is he the reason you want to stay?" James leaned over and whispered.

"Not the only reason," Siobhán said.

"Might that be the other?" James pointed. Siobhán was surprised to see Chris Gorden heading their way too. Siobhán and James stopped in front of Naomi's Bistro.

Macdara and Chris reached Siobhán at the same time, then stopped and stared at each other. Then they looked in unison at Siobhán.

"See you," James said, with a gentle shove to her shoulder. He hurried down the street, chasing after the young ones.

"Where are you going?" Siobhán called as James left her standing there all alone.

"Evening," Macdara said.

"Hello," Chris said. He looked at Macdara. "You go first," he said. "I'll wait."

"No," Macdara said. "I'll wait."

"But I assume yours is official business," Chris said. "Mine is of a more personal nature."

"Is that right?" Macdara said. "Well, I'm off duty."

"Then I'll have to ask you both for a rain check," Siobhán said. "It's been a hectic day."

"Are you alright?" They asked at the same time.

Siobhán couldn't help but laugh. "On second thought," she said, "you can both come in for tea."

As they headed back to the bistro, neighbors began drifting out of their shops, and by the time Siobhán had the tea kettle on, at least a dozen folks were gathered, desperate for details of what had happened with Séamus.

Poor Bridie; even though she had been having an affair, this was bound to shake her to her core. Siobhán intended to be there for her, just as Bridie had been for her. She'd leave out the bit about being convinced that she and Mike were the killers.

Oh, why couldn't the town go away so she could get her fill of being fought over by two men?

John Butler snuck up on Siobhán, almost knocking her over.

"I wanted you to know. I never once thought that James was a killer."

"Thank you."

"Actually," he said, leaning over and saying in a loud stage whisper, "my money was on you."

Siohán threw her head back and laughed. She couldn't believe the cheek of these folks. But that was Kilbane. You had to take the good with the bad. Folks helped each other out at times, and at other times begrudged one another behind closed doors. But they always came back. They came in for tea, and gossip, and brown bread. When she finally reached Chris Gorden's table, she couldn't see Macdara in the crowd.

"Are you interested in Garda Flannery?" Chris Gorden asked. "Romantically?"

"Funny," came a voice from behind them. "That's just what I wanted to know."

Siobhán whirled around to find Macdara standing there, looking as if he wanted an answer right here and now. She looked at Chris, then Macdara. She opened her mouth to give her answer.

Just then the back door burst open and Ciarán burst into the room holding the mangiest little brown dog Siobhán had ever seen. It may have been a Jack Russell terrier, but it was hard to tell underneath all the dirt. She wasn't even sure it was a dog until it began yapping.

"Can we go to London for the weekend?" Ann said, sidling up and taking Siobhán's hand.

Eoin poked his head out of the kitchen. "I want to go to New York," he said.

Macdara and Chris were still staring at her.

Gráinne entered from the back room. "London it is," she said before making a dramatic exit out of the bistro and up the stairs to her room. She stopped at the top of the stairs and flipped her hair. "If you say no, I'm going to ask James."

Before Siobhán could respond, her cheeky sister disappeared. She looked around for James. He was nowhere to be seen.

"Siobhán?" Macdara said. Siobhán held up her finger, turned around, and made a beeline for her cappuccino machine. She relished the noise as it churned the beans, drowning out everyone around her. Outside the window, a light rain began to fall. She grabbed her mam's apron off the wall and put it on. She frothed the milk and poured the cappuccino and turned to her brood, starting with Ciarán.

"Take the dog outside."

Next she turned to Ann. "We'll talk about London later. Nobody is going to New York," she yelled toward the kitchen. "James is a big boy," she said to the ceiling, in case Gráinne could hear from her room. "But I'm the one making those kinds of decisions around here."

She finally turned to the gorgeous American. "And, Chris, you're a lovely man, but my heart is already taken." She smiled, faced Macdara, who looked as if he'd just been struck by a stupid stick, and handed him the cappuccino. He met her eyes and smiled.

"Are you sure?" he said.

She held his gaze, and then smiled back. "Drink it before I change me mind," she answered.

The O'Sullivan clan of County Cork, Ireland, are thrilled to be catering the matrimonial affairs of a celebrity couple—until a cunning killer turns an Irish wedding into an Irish wake . . .

Any wedding is a big deal in the small village of Kilbane—even more so when the bride is a famous fashion model. It's also go for business. Not only has customer traffic picked up at Naomi's Bistro, Siobhán O'Sullivan and her five siblings have a full plate catering for the three-day affair. And Siobhán's own beau, local garda Macdara Flannery, gladly steps in as best man after the groom's first choice makes a drunken arse out of himself.

Even if he hadn't been disinvited to the wedding, the original best man wouldn't have been able to show. He's been found murdered in the woods, casting a pall over the nuptials. And when a second member of the wedding party is poisoned by a champagne flute engraved with Macdara's name, the garda goes from being best man to prime suspect.

With a killer at large and a string of robberies plaguing Kilbane, Siobhán feels more than a little protective of her village. She vows to clear Macdara's name, but the suspect list is as long as the guest list. Like the bride walking down the aisle, Siobhán needs to watch her step. For as she gets closer to unveiling the truth, the murderer is planning a very chilly reception for her . . .

**Please turn the page for an exciting sneak peek of
Carlene O'Connor's next
Irish Village Mystery
MURDER AT AN IRISH WEDDING
coming soon wherever print and e-books are sold!**

Chapter 1

As the sun rose over Kilbane Castle, it struck the stained-glass window in the highest turret, casting the grounds below in an unearthly glow. A breeze whispered through the grass, rippling the wedding tents, making them shiver down to their stakes. Neighboring hills shook off the morning mist, and wooly apparitions began to dot their peaks, grazing and bleating into the damp fall air. From a room high up in the castle, Kevin Gallagher lay in bed, battling the terrors. Pre-wedding celebrations were in full swing and a bit of drink the night before had loosened his tongue. Upon his stumbling return to the castle, he may have upset a few heads in the Cahill/Donnelly wedding party. He blinked at the ceiling and tried for the life of him to remember the carnage.

He'd told Paul Donnelly, the groom-to-be, that only an eejit would marry a beautiful woman. And Alice Cahill wasn't just beautiful, she was downright gorgeous. A proper fashion model to boot. She was *way* out of Paul Donnelly's league, and if his best man couldn't tell him, then who could?

"You always have to watch your back with a beautiful woman," Kevin slurred on the way home from the pubs.

They tripped along on the cobblestone streets of Kilbane as the morning birds began to trill, with the rhythm of the fella playing the spoons in O'Rourke's still thrumming in his chest. "An ugly woman, that's the way to go. Never have to be afraid of losing her. And that father-in-law! Who in his right mind would want to be related to Colm Cahill? If I were you, I'd do a runner and save m'self a life of misery, lad!"

"Shut your gob," Paul said. "You're bollixed."

"Would Alice still marry you if she knew all your secrets?" Kevin clapped Paul hard on the back, causing him to stumble.

When he recovered, Paul's eyes burned with rage. "What secrets are you on about?"

"I could tell Alice a thing or t'ree about her groom-to-be, now couldn't I?" Kevin joked. He and Paul had known each other since they were grasshoppers.

"I can't believe I chose you as my best man." Paul was practically roaring down the streets, his handsome face creased with rage. Kevin had never seen him so furious. He was only messing. Was Paul really worried about his secrets? Why, Paul Donnelly's secrets couldn't shock a virgin on her first day at the nunnery. If you couldn't take a bit of ribbing before snapping on the old ball and chain, then when could ye?

Kevin had had a falling out with Colm Cahill too. The father of the bride was having a cigar around the back of the castle, and the trail of sweet smoke drew Kevin directly to him. Colm was planted between a maze of shrubs, with his cigar in one hand and a glass of Jameson in the other. Ice cubes clinked and crickets chirped. The fat yellow moon hung low, and stars dotted the sky like diamonds. Reminded Kevin of the rock on Alice's hand. She'd better be careful flashing that yoke around.

Colm Cahill made his fortune on a start-up technology

company called Swipe-It. An app that allowed you to pay for things with the swipe of a finger. Made himself a pile of money. Can ye imagine that? Making money off taking people's money? The world was upside-down, it was. Kevin had tried to talk a little business with Mr. Moneybags——had a great idea for a new app called Alibi. If the wife was out of town and a man wanted to do a bit of sneaking around, he could send the missus a phony selfie showing himself doing the washing. Of course, she'd expect the washing to be done when she returned, but every new idea had a few bits and bobs to work out.

It wasn't until Kevin was nearly on him that he saw Mr. Moneybags was talking on his mobile. "Just do it. Send the confirmation to the castle."

"How nice to be bossing people around at this hour of the mornin'. Business never sleeps, does it?" Kevin called out.

The old tyrant whirled around. "What is the matter with you? Sneaking up on a person like that."

"I'm having a stroll. Just like you."

"Listening in on me conversation, were you?"

"Your conversation intruded on me, not the other way around."

Colm's face was scrunched with rage. He shook his fist. "Pack your bags and go home."

Kevin shook his head and glanced at the moon. A full one sure did bring out the strange in folk. Especially this crew. "I have another business proposition for ye," Kevin started in.

"Who do you think you are?" Colm approached Kevin, his large frame towering over him.

Did he really not know who he was? Why, the old man was completely off his head. He was starting to think the sooner this wedding was done and dusted, the better. Kevin pointed to himself. "I'm the best man."

"Not anymore. You're not needed anymore." Colm threw

a look over Kevin's shoulder, and Kevin whirled around to see Paul lurking behind him. Ear-wagging. Colm pointed at Paul. "Did ye hear that? Was I good and clear?" Colm stormed off. Paul stood staring after his future father-in-law, mouth agape. When he recovered, he turned on Kevin.

"What did you do?"

Kevin threw open his arms. "I am an innocent lad. Didn't even get a chance to pitch me idea."

"You're making things worse," Paul said. "For the love of God, just stay out of it." Then he whirled around and stormed off. Kevin didn't know what to make of it, but it made him feel a bit dirty.

Speaking of dirty, he might have made a pass at the mother of the bride. Susan Cahill was descending the steps to the guest rooms just as Kevin was sloshing up. He must have startled her for she cried out when she saw him. She had the look of a woman caught sneaking out. Kevin gave her a pinch on the arse and may have even planted a kiss on her middle-aged lips. Ah but sure, a woman Susan Cahill's age should be thanking him for the attention, she should. And he could see where Alice Cahill got her looks. Susan was a bit ripe, but you could still see the vestiges of beauty about her. Tall, the Cahill women, mighty tall.

There was at least one other person he had had a run-in with last night—who was it? Ah, Jaysus, for the life of him he couldn't remember. Alice, gorgeous Alice? He hadn't upset her, had he? No, she hadn't even joined the fun. Said she needed her beauty sleep, which was out and out ridiculous.

Brian? That whiny little wedding planner? Could be. Anyone who went around wearing little colored squares in their jacket deserved a bit of hassling. Ah, wait. The wedding photographer. Mr. Fancy Artist with a show coming up in Dublin. Eejit. The lad was in everyone's face with his fancy camera snapping and flashing away. It's a wonder he hadn't blinded anyone. Kevin had knocked the yoke flat out of his hands. The lens smashed to pieces on the cobblestone street. Lad should have had better reflexes. He went a bit mental from what Kevin could recall. Wailed like a woman. Said Kevin owed him five thousand euros. What a wanker!

Who else? He was forgetting someone.

Kevin sunk his sore head back into his pillow and stared at the elaborate crown molding rimming the ceiling. Such fine craftsmanship. Not like the shoddy estates going up today.

Kevin drank in the crystal chandelier, rose wallpaper, and arched limestone windows. His head throbbed, and he was damp right down to the bones in his toes.

The pints. The shots. A few pills. Oh, Jaysus. His head began to pound like a drum. Where were they exactly? Kilbane, was it? The walled town. Luckily the castle was outside the proper walls. Kevin couldn't imagine being so closed in, like.

A wave of panic hit him. Was the wedding today? It couldn't be today. He'd be puking down the aisle. No, no. T'anks be to God. The wedding was on Saturday, and today, why it was only Thursday. Lucky for him, weddings in Ireland were often three-day affairs.

Speaking of affairs—did he hear last night that someone was having one? A shocker, it was. Who was it? It was all a bit of a blur.

Something stirred next to him, and he nearly jumped out of his birthday suit. Slowly, he turned his head, and what a fright. Beside him, long blond hair fanned out over the pillow like a den of snakes. Medusa was in bed with him. Her face and body were hidden, burrowed under blankets. There was a colleen in his bed. Or was he in her bed? Perhaps every guest room looked alike.

"If I'm going to ravage anyone tonight, it'll be the maid of dishonor," Kevin suddenly remembered saying. She'd batted her eyelids and wiggled her full hips at him all night. He glanced over at the snoring beauty. What was her name? *Ah, right. Brenna.* Too bad she was nowhere nearly as gorgeous as Alice. Then again, who was?

How cliché. The maid of honor and the best man knocking boots. His eyes landed on the nightstand. His wallet. Keys. A folded-up piece of paper. He snatched it up. The message was typed and centered:

> More when the deed is done. Meet me at sunrise.
> Top of the hill.

Deed? What deed? More what when the deed was done? Once more he glanced at the nightstand, where his eyes landed on the answer, and it came as quite a delight. A thick stack of euros tied up with a little red string. He swiped it up and fanned through it. Why, there were at least a thousand euros here. He read the note again. The hill. The one behind the castle?

Kevin ran his fingers through his hair and plucked his packet of fags off the nightstand. He started to light up, then thought better of it. He might wake the bird. The last thing he needed was Brenna clucking around his business. It was almost sunrise. The note sounded a bit desperate. Parting desperate folks from their money was well within Kevin Gallagher's skill set.

He sat up, fighting the throbbing in his skull, and reached for the blue tracksuit hanging on the chair. Every member of the wedding party had been given the silly tracksuits. Alice had insisted on a group photo in front of the castle before breakfast. He'd have to hurry to the hill if he wanted to be back in time for the photo. Only thing worse than marrying a beautiful woman was riling one up. Especially one about to get married. He dressed, donned his trusty watch and gold chain, then shoved the money and note into his tracksuit pocket and crept out of the room.

He began to whistle a little tune as he wondered who would be waiting atop the hill. He couldn't shake the feeling that he was about to strike a killer of a deal.

Connect with Us

Visit us online at
KensingtonBooks.com
to read more from your favorite authors, see books
by series, view reading group guides, and more.

Join us on social media

for sneak peeks, chances to win books and prize packs,
and to share your thoughts with other readers.

facebook.com/kensingtonpublishing
twitter.com/kensingtonbooks

Tell us what you think!

To share your thoughts, submit a review,
or sign up for our eNewsletters, please visit:
KensingtonBooks.com/TellUs.